THE WINDOWS TO THE SOUL

"Did you know that you have a way of looking right through to a person's deepest thoughts?"

Victor had only meant to give her a scant revelation into the intensity of his feelings. There was no way to gauge what she thought of him now. She probably assumed he was an arrogant jackass and was just being civil for the duration of the dinner. But her unfaltering gaze held a kind of truth serum that he was unaccustomed to. Her eyes seemed to beckon, *If you tell me, you can trust me.*

Liza smiled, bringing her glass up to her mouth for another sip. "It's a gift—or a curse . . ."

"It's a gift."

After a long pause, she said, "Victor, I like to know who I'm dealing with. And for me, a person's eyes tell me everything."

He leaned forward and spirited her a light challenge. "And what do my eyes tell you?"

Liza took another sip of wine as she formulated her answer. Victor could tell that she had penetrated his guard somehow. It was in the way she raised one eyebrow, along with the wry, devastatingly sexy twist of her mouth. He could *feel* the power of something tugging at him. It felt almost like a current.

"Your eyes? What do they tell me?" She smiled sheepishly after a well-timed pause. "Oh . . . just about everything."

TIMELESS LOVE

Look for these historical romances in the Arabesque line:

BLACK PEARL by Francine Craft (0236-0, $4.99)

CLARA'S PROMISE by Shirley Hailstock (0147-X, $4.99)

MIDNIGHT MOON by Mildred Riley (0200-X; $4.99)

SUNSHINE AND SHADOWS by Roberta Gayle (0136-4, $4.99)

SUNDANCE

Leslie Esdaile

Pinnacle Books
Kensington Publishing Corp.

PINNACLE BOOKS are published by

Kensington Publishing Corp.
850 Third Avenue
New York, NY 10022

First Printing: October, 1996
10 9 8 7 6 5 4 3 2 1

Printed in the United States of America

This work is dedicated to the people in my life who believed in me along the way and who supported my efforts through encouragement and patience. There were many quiet souls who passed through my plane, the ones who said, "Baby, you can do anything you set your mind to," now all too numerous to name. They were also the same people who would get in a huff when I used the word "can't" and made me permanently banish it from my vocabulary. Many of those old souls are gone now, but for those who still remain, I say, *Thank You* for making one small child look up at the stars in wonder.

My work will always be a tribute to the Most High Creator, without that Universal love nothing is possible. And to the wisdom of the Ancients—those who told stories through the generations, and who knew that there was something out there greater than themselves. I had a lot of help and I believe!

To Aldine . . . my soul mate—the one who made me know that time is a continuum . . . You know the answer . . . "Never stopped."

To my mother, Helen L. T. Peterson, my guardian angel, who transitioned from this life to the next December 11, 1984. I miss you, Ma . . . you were, and still are, my best friend and source of inspiration.

To William T. Peterson, my father, friend, role model, and first hero! Thanks for setting the foundation.

To Lisa J. Peterson, my cheerleader and best friend—someone special who said, "Yes, you can do this. Just keep the faith, girl!" Without you, this would have never been possible.

To Helena, my daughter: May you be brave enough to follow the road less travelled, always seeking new answers while accepting no obstacles. Dare to dream—thus, live!

To Pat Nevius Sancho Peterson, Yvette Neir, and Susan Davis—real friends, true believers, mentors, and guides. Your support is immeasurable.

To The Esdaile-Hamilton Family . . . for loving me still, and especially to Lydia and Carlah for their ongoing support and positive energy. Special tribute to the best storytellers in the Universe, those "grand-masters" with whom I fell in love with at first sight: Pop, Slim, Luke & Wilbur, and Kenny. Thank you for the cherished stories, the serenades, and the connection to something wonderful . . . and those who have that special brand of calming patience which gives testimony to an eternity of wisdom: Mom E, Violet, Ernestine, Francis, Marcia . . . your eyes speak volumes. And, Michael, for the dreams we shared during the early years.

To Constance O'Day-Flannery, a true friend who taught me the fundamentals, hung in there through my craziness and kicked a few pebbles at the edge with me . . . What a Ride, Thelma! Thanks, lady!

Special thanks to Aunt Julia, Aunt Hetti and Uncle Harold, and Aunt Amy for making me remember the words of the grioles and loving me with their full hearts—*unconditionally!*

To my Kitchen Conference Crew: Those who helped baby-sit, listened to my sagas, and held my hand . . . Patti, Vicki, Michelle, Lynda, Rochelle & DJ, Marie, Pebbles, Kim, and Aunt Yvonne & Aunt J! They know who they are—Hey gang, we did it! Especially, Loretta Mary Cobb, another angel on my shoulder since 1985 . . . you taught me so much; I love you. And, my God-sister Terri, plus Tina & Andre, Maureen, Mom & Dad Page, Irene, Brandt, Javier, Darlene, Isabelle, Christina Klugar, Mary DuPont, Debbie & Mike Roundtree, Denise & Clay, Ruthann & Leonard, Asake, Janine, Muriel, TP, Jeff, Eric, Beverly Coleman, Ron Z, John Roberts, Marilyn . . . Karen . . . Kenya . . . Steve . . . Safee . . . Miss Jackie—the rest of the crew at All America Film & Video Company.

To my cousins, Abeo & Claudia, for getting in touch with the ancestors for me and for helping me hear their voices more clearly! Rhonda & Rev for their constant prayers and love—THANK YOU!

To Kensington Publishing, my editor, Monica Harris, and my agent, Vivian Stephens, who took the first big risk on my project. To Terrie Williams for her phenomenal inspiration.

. . . And, to Grandmom Pete, and Nana Thornton . . . The Ancient Ones, who are always there to guide me through. You've been there since forever . . . I remember your stories and how you told me to keep my eye on the sparrow. I love you.

If there is anyone who I left out, know that the oversight was not intentional. Your kindness and support was, and remains, deeply appreciated.

One

October 1996
Washington, D.C.

It was back again. Returning as always to manifest itself with a vengeance. The unprovoked feeling came without warning and, to her dismay, without regard for her schedule. And, as always, it brought with it a mild case of nausea accompanied by a dull headache as it reached full throttle.

This morning, like so many others recently, Liza would have to grant it a begrudging audience. At one point she had even considered therapy since the doctors couldn't seem to diagnose the source of her pains. But each time she lapsed into the uncomfortable decision to seek professional help, memories of the heated debates between her grandmother and her father would make her put off the task of finding a counselor just a little longer. Giving in to the possibility that there was something emotionally wrong with her was even more distressing than the headaches.

Psychic . . . a strange and inexplicable term, treated much the same way as mental illness used to be twenty years ago.

Those old images rose before her now, and Liza recalled her grandmother's indignant response to her father's suggestion that *something* about her was definitely not normal. She almost smiled as she heard Nana's words in her head.

"Bill, let me tell you one thing, son," her grandmother had always begun, not looking at him while she'd worked. "Ain't nothin' wrong with that chile that no doctor can fix. They can't medicate it away, and can't no minister preach it away. This gift comes to her jus' as natural as breathin'. So what cha gonna do, make the chile stop breathin'? That's probably what's wrong with her anyway. Nobody listens to the girl but me!"

The cryptic conversation had always ended the same way— with her father heading toward the door and Liza sitting on her grandmother's lap. Her mother had never wanted to hear of it.

When she'd been younger, she had been sure that whatever it was must have been strange or bad. It was in the way her father's eyes held a terrified intensity, making him back down. That was not Bill Nichols in any other circumstance. Yet, somehow, even though her adult logic now dictated otherwise, she had always remained a little unsure and oddly ashamed of the thing that she couldn't understand.

This *thing,* however, was hereditary. That much she was sure of and had always felt that truth in her gut. It was in the fragments of adult conversations, the ones where adults assume children are not listening.

Her father had been adamant. "Ma, keep your voice down!" he'd urged in a hushed command under his breath. "The child is probably already confused enough from that *mess* you've been telling her!"

Her grandmother's dignified reply had simply been, "God's *gift* ain't no *mess.*"

As the conversation replayed itself in her mind, Liza brought her hand up to massage her temple. Just thinking about the old memories seemed to make the pain worse.

Ancient thoughts and feelings created a visual blur before her. No longer mentally in her office, Liza allowed herself to slip behind the burgundy velvet drapes that guarded the entrance to her grandmother's parlor. From her childhood hiding place she'd seen the regal matron calmly prepare to do battle in a stance that was an unmistakable declaration of war.

Nana Ethel's response had been direct and unwavering as she drew herself up, straightening her already perfect posture. "You *know* this comes down from a long line of women in our family. Just because you done went down to Washington and got yourself a fancy position and all don't mean you can change what is. We *ain't* discussin' this *no more,* Bill."

Then it was over. The subject had been banished from the house. The vision ended.

Pushing away from the antique desk that had travelled with her since she graduated from Wharton, Liza allowed the rollers on her leather chair to propel her toward the expansive bank of windows in her office. The desk had originally belonged to her grandfather, who'd passed it down to her father. It was one of the few treasures that she had managed to save. Nearly all the rest of the sentimental relics had been auctioned off.

Her thoughts quickly became morose. So much had changed since her father's fall from political grace. The financial devastation that followed his eventual suicide had splintered her family over a decade ago.

She had to shake it. All of it. Daydreaming about what was, or what could have been, was pointless.

Upon retrieving a misplaced file, she paused briefly to take in the monument-studded skyline that made Washington, D.C. look so tranquil on the surface. She stared at the seat of democracy and fairness, then slowly blew out a long breath of anguish. Thoughts of the past were becoming inescapable. Trapped, the crush of those deeply guarded memories slipped into her consciousness now, giving way to another familiar wave of pain.

How ironic. Every time she remembered her home, sadness would creep to the surface, engulfing her in unwanted melancholia. She wondered if other people remembered their childhoods that way. Or whether the only emotion that thoughts of home conjured up for them were tears. Unable to turn off the fresh torrent of gloom upon demand, with another weary sigh, she gave in to the hurt while recalling the events that had changed her life forever.

Almost as a reflex, she braced herself for the scent of lavender. A delicate floral aroma always filtered into the room when these feelings overwhelmed her. The smell was both a comfort and a source of inexplicable fear. Something that raised the hair on her arms, yet stilled her heart at the same time. Closing her eyes as she absorbed the sensation, she felt her lids moisten against her will. "Nana . . ." she murmured quietly, tasting the salt of unshed tears. "Will you ever stop visiting me like this?"

Ultimately, a knock on the door provided the necessary jolt to save her from the daymare. The loud jarring sound stopped the agonizing visit back to the home and people that she had once loved so dearly.

"Liz, can I talk to you for a minute?" Maureen, her staffer, asked in a tentative voice.

"Oh, yeah, sure. Come on in. You don't look good. What's wrong?" Liza answered, brushing aside her own troubles to take a few minutes to listen.

Seeming as though she were about to cry, Maureen edged into the office and closed the door behind her. "It's Larry. You know about the divorce and all. . . . Well, he was supposed to take Danielle on her school trip today, but he just dropped her off without leaving her anything. That child doesn't even have lunch money, her entrance fee for the museum, or a way home. She called me from school in tears 'cause they wouldn't let her get on the bus. . . . I hate him for this."

Liza stood and walked over to Maureen, touching her arm as she spoke. "Listen, family comes first. We'll manage. Get out of here and go take care of your little girl." Then, as an afterthought, she added, "And take care of you. Okay? You don't have to come back in here today."

Maureen didn't look up as she answered, her voice still thick with emotion. "I hate to let you down like this, Liza. I mean, we're in the midst of the biggest contract this firm's ever had, and—"

Liza wouldn't let her finish. "Mo, hon, listen to me. You are the best networking guru around. You give a hundred and fifty percent. Regularly. But you also have a life. So, no more arguments. Go take care of your child."

Maureen gave her a quick hug and moved toward the door. Turning back before she left, she whispered, "That's why we work so hard for you, Lady. You're good people. Thanks."

Liza watched her friend leave, wishing there were some way to comfort Maureen. As she returned to her chair and peered out of the window again, it seemed that everyone's lives, marriages, children—everything—was falling apart and there was nothing that she could do about it. What was happening to the world? There had been a time when people could depend on each other or their extended families. It just seemed impossible to her that things had changed so drastically in only one generation. She wondered what her grandmother would have thought about the state of things today. If the stroke hadn't killed her, surely the sight of her old neighborhood now gone to ruin would have.

Trying to restore her sense of peace, Liza offered up a small prayer of protection for her friend, calling back the lavender to help focus her thoughts on the more pleasant childhood memories that she could scavenge. She hoped those positive feelings would follow Maureen and Danielle through their day. What else could she do? Her meditation was interrupted, and there was no way to get back to a still pace in her soul.

Connie's buzz on the speaker phone was the new intrusion to her senses. Giving in to exasperation, Liza hit the console button without turning away from the window.

"Mr. Duarte for you on line one," came the brief announcement, shattering the calm.

In an instant, the lavender was gone—along with the memories. The sudden change brought Liza crashing into the present, unable to repress the agitation that escalated into immediate fury. She hated the interruption, but that was her life. A series of unfinished business. It wasn't Connie's fault. She knew it wasn't anyone's fault. But when would peace be hers to claim? There was no telling when the bittersweet memories would visit her again. It was this uncertainty that always kept her on edge, fearful of her odd ability and expectant at the same time.

"Duarte?" she faltered, trying to regain her composure.

"Yup, on line one."

Irrational anger took hold of her. Hadn't he caused enough trouble? Swinging her chair away from the window, Liza faced the telephone console with unharnessed annoyance. Hearing Duarte's name was like cocking the hammer on a loaded pistol. Rattled, she could only respond to the affront with raw emotion.

"What does that arrogant . . . What does he want now?" she demanded. "He's already cost this firm three million dollars!"

Liza heard Connie pause and swallow, detecting the thinly concealed alarm in her hesitation. Connie had been caught in the cross fire between the two warring firms before, and Liza hoped that she hadn't taken this unprovoked salvo personally. What was wrong with her? No other client or competitor made her respond this way. What was it about this Duarte guy? . . . Every time she interfaced with him, something fragile within her snapped. She had to calm down. Pace herself. Get a grip.

Seeming to recover, Connie measured her answer. "I don't know, Ms. Nichols. Well . . . uh . . . he said that it was very important and insisted on speaking with you directly. I can tell him you're in a staff meeting or out with a client, if you'd like."

The daunted formality in Connie's voice made Liza quickly collect herself and prepare for the heated debate that always occurred between members of her firm and Duarte's staff. But she hated arguing. It was such a waste of energy.

Taking a deep breath, Lisa fought to mellow her next response. "No, Connie. I'll have to deal with him for the duration of this project anyway, so I guess I'd better get a handle on what the devil he's going to pull next."

Then, to reassure her shaken assistant, she added more reasonably, "And, Connie, I'm sorry . . . for yelling. Just buzz him through. I'll take the call."

Instinct coiled within Liza's stomach as she waited for the connection. Taking the offensive with a formidable opponent had always been her trademark in battle—if she had to fight. Yet something that went beyond pure instinct drove her. She'd slay him this morning. She was determined to win this round with the competitor that had plagued her firm for the past six months.

"Mr. Duarte—and to what do I owe the honor of this call so early on a Monday morning?"

"Ms. Nichols," he stated calmly, "I would *prefer* that you pick up the receiver so that I may speak with you . . . more confidentially."

The *nerve!* Victor Duarte's request was gasoline on an open flame. His rich baritone had filled every crevice of the console, but not before she'd detected a calculated pause. So he wanted to play games this morning. . . . Mentally, she pictured her confident adversary, with his thicket of ebony hair, tall muscular frame, cool poker exterior . . . the works. The more handsome, the more deadly, she grated to herself.

Snatching the receiver from the console, she nearly hissed into the mouthpiece through clenched teeth. "What's so confidential, Duarte?" As soon as the sarcastic comment slipped out, she regretted it. Why couldn't she hold a middle-ground position? Somehow, with him, it was possible.

She could hear him hesitate again before he spoke. A slight tremor coursed through her, bringing with it an irrational thought. Perhaps he was finally on a peace mission. Not likely. Besides, it was probably reverse logic. A strategy designed to catch her off-guard. They had never even been civil before. So why such formal politeness on a Monday morning? Did he think he'd find her more relaxed after the weekend?

As her adversary began speaking again, this time the tension in his tone was unmistakable. She smiled to herself. As always, she had penetrated his barrier. This game felt so much like an old dance . . . one that they both knew too well.

"Ms. Nichols, I'm calling today regarding the relationship between the two firms, which as you know has been strained for some time now—"

"I know you didn't call me for a history lesson. State your purpose."

"Excuse me," he grated back with impatience clear in his voice. "I obviously began wrong. Given the ferocity with which you've cut me off, I take it that this conversation is going to be like a tropical storm—sudden and violent, Miss—"

She didn't even give him time to finish before she went on, her ire gaining momentum against her will.

"We are only having any conversation at all because the client has unfortunately *forced* us to work together." This time her tone was more even, but no less sarcastic. "Let me refresh your memory, Mr. Duarte, since you want to take an *unnecessary* trip down memory lane. We were both at the final executive meeting where the client decided that each firm, as they put it, had a certain skill set. My firm has the computer networking expertise, and I *guess* your firm has the financial portion. Now we're supposed to act like one big, happy family while we set up a worldwide data base for this conglomerate to help them close their books."

When he didn't respond, she smiled again. Theater. He might have won the battle, but he'd have to endure the war.

"And, as you know perfectly well from those meetings, it is their objective to get, in *their* opinion, the best blend of available talent for the money." Liza pushed back in her chair, controlling the pace of her voice. "I happen to believe, and know, that Risc Systems could have handled the entire contract alone. But then, you and I have had this discussion a number of times. All of that is a very well-documented matter of record. So make your point, Duarte."

Victor could hear the rage in her voice as she acidly gave her account of the events that had led up to the joint venture. In an odd way, he actually enjoyed the stormy emotions that Liza Nichols had unveiled so regularly over the past six months. Although he hated her opinion, he enjoyed her raw candor—which had an undeniable quality of passion behind it.

Understanding that there was no way to stop a tornado, he decided to step into the eye of the storm and ride it out. As a distraction, he began to clear paperwork from his desk while she continued to rail without waiting for his response.

"And, despite the obvious professionalism and capability of my staff, your firm has continued to take the arrogant position that our Federal Minority Business Enterprise status was the *only* reason the client awarded my firm the controlling portion of that contract. Correction. A woman-owned firm. An African-American-owned firm. Thus, a disadvantaged business *given* an opportunity—not because we have an unparalleled level of excellence over here. Right?"

"¡Por Dios! She never even took a breath," he thought dryly. Leaning toward his desk, Victor looked for something else to absorb his vexation. Absently, he pulled one silver ball away from its brethren. Each one was suspended by a nylon thread which hung neatly from a chrome frame in a row of eight. As he let the first ball go, it clacked loudly against the next, setting off a hypnotic chain reaction of silver motion before him.

"And while we're on the subject, let me also remind you, from a legal perspective, that means your firm takes full project direction from Risc Systems—*not* the other way around! So here we are with a multi-million dollar contract between us, split right down the middle, giving your firm, a subcontractor no less, an unheard-of fifty percent cut! If anybody's been treated unfairly by this arrangement, it's us. *We're* the ones who were robbed in broad daylight. But then, that's an everyday occurrence in D.C. It was a damned drive-by, Duarte!"

Suddenly, in the distance he heard an odd clatter of destruction. Perfect timing. She'd obviously dropped something or, more likely, had thrown something in her office. Victor closed his eyes. It was as though he could sense her every move. It was the glasses. He was sure of it. High drama was Liza's style. And he loved it. The glasses would probably be the first casualty when she'd reached her endurance. The image made him smile. He thought of her standing now, her impressive height magnified by her anger. He could see her before him, just as he had in the many annoying daydreams that plagued him. Her full, voluptuous mouth drawn to a tight line. Her dark, almond-shaped eyes blazing. Her long, tapered hands clenching whatever she was holding so tightly that the color had drained from her knuckles. Magnificent.

When she paused for a breath, he seized the rare opportunity to get a word in edgewise. His strategy would be a logical defense. His objective, damage control.

"Ms. Nichols, *please* . . . As I have said before, the way this joint venture was forced by the client was perhaps not the best circumstances under which to form a working relationship. However, if both firms are going to be successful, we will, at some point, have to determine how we can manage to overcome the initial difficulties and misperceptions."

He had to regain control, to calm her down. He pushed back in his chair and tried to allow the irritation in his voice to dissipate, brushing an invisible fleck of lint from his knee as he gathered his thoughts.

"Peace is imperative, at least enough to allow us to complete our contractual obligations to the client. *Both* firms have some very talented people who, to date, have not been able to collaborate together effectively because of the personal issues that have disrupted their working environment. We need to declare some sort of truce or face the very real possibility of jeopardizing the entire project because of our lack of team integration. As a principal of DGE Associates, I am attempting to extend the olive branch at this juncture."

He hoped that this rational explanation would reign in the high-strung thoroughbred that was so determined to fight him.

Was he mad? Liza counted to ten before she spoke.

"You rob my firm of three million dollars, then offer a truce?" she fumed. "You're a real man of honor, *Victor.*"

"Honor? My honor has never been a question. Perhaps you're right about one thing—that we have nothing to discuss."

"Oh, but we do. You said so yourself."

It was his turn to think, and she could feel him trying desperately to disengage from the sudden fury that swept through him. That was it. The word *honor*. Something had happened before. She knew it like she knew her name. There was a breach of honor. But when? She'd just met him through this deal.

And, just as suddenly as he had made her angry, they had shifted roles. He was furious, and she couldn't repress the sardonic smile that crept over her face as she studied the irony of it all. Especially since it all seemed so vaguely familiar.

Taking a more strategic stance in order to think, Liza walked over to the window, slightly easing her grip around the sleek cordless receiver. She had to disengage from the anger in order to focus her thoughts—in order to use her *gift,* her ability to probe into the mind for answers. She closed her eyes and concentrated on the two seconds of darkness that she would allow herself. It took no longer than a slow blink.

He was right. There was no getting around it as the facts battered her senses. There were many aspects of the project that would have been completed weeks ago if the technical staff had felt more comfortable working in a cooperative environment. She'd have to relent and give ground. Why this whole process had enraged her so was beyond her understanding. It was as though Victor Duarte were some sort of catalyst that brought out the worst in her. Yet he had been equally as provoked in their many meetings, often causing his own partners to cringe . . .

"Okay," he said after a long pause. "Let's not get into this struggle again, Liza. We can agree to disagree, can't we?"

Hearing the way he used her name, she reluctantly smiled again. He was a pro. A worthy adversary to be sure. But she'd still win.

"Yeah, I guess so," she said, this time her tone mellow. Perhaps she was getting tired. Fighting him was such a drain. "Peace, huh? A Middle East accord."

"Peace. And a less stressful working environment."

Despite being outraged by the situation, she knew that she would have done the same had she been in Victor Duarte's shoes.

From a veteran's perspective, she had to confess that she liked Duarte's style, even admired the way he had skillfully put the ball right back into her court.

"Okay," she said grudgingly. "I would have to agree with you on that point at least, Duarte. Granted, we have to find a way to work together. There has been some unnecessary slippage on our deadlines which cannot continue to be tolerated."

More steady now, the full violence of Liza's storm receded slightly, giving way to her more calculating reason. She walked back to the comfortable leather chair which had been abandoned earlier, picked up her horn-rimmed glasses, set them very precisely on the bridge of her nose, and sat down. The chess game was about to begin. He had made the first move to vaguely apologize.

But he didn't answer her immediately. A negotiating ploy. It annoyed her that Victor's so-easily-detected strategy had worked. He had counted on the fact that she, too, was a pro and, despite her anger, would not let personal differences jeopardize the contract. She hated to be so transparent.

"Good, then at least we have the beginnings of détente," he said finally, grating her nerves even more with his confidence.

She'd heard Victor's voice lift to match what she was sure was another one of his deadly sensuous smiles. Civility within grasp, knight advances queen. Her move. She'd wait.

Caught at a slight disadvantage by the annoying pleasantries Victor had managed to maintain thus far during the meaningless call, she knew that the next move was critical. She hated the charismatic smugness that came through in his voice when he thought he'd won one of their matches.

But, before she could think of something curt to end the conversation, Victor quickly added, "This is why I had hoped that we could meet on neutral territory . . . for once. Perhaps you would be my guest for dinner tomorrow so that we can more fully discuss how to better integrate the team."

In the long silence that followed, she realized with alarm that his voice might have revealed a tinge more of expectation than even *he* wanted to admit. Without question, she knew that he had always respected her shrewdness and understood when she was armed. He could probably feel her studying the request carefully. He was vulnerable.

His anxiousness confused her. Why did he hope that she wouldn't detect how much he really wanted this meeting to take place? The truth was, if she had asked him directly why a dinner meeting was necessary, he wouldn't have had a plausible answer. Odd. She could sense it. Why did he suddenly now want to see her outside of the sterile business environment that had been a source of personal agitation for months? What was this man's angle?

"Dinner?" was all she could manage. Something was definitely wrong.

The shift in his mood, his strategy, his tactics—everything made her reinforce her guard. He was obviously employing some new strategy in the ongoing civil war between the two firms. Yet, she sensed no fraud or deception. It was weird. Focusing a little harder, she tried to uncover what it was that she heard in his voice. Her fingertips began to tingle.

"Yes, I'm sure that there'll be a number of logistics to nail down; and since we have a meeting Wednesday morning, we should start off on the right foot, a.s.a.p.," he faltered. "My schedule is booked for the rest of the day. So, since we are in agreement to enact a cease-fire, tomorrow night seems like the most expedient timeframe. Would you agree?" he added more tentatively.

Nervous? Victor Duarte? She smiled as he babbled on like a madman. What was wrong with him?

Her mind tore at the possibilities and trapped them. Fact: Victor Duarte had collected himself. Maybe a little too quickly. Smooth. Indeed, he had answered the real question that her tone had implied without giving himself away. But the strain of her silence would be the perfect weapon. "He must be holding his breath now," she thought as mischief rushed through her veins. Yes. Make him wait. The phone seemed to crackle with a new surge of energy. Strategy: Let a full two minutes pass before speaking. Liza looked down at her watch and began keeping time with the second hand.

Queen takes knight.

Discipline. *Wait* for her answer. Victor drummed his fingers on his desk, warding off the adrenaline. Remember the basics. It is imperative to gain control of the project and to ensure the success of the mission. He repeated the goal to himself like a mantra to steady his nerves. It was important to remain focused on the big picture: Control of the project direction in order to continue the mission which he had begun almost twenty years ago. No slipups. The vendetta was at stake.

Victor closed his eyes and let a deep breath escape from his nose. His request was insane. He'd been backed into a corner again, and it happened every time they clashed. No one could do that to him. He was one of the best in the business.

Forcing his mind to review the escape routes, it was easy for him to remember how he and his partners had sat gripped by outrage in the Chem Tech executive boardroom. Without warning, the small, savvy newcomer had pulled an unprecedented coup right before their eyes. She was good. Damned good, and fought like a pro. Only something more basic tugged at him now, mingling with the rage and clouding his perspective. For the first time, he couldn't remain safely detached.

This ill-conceived request, and his feelings, just didn't make sense. The dichotomy posed infinite variables, all too dangerous to consider.

An eternity seemed to pass as he waited for Liza Nichols' response to what on the surface appeared to be a very simple request. He could almost hear the gears of her well-oiled mind grinding and assessing the new data. It was painfully obvious that she was deciding whether or not to accept, how to accept, trying to figure out his angle, or, worse yet, formulating a practical refusal. She'd never go for it. A conference call would have sufficed, he groaned inwardly. Just fax her your position, let her fax you hers, strike what you can't agree on, and have a draft for the morning meeting. But *dinner?*

Years of executive-level negotiations proved worthless. Here he was, the senior negotiator for his firm, violating the fundamentals! Once an offer was out on the table, one should *never* make the first move or speak before the client has responded to the initial offer. It was simple. One-O-one level training. The fact that Liza was obviously well versed in the basics and had allowed a few tense minutes to pass with only a snort hadn't helped. However, despite all his years of experience, the wait for her reply was pure torture.

Unable to bear the strain any longer and fearing that her mind had already been made up to reject the offer of a peace dinner, he broke the silence.

"Liza . . . We *really* do need to talk. I sincerely hope that you will be able to get free tomorrow evening to meet with me over dinner."

Damn it all! He couldn't believe he'd said that! And she *still* hadn't answered him! The very call itself had been against his better judgment. Now the compounded discouragement of a probable refusal was overwhelming.

It unnerved him as he sat there taking in how truly disappointed he was. Until this moment, he hadn't realized just how much he enjoyed locking horns with his intemperate opponent. No one had ever seen him actually lose his temper—that is, until Liza's whirlwind of energy disrupted his structured, precise world. The only inkling of displeasure that he ever allowed anyone to witness was when the iron gate of annoyance closed down slowly over his professional exterior.

Colleagues and competitors alike knew that when his responses took on a tone of icy exactness, cutting through his otherwise controlled voice, that was when he became lethal. Yet, Liza Nichols never flinched. She would always look him directly, defiantly—electrically in the eyes.

"Makes sense to me, Victor. After all, this can't go on forever."

To his relief, Liza finally broke the silence that was strangling him. Her answer was casual and flippant. Typical. Victor's shoulders relaxed as the storm passed. Renewed confidence allowed traces of a smile to creep back over his previously tense face. *"Excellent.* I will leave the details with Connie and look forward to our discussion tomorrow night. Enjoy the rest of your day."

"Fine."

The phone clicked abruptly in his ear. She had hung up without the courtesy of a goodbye! Fury consumed him. She could be such a . . .

That, too, had been expected. Liza was in the driver's seat now, and he was certain that she derived a great deal of satisfaction from her position. Victor walked over to the long, black-leather sofa in his office and grabbed his briefcase. He had a client meeting to attend, and no more time to dwell on the Nichols problem. Somehow he had to vent some of this frustration before they met for dinner. Deep submersion into work might block her from his thoughts. Maybe. But one thing was for sure, he would not go into round two unprepared. Every aspect of his life hinged on this project.

As he took the back elevator down to the parking lot, his thoughts continued to crowd in on him. Their first meeting came into focus immediately. From the beginning, Liza had totally exasperated him in front of both the client and their staff—on more than one occasion. She had actually caused him to raise his voice and to openly confront her in the heated debates that were otherwise totally out of his character. Somehow, she had been able to repeatedly bring him to the edge of professional decorum, which always left him feeling quite off-balance and well outside his comfort zone.

Although her strategy was obvious, it was always effective. Try as he might, he couldn't resist the temptation to be drawn into open battle with her.

Each outrageous episode always resulted the same way. After effectively coaxing his temper out into the open, she would corner it, shift gears, and retreat into the calm psychiatric demeanor that always left him furiously vulnerable. Her greatest weapon seemed to be the ability to extract emotions from him that had been buried for a long time.

Victor stopped suddenly as a new reality assaulted him. He had to admit that he hated the battles, but also loved the challenge of them at the same time. With that thought, he became significantly alarmed by the new awareness of how very alive Liza Nichols made him feel. Fascinating.

Liza's grip eased around the receiver as she more gently returned the telephone back to its cradle, still looking at the console in amazement. She hadn't expected her own ambivalent response to Victor's suggestion to work out a truce. Over *dinner,* no less.

Could it be possible, she wondered, that she had actually grown accustomed to the daily verbal jousts with him? Or was it that she simply looked forward to the mental stimulation of the ongoing chess game that they so fiercely played? But somehow, she mused, this call was different.

Allowing herself to rest briefly in order to accommodate the dull ache in her temple, she finally admitted in a low chuckle, "Mr. Duarte, I gotta respect 'cha. You are most *definitely* a pro. An absolute, consummate professional!"

Shifting gears, she decided to call Letty. Maybe she'd even pop up to Philly for a taste of home. An hour-and-a-half Metroliner run along with some stick-to-your-ribs food would do the trick. Anything to get away from this stress.

Mentally envisioning her outrageous girlfriend, Liza hit the speed dial code on her console. Instead of a name showing through the clear plastic plate next to the auxiliary buttons, there was a little smiley face to denote Letty's number. After the second ring, Liza closed her eyes.

"Please, please, be home," she whispered. Her heart sank immediately when a rush of calypso music blared into her ear. She hated those machines. Prepared to leave a nondescript message, she was startled by the sudden break in the music.

"Joe's Pizza!" announced the familiar voice, followed by a laugh.

"Oh, Letty! I was praying that you were home and had Monday off. How did you know it was me?"

"Technology, Hon. Ident-A-Ring. Hey, you're the techie, Stranger. How the hell are ya? Where you been, Girl? What's the scoop?"

Liza hesitated for a moment before responding. She hadn't thought of what she would tell Letty. There really wasn't anything to tell, per se. She was just unnerved and wasn't even sure why. To go into a long, boring soliloquy about the Chem Tech deal was definitely out of the question. Letty hated corporate stuff and wouldn't have the patience to absorb what she was talking about anyway. She didn't want Letty to think it was a man thing. It wasn't. It was just a strategy question, she told herself. Letty was good at knowing where people were coming from.

"I, uh, have a situation here and could use your advice. . . . I dunno, maybe it's me, but—"

"It's a man! I knew it! I could tell in your voice as soon as you said my name!"

Liza groaned. "No, no, no. It's not a *man*. Not really, but it's a situation that involves a man. . . ."

Liza heard the familiar exasperated breath that Letty expelled into the receiver, which was always followed by the soft tick of Letty sucking her teeth.

"So, we gonna spend the first twenty minutes of this long-distance call with you trying to convince me that I can help the queen of business negotiations with a bizillion-dollar deal? Okay, sell off the IBM stock, buy AT&T, and—lemme see—invest in pork bellies. Now, can we continue with the reason you called? It's your dime; spend how you like, Lady."

Liza smiled, this was indeed why she had called. Only Letty knew her this well. Well enough to get past all of her insane barriers in ten seconds.

"All right, already. You win. But he's not *my man*. Not by any stretch of your overactive imagination. Okay?"

"Doesn't have to be," Letty piped in, chuckling. "Is he fine? Of course he is or you wouldn't be trippin' like this. So what's he do? Or, better yet, how's he do it?"

"Letty, please! Are you going to let me tell you what the problem is or are you going to tell me the whole story yourself?"

"I'm sorry, Girlfriend," Letty soothed, her voice still resonant with mischief. "Suppose I was just hopeful 'cause you haven't said anything to me about any man for a long time. I haven't heard you like this since the whole Barry thing a couple of years ago. Talk to me, Hon."

Collecting her thoughts slowly, Liza closed her eyes and allowed her head to drop forward and massaged her neck. Barry Walker had been the last thing on her mind. How in the world had Letty made that vertical leap? She hadn't dated Barry Walker in years and had left that heartache folded-up neatly with all the other disappointments of her life. Leave it to her friend to drive a stake right into the heart of the matter.

"Can we just meet at Thirtieth Street Station after work and go to a joint around the way? I miss home. I miss everybody. Just for a couple of hours, then I gotta jet back to the business to finish up . . . around eleven."

Letty was quiet for a moment. "Girl, c'mon up to Philly. We need to talk about a lot of things."

The throb in Liza's temple intensified. "I'll be there by 7 P.M. Find us a good soul-food place, okay? I'll make it up to you."

"Don't worry about it. I'm your home-girl. Remember that. Love you, too. Bye."

Liza looked at the receiver as she set it down. "Yeah, bye," she murmured into the quiet, closing her eyes again. "But what am I going to do?"

Two

Numerous issues converged on Liza's brain as the train plowed forward. There was no possible way to salvage her concentration.

Leaning back in her seat, she focused on the lesser of two evils. Connie had given her the facts about Duarte's dinner. They were to meet tomorrow at 7:00, just after she finished up for the evening. Unfortunately, that meant she'd have to deal with the unsettling feeling of nervous intrigue *until next evening.* Her fault. She shouldn't have broken through his defenses. Using that so-called gift the way her grandmother had taught her always left her feeling tired, wrung-out, and jittery. Her own secret weapon had obviously backfired, leaving her in its wake.

"Why?" she wondered again aloud, annoyed by the new issue that had taken priority over her other thoughts. She had more serious work to do, but . . . then again, what was more serious than a threat to her firm?

Still caught up in the process of evaluating the call, she found a sudden new insight crashing in on her. The reservations that Victor Duarte had made at the exclusive French restaurant, chosen on a supposed whim, had most likely been arranged and confirmed at least two days in advance. Once again, Duarte's confidence totally infuriated her. Then it hit her—she had picked up a distinct interest from him, and not a business-oriented one.

It had felt like a deep rumble beneath the surface of their exchange. "Oh, God. I knew it from day one." The information congealed in her brain and forced the whisper from her lips. It was impossible to ignore, just like thunder in the distance . . . and just as strong, just as difficult to deny. Worse, she'd felt him grappling with his own denial, repressing the torrid energy that ignited both of their tempers beyond reason and professional bounds. This was a serious problem.

She also didn't enjoy the personal admission that accepting his invitation meant that he'd won their short telephone match. Which also meant that thus far his *moves* on the board today had gone unchallenged. To steady herself, she rationalized that she could afford to lose a few pawns to get to his larger pieces during the game.

"This dinner will be his mistake," she murmured to herself while clearing out one section of her briefcase. She would not give in to this *other issue* that went far beyond business. Duarte might want to, but she wouldn't even acknowledge it. Liza smiled as she chiseled away at the mountain of paper before her, delighting in the mischief of her strategy. She could handle it. Wouldn't be the first time some guy had an agenda that she ignored. It went with the territory of being a woman in the business arena. Somehow, having a definite competitive edge—the ability to use *her gift* to stay one step ahead, even if she decided not to use it—had enabled her to relax enough to deal with the business at hand for the balance of the day.

Yet, as the workday had drawn to a close, she'd even found herself in the ladies' room, freshening up her makeup and retouching her hair. Why couldn't she disengage from the broiling thoughts that Victor Duarte conjured in her mind? With other men, she could. Almost three years of celibacy had not been a problem until now. She didn't even allow herself to think those useless, frustrating thoughts. But this guy . . .

The monotony of the train engine and the industrial wasteland of scenery drilled a hole in her brain. Nothing had seemed to make the cranial-splitting headaches stop today.

Still fussing at herself as she cleaned her glasses, she took out a small compact and looked into the mirror, then flung it back into her purse. The fleeting thought that she should have worn something different to the office was an unnerving irritant. She already had on her favorite, knock-out-red power suit. So, what the hell? Of course, the run in her stocking took away some of the power. But tomorrow, she told herself, she'd be together.

How could one successful chick be so insecure? she wondered, tugging at the hose. And for what? A dinner with an arch enemy? She was obsessing about this, yet the question remained—why?

The swirling thoughts were making her head hurt, and she felt herself becoming queasy again. Shaking four Advils into her hand, Liza let the tiny brown pills hit the back of her tongue and swallowed hard. As they slid thickly down her throat, she gagged and stood up. She had to get into the bathroom before she wretched. What had she been thinking when she'd done the psychic probe on Duarte? It really wasn't fair to invade the man's mind like that, but, then again, it seemed like necessary self-defense.

Finally inside the tiny cubicle, she turned on the cold-water faucet. She hadn't eaten all day. Cupping her hands beneath the cool stream of water, Liza peered into her palms, watching the water overflow into the sink. Her thoughts crystalized in the clarity of the water, and she stood transfixed, unable to move.

Why had Aunt V, her mother's sister who'd raised her, and the bevy of formidable church ladies acted like she'd committed murder when she'd told them that she wasn't in school to get a husband? she wondered, taking a sip from her hands.

Liza dried her hands and went back to endure the ride. Pain still shot through her temple, and she sat down with a wobbly thud to avoid falling. It had never been this strong before, and she had always been able to stop any thoughts that attacked her. Her equilibrium was off, and she was near tears. What did they want from her? Working and getting good grades had been her only ticket to freedom during college. Why was she thinking about that now anyway?

Her mind jumped to how frantic she had been to get a job. A *good* job. It had been the only thing that she could think of to rebuild what they had all lost. Yet, none of them seemed to believe that she was capable of restoring the family to good financial health. They thought that her brother, Gerald, should do that. And poor Gerry, he just wanted to dance. Now her brother was too sick to even lift his head from his hospital pillow these days, let alone take on some family-restoration challenge.

She had known since the moment she'd been shipped off to her aunt's house that she had to get out of there. Aunt V, just like Mom, couldn't stand to hear a word about the paranormal. Nor could she cope with an energetic, aggressive young woman full of hope. Auntie's way of dealing with it was to send her to church and refuse to discuss any of it.

The whole decade of the eighties had been a trial of horrors. Giving in to the pull of her thoughts, Liza focused on the pain and looked out the window. She knew that *they* were making her face herself today. But why her thoughts were being so relentless was beyond her. Hadn't she admitted from the beginning that the corporate world wasn't the answer? That it had just been a necessary means to an end. Something to give her the cash flow and experience to start her own firm.

Liza shook her head. Her mind was careening from subject to subject like a top out of control. Corporate America had more rules and prejudices than her aunt and demanded the same level of excellence. But the jobs she'd had only required that she show up every day, wear conservative clothes, sit in a tiny cube facing a screen, and program until she was cross-eyed. Okay, she had done that, despite the fact that they rarely gave her credit for her efforts. Then, there was Letty to contend with, who was appalled by her career choice. The corporate world flew directly in the face of freedom fighting, according to her militant friend. She wondered if Letty would consider it okay now, since she had turned those years of angst into a business which employed *The People?*

Rubbing her temples and massaging her neck, Liza let her thoughts roam to her mission. She had stayed on track until Barry had entered her life. Liza groaned and shut her eyes tight. She didn't want to go where her brain was hurtling . . .

Before that madness with Barry, she had had a few dates,

endured a few crushes, but mostly enjoyed her male friends who were always there to pal around with on platonic outings. But Barry had been the big one. The one who seemed to believe in her. The one who encouraged her to dream. At one foolish point, she really had thought that she could have it all. Maybe even live like a normal person. Together, they would be a team to conquer the world.

"Please stop," she whispered to herself. "I don't want to see it again." But the mental muscle was already in use.

It had taken Barry over a year to convince her that he had truly chosen her out of all of the other possibilities. A whole year for their relationship to go beyond mentor/protege to an intimate encounter . . . where he'd promised her forever. Liar. It was still hard to deal with the reality that all he'd wanted to do was to use her best work to land contracts of his own, which had offered him a foothold into the lucrative Chem Tech Conglomerate. Then, it was over.

Liza opened her eyes, but the motion of the train made the thoughts slam against her skull. Barry had announced that he was getting married to a more "well-healed" female who could finance his endeavors. She hated that she had only been his brains and his challenger, Cherrell, had been his banker. But in the end, she had still won out the contract over all the others, so maybe there was a little justice in the world—if not revenge.

Now, she faced Duarte, a man who had clearly impacted her financially, with her firm doing the lion's share of the work for the contract. They were the brains, not DGE. Maybe she was going from bad to worse, getting both her brain and her pocket picked. And on top of it all, Duarte now wanted to get personal, to take her to dinner!

Liza's breaths were coming in short rasps now. She felt ill, and a clammy moisture wet her back. Then it hit her. That's when the *thoughts* had first started coming to her in sequence, bringing the nasty headaches with them. Duarte! They had just invaded her life without permission, forcing her to use her gift. They started coming in dreams, making her see visions. . . . Nana

Ethel had told her that the ancients would talk to her one day and that she had an important job to do. The ancients? That was insane! She wanted them, or it, out of her life! She refused to be pushed around, even by spirits. Oh God, she was starting to sound like a lunatic!

Swallowing down another wave of nausea, Lisa reached for her compact and looked at her now-paling complexion. Thirtieth Street had been called, and she added a bit of color to her cheeks. When her probe was on too long or the subject matter was too terrible, it totally drained her. Studying her face, she lamented over how tired she looked. She was positively grey. After she'd finished the Barry situation, which she refused to call a relationship, she'd promised herself that she would never probe an emotionally charged situation again. If it were business, then fine. That was easy and didn't take a toll. But when her heart was involved . . .

What was she saying? Her heart wasn't involved. The thing between her and Duarte was just business, angry business, wasn't it?

Standing quickly, she looked at her transformed image in the window as the train lurched into darkness. Happily-ever-after was all a big lie. All of it. She would stay on her mission and uncover the people who'd brought her father to ruin. That was the only truth here. The key lay in Chem Tech, she could feel it. She knew it. Her childish wants and needs be damned. Having a person to love her, cherish her, stand by her side forever . . . children, a home—not a house . . . The bleak thought shook her, and she felt hot tears threatening her composure.

Revenge had its price, though. Now she was damaged goods from the inside out. That was one thing she'd never forget. How could she? It was only *after* she'd changed, become a worthy adversary with her own lucrative firm, that Barry had wanted to see her again. Ain't that nothin'? Power was the only thing that people respected. What a painful way to learn a lesson.

Two big tears rolled down Liza's cheeks and made her cringe. Damn. She would have to start fixing her face all over again.

What was wrong with her today? The last thing she wanted to do was meet Letty looking as if she'd been crying. And she could just imagine the smug look on Victor Duarte's face if he had even an inkling that she was this upset.

Ever since she'd re-invented herself, changing from a slightly overweight, conservative geek to a successful business woman, she'd gotten her fair share of male attention. She had also put every would-be liar in his place . . . which meant for some very lonely nights. But she also wasn't about to risk her heart or her integrity again in any equation. For what? A few moments' pleasure? A fleeting glimmer of hope? Besides, she prayed that that wasn't one of the dynamics going on with Duarte. If it were what she suspected, then at least she could ignore it. Anyway, it was bad enough that she had to wrangle her contract money out of him. Anything else would just be too intense.

Protocol aside, she dabbed on concealer while swaying in the aisle and angrily blended her makeup in to cover up the smudged mascara. She liked winning. But the victories had all been hollow. She didn't want the attention if it only hinged on the way she looked on the outside. Who she was, was who she was. She wasn't going to humiliate herself again, be made a fool of, nor was she about to deal with someone who liked her only because she now had a great pair of legs. Liza peeped at the reflection of her profile as passengers began to exit the car.

So, why was she still locked into her exercise regime and daily application of makeup ritual? She could justify the exercise. It gave her more energy for the long days she put in, and supposedly exercise extended one's life. Okay, that was rational. But the other stuff . . . the makeup, the hair . . .

Impatient to get off the train, Liza blotted her face with the back of her hand and winced at the oily T-zone that had reappeared. What had she expected? It hadn't gone away since high school. She had to remember that tomorrow was, after all, just a business meeting, not a social outing. Frustrated by her own inability to banish the last wave of nagging self-doubt, she hurried herself, muttering as anonymous briefcases hit her legs.

Sardines trapped in a can. She breathed in, invoking mental affirmations to help her relax. Yes, she would be in control tomorrow night. She would *not* be pushed around. Her company had won the bid fair and square. Though, why she now felt so nervous about a *business meeting* was completely beyond her scope of reason.

Yet, she just couldn't put her finger on what it was that had shifted her own perspective on the board at this moment. Whatever her nervousness stemmed from, it was making her unsure and curiously expectant of the meeting. She had to get out of the throng. Their thoughts were crowding in on her within the small confines of the stairwell.

She briskly walked across the wide expanse of marble floor. Freedom. The high ceilings and light filtering into the station made her take a deep, cleansing breath.

Liza glanced down at her watch. She hated being late. It annoyed her that even by 7:15, she still hadn't broken the code on the tone of eagerness in her opponent's invitation. There was also something more about Victor Duarte. She was almost positive that she had detected something different in Duarte's voice. Perhaps it was the unusual hesitations that made him sound so uncharacteristically vulnerable. Maybe it was the extra emphasis he placed on every word that had raised her antenna. She just couldn't put her finger on it. But, then again, it really wasn't important.

Brushing aside the queries, Liza immediately reminded herself that she was early—Letty was always late. Fifteen minutes was nothing. She had to relax.

"Chile! I was running to make it here as fast as I could!"

Liza looked up from her *Wall Street Journal* and laughed. "Yeah, I know. What 'cha got for the blues, Girl?"

They hugged, and Liza held her friend back to look at her. "You are a knockout," Liza beamed with affection. "I love the look," she added, marvelling at Letty's sleek olive tunic and pants suit.

"It's a total package . . . had to polish up my act to get a job,"

Letty chuckled, turning around and making her short frame chime from the hundreds of beads around her neck. "I had to convince them that the braids, the cowrie-shell earrings, and my Afrocentricity was not a threat to their establishment. I'm now ethno-chic, Girl."

"Well, it works. Wish I could do the same. I still have to contend with a bunch of old geezers down in the District to get my business rolling. But, I swear, one day I'm hanging up my pumps."

Liza was truly in awe as they began a brisk pace from the station. Only months ago, her friend had donned slogan tee-shirts and baggy pants. Now she looked like a dark Isis with a touch of Madison Avenue.

"Lady, you look and sound a lot better than I expected. You had me worried," Letty admitted when they approached the cab-port.

Liza threw an arm around Letty's shoulders as they stood waiting for a cab to pull up. "Just, plain, old beat, Girl. Needed some laughs, TLC, and—"

"I know what you need."

Liza laughed again. "Yeah. Could use that, too, Hon. But do you know where to get it clean, neat, no strings attached, that'll take coffee in a go-cup? If so, let me invest there."

"Chile, you ain't said a mumblin' word! But coffee in a go-cup was never your style, so stop frontin'. Long-term, steady, love-of-your-life is what's making you so picky. If we could find that on a regular basis, then we'd start a new market. Better than Lotto—we could both retire!"

They both looked at the disgruntled expression on the cab driver's face and laughed.

"Sorry, m' brother," Letty soothed, patting the man's shoulder as they slid into the back seat. "See, my girlfriend here is a serious workaholic and she ain't got time for no games. This lady is takin' care of bizness. Problem is, she needs somebody to take care of *her* bizness."

"Letty!" Liza screamed as the cabby laughed and shifted into gear. "Don't pay her no mind. She's no longer my friend. I don't know this woman."

"Well, it's true," Letty protested through giggles.

"Well, if de lady is in need of company . . ."

"Don't pay her no mind, I said. I'm fine."

"Yes. You are very fine, I would agree. My name is Gregory. You from dis country?"

Liza smiled weakly and groaned. "Yes. Hi. Nice to meet you."

Jabbing Letty with her elbow, she forced light conversation until they pulled up to the Caribbean Soul restaurant on Baltimore Avenue. "I'm going to kill you when we get inside," Liza whispered through her teeth and fought hard not to laugh when Letty winked.

"You take care, m' brother," Letty said and closed the door, squealing as Liza pinched her side. "Now, he was *fine*. . . . See, that's why you gotta come home, Girl. Ain't you tired of all those foo foo la la people yet?"

"Those foo foo la la people pay the bills," Liza chuckled as they made their way to the counter. "Gotta work to eat. Gotta eat to live. Know what I mean?"

"Yeah, I'm gonna quit though one of these days, Liz. I want to open up a jazz dessert house or something. You know, where artists can groove and unwind. People can talk . . . get their work seen."

"Like I said. Takes money, time, and—"

"Okay. Okay, Miss Black Enterprise. Stop killing dreams before they're born. Let's get some greens, coconut peas and rice, some conch fritters, some curry chicken, iced tea, and sit our tired butts down. Then you can tell me 'bout why you had to escape from Alcatraz."

The place smelled like heaven on earth, and Liza settled into a broken red-plastic chair with relish. "Oh, Letty . . . I miss the pace of home . . . where I can let my hair down, talk like I want, be like I want. You know?"

Letty gave Liza's arm a squeeze. "Being bilingual is a trip, ain't it? I know. But you should be used to it by now."

"Hey. Trust me, just because you can do it, doesn't mean you want to."

Letty shook her head as they walked back to pick up their orders. Just standing up had become a chore.

"So, when you comin' out of the concrete jungle?"

"When can I afford to?" Liza picked up her tray and moved toward the table again. "I feel like I've been burning the candle at both ends and there's no wick left."

"So, who's been burning up your stuff, Girl?" Letty said, shoveling a forkful of peas and rice into her mouth when they sat down. "Hope he's better than that other—"

"I keep telling you. This isn't a Barry situation. I haven't gone out with the man. It's not like that."

Liza felt a sudden defensiveness sweep through her. "I need to run to the ladies' room. Haven't gone since I left the office."

She needed an escape. Liza's face grew solemn as she paced away from her friend. Where had that come from? Impatient with herself, she walked faster. She needed to burn off the nervous energy that felt like a live wire running down her back. Couldn't she ever have a thought that didn't pull up a whole mess of sorrow behind it? What did Barry Walker have to do with going to dinner with Duarte?

Tossing her purse on the sink, she searched for her comb. Momentarily stopping her search, she stared at her reflection. After Barry left, it was sheer defiance of the concept that she was not to be contended with that had made her buy the red outfit—which was now two years old. Silly, feminine revenge that was never even noticed by anyone but herself. A waste of time, energy, and money. She hated the way the whole thing had gone down.

Liza's shoulders slumped. What was she doing? There were higher stakes with the Chem Tech deal than this. Yet, one stupid reference to her past had again dredged up a string of sad memories. It was as though her thoughts had become a kaleidoscope today, each memory triggering another in an endless array of pain.

Barry. What a laugh. Liza adjusted her blouse and blotted on a final matte finish. She'd have better answers for Letty when she returned. They'd eat and enjoy each other's company. The Barry fiasco was over. Duarte had nothing remotely to do with it.

"In fact, we positively hate each other," Liza said, sitting down hard as she returned to the table—a strategy designed to make her point before Letty could make her think. "We've been fighting like dogs for the past six months over a contract, which I won but had to split with his company. And it was okay, as long as it stayed like that—I mean, being at odds. That way, it was easy to keep everything organized . . . in my head. But something strange happened today. The guy called on a serious peace mission. He also asked me out to dinner when we could have just faxed each other the info. I don't know why I feel so weird about this."

Letty had set her plastic fork down and had stopped eating. After a long pause, she twisted one of her micro-braids behind her ear and adjusted an earring. Smoothing the front of her tunic, she then untangled her silver bangles before her hand went to her hip. It was a production. Like watching a prophet get ready to deliver a sermon, maybe the tablets. There was no rushing her friend's advice.

"Liz," she said, hesitating for emphasis and glancing around the room to the interested ladies behind the counter. "You mean to say that you've been battling this tall, gorgeous hunk for six months . . . and nothing's kicked off yet?"

"Shhh. Keep your voice down, will you?" Liza felt her face get warm.

"Allow my editorial comments. So, you beat him. Fair and square. It's simple. Right?"

Neither woman spoke as they ate. What was there to say about the oldest reality? Liza felt a deep ache rekindling as she thought back on how she had learned the hard way that it wasn't enough to be a nice person or to be smart. People didn't hand you things just because you quietly deserved to have them. You had to *make* things happen in your own best interest, especially if you were a woman. Especially if you were black. But being a woman these days meant that you also had to be pretty, marry well, have perfect children, have a great career, be socially, politically, and environmentally responsible, well read . . . Superwoman. Who could live up to that bill of goods?

"I guess I'm just trying to . . ."

"Make sure you don't get interested in someone you work with and put yourself in the same position that you found yourself in before. Right? You have to admit that there is some basic level of attraction or you wouldn't be this blown away. I can always tell when it's a man thing with you—you get all weird and super professional and go into denial. Am I right?"

"Wrong. This time. And what you've described has only happened to me once, so how can you make a blanket statement like that? No. I'm having problems working with a difficult subcontractor on an important job. That's all."

Letty smiled and took a sip of iced tea. "Denial."

"I'm not in denial. It has nothing to do with it."

Liza knew that she had issued an intellectual defense, but then, why had she shied away from the numerous opportunities to date the eligible men in her circles? Her motives were too complex to face at the moment, and an argument about it over curried chicken and rice was out of the question. She'd think about it later. Much later.

Letty rolled her eyes. "Has everything to do with it."

"I don't want to debate that tired topic again in life."

"All right. Just checkin', anyway. You won a contract he wanted. Right? Now that the dust is settled and both of you can see straight, he asks you out to dinner. It's as plain as the nose on your face."

"I can't see the nose on my face, Letty." She laughed, feeling more at ease as her friend oversimplified the issues.

"Tell me that you don't want *somebody* in *your* life. That's the issue, Liz. You do, but don't want to admit it. Your body, mind, and soul are raging against the Universe. And—"

"And, it's not fair that people play games, and I won't—"

"Chile, why are you wearing yourself out over this? He's just a little ole man. Lord have *mercy,* Girl! He hasn't said anything to you out of the way, and I take it that he's one of those suits that's too professional to put his hands on you without a serious green light."

"You haven't heard a word I've said!"

"I think you're going overboard with—"

"Overboard? Overboard? He beat me out of three mill. This ain't philosophy!" Liza lowered her voice as the entire restaurant stopped moving.

"Three million dollars?" Letty whispered. "I'd a kicked his butt."

Liza laughed. "It might make me feel better; but legally, I can't do anything to him. He won. Just like that. Because he was in the ol' boys' network. My staff has most of the programming work, and as a distributor, my firm also has to deliver the equipment—all on our half of the money. That's salaries *and* equipment. His firm only has to go in and toodle around on a small part of it—the financials. *But they got half of the contract money!* If I didn't have outstanding bills, I'd take my half down to South Philly and have his legs broken."

Liza sighed. "I don't know who to be angrier at, him or the client. There's no place to vent this frustration."

Letty's expression was still full of mischief. "Probably toward the client. If you could have won a sweet, minimal work deal for your firm, you would have taken it. Right? So, how can you blame this guy? He did what came natural. It doesn't sound like it was a personal thing. Now the guy wants to take you out . . . maybe get in your pants. You can say yes or no and not be compromised. Your decision, based on all the facts. So?"

"So, hell . . . I'm not trying to go there again."

It was Letty's turn to sigh, and she took a few bites of food while shaking her head. "You know what the problem is? You never brought closure to that other mess like I told you to.

Shoulda gave Barry Walker a left, then a right. Or maybe poured bleach on his fifteen-hundred-dollar suits. Yeah. But you told me that wasn't how the rules of business decorum went, so you had to let it go. *Had to be a lady.* Peacefully. Now, you're still mad and he's still rich and married."

"Rules," Liza said in a low voice with a smile. "Were made to be broken. I probably would have felt better if I'da decked him."

"Yeah, right. Coming from a conservative sister like you? What rules have you broken lately? The most I'll give you is, red. It's a dramatic departure from your earlier drab blues, blacks, and browns. But, I hate to tell you, the earth tones are back in vogue, Girl."

Liza groaned. "I know. But I already spent a mint for this stuff, so I'm wearing what I bought till it dry rots." Annoyed at the thought of how well she had followed the rules, Liza defiantly snapped open her purse again and added more lipstick. What did doing everything by the book get her in the long run anyway? It had been safe, but boring, and she supposed that she should be thankful for her success . . .

"I'm just tired of fighting when everything is stacked against me. Why make myself any more vulnerable than I have to?"

Letty didn't respond. They both knew that following the rules hadn't kept her safe from the tragedies or the pain. Her father's nightmare had taught them that much. And Liza had been glad to finally get out on her own. At least that way, any mistakes she made would be her own private issue. Not something to be held up in her face by anybody else. Especially not by Aunt V—or the world, for that matter.

"You'd be surprised," Liza said finally, downing her tea. "I've fought a lot of quiet battles."

"Yeah . . . but, that was a long time ago when you corn-rowed your hair and marched in the last campus demonstrations known to the U.S. Eighty-one. Right? In a minute, we're talking fifteen years, Hon. Only thing that did was send Aunt V into instant apoplexy."

Even though she laughed, a crush of depression weighed on Liza as she considered Letty's words. Her reflection distorted in the metal napkin holder on the table as she avoided Letty's gaze. Just like everything else, she thought, her life was distorted. She needed to steady herself before going back to Washington, before the dinner meeting in Bethesda. Just a moment of privacy to clear her head. When had she ever departed from the norm, from that which was expected of her? And there had been so many expectations to contend with over the years.

"Maybe you're right." Liza's voice was barely audible. "I simply hate injustice, that's all. I still do." Victor came to mind for a moment.

Liza didn't invite Letty into the more fragile areas of her emotions. If they could stay on the surface, on the philosophical, then maybe she wouldn't have to examine the complex interiors of her own soul. Not now. She just wanted the companionship, the warmth of friendship and home—without opening up a jugular vein.

Yet thoughts besieged her without mercy anyway. She recalled that when she had been accepted to an Ivy League school, they hadn't just been proud of her. No. She had been lectured about her duty to further the race, reminded about how many people had died in the marches so that she could go there, told that she mustn't do anything to tarnish her reputation so that others could follow in her footsteps. . . . That's probably why she had helped to lead every campus demonstration around. If she were going to fight for what she believed in, *she* would be vocal. Positioning her glasses on the bridge of her nose with annoyance, she straightened her spine and collected herself.

Letty hadn't been looking at her, but it felt as though they were locked in the same thought.

"Liz, this is life in America, and you're in two non-protected classes," Letty reminded her. "So, you just give 'em a run for their money, is all. Hon, since I've known you, if it was a battle for yourself, you'd always get beat up. But if you were fighting for somebody else, you were sure to win. Strange how you operate. You've got to learn how to fight as hard for yourself as you do for everybody else. Understood?"

"I got beat up pretty bad with Barry," Liza admitted quietly, fidgeting with her paper cup. "He dumped me for one of those D.C., Capitol Hill Miss Perfects remember? Aunt V forgot to tell me how that game worked. She never groomed me to become a charming, D.C. socialite. I don't go in unarmed anymore."

"But you lost forty pounds, Girl. Re-did your entire thing. That's something. Isn't it?"

Looking down at her new figure, Liza blew out an impatient breath. The male, alien species. The change that she had fought so hard to make now seemed so worthless. She had never bothered to learn how to carry on witty, feminine conversation. She'd probably bore them to death with mathematical vectors and arrays. She also hadn't learned how to pull together all the details associated with the so-called feminine mystique. She'd been too busy to pay attention to *that* while she was working her way toward a full scholarship for college.

"A hollow victory, Letty. Trust me. Just like my Chem Tech win. Let's drop it." Smoothing her suit front and closing her purse, Liza became more introspective. She was stalling. She knew it. She needed a way out.

"Accepting a dinner invitation was the most foolish thing I could've done," she pressed on, hoping to end the questions once and for all. "What are we going to talk about? The weather? Or current events, perhaps? We have nothing in common except the fact that we hate each other. Now there's a topic for pleasant dinner conversation."

"Okay," Letty said finally, throwing up her hands. "So, you didn't protect yourself from one man. But when people hurt somebody you care about . . . Liz, you get downright crazy! That's why you Taurus people are dangerous. You go along peaceably, smelling the flowers until a bee stings your butt. Then, y'all air the joint out—like a bull in a china shop."

"Well, that's just what I can't afford to do now. I can't go around airin' out, as you say—even if I'm right. Sometimes a little strategy is called for, you know?"

"Back to the problem at hand—this man. So, what's the problem with this guy?"

"Other than the fact that he stole half of my contract? Isn't that enough?"

"All right. A business barracuda, he is. But, truthfully, if you could've done the same, wouldn't you have?"

"Depends."

"An even match. Same ice water runs in both of your veins when it comes to business."

"That's what I'm afraid of. He may be worse than me."

"What 'cha 'fraid of, Doll? Just put your pea brain on automatic, go to dinner, and have a good damned evening. 'Sides, you go to these clink-clink-more-champagne dinners all the time. There's more to this story, I can feel it. . . . Make him pick up the tab, too."

Liza had to laugh as she looked at Letty's expression. But also wanting to stop the uncomfortable discussion that she'd started, she shifted to a decided retreat.

"Yep. You're right. Well, that's all I wanted to talk about. How's your Mom? Tell her I said—"

Letty studied her face hard. "Hold it, hold it, hold it, Miss Thang. Don't *even* try it. I'm not letting you off the hook like this. You didn't ride all the way to Philly to eat some Jamaican food and chitchat. We could have done this over the phone." After a long pause, she asked, "It isn't Gerry, is it?"

Her friend had her. She was busted. They knew each other too well, and Liza gave in to defeat. An escape attempt at this point would be futile. Although she hadn't kept many friends throughout the years, Letty went back to the old neighborhood. With that kind of insight, Letty was the only one who could ground her. "He's doing fine," she lied to protect Letty's heart. How could she tell Letty that Gerald wasn't getting better, that the HIV was now full blown and his time was so short? Letty didn't deal well with death, sickness, and dying, having never lost anyone significant in her life. Liza had lost everyone but Gerald. A time would come when it was inevitable to tell Letty, but not today. Not when she didn't even want to think about losing him herself.

This time, Letty leaned in and lowered her voice. "Good." Her posture relaxed. "I'm glad that this man thing is the only thing bugging you."

Liza hesitated and tried to keep her gaze steady. Letty's comment was more of a question looking for reassurance than a statement. It was difficult to explain to her friend that a myriad of concerns weighed on her . . . Gerald, the future of Risc Systems, the mission to uncover the men that ruined her father, and the Duarte problem—all at the same time. Oddly, right now, the safest topic seemed to be the most uncomfortable one.

"Then, tell the truth. You *probed* him, didn't you, Liz? You picked up more than your basic business interest, and that's what's got you so spooked."

Liza didn't answer immediately. There was no need to confirm the obvious. Only Letty and her brother, Gerald, knew about her gift, or curse—depending on one's point of view.

"Letty, I didn't *want* to pick up any interest from this guy, okay. I don't need this in my life, not after what I went through before. One simple little peek into his mind has had me screwed up all day. Normally, I can shake it . . . but something happened. Maybe I was too tired to do it, and I usually don't go into anyone's thoughts directly. It's not right. But when I got in there, I felt a strange darkness around him that scared me. I don't know." Duarte was definitely an easier subject to cope with than Gerald at the moment.

Letty swallowed hard and was quiet. At least the less pressing issue was out on the table and her friend could do with it as she pleased. There was no need to discuss real problems like death.

"Besides," Liza continued in a forlorn voice. "I always pick the liars . . . and I don't have any more luck using my second sight than anyone else has using common sense. Why do things always have to be so complicated?"

Letty still didn't answer, but began eating again.

"Hello, are you there?" Liza whispered, ignoring the nervous roll of acid in her stomach.

"Only if you're finished." Letty sighed, exasperation clear in her voice. "Why do you do this to yourself, Liz? You are a gorgeous, intelligent, successful woman with a good heart. A soft heart, I might add, that unfortunately nobody but family and close friends get to see. Have you considered that the darkness is your fear keeping you from seeing what this guy has to offer? Maybe you should just force yourself to look past it."

She couldn't respond. How could Letty understand what this felt like? She hadn't confided in anyone about her mission to avenge her father's death. Nor had she confided that she'd had dreams about her nemesis. Sensual ones. Hell, she could barely admit that to herself. Letty's comment only made her feel worse.

"You cannot, I'll say it again for the five-hundredth time, cannot continue to live like a nun, scared that somebody's gonna hurt you again. You also cannot go around thinking that the only way to remain safe from your feelings is by working yourself to death. You gotta get some balance in your life—maybe I'll send you some herbal stress remedies. But, in the meantime, with that said, stop worrying about what's going to happen at dinner. He won't bite you, at least not in the restaurant. Then take it one day at a time from there."

"I don't want him to bite me."

"Might get good to you, huh?"

Liza ignored the comment. "I want him to get up off of my contract percentage due my firm. He's a robber baron and got over just because his firm is larger than mine."

"Are you finished?"

"Yes."

"I think it's the chemistry that's blowing your circuits," Letty said with a chuckle.

"Uhmm, hmmm . . ." one of the old women behind the counter chimed in. "Julia. It's a man. I told ja."

Liza wanted to die.

"I been tryin' to tell the girl," Letty laughed, moving her leg out of the way before Liza could kick it. "Miss Julie, Miss Ruth, tell her to stop worrying about a dinner date."

The second woman laughed and wiped her hands on her apron. "Same dish served up a different way. Man'll give ja heartburn more so than de curry. Too pretty to worry about one fish in de sea."

If she could have reached across the table, she would have strangled Letty. "See," Liza said in a whisper, "you done told the whole place my business. Girl, I—"

"I know," Letty laughed. "It ain't no man thang."

There was no arguing with her friend. Once Letty made up her mind on a subject, she would not be moved. And Liza knew her friend had made this declaration too many times in the past for the outcome to be any different now.

"Here, take the man some Key Lime pie," the first woman chuckled. "Is still true about the route to a man's heart. De odher way gits ja in deep troubles."

Liza covered her face with her hands and laughed. "All right. I give in. You all win. I was worried about some attraction I felt. Pie is out, though, Miss Julie. No disrespect intended. He already owes me *a lot of money*. So, *I'll* eat the pie, okay?"

The old women laughed and sucked their teeth, joining Letty's chuckles.

"Owe a woman money?" Miss Ruth said, totally disgusted. "Den, no pie. Leave dat deadbeat alone. Woman can do bad all by herself! Just ask my sista."

As a squabble ensued between the two matrons, apparently over the reference to somebody's ex-husband, Liza tried to urge Letty to leave. The row was a good cover. They'd sneak out under heavy verbal artillery.

"Okay. Okay. You rushin' me, Girl. Let me get my pie first." Letty dumped her plate and paid for two slices of dessert.

"C'mon," Liza said, pulling her by the elbow and leaving a generous tip. "Let's roll."

Once outside on the curb, they both looked at each other and burst out laughing.

"See, now, when I come back in here, they'll be asking me about some man that I'm not even dealing with. They'll feed on it forever!"

"Liz, they've got so much drama kickin' off in that place, by the time you come back, they'll be tellin' you somebody else's business. Girl, you know it's like the beauty parlor in there. And that's where you need to go before that dinner. Chile, I'd blow his mind."

"We are not back on that subject again, are we?" Liza shook her head as they walked toward Spruce Street to hail a cab while Letty waited for the bus. She was almost glad that they had to travel in two separate directions.

"Letty," she said after a while. "How come I don't feel so beautiful, and successful, and all of that nonsense? I feel nervous, and stupid for even worrying about the improbable. . . . But that's crazy, because I hate this arrogant jackass . . . no matter what you say. So, who cares what I look like? It's just a business meeting anyway."

"Just pull yourself together, go to dinner, and work him the way he thinks he's gonna work you. Keep your skirt down—especially if you have to wear those beat pantyhose tomorrow. Take off those schoolmarm glasses, and flash those pretty eyes. If he wants to play games, play to win. You've got a secret weapon. He'll die. Then call me in the morning with the coroner's report."

Still giggling as the forty-two bus approached, Liza fussed back, "Yeah, and what if *I* die? You gonna be the one to read the tag on my toe, Lady?"

"That good looking, huh?" Letty called over her shoulder as she waited in line to board. *"Girl,* you better call me with every single, ingle tingle of the details tomorrow!"

Laughing, Liza relented. "Okay, okay, already. I'm gone before you tell my *bizness* on SEPTA. But, you're wrong," she added, trying to get a last word in edgewise. "It . . . Is . . . Not . . . A . . . Man . . . Thing! Got that?"

"Mister, shut the door on my girl, will you?" Letty laughed. "Oh, yeah, and wear that *bad* jewel blue suit and blouse I helped you pick out. Those crystals for luck, and your best silk underwear. And, please, take off those glasses!"

"Shut up and get on the bus. I ain't thinkin' about you."

"Love ya, Hon. Call me tomorrow. Give Ger a kiss for me!"

"You got it. Hi to your Mom! Love ya!"

Liza stood and watched the bus pull off. Her friend had thrown her a lifeline of comfort, made her laugh . . . made her angry . . . made her almost cry . . . then made her laugh at herself in two brief hours. They had time-travelled together to a place where tears were for things less serious, where laughs came from deep within the belly, and fears could vanish with the smell of pie.

If she could just hold onto this little piece of heaven . . .

Three

"G'night, Hon."

"Yeah, Betsy. You, too. Another day, another dollar."

"Aw, it's not so bad. Least the only person driving you is yourself. Why, in my day, nobody thought that would be possible. 'Specially not a young woman like yourself. Know what I mean? Count your blessin's, chile. We're all proud of you."

Liza smiled weakly at the older woman. "Yeah. Thanks, a lot. Have a good evening, Miss Betsy."

When she finally turned off the lights in her office, the rest of the team grunted an unceremonious goodbye without looking up. It was only Tuesday, but everybody was already whipped. They didn't formally acknowledge her departure for Duarte's dinner, just sat like zombies in front of the bank of flickering workstations that framed the technical area. Even though she knew that their response wasn't personal, just an extension of their fatigue and frustration, she still felt guilty.

It was a rarely taken luxury to leave before 10:00 P.M. Twelve-to-fourteen-hour days had become the norm since they had landed the project. Dinner was usually stale pizza left over from lunch. Their beverage of choice—coffee which had turned into espresso on the warmer. Liza cringed at the thought and decided to surprise them with a deli tray. Although long hours were her normal routine, she couldn't expect her staff to continue like this forever. After all, they had personal lives and families.

Pulling herself together, she focused on what was relevant. Her team's level of dedication and excellence was the cornerstone of the firm. That's why it had absolutely outraged her to see the team robbed of any contract percentage due them.

As the chrome elevator doors closed her away from the staff, for the first time she allowed her mind to quietly admit the truth with a resolute sigh. Who in the hell was she fooling? She would have taken that account for a dollar and fifty cents if it meant that she could expose the men who had ruined her father years ago. Her fury at Duarte was complicated by elements that went far beyond the money, yet the money had initially been the only tangible issue for her to confront. By now, the team deserved a break. They simply couldn't go on like this.

Fearful that her father's death would flash before her, Liza focused on the call and nervously fingered the car keys in her hand. She would not allow herself to spiral into that depth of melancholy tonight. She didn't want to see the blood, the letter, any of it ever again. The rare times when these visions occurred, they brought a level of emotional paralysis that she couldn't afford to give way to this evening. She wanted justice, but not at the price of her sanity. Early on, she had made the decision to use her intellect, not her gift, to right the wrongs of the past.

Leaving the building, bogged down with paperwork and fatigued from the drain of the day, she also realized with alarm just how close she had actually come to allowing a stupid grudge match to interfere with her primary objective. "Winning the battle and losing the war . . . Hmmm, where have you heard that one before, Liza?" she mused absently while pitching her arm-load into the already overstuffed trunk of the car. Duarte. He'd said that to her once before in one of their heated debates.

Immediately, the many nights she had spent upstairs with the team, sharing lunch leftovers and horrible coffee, became important. Dinner sent up might help soften the sting of her early departure. "Call the deli," she told herself, "and stop worrying about Duarte. The hell with Duarte or his motives." He was messing with her money. Deal with what's relevant. Her team. Her firm. Her contracts. Her mission. Her life.

Just as leaving the building with paperwork seemed to lessen the guilt, she also felt better knowing that at least her team would eat some semblance of dinner tonight. Control. Get back in control, and stay there. Take care of your own.

As she returned the car phone to the jack and shifted into gear, the edgy feelings that plagued her all day were quickly replaced by outright indignation. She was tired. The day had been long enough without having to endure some new game that Victor Duarte was playing.

Skip dinner. Call Duarte and cancel this nonsense—just as soon as the reception cleared up. That was the only thing that made sense. Negotiating the black Volvo sedan past the numerous concrete columns and turns of the underground parking ramps, she became more adamant about her decision. It was safer that way. Why play with fire just because she was curious? She didn't have time to get burned.

Deftly punching in the general switchboard number for DGE while rummaging in her purse for an elusive monthly parking card, Liza quickly put the receiver back in the jack and set the mobile unit on speaker. By the seventh ring, she was furious. "Where is everybody! Risc Sys people are *never* gone this early!" she bellowed, outrage replacing irritation.

But before she could reach for the off button to terminate the call, Ed Gates' conservative, professional salutation caught her by surprise.

"Good evening, DGE Associates," flowed the easy tenor greeting.

Still feeling off-guard, Liza tried to meet his calm, deliberate tone with an upbeat response. "Oh, hello, Ed. This is Liza Nichols from Risc Systems."

She hadn't expected one of the partners to pick up. Either voicemail or a secretary would have been better. Especially since she hadn't come up with a good reason for cancelling. If Duarte had answered, she could have been direct with him. Now what? Feeling forced into a cordial conversation, she hesitated before pressing on. "I was hoping to catch Victor Duarte before he left for the day."

"Really?"

The question took her by surprise. Or maybe it was the tone of the question. Was she getting paranoid? Cringing inwardly, she hesitated again and tried to recover.

"Duarte and I have been playing phone tag. I'm returning his call."

"I'm surprised, frankly. Well, maybe I can locate him. I'm glad that he's at least begun to establish communications."

Ed's response was not sarcastic; it was genuine. That pleased her. He was a good guy. Too bad he worked for the Devil. She would love to have someone of his caliber on her team. Ed's keen financial mind had garnered her respect early on, as well as the respect of the rest of her staff. The added bonus was that somehow the stress of those meetings never seemed to ruffle him. They certainly needed one peacemaker in the group and, above all else, Ed could always be counted on to maintain the polite decorum often absent from those sessions. She took a deep breath and plunged forward.

"I know things have been strained, Ed," she began tentatively, "but there are still a number of logistics to nail down."

"I didn't mean to pry. I was just surprised and wanted to help if I could."

Ed sounded embarrassed, and that dismayed her. She had waited too long to answer him, caught up in her own crazy head-talk. He was one of the few people that she actually liked at DGE.

Before he could continue, she took the rare opportunity to rush in a compliment, hoping to put him at ease. "Thanks Ed, I should have known that you would still be there burning the midnight oil. Has the rest of the group deserted you?"

"Yes, I'm afraid it's true. They left me to my numbers tonight, much to my wife's chagrin. Vic said he had an important impromptu meeting this evening, so I decided to take full advantage of the quiet."

She could almost hear a modest smile in Ed's voice and was sure that he appreciated her honest recognition of the tireless effort that he was contributing to the project.

"Shall I leave a message that you called? Or, if it's urgent, I can try to reach him at home later."

"No, no, that won't be necessary," she cut in quickly. "It's nothing that can't wait until our joint team meeting in the morning. Uhmm, I just had a few ideas about a new approach to the data-base issues that have been plaguing both firms and wanted to get some input from the group."

Why had she lied? She hated how contrived the whole thing sounded. Now she would have to come up with some plausible new idea to a problem that had stumped both teams for weeks. *Damn*.

"Well, Liza, if there is a new perspective on this problem, I would have been totally surprised if it came from anyone but you. Take care, and don't stay up too late yourself. Have a good evening."

When Ed hung up, she sighed a breath of relief. She was glad to end the mildly disturbing phone call, especially since Duarte hadn't even told *Ed* that they were meeting tonight. Why had he added an unnecessary layer of secrecy to this meeting? For that matter, why hadn't *she* just mentioned it to Ed, or to the other members of her own staff? The whole thing was becoming murkier and murkier.

As her sedan pulled away from the mouth of the garage into

the open evening air, Liza rolled down the driver's side window. She loved the way the chilly night stung her face as she darted between the slower-moving vehicles.

Driving fast, with the wind rushing in all around her, had always given her an ephemeral sense of freedom. She was sure that the sensation simply could not be duplicated elsewhere. Driving was the time to clear her head and to do her best planning. It was an intensely private time where she could allow her gift to run free range.

Aggressively managing the stick shift, she negotiated through the bog of local traffic. Usually, her entry onto the Beltway was when she felt most in control. It was an illusion that she loved to experience. She'd imagine that the ramp leading up the interstate was the beginning of an airport runway. That's where she could really take off into flight and lose herself in the euphoria of becoming airborne.

But that was just one of her daily rituals. She took great pride in the regimented schedule that she had developed over the years and strictly adhered to. The simple consistency offered her a sense of security. It had become an effective shield against the painful aftermath of events which were always associated with unplanned, spur-of-the-moment decisions.

Drive, swim, meditate, work, attend client functions, sleep, exercise again in the morning, then work. These things were all safe and well-planned activities that kept her life on track. Most importantly, they kept her anesthetized from the pain.

As she careened into a small void before her, the night air caught Lisa's hair and viciously whipped her cheeks, bringing tears to her eyes. When she blinked them back quickly, a thought, or something more like a presence, came to her in a flash. The eerie scene made her sit up straighter and rub her eyes violently.

Oh, God . . . It was happening again. Never before . . . not while she was driving! She couldn't see the road. . . .

Was she losing her mind?

Wood, wood all around, a very small space had captured her.

*She couldn't breathe. Then there was a scent. . . . The specter's
deep, masculine, spicy aroma, that drew her to it and mingled
sweetly with her own. But her dress . . .*

She wasn't wearing one! She had on a suit. What in the
world? . . .

Liza cast her gaze around the·interior of the car anxiously.
How did this random, insane thought encroach upon her mind?
She was trying to concentrate on Duarte! These meaningless
snatches of information had assailed her all day, totally confusing her and throwing her off-kilter. She was tired. That had to
be it. She would just have to wait until she was within closer
proximity to turn on her probe. Her sixth sense had always been
dead accurate. But everything coming to her now was pure nonsense.

Approaching the jammed entrance to the Beltway, she
strained to shove memories of the vision aside. Anger would
keep her focused. All she had to do was think about how much
of a percentage his firm got. How it should have gone to her
people. How hard she'd worked to land the deal. Why she needed
the money. The things he'd said . . . his arrogant position.

Whipping herself up intentionally, she was relieved when the
eerie feeling began to pass. Unfortunately, tonight, because of
Victor Duarte, she would have to endure a short, jerky, rush-
hour-laden run on the road, then tolerate an unnecessary dinner
that would ultimately make her miss her swim. Another stupid
inconvenience!

It was working, and she let her breath out slowly. Close call.
She had never had one of these blinding episodes while driving.
What if she couldn't see the road before she killed herself? What
if she hit another vehicle . . . all because her vision was skewed
to something amorphous? Before, she had had relative control;
now, there was no telling when she'd have to shove it to the
background of her mind. And what if it happened in front of
someone—a client? It would be embarrassing, debilitating . . .
almost like a form of epilepsy.

Liza pressed her palm to her chest. She had to calm down.

* * *

Parking was always a problem in the area. One last circle around the block before capitulating to the eager valets outside of the establishment would give her the necessary time to collect her thoughts. She felt shaky and just wanted to get her bearings before having to deal with Victor Duarte.

She expected him to be waiting smugly for her in the lounge area, which would give her even more time to survey the establishment. She just wanted to get a bead on his strange temperament before actually having to confront him.

Instead, she almost knocked him down as he unexpectedly opened the door for her to enter the grand foyer. The worst part of all, he was smiling! Then in a flash, she saw *it*. The vision. Again.

His outline, the way he stood in the arc of the door, one arm nonchalantly holding the brass handle, the white shirt . . .

"Ms. Nichols, I'm glad you were able to join me on such short notice," he beamed, accurately anticipating that she might try to cancel at the last minute.

Catching her by the elbow, Victor's smile broadened as he escorted her into the lavish interior. She felt positively undone, a nuance that she was sure had not gone unnoticed.

He seemed to be monitoring her glare, which was the only suitable armor that she could muster at the moment. Ignoring it, Victor continued in a smooth, controlled lilt.

"I do appreciate what a disruption this could have been to your schedule, Liza."

Not only was she unprepared for their collision, she was totally unprepared for his open, friendly response. The collision had placed her in close proximity to him, much closer than she had ever been before. Because of her height, it was rare to have any man tower over her. The fact that Victor Duarte did so was disconcerting.

She backed up a few inches to give herself a more comfortable range to negotiate, just a little distance for clarity. She had to stop staring at him. At the very least, she had to close her mouth. Then her vision blurred. She was somewhere else and had to get back.

The brisk movement to realign herself drew the subtle, spicy scent of an expensive men's cologne into the small void between them. Just like the scent in the car. It couldn't be the same . . .

At close range, Victor Duarte's voice reverberated through her bones. His deep set, intensely black eyes seemed to have a lethal, charismatic quality to them.

She felt his predatory assessment and hated that he was probably reveling in having caught her completely off-guard. She saw it in his eyes, which hardly matched the controlled calm of his voice. They were absolutely gleaming with the satisfaction of having temporarily disarmed her. His expression perfectly complimented the slight smile threatening the corners of his full, sensuous mouth. She had to regain control.

Taking a more aggressive posture, which was a poor cover for her distress, she tried to regroup with a curt reply. "Well, Victor, I do have to eat sometime tonight. So, I don't suppose there has been too much of an impact to my schedule," she snapped. But her snipe only seemed to make his eyes twinkle even more as he ushered her toward the maître d's podium.

Unaccustomed to receiving this level of overt chivalry, she found the closeness of Victor's escort a sudden invasion of her personal space. He seemed to consume all the available air around her as she struggled to appear calm.

Fixing her gaze dead ahead of her, Liza straightened her already rigid carriage, determined to ignore the tremble that crept down her spine. He was positively gorgeous, but notwithstanding that fact, he was also the enemy. At least her mind still worked on a perfunctory level.

She graciously, but skeptically, accepted his lead to the podium. They were collected promptly and bade to follow their host to a perfectly placed table by the window.

As soon as the tuxedoed gent left their side, she mustered up her most direct glare, rearmed, and fired. "All right, Mr. Duarte. This has been bugging me all day. Why did we have to meet for dinner? Especially all the way out here?"

Although taken aback, Victor allowed the cannon blast to pass over him. His only response was to calmly open the wine list and to begin evaluating their choices. After what seemed like an eternity, he answered, avoiding her question entirely, using the same tactic that she had employed with him only two days earlier.

"Grgich Hills produces an excellent chardonnay. Or would you prefer a nice chablis? I would suggest François Raveneau or Rene and Vincent Dauvissat."

Exasperated by the uncamouflaged evasion and by the way he arrogantly threw out all of the best name-brands, Liza reinforced her position: Pompous jackass!

"The *chardonnay* will be fine, and I'm sure you'll decide on the appropriate vintage. However, you have not answered my original question."

"As you prefer. Chardonnay it is," Victor replied casually, still referring to the wine list without looking up. Motioning to the poised maître d, he returned the list to the host and selected a bottle of Grgich Hills. Before she could start again, he simply held up his hand, indicating that he would answer, but only when *he* was ready.

Liza watched him formulate an answer. To her, Victor seemed entirely out of place in the twentieth century. His Old World speech patterns, his sense of gentlemanly conduct, his arrogant assessment of women . . .

"You are a very direct woman, indeed, and I suppose the only way to begin our discussion is at the beginning," he mused, still avoiding her unfaltering glare.

Direct eye contact was Liza's forte, paled only by her forthrightness, and she was not about to relent or lose her position.

"So please begin at the beginning," she volleyed, allowing obvious annoyance to singe her voice. "And let's not play games here, Victor."

* * *

Games, Victor thought. Why did this woman think peace was
a game?

Liza's response was almost a hiss, and he could see her mood
taking a familiar turn for the worse. Despite all the rancor and
animosity between the firms, tonight he wanted peace. He had
important information to share with her, and he had recognized
awhile ago that both teams needed a break. Especially her
smaller staff. Keeping that objective in front of him now would
be the only way to sort through the personal confusion that momentarily assailed his logic.

But as he looked at Liza, then back down to the elaborate
leather-bound menu before him, his objectives seemed vague.
It had taken every ounce of discipline to keep his expression
from changing when she had literally fallen into his arms at the
door . . . flustered, angry as a hornet, and absolutely breathtaking. He more than admired her. He wanted her. And there was
no appropriate explanation for those feelings.

"Let's review our choices for dinner first," he hedged. "It is
far better to do battle on a full stomach, if we must. But, if you
must know, I had truly hoped for a peaceful discussion tonight."

He wanted to lighten the mood and get her to smile. Unfortunately, Liza only offered a neutral, unreadable expression as
she looked down briefly at the menu before closing it. She was
tough. Maybe that's what intrigued him so. She never gave an
inch.

Falsely engrossed in the entreé choices, he thought about the
distrustful woman who sat across from him. Her lean athletic
carriage had a regal quality to it, especially when she straightened her spine to make a point. Yet somehow the lush curves
that she seemed determined to hide beneath her conservative,
tailored suits gave an inkling to a softer side of Liza. The collision had confirmed his suspicions. She was, indeed, all woman.

He was grateful that the wine had come to their table quickly.
Perhaps the libation would help her to relax. Going through the

motions to stall for time, he surveyed the label, tested and sniffed the cork, then took a sip, swishing it around his mouth for emphasis before dismissing the attendant. He hadn't thought about it much, but possibly Liza was as nervous as he. After all, she had no reason to trust him.

Without looking up, he could feel her tension. She was impatiently, and rightfully, waiting for an answer to her very logical question. The problem was, he hadn't formulated one yet. Or, perhaps, it was because the pieces were moving so rapidly on the board that he hadn't had time to shift his perspective. A quick mental review of the fundamentals helped—a little.

Finally, with not much room left for evasion, he knew it was best to answer her question directly, using an open appeal to her reason as a beginning. Slowly returning the menu to the edge of the table, he took another long sip of wine and studied her face carefully.

Her warm brown eyes held a passionate intensity that arrested his judgment. The firelight from the candle caught in them, making her eyes appear to blaze with fury while at the same time turning her even, toffee complexion to dark gold. If Liza Nichols could be this passionate about business, he couldn't help but wonder how deeply her other passions ran. A mistake. Don't even think about it. Quickly cursing himself for the thought, he wrestled the subject of business to the front of his brain. He had to get back on track, but it was going to be difficult.

However, Liza's rigid position could not be ignored. Despite his momentary lapse into an appreciation of her beauty, he was certain that she was not about to accept some inconsequential discussion. This would be a very delicate negotiation, indeed.

Collecting his thoughts, he began in a low, even tone. "Ms. Nichols, why are you making it so unnecessarily difficult for me to pass the olive branch? I am only trying to establish an honest truce with my very reluctant partner on a very important multimillion dollar project. I suppose, I, too, am tired. Just as my entire staff is tired. I can't deal with this unending hostility any longer. I'm tired of playing poker with you, your firm, our client . . . everybody, really. I just want a peaceful finish so that we can conclude our business and have both firms save face in the industry."

Expressionless, Liza sipped her wine, staring at him intently. Seeing that she was in no mood for evasive posturing or long speeches, he steadied himself and continued.

"Up until now, it would appear that we have both been expending a lot of unnecessary energy fighting each other instead of tackling the problem. This cannot continue since neither one of us has the unlimited resources to keep our battle stations manned on constant red alert."

He had struck a chord. Liza's focus narrowed on him, and he dug in his heels. He was right, damn it!

Undaunted by her challenging glare, he pushed his point with more conviction—although the light glistening in the highlights of her rich, dark hair created a momentary distraction.

"Look, we both know that Chem Tech is your only major client focus at the moment. That's only because your firm is smaller. But DGE has the additional resource drain of having to service a large portfolio of accounts. So our manpower is equally strained by the duplication in effort."

After a long pause, he softened his tone in an earnest attempt to make her understand. "I will honestly tell you, I wish that they had only awarded us the going rate of twenty percent if foregoing the extra money could have avoided this hassle."

She took another sip of wine, deliberately, without losing eye contact. There was an unexpected honesty in his statement; her mental magnet detected no fraud. But there was more that he was not disclosing . . . something peculiar that made this project so vital for him, which went well beyond the issue of money. Odd, she could feel it, along with a more primal pull that was difficult to ignore. What she needed was time . . . time to relax enough to really get a sense of the issues competing for priority in her brain.

Although she had been thoroughly rattled when she'd first arrived, the change of venue and the brief exchange had given her the chance to mellow. Focusing on every muscle in Victor's face, she concentrated on his words as a dull ache overtook her temple. She was fully engaged now, her probe activated, and her guard unwavering. She was going to risk a peek deep within the recesses of his mind.

"If the money wasn't the issue, then why did you battle me so hard for control of the account? I need to be able to trust those that I do business with, at least on some basic level. No games."

"That's the last thing I would do, Liza, play games. Perhaps complete trust is out of the question at this point, but we do have to come to an accord."

Victor's voice still registered a quiet urgency. He was playing a very bad hand of poker, and her mild comment had made him visibly cringe. He was hiding something and hadn't answered her question fully. But why had that sent a volt of electricity through her?

Somehow, Victor's logical defense of her earlier attack was totally unexpected. His stare had now become so direct and the exasperation in his voice so blatantly recognizable that her only conclusion could be that his attempt to stop the war was real. Even the part about not wanting the money seemed real. Yet . . .

"All right. Maybe you do respect the expertise of my firm. Let's not even get on the subject of the percentage. That has been a sore point with me since the beginning. That's done. It's too late now, anyway. Besides, it was the client's call, so I have no choice but to let it drop." What else could she say?

"Ah, yes. The money," he said in a tone that almost sounded wistful. "They say it's the root of all evil. I am sorry that it came between our firms. Really."

"That issue doesn't concern me any longer."

His expression was one of amazement.

"But isn't that what we've been battling about? The money."

Her response was cool. "No. Control. Why is it so important that you control the account?"

No one had ever stared her down from her position. But as she continued to look at him, she saw in the depth of Victor's eyes a level of inexplicable, passionate desperation that made her look away. The momentary confusion forced her to move to an evasive posture where she could better analyze the new information. She was in deep, much deeper than she had ever tried to go into anyone's mind before. It was uncomfortable. Eerie. She could almost feel him breathe through her own skin.

It was his turn for a non-answer as he picked up his wine glass and took a sip. "It's almost like you can read my mind. This dance that you and I do is riveting."

Opting to shift gears and break the tension, she finally looked up and smiled uneasily.

"I can see that you're not going to answer that question, but if we have to work together, I might as well tell you that I have a lot of respect for Ed Gates, your financial man. Now, *he* is a pro and an excellent asset to the team. Despite the circumstances, I do enjoy working with him immensely."

She could sense that every muscle in Victor's well-toned body was keyed as he tried to remain detached before her. The sudden compliment and change of focus had the desired effect of immediately disarming him as he began to visibly relax. She needed him to relax, to drop another level of internal barrier for her to get in. His style was predictable. Gallantry had obviously become second nature to him over the years. Thus, a polite return volley was to be expected.

"I also have a great deal of respect for your data-base man. I think your Ron and my Ed are made for each other. They could be like Romeo and Juliet, just waiting for the approval of their two warring parents to allow them to get together. Shall we let them work together in earnest then, Liza? Especially since we do seem to be coming to an understanding."

Victor's hopeful return contained the same intensity that had gripped her earlier. Now the volley was in her court again.

She seriously considered his offer while quickly arranging

the facts in her mind. "We have arrived at our destination, gotten to the main issue, exchanged mutual compliments. . . . Now what?" she thought impatiently. Realizing that she was also tired of the war and since Victor *seemed* to be making a semi-honest attempt, she decided to generously concede to letting the staff work unhindered. What could be so dangerous about that at this point?

"Yes," she offered cautiously. "It would be a crime to stifle two such creative energies. They would positively feed off each other and produce brilliant work. Besides, I know Ron is just dying to collaborate with Ed. Okay, Duarte. Let's get down to business. Divvy it up."

The smile that eased its way out of hiding from behind Victor's previously serious expression told her that he did appreciate her acceptance of his proposal—even if it was a little late. She knew that he respected her too much to take the gem that she had just slipped to him for granted and that he fully understood that the additional compliment was her way of accepting the olive branch. She was also sure that he appreciated the genuine respect that she had always shown toward his best friend and knew that her words were sincere. This could work.

"I know that Edward has been hoping for a peaceful resolution so that he can work well into the night with someone of the caliber of your Ron," he said after a moment of hesitation. "Thank you, Liza, really, for coming here tonight to work this out. . . . And I want to apologize for any unpleasantries that I may have personally caused from the DGE side."

Returning the generosity of her honesty, Victor had offered an open compliment of his own—although this one was apparently not quite a planned, strategic move. But she had to remember how to do it, how to focus on that gut feeling of truth the way Nana had taught her. Sometimes it worked, sometimes it didn't. But she had to know what wasn't mentioned in the content of Victor's speech. Just focus on the eyes, concentrate on making the truth flow out with the words. Hear the voice telling you what you need to know . . .

Within seconds, Victor's posture changed. He leaned forward so intently that it startled her.

"Liza, everything is so utterly *complicated* with you! I am thanking you, and even apologizing, because under different circumstances . . ."

They both sat back in their chairs, trying to regroup after Victor's sudden outburst. The expression on his face said it all. It was as if he were standing in the middle of the restaurant totally naked. She looked away to give him room to recover. This was certainly not one of his cool, planned chess moves. The depth of the emotion that came with it had obviously left him thoroughly mortified.

Something had happened here that was not on anyone's agenda. She had merely been mentally fishing for the truth, not a total confession, for God's sake! It was as though her light mental probe into his thoughts had become a giant magnet, pulling information from every crevice within him—but the one fact she needed was severely blocked by shadows. There was also a flash of recognition as their gazes locked, and it frightened her. It was too close, too familiar. She knew him from somewhere.

Oh, Nana, why aren't you here to help me?

Beginning slowly and softly, Liza looked down into her wine glass. She didn't know what to say. All she could be sure of was that she wanted to avoid any further embarrassment for either of them. She knew that the only thing to do was to counter with a fair and reasonable response. Victor Duarte had given an inch, the least she could do was match it.

"Victor, may I call you *Victor?*" she stammered, not quite sure how to begin. Accepting his tentative nod, she continued. "Listen. . . . I don't know how to explain this, really. But I *know* when people are hiding things from me. I'm concerned because I can't put my finger on what it is with you. Plus, if you haven't already noticed, we've both seemed trapped in this very charged exchange since the day we met. . . . I mean, you've lost bids, and so have I, but I'd dare guess that we've never carried on this way with a competitor. It's been unprofessional—on both sides. What gives?"

Four

His head throbbed, and he felt as though an unseen centrifugal force was rushing the blood through his veins. What on earth . . .

Somehow, he sensed that Liza had *allowed* him to recover gracefully to save face. When the quiet return of their waiter disrupted her probing line of vision, relief swept through him. Although he had been subjected to her intense visual exchanges in the past, he was still unprepared for her searing glances tonight. It was literally impossible to ignore the hypnotic quality of her eyes, which seemed to beg the truth from him. He found that even a brief look into them caused him to expose much more than he ever intended. Each time Liza had engaged him, she had been able to elicit a new, totally raw, emotional response. His detached negotiating veneer wore thin as he felt himself utterly losing control.

"May I review our specialties with you this evening?" charmed their server, who was patiently waiting for their attention.

Quickly recovering from his mild trance and trying desperately to clear his head, Victor nodded toward his guest. "Only if the lady is ready."

Receiving Liza's approval, the waiter began a delicious description of the menu choices.

Still studying the tilt of her head and how the candlelight warmed the rich, caramel color of her cheek and throat, he had hardly noticed the elegant young man politely waiting for a response. In the soft light, with peace between them, Liza was positively captivating.

Although he knew the menu already by heart and was sure

that anything he chose would delicately arouse his appetite, he found himself suddenly unable to decide. His intense awareness of Liza had dulled his hunger, replacing it with a more basic urge that disturbed him.

Waving the waiter away with a deferring plea, he successfully dismissed the young man. "Jorge, your choices have over-whelmed me tonight. You decide . . . please." Lame, but that was the only suave request that he could come up with to mo-mentarily cover his inappropriate distraction.

Accepting the direct compliment with obvious enjoyment, the waiter removed the menus and turned to Victor again. "I am sure that you will be pleased with our choice, *monsieur*." Then he strode confidently away.

Liza laughed. "Victor, how long have you been in the States anyway?"

"Many years. Why?"

"I thought by now you might have noticed that American women are fairly capable of making their own choices for din-ner."

"I'm so sorry. Would you like me to call him back?"

"No, let's be surprised," she said, picking up her wine and smiling as she took a sip.

What in the world was wrong with him? He knew better than that. Had he been home in Peru, it would have been perfectly acceptable. But then, social customs between men and women had not changed there in the last few hundred years. There was still an Old World formality when a man and a woman were out together. Why, now, with this very independent woman, in a business setting, would he pull out old traditions? It just didn't make sense.

With the menus no longer on the table, Liza casually removed her glasses while brightly telling him about her mild case of nearsightedness and the escapades that had finally made her concede to wearing them. He was glad that his social *faux pas* hadn't returned her to her previous state of indignation. She only chuckled in a confidential, easy tone, leaning forward to fully dramatize the secrecy of her confession.

"If you don't mind, I really do have to take these off so you're not sitting in my lap. There, that's much better. Now we can split up the project details without your being two inches in front of me."

The way that she carefully placed the conservative horn-rims in her purse seemed so natural and easy. Liza's voice had become the same way, making the effort appear to be something that she did regularly without a second thought. But he accepted this gesture as yet another peace offering. The simple act of removing her glasses made Liza appear to relax even more. It was almost as if she had willingly dropped her guard in an unspoken acceptance of his peace offer. After months of warring, this change in Liza was both welcomed and startling.

Not wanting to interrupt her, he enjoyed the light cadence of her voice. That, too, was soothing and had lost its once-strident quality. Oddly, he found himself smiling at her when she had finally settled back comfortably in her chair. He wanted to compliment her on how lovely she looked without her glasses, but thought better of it. He had gone too far already.

Taking a sip of wine, he gave her question serious consideration. It was becoming increasingly difficult to stay focused or to think. Liza's peace offering was turning out to be the most lethal weapon in her arsenal. Without the obstruction of glasses on her face, she had unveiled two deep, warm, brown pools that he could positively drown in. Her expression-filled eyes, combined with her rich genuine laugh . . . It was almost too much to bear.

"I know that trust is important," he began softly, "but, some issues are personal and one should have the right to keep them that way."

He was surprised when she nodded and appeared to accept his response. It was becoming impossible to continue to view her as just a necessary chess piece to help him complete his goal to ruin Chem Tech. He actually liked her. It was strange. He felt a surge of protectiveness toward her that was unnatural. Where did these odd emotions stem from, especially with regard to this previous adversary—this person who had, to date, thwarted his goals to control the project and kept him from getting to their precious data bases?

Yet the more he absorbed Liza and listened to her voice, the more his body tensed with unwarranted desire. The physical discomfort forced him to look away from her repeatedly as they chatted about the new logistics of their working relationship. He had to regain control. This was ludicrous!

So far the evening had provided more than he had ever bargained for when he'd first invited Liza Nichols to dinner. Silently cautioning himself, he tried to summon discipline. His godfather said to always factor in the variables. That this one was truly becoming an exquisite surprise was irrelevant!

Desperate for any distraction that would allow him to recover, he averted his gaze to the wine stand. "More chardonnay?" he asked softly when there was an appropriate break in their conversation.

Not giving Liza the chance to respond, he deftly brought the bottle neck to the lip of her glass. He felt sure as he poured the wine that she knew just how pleased he was by her acceptance of a truce and swiftly became annoyed with himself. Surely she could sense the effect that she was having on him.

Unable to avoid looking at her any longer, having taken as long as the task required to pour two glasses of wine, he braced himself to meet Liza's steady, serene stare.

"Did you know that you have a way of looking right through to a person's deepest thoughts?"

He had only meant to give her a scant revelation into the intensity of his feelings. There was no way to gauge what she thought of him now. She probably assumed he was an arrogant jackass and was just being civil for the duration of the dinner. Common sense would have made him feel her out more, take it slowly, and get a sense of mutual interest first. But her directness made him want to say so much more. It was as if her unfaltering gaze held a kind of truth serum that he was unaccustomed to. Her eyes seemed to beckon, *If you tell me, you can trust me.* Having no plausible reason to believe that, but feeling it so strongly in his gut, just added to the collection of things making him uneasy this evening.

Liza smiled, bringing her glass up to her mouth to take another sip. "It's a gift—or a curse . . ." Her voice was almost inaudible.

Victor looked at the damp trace of wine on her lower lip. It made the dark, ruby color of her mouth glisten. He swallowed hard. "It's a gift."

Liza didn't answer, choosing to take another sip of wine instead. He was locked into her gaze and a silent understanding seemed to pass between them. It was pure agony. He couldn't look away, but wasn't sure of how much more he could take. No woman had ever made him feel this way. Ever.

The confusion that he wrestled with was new. He had truly only seen Liza's level of directness in a few people's eyes, and most of them were much older. They also had a strange quality of fire beneath ice, when not burning with the intensity of anger. Oddly, her luminous eyes reminded him of the large, smoky topaz gems that were set in his mother's priceless earrings. Both were beautiful, of mysterious origin, catching the light in every facet while penetrating the soul. Now that was a crazy thought! He remembered not being able to take his eyes off the stones when his godfather, Helyar, gave them to him in London. It was the same way tonight with Liza.

After a long pause, she interrupted his personal thoughts. "Victor, I like to know who I'm dealing with. And, for me, a person's eyes tell me everything."

Liza seemed unsure about the cryptic statement that she'd made. It was as though she had started down a path, then immediately seemed to retreat. He was intrigued, and not about to let her stop now.

Half afraid to ask the question, he leaned forward and spirited her a light challenge. "And what do my eyes tell you?"

Liza took another sip of wine as she formulated her answer.

He could tell that she had penetrated his guard somehow. It was in the way she raised one eyebrow, along with the wry, devastatingly sexy twist of her mouth when she gave him that very strange response. What was worse, he could *feel* the power of something unfathomable tugging at him. It felt almost like a current.

"Your eyes? What do they tell me?" she smiled sheepishly, after a well-timed pause. "Oh . . . just about everything."

Although she had obviously tried to mellow her response with a little laugh, his guard was already in shreds. Victor swallowed hard, his mouth becoming dry. Good God, if she only knew.

She had been right. Hell, Letty had been right. The thing that had accosted her all afternoon was undeniable now. How was she supposed to handle the strong emotions that she was receiving from Victor Duarte, coupled with this portion of him shrouded in mystery? The passion and desire that reflected in his eyes made her again question her ability. This time her own probe had betrayed her. How could she be so suddenly attracted to a man that she had literally despised earlier in the day?

She had to turn it off.

But it was stronger this time. Frighteningly strong. Never before had she been able to probe this deep this fast. It was as if Victor were a lightning rod, drawing current from every available energy source within her. Unable to control her thoughts, she descended on the blatant desire that had resonated in his voice. This proved to be a dangerous prospect, however, as another familiar volt of electricity ran through her. Shaking it off, she shivered, yet continued to toy with dynamite. It had been so long since she'd felt this way, this aroused, or this intrigued. No doubt, it was going to be more than a notion to collect herself and go home, she thought ruefully.

"Then I hope you're prepared to deal with everything you see," he said finally without losing eye contact.

Victor's voice had dropped an octave. A sexually charged,

thick octave that was unmistakable. She didn't need a probe to
read between the lines.

"I could be."

Without question she was sure that he had picked up on the
unintentional double entendre. The words had just slipped out,
and she was actually flirting with him. She. Flirting? At a business dinner? Dread overtook her, but she was still finding it
exceedingly difficult to stop.

"Then I guess from here on, everything will be out on the
table between us," she whispered.

Dear God, where had that come from?

Victor didn't move or respond. The muscle in his jaw twitched
and his gaze became more intense. It was clear that she had
successfully penetrated his armor. Since Victor prided himself
on his stoic negotiating facade, he was probably debating
whether or not to respond to the comment, how to respond to
it, or trying to figure out if she were just bluffing. They were
dancing around an unspoken, inappropriate subject and it had
to stop. How had they gotten so far off track? And why had she
allowed it, welcomed it? Even alluded to her gift. Was she crazy?

"Then there is no need to continue avoiding the *real* discussion, is there, Liza?" he said after another tense moment, leaning
toward her and looking as though he wanted to eat her alive.

Oh God! He had openly given himself away! It was all too
direct. The way he stared at her was embarrassing. Had she given
herself away, too? Perhaps she was reading too much into a
benign comment. Whatever the case, Victor was obviously interested. But why had she started talking about this dangerous
new subject? She had no intention of getting into this discussion
with Victor Duarte, of all people!

Prying further, Victor approached the topic delicately. "I hope
that you can see how very much I would like for us to work
together peacefully . . . and how glad I am that we were able to
subdivide the tasks before us during this meeting without the
usual rancor and animosity."

He's good. Real good. Her brief panic had given Victor

enough room to pull himself together. Nodding in the affirmative, she extended her hand across the table, intentionally breaking the charged sexual aura that enveloped them.

"Yeah, if I'd thought you were lying, I would've left— abruptly and with *lots* of rancor and animosity," she said, smiling. "Let's shake on the new spirit of détente."

She had broken the mood. She could get through this.

When he rose to accept her hand, she had to laugh. "Victor, you *are* really *Old World,* aren't you? That's probably why we clashed so in the beginning. It must be quite an adjustment, huh?"

Victor laughed as he sat down awkwardly. "Sorry, it was a reflex."

It was odd, but when he'd risen to take her hand, she'd known that he had hesitated, thinking better of kissing the back of it. She was grateful that he hadn't, because she would have melted right there on the spot. Her turn. She had to say something. Anything! At a loss for words, she felt the tension building again in the quiet.

Still enmeshed in Victor's thoughts, she checked herself and tried to disengage her probe. But that smile . . . those dark, intense eyes . . . His presence loomed over their small table.

Becoming unnerved by her own responses, Liza strained to smile and remain appropriate. It was not her objective to offend him or possibly scare him or to make a complete fool of herself either. So, the only option was to elaborate. Diplomatically.

"I probably owe you an apology," she began nervously, "and not for the reasons you'd suspect."

She felt her throat getting tight again, but Victor appeared to take in the information peacefully. He didn't seem smug or detached, and his expression offered a glimmer of hope.

"Liza, please. I want you to know that I understand what this contract meant to your smaller firm. I have been there, starting from the ground up without many resources. As I said earlier, I wish this whole dispute could have been avoided."

Convinced that he was being truthful about wanting to understand, she elected to tell him about the impact of the deal to Risc Systems. If they were going to work together, she had to get it off her chest. Letting out a long sigh, she continued with weary resignation.

"I had envisioned being able to really make a difference during this five-year contract since we were supposed to get one-point-six mill annually. That three million dollar differential, the extra amount DGE was unfairly awarded, well . . ."

"I had no idea," he said quietly, his expression troubled.

"Yeah, well, it was a very personal loss . . . but I'm apologizing about more than the feud."

She watched intensely as Victor carefully considered her words and measured his reply. No fraud. She knew he understood. Finally. Maybe they could work together.

He could sense that she trusted him. A little. It was a start. A good one.

Instinctively, he knew that they were at a critical turning point in the discussion. It had to be handled carefully. He would have said the same; it was honest.

"What else is there to be sorry about? I also added my share of rancor to our meetings. But thank you."

Obviously, there were many things he had to learn about his strange reactions to Liza. Only recently he had begun to understand the full depth of her fury. Not unlike his own, it, too, went well beyond the money. The core of their debate centered around the matter of principle involved. With that in mind, he lowered his guard a little more and offered her some reassurance.

"Liza, it's true. I was not raised here, and I'm not accustomed to the level of exclusion that I imagine you've faced," he said, pacing himself. "Since I have experienced people who did indeed require an attitude adjustment, I imagine that it was a major loss."

He sensed that she was hinting at something else, some aspect of the unspoken that was not out on the table yet. Needing to know, he offered her more chardonnay with a smile designed to put her at ease. The logic of his statement was sound and, based upon Liza's own experiences, she would probably accept his comment.

Graciously conceding, she gave him an affirming nod. "I honestly hadn't thought of it that way, Victor. I'm sure you've had your share of incidents . . . with trying to establish a firm in Washington, D.C.—the town of blue bloods and *old* money."

He loved her direct approach and the way her mind really took in new information. It was not naivete, but openness. A rare quality that compelled him to do the same. Rather than let Liza imagine that he hadn't heard the unspoken, he opted to press on.

"But, as you said, you are not talking about the feud. You also said that you didn't want games between us for the duration. Let's at least establish that tonight."

Nervously, he watched her studying him. He could tell that she was still trying to make up her mind about how far to go with a response, but relaxed when Liza finally nodded at him over her wine.

Her voice was barely above a whisper, and her eyes remained sad when she added, "Yeah, I'm tired of fighting with people. I'm tired of always having to keep up my guard, and sometimes I . . . It must be nice to grow up totally unencumbered by crazy stuff. I'm sorry, I shouldn't have invaded your thoughts without permission."

Perhaps it was the melancholy that rang through her sad tone or the openness with which she lifted her face to him. Liza's last comment got to him. Somewhere within the deep recesses of his being, it made him want to reach out and protect her. It was as though they had had this strange conversation of half information before, sitting across from each other in the candlelight while the fire glowed against her high, regal cheekbones.

He felt compelled to connect with her on some level and give her more of his own experiences to draw the vague parallel.

"Liza, while I may not be personally familiar with some of

the events that have taken place in this country, I am no stranger to oppression. Whether it's racially or militarily motivated, the effects upon the human spirit are horrendous."

He hadn't meant to go so far and hoped that Liza could accept his cryptic response as the truth. Her warm smile back was an immediate indicator that she had. But her eyes continued to haunt him to go further. They were devastating.

"Tell me, Liza, where did you learn to uncover the core of a person by simply looking at them? When not in battle mode, you can be truly interesting."

His honest, but backhanded, compliment made her laugh now. He was glad that the levity she exhibited had allowed the small slight to pass without incident.

"Well," she began, amused, "I have the unfair advantage."

Liza's smile was infectious, and he found himself chuckling at his own awkward comment.

"Since we are establishing détente here, it's only fair that I warn you up front, Duarte. My advantage is *very* strategic."

Noticing that she was back to calling him by his last name, he smiled, wondering whether it was a good sign or not. Non-plussed, he studied her over his wine glass, thoroughly intrigued with the possible new direction that the conversation could take. Vaguely, he hoped that Liza might be wandering down the same mental path that had captured him this evening. A sly smile had overtaken her lush mouth, and her eyes sparkled with mischief as he watched her speak.

Her gaze warmed him, and he struggled to appear impassive. If he had been foolish enough to stand up, it would've been immediately obvious what Liza's advantage had become. His armor in ruins; he let down his guard even more. What the hell . . . It was getting in the way now, anyway.

"Yes, your advantage is indeed strategic, or so I have gathered thus far this evening," he admitted, heady with wine. "And you have invaded my thoughts without permission."

"No, I'm serious, Victor," she pressed on, slightly more cautious, but still seeming comfortable with the exchange. "I have, shall we say, an ability. Sometimes I probe too deeply . . . and people get nervous. I rarely use it because it represents sort of an unfair advantage, as I said. But when I'm really curious, like tonight, or sense that I might be in danger, I do. I really should've asked you first. I'm only saying that I *know,* gut level, that you do want peace and you'll abide by the things we agreed upon tonight."

She looked away, quietly adding, "I just couldn't resist. If it will make you feel any better to know, I'm paying the price, too."

Her comment sobered him instantly, removing the relaxed haze from his mind. Sitting bolt upright, he pressed her for a direct explanation.

"We aren't just talking about the feud, are we?"

Victor knew there was an unspoken cue here. Something that was distantly familiar, heralding from the *old traditions* that he had left far behind with his Western education.

Looking at him with the most serious and open gaze that he had ever seen, she answered him simply. "It may be weird, Victor. Who knows? I don't want to offend your probably staunch Catholic background."

"Try me. My people have resolved the complex blend between religious concepts."

"No. It's stupid. Just trust me. I can tell things."

He set down his glass and rubbed his chin. "Talk to me."

Liza just smiled. It was going to be a stalemate.

"You know there are many things that we don't understand. But I have learned to respect what I don't know," he said evenly, hoping to draw her out. It was just a hunch, but he could almost swear that Liza was going down a path that he wouldn't have expected from the conservative businesswoman who sat before him.

"Okay. So, you want to hear something crazy, huh? The adventurous type. Figures."

He had to chuckle. "Very. Try me."

"Well," she started slowly, "my grandmother used to tell me

when I was a little girl that I had a gift. Okay? I generally don't tell anybody this stuff because they'll cart me away or definitely suggest serious analysis. Why I'm telling you now is beyond me."

He could feel her studying him to be sure it was safe to go on. It was.

"Maybe you have to tell me, now that you've started without my permission. That's only fair. My grandmother's wisdom. *Comprende?*"

It was the only short encouraging reply that he could think of. He understood that he had to give Liza something to let her know that he hadn't totally dismissed the unspoken concept. If she could really do what she had been alluding to all night . . . he was definitely in trouble.

She could trust him. She knew in her belly that this man was on the level. It was something about the way he asked the question that made her know he didn't think she'd lost her mind. There had been an urgent curiosity in his voice that held her. It had also shone in his eyes.

Shifting to get comfortable in her chair, she continued her story haltingly while holding on to the awareness that there was no appalling silence or disbelief in Victor's tone. She *knew* he would believe her. And he'd be the first person who ever had since Nana, other than Letty and Gerald.

"Let's just say I can tell when people are lying to me. That's a gift. End of story."

She ventured a peek across the table. Victor sat transfixed, trying to take in this bizarre new information. Why, she asked herself, was she telling Duarte? Something had her. Some strong indefinable pull to this man had her, and she just couldn't stop.

"I have heard about this, but never expected a business partner to exhibit it. Interesting . . . so, is that how you beat DGE?"

Liza laughed. "Nope. We just whipped your butt with old-fashioned hard work."

"Then when do you use this so-called gift?"

"When I need to."

"Ah, so something has made you activate it now. And what, may I ask, would that be?"

Cornered, she retreated immediately. She had gone too far, and he was decidedly inside her hidden territory.

Peering at Victor nervously, she shrugged, but his gaze never faltered. He seemed mesmerized by her admission.

Liza dropped her gaze, totally confused about why she was telling Victor Duarte, her recent nemesis, about this madness. She had let this insane information just tumble out of her mouth for no apparent reason! It was so odd, and terribly unsettling. It was just as crazy as the confession that Victor had blurted out earlier. This stranger, this opponent, had pulled as much out of her as she had pulled out of him. The question was, how? But more importantly, would he ever use what she had just told him against her?

"I was interested. Curious. About the shadows that I couldn't see through. There seemed to be danger there . . . but, not in the other areas I saw. Which creates a dilemma."

The sudden gush of truth had now left her exposed, entirely too vulnerable for this situation. Retreating again, she neatly folded her hands in her lap to keep Victor from seeing them tremble. When she finally looked up, she was totally surprised that he wasn't looking at her like she was insane or with the customary amused disbelief. His mind seemed to be racing ahead of her, full of questions and possibilities.

His reaction was one of pure fascination, not contempt. After a long pause of consideration, he assailed her with rapid-fire questions.

"Liza, tell me, how do you know that you can do this? Can you control it? What does it feel like when you do it?"

Victor responded with awe, and she deeply appreciated that he didn't tease or make fun of her. The fervent look in his eyes which belied an intense curiosity soothed her and she found she wanted to tell him more.

"No, I can't control it really. I mean, sometimes things come to me, sometimes they don't. But usually, if I am relaxed enough, I can do it. It's funny . . . if I sense hostility, I tense up and lose it. Or if I see something terrible, I mentally block it out and it's gone. But if it's something non-threatening or cut and dry, I can usually call it on a dime," she remarked casually, as if she were talking about something in the newspaper.

She had told him enough and was not about to reveal her Achilles' heel, the headaches.

Confused, she looked at him directly. "How did we get on this crazy subject anyway? Tell me about the next stages of the project . . . like, after tomorrow."

It was time to let it drop, to pass herself off as an eccentric "New Ager." The problem was that Victor kept staring at her and she couldn't turn off her secret weapon. It was as if the missile had turned on her and he was the one doing a probe. She'd die of friendly fire, that she was sure of. Her body tensed as she waited for it to hit ground zero.

When the waiter returned with their salads, she relaxed. The sudden shift momentarily interrupted the intense exchange. She had to get something in her stomach. The wine was clouding her judgment. That had to be it.

Extra Sensory Perception. The words reverberated inside Victor's head.

He studied Liza carefully. He hadn't dealt with such extreme beliefs since he'd left Peru, and Liza Nichols was the last person in the world that he would've ever expected to engage him in the topic of paranormal experiences. It was another exciting variable indeed. A wonderful caveat that he had to explore. He was not about to let Liza Nichols skillfully change the subject.

Looking down at his salad with disinterest, he softened his tone. "I was always told that if you have a gift, it is a sin to waste it. My grandmother's wisdom. So, why are you afraid of it?" he asked cautiously.

"Because, I'm also picking up more than a business interest from you."

He watched her focus narrow on him. She was still obviously trying to detect any fraud in his intent—this time, on a personal level. With no small measure of enjoyment, he could tell that Liza's probe was fully engaged and he hoped that she would never stop making him feel this way. Without question, he had never found a woman more captivating in his life.

Considering her comment, he savored the wine, still ignoring the salad. "It is a part of my cultural upbringing to leave one's mind open to certain *possibilities*. Your ability is, indeed, a gift, and you are accurate to view it as such."

Did he dare propose that she help him uncover critical parts of his mission by using second sight? It was an insane proposition. However, curiosity had the best of him. As long as he remained in control, Liza need never know why this information was so important to him. He had to find out who was behind the assassination of his family. Every clue led to Chem Tech and the men who ran that conglomerate. But for two years, he'd run into dead end after dead end. Landing the deal to work inside the corporation had been a desperate, last-ditch attempt. He had little concern for the business deal; he was engaged in a vendetta. She could keep the money. It had taken him over two decades to get this far. However, he now faced a new interest: The woman.

Leaning forward again, he proposed another challenge. "Listen, if you have this gift, you should develop it. It could be a great asset. I will teach you how to play chess like a master, which is a non-threatening way for you to strengthen your skill. Chess teaches you how to understand your opponents' possible moves two or three plays in advance of their actions. It was actually the backbone of my financial education. In return, if you do, indeed, have this gift, you may possibly be able to help me on a personal project one day. Guaranteed, it has nothing to do with personal gain. We may even be able to re-negotiate some of your lost-contract per-

centage. That is open for discussion . . . just between the two
of us. I will assure you that my priorities are honor and justice.
Deal?"

Was he mad? Why on earth would he even let her get that
close to the subject. Victor sat back and steadied himself.

She weighed his offer, but hesitated. There was no need to
tell her more. Yet if she did have second sight, he only hoped
that she hadn't picked up on the blatantly physical urge that now
accosted him. Unfortunately, there were several very personal
issues swirling in his mind at once—none of them appropriate
for this meeting. He had been in her presence before and had
felt the attraction. But tonight, he was obsessed. His original
objective had been to get to know her better and to clear the air
so there wouldn't be any more project interference from her
team. That way, he could go on with his plan unhindered. Now,
his interest in Liza was not so icily removed. No longer could
he view her as an obstacle to get out of the way. She was seeping
into the wrong side of his brain: The personal side. And there
was no room for a woman or a relationship now. Yet, God help
him, he still wanted her.

Seeming intrigued, Liza tentatively approached his challenge
after a long, thought-filled pause.

"And how will you know whether or not I'm worthy of all
of that time, energy, trust . . . and money?" she mused nervously, apparently delighted by the game of chess to strengthen
her skill, but still unwilling to commit to play it with him.
"It'll cost you."

He understood Liza's position well. For all she knew, she
could be forging a pact with the Devil. The mere thought made
him smile. Perhaps she was.

Encouraged by her ambivalence, he seized the opportunity to
press her for an answer. "I'm prepared for the cost. Are you?"

"You've got to pay the cost to be the boss, Duarte."

"How much?"

Liza didn't answer, just smiled and sipped her wine.

"Not sure, Liza? Well, one way to know is to try to read me

now while you're relaxed. But promise not to hold back any information. Agreed? No matter how disconcerting. Although I may not tell you, *I'll* know if you hit a direct bull's-eye."

Despite her claims to have an uncanny ability to read minds, he could tell that a shadow of doubt still remained. Maybe she was afraid of the challenge or maybe the gift she claimed was just a bit of parlor room showmanship and he had called her bluff. Yet, as the last part of those thoughts crossed his mind, her saw her brow wrinkle. Coincidence? Nah. He was starting to scare himself.

"Aren't you going to eat your salad?" she evaded. "I haven't eaten all day, and the wine . . . well, I need something on my stomach first."

"Where are my manners? Of course, of course. Please, do not let me stop you," he said softly.

He could tell that she was buying time, but he had lost all interest in the meal. Pushing his plate to the edge of the table to signal the waiter to remove it, he watched Liza intently as she took a few nervous bites then pushed her plate away as well. He had hoped that it would be too late for her to disengage. Perhaps the challenge of the game would hold her. It already had him in its grip. He had to know.

"Victor, are you sure? This could get uncomfortable if you want to know *everything.*" She eyed him cautiously.

At this point he was no longer sure of anything, except that something totally foreign was drawing him out. He was also unsure of whether or not this game would create more side issues than it was worth. He hesitated, then decided to press on.

"I insist on total accuracy to the best of your ability or I will consider it a breach of contract," he said, smiling openly and waiting for her to get comfortable again.

"We haven't established terms yet."

"I think we have," he contradicted, leaning forward.

He watched as she warily considered the implications.

Liza shrugged, but her eyes still held a mystical quality. She had been baited and hooked.

God, she was beautiful!

Five

The night guard nodded sleepily as Liza passed the lobby entrance to her building. Three intense hours of negotiating with Victor Duarte, a true confession of her ability, and a near-sexual collision . . . What a night!

She was thankful, the lights were still on in the office, where she could see that a few members of the programming staff were still hunched over their tubes. Although she hated to see them there so late, she was glad that she didn't have to pass by vacant cubicles alone at this time of night. Hailing them briefly and again getting only a few disgruntled responses, Liza tried her best to get them to go home before she closed the door to her own office.

Tucked safely into her sanctuary, she clicked on her tube and waited for the system to boot up.

Weird. The whole night had been weird.

As grids of information filled the screen, her hands moved deftly across the keyboard.

Too coincidental. He's emotionally tied to Chem Tech . . . somehow . . . as am I. But it's a dark emotion. Like mine . . . full of hurt, pain, anger . . . The contract—the money—was never the main issue. That was the ruse on both our parts.

As she studied one computer window, Liza moved the mouse to overlay another file next to the on-screen document for comparison.

No more rage directed at me. No more rage directed at him. Anger has been transformed to a new, more dangerous emotion. There is still a link between us. From where?

Liza sat back from the screen and tried to allow the acute arousal that had haunted her throughout their dinner to subside.

Throughout the meal, her mind had kept descending upon that feeling, which had blocked the real information she wanted. It was almost as though his desire created a blanket over any other content, which was why she'd left the conversation hanging, finished her meal, and returned the balance of the discussion to business. She was glad that he'd accepted her retreat, almost as if he, too, understood that they were treading on dangerous ground.

But he'd also believed her, believed that she could probe his mind. What in God's name had made her reveal that to him? And it hadn't even been an option. Once she'd skirted the subject, he had actually *pulled* it from her. Something strange was definitely going on, and her curiosity had the best of her.

She closed her eyes and let out a slow breath. "Think, Liza. Think. Get back to your work. Let it go."

A buzz on her console almost made her jump out of her skin, and she picked up the phone on the first ring.

"Liza. I need to talk to you."

She immediately recognized the male voice that resonated on the other end of the phone. But how had he known that she'd gone back to the office. Had he followed her?

She answered slowly. "Victor, what's this about? Is something wrong? How'd you know I'd be here after dinner? It's eleven o'clock at night."

She could hear the crackle of static through the receiver and light street traffic. He was on a cellular. He wasn't . . .

"Yes. Something is very wrong. When I left the restaurant, I got into my car, but then there was a wood-paneled room. Flashes. Pictures. I don't know what's happening."

His voice had a desperate quality to it that she understood. She had lived with this vertigo all her life. Terror engulfed her. How could they have had the same vision?

"Where are you?"

"Outside. Outside your building. Please. Make it stop."

"I'll be right down. I'll get my car. We'll go some place to talk."

"No. Just come down. Now."

He didn't even wait for her response; he hung up. Adrenaline propelled her as she grabbed her purse, shut off the lights, and hastily left the office without saying goodbye to her preoccupied staff.

It seemed like an eternity for the elevator to come, and she paced in front of the doors until they opened.

Time. Time expanded and crept as each floor lit on the elevator panel. She had to get out.

"C'mon!" Yelling into the vacant space just made time seem to move slower. The tiny confines made the walls feel like they were moving in on her.

As the doors opened, she jetisoned herself beyond them, half running, half walking quickly past the guard, down the front steps, and out to the curb line. She could see Victor sitting in his steel-gray SAAB, clenching the steering wheel with both hands, and looking ahead without expression.

She was almost afraid to tap on the window, but did so lightly to let him know that she was there.

He motioned to the passenger-side door, and she leaned in, but didn't enter immediately.

"Get in."

"Are you all right?"

"Get in. Please. I have to talk to you."

Nervous energy moved her limbs without consulting her brain. His voice held a command quality that she couldn't ignore, yet she resisted the impending discussion.

Victor moved the stick shift and engaged the idling engine. "I'll go around the corner and park. I'm not ready to drive yet."

His face was covered with a damp sheen.

"Are you all right? What happened when I left?"

He didn't answer immediately, but pulled over to the side of the street and put the car in park. Victor took a deep breath, ran his fingers over his hair, closed his eyes, and leaned back, allowing his head to fall against the headrest.

"Talk to me, Liza. You owe me my sanity, at the very least."

The process of assessing Victor was electrifying. She could tell that he felt it, too. As she peered at him, he seemed to battle for composure as he began to literally struggle for air. His intense expression, gave her the impression that something was sending a vertical current through him, linking them in some strange, unfathomable way. When he suddenly gripped the steering wheel tighter, she flinched involuntarily. Warmth radiated through her abdomen, connecting with a sudden heat that spread to her thighs.

"Were you on a ship?"

Victor took in a gulp of air, but didn't open his eyes. "My God, how did you know? Every night, it's the same. Recurring. But never this strong. I'm awake now, but I can actually feel it . . . like when you did it at dinner, when you went into my mind. I can't disengage."

Inconceivable. They couldn't have had the same dreams.

"Where are you now?"

His voice was barely audible. "I can't . . . Please. It's too intense."

New fear took hold of her as her body swayed from an avalanche of erotic awakening. What was happening to him—to them?

"I'm not doing it. I don't know what you're experiencing. You have to talk to me."

Victor's breaths were coming in deep rasps. "There's a storm. Wood. Wood in a small room. Your hair. You smell so good. Your skin . . . never in my life . . ."

When a low moan escaped his lips, she shut her eyes in reflex. Each fiber of her skin tingled as the sound of his voice went through every pore. The darkness behind her lids burst into color, a collage of images. . . . She could taste the salt of his skin as her lips brushed his neck. . . . Her hands revelled in the texture of his hair. . . . His weight pinned her, moved against her, forcing a gasp to escape from her lips.

"I can't break it either," she exclaimed, wrestling with her will to open her eyes.

From her position in the passenger's seat, she peered at him and gently shook him by the shoulders. Slowly, he came around and opened his eyes, breathing heavily through his mouth.

"You never touched me, but I felt it. I'm at a loss . . . I actually felt it. Your touch is echoing through me now, even as I speak."

All she could do was look at him.

"Liza, has this ever happened to you before . . . when you've done a probe?"

"No. Never." Her voice was a mere whisper. "I can still feel it, too. Everything with you seems volcanic. The fights feel familiar. The touch feels familiar. Known. Do you understand what I mean?"

Victor nodded slowly. "I have to understand this. I've never felt anything so powerful in my life. I don't want to have this conversation sitting curbside in the District this late at night. Will you talk to me? Tell me what you did . . . how you did it. When did you know that you could? I'm . . ."

"No. I don't want to go into this now. It's too charged and too compromising. I honestly don't know what just happened."

Liza placed her hand on the door handle. She needed space, time to think, a place to recalibrate and get rational. Who was this man? How could he manifest such feelings? Shared visions? Shared dreams? It was as though he were some eerie catalyst that took her inate ability to a new level that she wasn't ready to explore.

Leaning over slowly, he covered her hand with his own. The contact burned her, sending searing waves of want through her body.

"Please, Liza. I have to know who you are to me. This goes way beyond business."

The intensity of his gaze, combined with the familiarity in his voice and the ache that his touch created within her, made her close her eyes again. As she slipped behind the dark curtain of her lids, her lips parted to speak, but she felt his mouth close over hers. . . . His tongue slid across her teeth, the bridge of her mouth, tangling deliciously with her own. Yet when she opened her eyes, he hadn't moved near her. She had only sensed it.

Victor removed his hand and allowed his head to drop forward against the steering wheel briefly before straightening himself. She watched him struggle for composure within the small space that separated them.

"I will endeavor to be a gentleman, but we need to talk about this."

Without looking at her, he clasped the stick shift and moved it into drive. . . .

He had heard her silent acceptance.

Somehow breaking the sound barrier undetected, Victor had managed to compress the normal twenty-five-minute ride into fifteen harrowing minutes. Initially, the speed was exhilarating, combining with the tension and fear that enveloped her.

Unable to think, Lisa closed her eyes to the lights of the landscape. Everything was a blur as they flew along the deserted roads. She could mentally feel Victor taking her with anguishing pleasure, and abruptly opened her eyes. There was no escape from his thoughts or the visions which now laid claim to every inch of her. It had been so long. Two years, seven months, and twelve days to be exact. She was helpless to stop it.

In her mind, he kept taking her over and over and over again until she almost cried out with her own physical need. That was still not enough reason to rush into anything. This was not real. It was only a vision. For the first time in her life, she could not shut it off. She reprimanded herself not to do anything this crazy. At least not something this volatile, this close to her business!

Letting the window down slightly, she hoped that the wind might snap her judgment back into focus as they cut through the crisp evening. As they careened past slower traffic, he seemed impervious to the distraction of the cool air that filled the cab.

Peering at Victor, she watched him aggressively take out his pent-up frustration on the gears. Rapt, she continued to study every detail of the male hands that controlled their flight. This was not she, Liza Nichols. This was not happening . . .

However, as their journey transitioned onto the winding roads that laced the waterfront residential district near the Potomac, she became even more unnerved—if that were possible. For the first time, in a very long time, she actually feared for her personal safety. If they didn't slow down, they were surely going to die.

She wanted to say something. Something plausible that would give them a face-saving out. There was no reason why she had to turn on the damned probe in the first place! Millions of people lived their entire lives without the benefit of second sight. Now, everything she thought of to say sounded trite. But her dignity was on the line.

"Maybe we should go to someplace neutral for coffee?" she suggested softly, angling for an eleventh-hour, fifty-ninth minute escape.

Victor didn't answer immediately or look at her, but he drew in a deep breath through his nose. "I'd prefer to be somewhere private, someplace where neither of us has to be embarrassed if this escalates."

Her stomach muscles contracted with the sensual tone of his voice and his underlying meaning. She would have to put her foot down! True, she was extremely aroused, but she wasn't out of her mind. The probe was affecting them, that was all. She would do the honorable thing and give him room to not be humiliated. She would not let this happen . . . at least not yet.

Although she rummaged through the cobwebs in her brain for something acceptable to say, nothing came to mind. In response to her silence, Victor accelerated the vehicle to the limits of its technical capability. The car repeatedly left the ground, registering each deviation in the road with a soft thud. *We're practically flying!* she screamed to herself, edging toward mild hysteria. *He's going too fast! This whole damned thing is going too fast!*

Intermittently, she looked over to see if Victor's expression had changed. It hadn't. He was totally focused, and never once did he look in her direction or acknowledge her growing distress. Only the twitching muscle in his jawline gave her any indication that he was acutely aware of her presence, marking the explosive emotions that he was hopelessly trying to hold in check.

As they hurled into the driveway, Victor reached over her lap while the car was still in motion. The sudden action startled her, but she tried to remain calm. In one easy move, he'd deftly popped open the glove compartment to activate the automatic garage door opener.

This is it! her mind screamed again. She had one last chance to make a break for it. She couldn't let this happen! Yet, it was all so familiar—so curiously tempting to play the whole experience out to the end. The conflict tore at her. She was afraid; but at the same time, she wanted to know him, all of him, in one exhilarating moment. Somehow she had been pushed beyond the border of shame, in exile from herself, and was now immersed deep within the territory of raw emotion.

That's when she saw him again. Saw it. Them.

It was vivid, yet fleeting, like the momentary flash of light in a thunderstorm.

He was making love to her recklessly, pushing her long skirts up past her hips. She scrabbled violently at the loose, white-linen shirt that he wore, intermittently tangling her fingers in his hair. He took her mouth in a harsh caress, opening her legs with his knee Yet, it was in his eyes . . . a gentle entreaty which begged for the permission that she had already given him. Everything happened so fast, so furiously, against the wall of a wood-panelled room. He choked out her name; she heaved and climaxed against him. He repeatedly called her Querida.

The vision stoked Liza's own need, quelling her fear for her safety, making her bold, fusing with the devastating warmth that radiated up her thighs. It was Victor. It had to be. But under what circumstances? Where? Surely she was mad.

* * *

Forced to bring the vehicle to a screeching halt, Victor idled the engine impatiently while waiting for the painfully slow process of the garage door to open. The agonizing wait brought some semblance of clarity to his mind, and he repeatedly told himself ridiculous lies. He had *never* lost control, and didn't intend to tonight. They'd have coffee. . . . He'd learn more about her strange ability. . . . What he wanted from Liza was strictly related to the mission. Nothing more. If she had gotten this close to him, what else did she know?

As he more cautiously brought the vehicle over the threshold of the entranceway, he reminded himself of the dangers. Liza was there for a discussion. *That's it. Don't be stupid!* he instructed himself. Was he out of his mind? He'd told her he'd be a gentleman. He had to pull himself together. This could jeopardize everything.

But once inside the spacious three-car garage, all of his admonishments evaporated instantly. With the motor still running, he found himself compelled to turn to her, bringing his hands to either side of her face. His passion was undeniable now, and he pulled her to him to devour her mouth.

Liza groaned unashamedly when his lips made contact with hers. Her response shook him, as did her ruinous, immediate warmth. He was already heady from the combination of her inexplicable gift and raw beauty, but her touch and her feminine scent was simply too much to bear. Her tongue tentatively grazed his teeth, sliding easily to find its mate, dancing with his in a familiar embrace. Never in his life. *Never* in his life!

Traces of chardonnay and the sweet hint of Grand Marnier continued to batter his senses. The warm fervent question of her compliance answered him without further negotiation. Her consent also shone in her eyes, he was sure. He watched it positively mirror back to him from her deep-brown centers of gravity.

What are you doing, man? His intellect screamed out to him while his desire raced wildly in the opposite direction. Holding on to his last shred of reason, he withdrew. He had to stop before it was too late. His breathing labored as his mind became completely besieged with reality.

Thoroughly expecting to receive a well-deserved slap, or worse, a probable lawsuit, he turned to rest his head on the steering wheel. He needed to recalibrate himself, take this woman back to her office—immediately, before it went any further.

"I'm sorry . . . . I promised . . . but . . . I'll take you back if you want to leave . . ." He couldn't breathe, each word had escaped from his mouth separately in a string of adolescent longing. He wasn't making sense.

Without recovering, he turned to Liza, still unable to catch his breath, and tried to wrestle the balance of an apology from his throat. But instead of apologizing, he found himself reaching for the woman again, aggressively searching for her tongue.

What should have been a chivalrous retreat became an arduous advance of his passion. Staking his claim on this wondrous new territory, he offered an admission as he groaned deeply against her cheek. "Oh, Liza, I want you *so badly* it hurts. Please don't ask me to be a gentleman tonight."

He had lost it. He was mortified by his own behavior and expected her to be utterly insulted. He could only hope that his admission gave her room for the positive response that he so desperately needed to hear. The situation had possessed him. He'd plead insanity for sure.

His eyes scanned her face rapidly as another wave of hard want overpowered him. Without waiting for her reply, he buried his face into the delicate flesh of her neck, absorbing all of her. His nostrils filled with her deliriously intoxicating scent. He felt weak. Liza's short gasps were the only audible acceptance of his advances that his mind registered. Before she could formulate a refusal, he found himself rapidly spilling kisses down her neck toward the firm swell of her breasts. She felt so good. Too good to be true. But Jesus, he was scared. How could he stop now?

* * *

Liza begged him with her mind not to stop. The joining of their mouths was too brief, providing only a short breath of life for someone who was drowning. She needed more and sought Victor's mouth again, her lips parted. It was an invitation . . . a request . . . a plea for him to go further.

She was hurled into a terrifying void of pleasure, unable to assess the delicate nature of her precarious situation. Every warm, vital kiss that brushed her skin made the over-sensitive tips of her breasts tighten and sting, aching to be touched. She whimpered when he brought his mouth down over each erect peak through the sheer fabric of her blouse. She was alive again. Painfully alive. But she had to stop.

"Please . . ." she breathed. Even to her own ears, her words sounded more like a request than a protest when she uttered them.

Returning repeatedly, Victor punished her mouth with harsh kisses. Fiercely devouring all the venom she had visited upon him for the past six months, he now demanded restitution. Suddenly, there was no such thing as propriety or tomorrow. In Victor's arms, there was only the immediate descent into a powerful ecstasy designed to drive her mad.

She felt herself open to the raw need that he elicited so deeply from her core. To be touched and held, with—or without—love, became a necessary part of her existence. But somehow, crazily, insanely, she felt love. How had she survived without this attention to her body and her heart for so long? Unable to fight against the sensations he unleashed, she writhed under each caress. Indeed, they were necessary. Basic-peristaltic. But this had to stop.

"We can't . . ." she finally managed, taking in large gulps of air.

"I know. . . . This is insane. . . . But, God as my witness . . . I've never . . ." he said, gasping.

She watched Victor struggle with himself and withdraw. His pain became hers, the tide of emotion too overpowering for them to fight.

"I want to as much as you do," she whispered hoarsely, hoping to ease the embarrassment that she was sure would follow. "But . . ."

Her words trailed off as Victor's gaze burned her. He answered with an intense look before reaching toward her again. His hand moved through her hair until it reached the nape of her neck. As he drew her to him more gently, he took the lobe of her ear between his lips, slowly pulling at the tender skin.

"How can we stop . . ." he murmured breathlessly, ". . . when this has consumed us both since the very beginning?"

She knew that what he said was too true. There was no way for them to stop. Not when it felt this good, this right. She had felt this desire before, but had fought angrily to ignore it. She placed her hand on his chest, feeling the hard thuds of his heart beneath her palm. Her body was not her own, and she felt herself lean into him more closely, absorbed by the warmth that surrounded her. Everything they'd ever felt toward each other had evoked passion. Whether it was anger or attraction. Victor was right. It was all-consuming. When she allowed her head to drop against his shoulder, the muscles in her thighs relaxed and her knees parted without consulting her brain. It was another nonverbal invitation that her body willed against her mind.

His hand answered, slowly caressing her inner thigh in response. As he touched the damp silk undergarments that covered her throbbing center, she heard his breaths come harder. She gripped his lapels, bracing for the shudder that was sure to devastate her when he slid his fingers beneath the soft fabric.

Involuntarily arching against the contact, she pulled him in closer as she lost control. As though reading her mind, he focused his caress into a gentle, rhythmic tease. That did it. Her reason snapped.

"Victor . . . please . . . Let's go inside. . . . I won't hold you to your promise tonight."

She wanted to be with him regardless of the consequences. It felt right, and there was no going back.

Her urgent declaration released him from the bondage of honor. Without hesitation, he left her and bolted out of his side of the sedan. Cornering her halfway between the car and the door which led to the house, his eyes said everything. He seemed rooted where he stood, as though unable to go another minute without touching her.

She stepped toward him, close enough for him to reach out and forcefully pull her to him again. His swift approach left them unbalanced, and to break their fall, he caught her in the sway of her back as they stumbled against the cool garage wall.

Pinned beneath him, she felt each vertebra separate, bruising under the force of his crush. Her spine flattened as she reached up to him. She sought retribution in his back, clawing the length of him until he arched in pleasure and brought his mouth down upon hers. Neither could relent; neither could pull away—despite the ultimate destruction that lay in their wake.

Somehow, as Victor reached out to catch her, he had become hopelessly entangled in the lengths of baubles that draped her neck. His focus had become singular and penetrating, and he seemed only to care that he had her in his arms. Driven to distraction, he tried impatiently to extricate his cuff link from its snare, but it was only a matter of seconds before the strands of pearl and crystal broke, wildly scattering hundreds of tiny beads across the hard, cement floor. She shattered with them, reality bouncing angrily away from her.

"This is madness," she whispered breathlessly. "Complete madness." Yet her words were hollow. The thought of tomorrow had already been banished by their desire. There was nothing but this moment . . . his touch . . . her need.

"I can't stop," he breathed back rapidly. "Even if I wanted to."

She felt the same raw passion that made Victor oblivious to his surroundings and the circumstances. Now there was no danger, no restraint. Propelled by the reckless emotion that they shared, he bit into her neck, lavishly fondling her breasts. She tugged at the buttons of her own blouse, needing to feel his skin against hers. His cheek, his mouth, his hands, all grazed every sensitive inch of surface on her torso. She rubbed against him feverishly, forcing the ache between her thighs to ignite an explosion of pleasure.

Blanketing her, Victor moved against her body as though he were already inside her. His tempo increased with his own mounting need until her ardent, willing responses scorched him.

Finally, in a harsh staccato whisper, he admitted what they had both known for hours. "Now. Liza. Please. I can't wait any longer. I need to feel you. It's . . . just been . . . *so long.*"

Totally consumed with need herself, she could barely answer him. A low throaty groan was all that she could muster as she worked furiously at his zipper and belt. Once past the complicated fastenings on his trousers, she freed him, moving her hand across his length. Her fingers burned with a contrast of textures as her hand molded his form, singeing them anew with relentless urgency.

He responded to her sudden touch with an immediate, violent shudder. His breaths became more labored, matching her irregular rasps, and she was sure that she would collapse as waves of pleasure resonated through her soul. It was too much. All of it. Never before had she felt like this with any man.

It was impossible to keep their mouths joined as they fought for air. Suddenly, without regard for the consequences, he pushed her skirt up past the tops of her thighs. It was happening again. This time, it was real. She had no will left to stop him. She wanted him. Needed him this way. There was now only one goal that they both shared—to connect, to complete. Just the way it had happened before . . . in the vision.

He was no longer in the garage. He was in a wood-panelled room, and his restraint crumbled as he gently stroked Liza's long, shapely legs. With each caress, he revelled at the touch of her skin beneath his hands. His mind registered every glorious detail as he moved from the bare skin at the top of her thighs to the smooth silk stockings that adorned them. It was all so devastatingly familiar. Beyond control, he tugged roughly at the thin barrier of lingerie until it gave way to the exquisite feel of Liza and he lost the ability to reason.

"Victor . . . let me help you," she whispered hoarsely, then used her hand as a gentle guide. Her touch quaked him as she tilted her hips forward and brought one long leg up around his waist.

His breathing stopped as he absorbed her inner warmth, filling her forcefully to unite them in the timeless bond. He could feel Liza's heart beating inside him, throbbing its ancient rhythm through his body, beginning where they had joined. Yet when he fused to her violently with a moan, he could no longer move or stand it. He was totally overcome as his intent fractured. It was happening too soon.

"Oh, God, Liza."

The depth of the long-awaited sensation had forced him to cry out to her, freezing him in an abyss between agony and pleasure as he held her savagely. Closing his eyes against the rapid need that assaulted him, he could barely choke out the truth between each massive breath.

"I know you, *Querida. I know you!*"

Still pressed against her neck, his cheek burned as his objective splintered from the uncontrolled fission. She did not answer him, but squirmed under his hold, making it impossible for him to regain control. He understood how desperately she needed to arch, to take more of him into her—needing him to begin. But his response to her struggle was to grip her more forcefully, grinding out his resistance to her movements with the pulsing muscle in his jaw. He was beyond speech, yet held out the hope that she could hear his mind screaming. *Don't move. Please. Just for a moment!*

To his dismay, she ignored his silent entreaty and bore down hard within the small space that his hold would allow. The sensation made him close his eyes tighter as she used only an agonizing sliver of movement to quench her body's thirst. He wanted to please her, to make it last, to give her his soul until her womb gave way to his invasion. But now gloriously inside Liza, he knew that if he moved it would be over in an instant.

Each violent tremor that wrecked his body brought with it a new wave of distress. Outright panic coursed through him, making him afraid to begin. Torturously aware that he could explode at Liza's slightest movement, he trembled as he tried to slow his breathing to regain control.

The tension that vibrated through his groin betrayed him without mercy, mounting swiftly against his will. Between each ragged breath he bit out his caution to her. "Please . . . not yet. I can't . . ."

He felt her answer as she clutched the back of his jacket, passionately ignoring his plea. With a deep moan, she continued to arch rhythmically to bring him into her again and again.

"But I want you," she breathed near his ear, "and I don't care how long it lasts."

The connection was instantaneous. She had become his other half, that which could make them whole—if only for a brief spark in the continuum of time. Without warning, Liza shuddered beneath him, burying her head against his shoulder. This time, he read her thoughts and kissed her face passionately, allowing the familiarity to wash over him.

Tangling her slender fingers through his hair, she forced him to stop and look into her eyes. She gazed at him intently as she fought unsuccessfully to steady her breaths.

"I know you, too . . . since forever . . ."

Broken by her words, he took her mouth instantly while thrusting without restraint. It was impossible to control himself, to be gentle, to take his time. Each moan that Liza released drove him onward. He feared that her spine, now bludgeoned by its merciless contact with the garage wall, might fracture under his weight. Yet he was unable to stop. He was so close . . . and she still seemed to need him, more of him. She pulled him to her as if the barrage would rescue her, and he groaned as he felt her teeter on the edge of another completion.

When she wrapped both her legs around his hips, he quickly

responded, shifting his hands under her bottom, supporting her weight without interrupting his stride. His responses began deep within his chest, mixing eerily with the familiarity of their embrace.

Broken, he simply uttered, "I can't stop . . ."

That admission, combined with Liza's body, was too much. He felt her stomach wrench as she clutched and released him inside her, letting out a low spasmodic wail of pleasure.

Again and again, her warmth engulfed him as she trembled beneath him. He was unable to delineate the boundary of where her climax ended and his began. Every nerve ending was alive, merging into the delicious harmony of their rapture. Hot tears streamed down her face, combining with the perspiration on his own. There was no recovery from this final, utter destruction.

Liza's unbound response drove his tempo as she matched his demanding rhythm. When she continued to climax in a wave of shudders and moans, he could no longer hold back. In one agonized gasp, without warning, his body convulsed in a powerful release into hers. The impact of his sudden explosion elongated her name in his throat, and he buried his face against her shoulder. He could feel each syllable ripple through him as it made its way up from the depths of his being. Shivers of pleasure repeatedly shot through him, jerking every taunt muscle of his frame. He felt his head fall back in the torture of passion, his movements no longer his own. The unceasing sensations battered him, shattering time and space.

Tears threatened the corners of his eyes, which he shut tightly against the wonderful agony that threatened to annihilate him. Liza felt so good and so . . . familiar. He had needed her this way for a long time, and in an instant, a flash of recognition thawed the icy regions of his soul. He knew her! *Dear God in heaven, he knew this woman!* . . . and he cried out again as he finished deep inside of her.

The extended delirium sapped his strength until he was almost unable to stand. The violence of his release had been sheer destruction. He had died for her—only to be resurrected from the ashes of his decimation by her kiss.

Finally, he gave way to exhaustion and collapsed against her for support. It was madness. A breathtaking, exquisite, madness.

He sucked in huge gulps of air while tiny rivulets of perspiration coursed down the center of his back. He had no defense against the sensations as he held her close. The glorious torture continued, sending wave after wave of aftershock tremors to wreck their bodies. Only after the last violent quake slowly subsided, ebbing with Liza's soft moan, could he shift his weight imperceptibly to give her more room to breathe.

With the temporary shift of his weight, the night air played over their damp clothes and they both shivered as the last of the tremors abated. He pulled her to him again, closing off the cool air that rushed between them. Still nuzzling her neck, he could not bring himself to withdraw from her warm, wonderful body.

"Are you cold?" he asked tentatively. Her expression was so tender that it brought a tightness to his chest.

"No . . . not anymore," she whispered, looking deep into his eyes.

He knew that she was searching for something in his voice, something in his face, that flash of recognition that had been eclipsed as quickly as it had been revealed.

The fear reflected in Liza's expression was all too familiar, mirroring the sad understanding that comes from saying goodbye. But as he took her face into his hands and kissed her gently, an emotion filled his being that he could not describe.

Lightly stroking her moist cheek, he allowed himself to dive into her liquid-brown eyes and absorb her pain until he was totally overwhelmed. He detected something ominous, yet compelling, behind her wide irises. Something in Liza pulled him into a terrifying reality.

Saddened, he shook his head. Too much still stood in the way of any other possibilities for them beyond this accidental encounter. Roughly, his eyes searched her face for answers, and his voice became almost a whisper.

"Liza . . . This has all happened so fast . . . so, unexpectedly. . . . Tell me, what are we going to do now?"

She looked down, overwhelmed by the depth of his honest confusion—and her own. He was sure that terror now blocked her gift. From a remote place in his mind, he watched her struggle with the after-the-fact impropriety of their behavior.

"I don't know, Victor. This wasn't supposed to happen. There's so much that we don't know about each other. . . . Everything was too intense," she said quietly, then rested her forehead on his shoulder.

What else could she do but steel herself against the reality of their horrible mistake in judgment? His worse fears had been realized. She regretted the impropriety. So did he. He should have never let it happen.

He felt her withdraw—not in anger, but to protect that soft, vulnerable center in her heart that he had unwittingly uncovered. As her body tensed, he released her, knowing that her instincts about him were probably correct.

With one finger under her chin, he forced her head up gently. "Liza, that's not what I meant," he protested in a quiet voice. "I don't know what's possible. There is so much in the way." Unable to look into her eyes any longer, he traced her neck to find the remains of her broken pearls.

Stray beads bounced and scattered as he loosened them from the soft folds of her blouse. "I'm truly sorry. . . . I'll have to replace them. I didn't mean to be so . . . rough . . . I should've been more careful. I've never behaved this way with a woman," he began haltingly, then trailed off. There was nothing to say. This had definitely been a mistake.

She placed her fingers to his lips to stop his awkward apology. "It's all right, Victor. I enjoyed every moment of losing them."

His heart wrenched. She was going to play fair to the end, he thought gloomily. Even if it killed her.

His apology went beyond the scattered pearls, but she clearly understood. They had undoubtedly both been here before, watching broken promises dance away. But that was insane. He'd made no promises. And she was a grown woman. But, an immediate, irrational sense of loss gripped him.

He read the sadness on Liza's face at his equivocation. Yet what was the truth? he wondered. What they had so magically found probably wouldn't go on. The anguish that filled his chest was strangely different this time, like the intense pleasure that he had never allowed himself to experience before had been.

Quietly collecting herself, Liza began another purposeful retreat. "I'd better go. We have a staff meeting in the morning, and it would be best . . . if we just left things . . . *simple*. Would you take me back to my car?"

There, at least she had been the one to say it. Perhaps the subject would be closed, as if this spontaneous, ill-conceived situation had never happened. He would numb himself again, go back to his cloistered, unfeeling existence, and futilely try to forget the instant passion that Liza Nichols had aroused.

Morose and bewildered, he had no explanation to offer her, and they separated awkwardly, smoothing their disheveled clothes. With her eyes still lowered, she picked up her tattered silk panties and tucked them into her pocket. In the silent aftermath, he felt that he had violated her. Emotion caught in his throat when he saw her bottom lip tremble, and he turned away to offer her some small semblance of privacy in which to collect herself with dignified resignation.

But despite his newfound reserve, irrational thoughts besieged him. How could he simply walk away from her after the way she had made him feel? He had called her *Querida,* love of his life, and he had *never* used that term of endearment with any woman before. And when he had held Liza in his arms, she had seemed almost . . . familiar. Emotionally battered, he could only chalk the sensation up to his recent monk-like existence and the vestiges of superstition.

Solemnly returning to the car, he felt lonelier than he had in a very long time. Unchecked, his emotions would have raged until they would have made him blurt out, *Lisa, I'm crazy about you and I need this . . . you . . . in my life!*

But his intellect, reawakened, chided him for his foolishness. How could he be this drawn to someone he hadn't even known, much less liked, before this evening? Not being one given to rash impulses, he was astonished at his own erratic behavior. This was supposed to have been *just* a cordial business dinner, not a spontaneous combustion of his emotions.

Moreover, the reality of his past and the mission that loomed before him held close guard over such ravings. No matter how he felt, it was impossible—and far too dangerous—to start getting so deeply involved at this point. Especially with a potentially lethal task before him.

The return drive was subdued. Yet the silence was excruciating as she gazed out of the window to avoid looking in Victor's direction. At last they pulled up to the garage, and she prayed that none of her staff members would see her. The possibility of being discovered frayed her composure.

How could she have let this happen? It had been so unplanned, so erratic. For God's sake, she barely knew this man! Fighting against tears, she locked her jaw in a decided display of strength, hoping for Victor's discretion. If they never mentioned it again, maybe it could pass as an unfortunate incident.

But how could she pretend that she didn't feel anything? There had been a connection, something deep. But then, that was probably her own stupid, wishful thinking. She had let down her guard and cheapened herself. She was truly going to die.

While she tried in vain to smooth her rumpled suit one last time, Victor broke the strained silence, lightly touching her arm. *Please,* she prayed, refusing to look at him, *just let me get out of here.*

"Liza, are you all right?" he asked, sincere concern evident in his voice, as if he desperately needed confirmation that she didn't feel used. She thought he wanted to hold her, but she wouldn't allow it. That fraud would bruise her even more.

Nodding, almost unable to speak through the tears that constricted the back of her throat, she smiled weakly and answered him flatly. "Yeah, Victor. I'm always all right."

Although she had not intended the sarcastic sting, she knew

her words had hit their mark. He looked down at the steering wheel, offering no further response.

Focusing beyond the dull ache that nagged at her temple, she could sense Victor's defeated acknowledgment of the truth. He *had* asked others that same trite question—too many times in the past. Was she going to be all right? Would any woman be all right after this? But he had warned her and she had practically begged him to take her. She couldn't blame him. This humiliation was her own.

To avoid any further discussion of an encounter that had decidedly never happened, she quickly hopped out of the sedan without looking back. It took a great deal of effort, but she kept her head held high as she walked toward her car and escaped.

She fled from Victor mentally as well, leaving him to his pain. She had to get away. She would not be hurt again. Never. But she noticed that although he probably wanted to escape immediately as she had, he was gentleman enough to stay until he saw her safely get into her car.

Without turning back, she felt a pull from some remote part of his mind. She sensed that he was watching her closely and knew that he was hoping for a last acknowledgment that she would never give him. This had simply not happened.

Only when they had both pulled off, did she finally allow the tears that she had been holding back to soothe her mortally injured soul.

This was no gift. What she had was definitely, undeniably, a curse.

Six

The bright fall morning made Liza feel even worse, and her overcast mood only became more somber as she entered her office. Unable to really sleep the night before, she had opted to come in extra early. She needed a few moments to herself before beginning the day. That was her only salvation, to completely deny what had happened last night and purge herself of the memory. The thought of having to face Victor in the new spirit of détente, especially after the intimacy of the night before, absolutely horrified her.

Up until now, she had been able to ignore her sexual needs and safely remain detached from the world. This melding of body and soul was all too sudden. Too intense. Too unexplainable. Being with Victor had totally wreaked havoc on the discipline and order in her life.

She had chosen to wear royal purple and made sure that every hair was in place. She needed to exert her authority today. Looking well put together was her only placebo for warding off chaos.

Tears threatened to spill over Liza's damp lashes as she closed her eyes against the horror that magnified itself in the cold light of day.

"Hell, you don't even *know* this man," she cried out loud, holding her arms around herself. With her eyes still closed, she murmured a prayer. God, help her.

She couldn't even share this fiasco with Letty. In an act of sheer cowardice, she had opted to call Letty's answering machine last night, knowing that her dear friend probably wouldn't be home at that hour. For once, she was glad that Letty maintained a perpetual party schedule. Her message had been falsely upbeat and gave no hint of what had really happened . . . although she would probably tell Letty about it later—much later; it was all too fresh to cope with at the moment.

Totally engrossed in her thoughts as she slowly opened her eyes and peered sadly out the window, she was startled by the reflection of a figure in her doorway. Immediately dropping her arms to her sides, Liza stiffened at the invasion and spun on her intruder.

"Ronald! You could scare the life out of somebody! What're you doing in here so early?"

Although she was taken aback by his presence, Ronald was a much-needed source of comfort to her, despite his often irritating way of showing it.

"You look like hell, Boss," Ron answered in his normal, surly tone, moving into her office without an invitation to enter. "The question is, what are *you* doing in here so early?" he quizzed.

She was being stalked for personal information. She could feel it. The sensation made the hair on the back of her neck stand up.

"Ron, listen, I'm not in the mood this morning for your sarcasm. I have a lot on my mind and a lot of work to do before DGE gets here and—"

"Liz." He cut her off more gently, easing toward her in a less-threatening manner. "We've been friends a long time. Is there something wrong with the project?"

As Ron passed her desk and leaned against the credenza, totally disregarding her attack, she knew that he was not to be moved until he had a rational explanation.

Weary beyond words, she sighed. "Why do you harass my life like this? *No,* nothing is wrong with the project."

Hesitating, she collected herself and then began again more calmly. "In fact, I met with Duarte last night and we struck an agreement to let the teams work in harmony. We're going to discuss the new arrangement at the meeting, which will balance the work load so we can all hopefully get this abominable project finished." Turning away from Ron, she tried to end the conversation with a terse close to stop his interrogation. *"Now,* may I get back to work?"

"First of all," Ron started, hopping up to his favorite perch on her polished furniture, "you know you love it when I *harass* you." He smiled, openly reveling in his ability to needle his best friend. "Second, you never told me that you were meeting with General Noriega," he continued flippantly.

Before she could censure it, Victor's image flashed across her mind. And regrettably, she found herself taking a defensive posture.

"Look, Ron, since when do I have to disclose my calendar to everybody in this office? The discussions were sensitive until something could be worked out . . . and from now on, I don't want to hear any disparaging description of our partners. Agreed?"

Her voice had become a pitch higher than she had intended. Grabbing a few folders, she struggled unsuccessfully to disguise her annoyance.

"Boy! We *are* testy today!" Ron continued, unwilling to let her off the hook. "I thought we were at war with DGE."

Unaffected by her glare, Ron took a sip of day-old coffee that made her cringe for him as it oozed thickly down his throat. She tried to ignore him while pulling print-outs from her IN bin. Her position was tenuous at best.

Restoring her frail attempt at nonchalance, she offered a blasé response. "I don't know. I guess it was just time. . . . We're all tired."

Ron appeared thoroughly unconvinced, and he adjusted his roly-poly frame to a more permanent position on the edge of the furniture. Looking up at him briefly, she knew that he was not going to just *go away.*

Exasperated, she finally gave Ron her full attention, ready to close the subject once and for all.

Starting over in earnest, she tried to make him understand— without going into the gory details. "Ron, I *really* . . . just don't know. But I *am* tired, and peace within the team makes good business sense."

Unconvinced, Ron raised a suspicious eyebrow and continued to grill her. "Lizzy, you're my favorite girl and you look like something has thrown you into a total tailspin. Don't let this geek exterior fool you. We've been through too much together, and I know the difference between stress . . . and duress. So what the *hell* happened?"

Lisa knew that Ron was one of the few people who really understood her and, for all of his eccentricities, he also really cared. But she could never bring herself to tell him that she was rattled because Victor Duarte, their firm's recent arch-enemy, had just made the most intense love to her that she had ever experienced.

She couldn't answer him immediately for fear that her voice might crack. Shaking her head no, she looked down, blinking quickly to stop the tears. "Nothing's wrong. Please, Ron, can't I have a minute to pull myself together this morning? I'm tired, that's all. Really, really tired."

He looked deeply concerned and didn't respond for a moment. Since Ron tended to resort to sarcastic MASH Unit wit to solve everything, she assumed he was at a loss. That she hadn't regained her control since she'd lost it the night before was humiliating to her. Would the floor be so kind as to open up and let her crawl in?

"I'll figure it out sooner or later, Liz, and I'm not about to let anything happen to your firm unless you want it to. Just know that I'm in your corner . . . If the guy tried to pull a fast one, we may be small, but we can take him."

She wanted to die. Ron was clearly ready to defend her honor; the problem was that she didn't have any left. He obviously thought that she was upset because she'd blown the negotiations. Liza cringed inwardly. Ron's opinion of her mattered deeply and, in truth, even she didn't have a clue as to what had actually *happened.* How could she answer him when that very question had kept her up all night long?

"I gave away a little more ground than I had intended to last night, but I'll recover the losses. Don't worry. All right?"

There. She had told him the truth. Well, part of the truth. That *was* what had happened. She had given up *much* more than she had ever intended to. Perhaps a half truth would be enough to satisfy Ron, she thought perversely.

"Is that all? You are such a control freak, Liz. I bet you got more out of him than he got out of you, but you're just upset because it wasn't a hands-down victory. You really scared me for a minute there, kiddo."

Liza continued to sort through her desk, opting not to look at Ron as her mind echoed the complete truth. It was so horrible that she almost laughed. What had happened was that she had lost *all* control. Her mind screamed violently while she rooted for another misplaced file.

Near tears, she prayed for Ron to leave. She wanted to tell her friend that she was scared to death, that something terrible had happened, and that she didn't want to face the guy. The shame was killing her.

Trapped, she tossed out another casual comment to throw Ron off her trail. "Well, you win some, ya lose some, I guess. Trust me, I never plan to lose like that again. Case closed."

"I'm glad you confided in me, Liz. It's probably not as bad as you think, really. I'll help out. Just give the word, okay?"

All she could think of was the probable expression on Ron's face if she told him the real facts. She had never lied to her best friend, and the weakening of the bond between them through this omission wounded her deeply.

Steadying herself, she responded quietly. "I didn't expect him to be a decent person, and I'm perturbed that I let our team suffer this long without bringing the whole thing to resolution. It was unprofessional—the war, that is—and I could have jeopardized the contract. *That's all.*"

Her eyes never made contact with his as she continued to sort through her files. While her story was plausible, the words sounded false, and her tone was much too brittle.

When she looked up, unable to bear the strain of the silence any longer, Ron's bright-blue eyes had narrowed into a droll expression that almost made her laugh despite her morbid state. As he pulled his plump little body off his perch to take a seat closer on her desk, she knew he was there for the duration. Oh, God.

"Now, *Liza,* I want you to tell me that you aren't smitten by this suave, Latin American son-of-a-bitch."

Ron had her. She was busted. She didn't want to lie to him, but without warning her face flushed and her motions became too animated for the boring task on her desk. "Honestly, Ronald, you are incorrigible!" she shrieked, half laughing in disbelief, then swung away from her desk towards the credenza. "One day your mouth is going to be the one thing to get you in trouble!"

"I see," he continued, unperturbed at having struck a raw nerve. " 'Methinks the lady doth protest too much,' " he quipped, enjoying himself at her expense. "I hope you at least wheedled the other half of our contract out of him."

"Get out of my office!" she exclaimed, still smiling as Ron winked at her again. "I am not speaking to you anymore until the meeting. I have work to do, and you are giving me grief this morning that I *do not* need. Out!"

Unmoved by her outburst, Ron questioned her more seriously. "Lizzy, sweetheart, you know I really do love you and we've been together a long time. You're the only family I have in this world, and I won't see you hurt. I mean I'd do anything for you, just as you've done *everything* for me. . . . So just give me the word and I'll cut this suave señor's throat for making a false move on my favorite girl. No biggie. I'll just go to a psychiatric clinic for disturbed ex-Vietnam vets. I'm sure they'll give me a P.C. or a terminal as a therapeutic device. You'll still get the project done. So don't worry, love of my life."

They both laughed now, albeit hers was a little less vigorous than his. Once again, Ron had been able to get to her. Although his last comment had been mildly disconcerting, his offbeat humor had begun to lift her from her previously morose state. Laughing at herself would be the only way to get through the morning. It was crazy, but she was glad that if anyone had any suspicions, at least it would only be Ron.

Their bond had been forged long ago by an unspoken balance. Ron provided her with some of the most exceptionally creative work ever seen in the industry—along with *occasional* respect. In return, she allowed him the creative, unhindered flexibility that had prompted him to leave the confines of the traditional organizations which smothered him—along with a *lucrative* salary.

The ultimate terms of their unspoken contract were clearly

understood. They would offer each other a trusted friendship, unwavering support, and a loyalty unmatched anywhere else.

"Why do I put up with you? I should be the one in therapy," she groaned, finally recovering from the giggles. Perhaps it was only hysteria, but she was becoming elevated from the depression that had ruined her disposition earlier. Maybe it wasn't so bad. At least she was getting to a place where she could laugh at herself.

"Because you love my sexy body and know that I'm the only man in the world for you," Ron chuckled back defiantly, popping off her desk with a wink.

He's satisfied! Totally relieved that *The Inquisition* was over, Liza let her shoulders drop two inches as Ron moved to leave.

His short chubby frame lingered in her doorway as he added with a twinkle, "I have a big surprise for you this morning that will take your breath away! I may not be as good looking, but I'm good, Liza. Really, really, *good!*"

Before she could respond, Ron vanished down the hall toward the technical work area he called home.

It was another hour before the rest of the team began to arrive in a slow filter of disgruntled good mornings. They looked positively wiped out, and Liza knew that they had worked late.

Maureen was the next one to invade her sanctuary.

"Hey, Fearless Leader! Do we all look as bad as we feel?" Maureen grunted merrily, flopping into the overstuffed antique chair that faced Liza's desk. "I came back late last night. Mom said she'd watch Danielle for me, and I really appreciated the break during the day you gave me. Thanks, Liz."

"Vunderbar!" Liza teased back, taking on the phony accent to dramatize the point and to disguise her mood.

"That bad, huh? Yeah, well, we were all in here till 1:00 A.M. with that madman Ronald. Thanks for the deli tray; I couldn't have taken another pizza!" Maureen laughed again easily and sprawled comfortably in the chair.

"Well, take heart, my dear; we'll all start working more reasonable hours after today. . . . I think we've been able to gain cooperation from DGE," Lisa said in a cautious voice, watching Maureen's expression.

"Get out of here! You mean you made a pact with the Devil for the team?" Maureen's face was incredulous as she sat up to take in the full meaning of the new information.

Afraid Maureen would begin another series of hard-to-answer questions, Liza added a quick clarification to stem the tide of uncomfortable queries. "Yeah, Mo, it was time. Even I know when to cry *Uncle*. Who could take it anymore?"

Maureen studied her face carefully before responding. "You know, Liz, we're all aware of how much this deal meant to you and everything. For you to back off from the feud for us . . . well, that's why we love you. I mean, if you want to continue to rally the troops, we're with you all the way."

The confidence that the staff had in her judgment was what had infuriated Liza about the unfair arrangement in the first place. She knew that they'd turn themselves inside out to produce, and she hadn't wanted to let them down. Now things had become unnecessarily complex and it wore on her as she struggled to give Maureen an answer that was acceptable.

"Mo, even I know when something has turned into a suicide mission, and you guys have been through enough. We were going under with the work load. I just want to be sure that everybody is okay with this, and then we can go forward. Hopefully, after today, they'll be no more 1:00 A.M. stints."

Maureen's expression was serious. It was the first time that Liza had been able to gauge how the team would take the change. She wasn't managing her life or the firm. Events were managing her, and it was her own stupid fault!

Maureen appeared unruffled after briefly considering the issue, and Liza knew that everything would be all right when her colleague made a funny face while swallowing a bad sip of coffee.

"Liz, if this is okay with you, it's great for us! You know they say that politics and business makes for strange bedfellows. Speaking of which, this project has put a serious dent in my love-life. How's a single mother supposed to date when a computer is the only thing she spends the night with?"

Then, just as abruptly as she had entered, Maureen laughed at her own joke and bounced out the door. The unrelated reference to lovemaking brought another flood of guilt as Liza tried to shake the recent memory. She knew that her team would loyally follow her through any crazy project she could land, and she felt weighted by the full impact of that responsibility. Dear Lord . . . what in the world had she done?

Liza shivered and clasped her arms around herself again, suddenly feeling seamy and unethical. Maybe she should have worn black. It was the appropriate color to mourn the death of her dignity.

Her thoughts reeled as she tried to get back her perspective. No, what had happened was not some well-calculated plan that she had devised to seal a deal. She had really *seen* something there . . . for an instant. Closing her eyes to visualize the events of the previous evening, she tried to focus on any possible deception on Victor's part. Nothing registered.

Bewildered, she became more rueful about the possible consequences of seeing Victor in an open meeting with both staffs in attendance. She had compromised herself and would never allow that to happen again. There had been only one time in her life that she had totally misjudged a situation . . . And that had been because she'd kept blocking the information that was coming to her. It was a morbid recollection.

Warding off another uneasy shiver, Liza bitterly forced herself to drop the subject, hoping in the quiet recesses of her mind that history was not about to repeat itself. It wouldn't. She was much smarter now. Much more secure. She wasn't about to delude herself into believing that Victor Duarte had put anything more than casual emphasis on the *situation*. But if she were so together, why did she feel so rotten? That was real.

It was only a little past eight in the morning, and thus far, she hadn't been able to make a dent in the pile of work facing her. Continuing the trip down memory lane was totally out of the question. She just needed to "fake the funk" for a little while to get through the meeting. Then, she would be outta there. She could work from a system at home and hide and lick her wounds.

Connie arrived, effortlessly bringing order to the office melee. Chaos was the norm until the group was harnessed into a procedural flow that only Connie could direct.

Liza was honestly elated when her assistant stopped in with her cheerful greeting. As always, it immediately stemmed the tide of despair that repeatedly crept into her consciousness.

"Good morning, Ms. Nichols!" came the familiar sing-song greeting from the outer office. "I can always tell when you guys were in here late . . . messin' up my files, leaving coffee to burn up in the pot, papers everywhere. . . . What am I going to do with you?"

Connie fussed about good-naturedly, not waiting for a reply. "I think the DGE people may be a little early today, because I saw them in the lobby as I came up. Do you want me to ask them to wait while I round up the gang?" Connie asked, poking her head into Liza's office.

Liza looked up from the stack of papers on her desk with alarm. Dread made her heart skip a beat. They were early! She hadn't even had time to pull together her thoughts for the meeting, let alone decide what to say to Victor.

Taking a deep breath to swallow down the dry heaves, she answered calmly. "Good morning, Connie . . . uh . . . no. You can show them in when they get up here . . . but could you order in some pastries or something? If you haven't heard, we're no longer at war. So, we won't be in here so late to mess up your office." Liza forced a smile under the strain, genuinely thankful for the early warning.

"Oh, that will be wonderful!" Connie responded with earnest relief in her voice. "I can't tell you how all of that cussing and fussing was working on my nerves!"

Liza agreed wearily, "Yeah, the whole thing has gotten on my nerves, too, Connie. You just don't know."

Twenty minutes later, the Risc Systems team had assembled

in the large conference room at the end of the hall under Connie's effective command. As Liza walked down the corridor to join them, she caught the reflection of Victor's well-dressed staff through the large glass panels framing the entryway to her office suite.

She had been unable to stomach breakfast; and now the coffee, combined with a bad case of nerves, was making her stomach churn. In a flash of terror, she realized that she had forgotten all about the contrived comment to Ed during their brief conversation.

Swallowing hard, she shrugged off the discomfort and wiped her moist palms against the fabric of her skirt. Her mind was in no condition to develop some plausible new strategy to satisfy Ed's curiosity about her call to DGE last night. Moreover, she hoped desperately that Victor would at least be discreet, especially since remaining a gentleman had been such a problem.

Taking another deep breath to steady herself before pasting on a civil business-like smile, Liza hastily slipped into the conference room to position her staff for the meeting. In a matter of minutes she knew Victor's team would strategically disperse into the room with military precision—all donned in the same immaculate, dark-blue suits that made them uniformly look like high-priced, professional assassins.

Carefully monitoring the tension in her stride, she watched Ron for any hint of sarcasm. She couldn't take that. Not now. Not in an open forum. But instead, she was relieved when he sidled up to her as she moved farther into the conference room. His only gesture was to give her elbow a discreet, reassuring squeeze.

Ron squeezed her arm one last time as Victor entered the room. She felt sure that she must have visibly blanched when she saw him and was relieved that her buddy was there for moral support. Correctly sensing that she was in some sort of unspoken distress, Ron had opted to stay nearby, staking out a seat next to her at the polished, oblong table.

For once she was glad that Ron had been impervious to her

rebuffs and appreciated his gallant show of friendship that made him an ally at the table. It was going to be a long morning, no doubt, and she cringed again inwardly as she fought down another wave of anxiety.

Leaving Ron at the guard post that he had set up to her left, Liza crossed the room to welcome the DGE staff and to perform the basic greeting ritual. She took a deep breath. Victor was positively magnetic as he stood before her, intensely boring through her facade with *those eyes*.

"Victor, Ed, Stan, Walter, Donald . . . Gentlemen," Liza intoned robotically as she extended her hand. Noting the mild stir in the room, she continued undaunted. Things had gotten so bad between the firms that the mere act of offering a handshake was enough to cause a fervor amongst her staff. Since the relationship had deteriorated well past the point of professional courtesy, it was a beginning, she thought critically.

Without missing a beat, Victor crossed toward her. "Liza, it is a pleasure to be here this morning and my colleagues and I are eager to begin work within the new atmosphere. I hope that our early arrival has not caused any undue inconvenience."

Damn, he's good! she thought quietly, admiring the way Victor dispensed the light civil discourse without as much as a flicker of recognition beyond business pleasantries.

"None at all," she answered curtly, then looked toward the conference table. It was all she could do to hide the stain of embarrassment that she felt. Her humiliation was only made worse by the intense pleasure that she found in hearing Victor's voice.

"Then I'm eager to begin." His reply had been pleasant enough, but his tone contained perhaps a little too much familiarity. The double entendre was implicit. Or was it that she was hearing what *she* was thinking? Oh, God, her probe was on and she hadn't even tried! Perhaps it was the fatigue and that her defenses were down. What was happening to her facade? It was crumbling at her feet! She admonished herself quickly. *Don't do this to yourself, Liz. Do . . . Not . . . Do . . . It!*

Looking at the team, she saw that the possible duplicity in Victor's meaning had passed undetected. She felt him breathe in and knew that he was just as hopeful as she to avoid another calamity. Strangely, that observation was comforting. At least she wasn't the only one a little nervous and off-center this morning. Actually, she was more than relieved. She was flattered.

Motioning for the DGE team to take their seats, Liza forced another smile. "Ready when you are." It was a perfectly cloaked response. She could deliver hidden messages, too.

"After you." Victor's return volley had gone smoothly, although it totally belied the turmoil that she detected behind his poker exterior. He gave no hint of the deeper issues, and he was going to be a gentleman. That thought made her feel more at ease. *Thank you.*

However, taking a seat across from him during the meeting was definitely going to be interesting. Liza felt her carriage stiffen as she approached the table, immediately steeling herself against a mild internal stir that was inappropriate. She didn't sit down. After all, this was her meeting. With a discreet nod, Victor conceded and sat across from the chair that she stood behind.

His dark eyes reflected back the deep purple that she wore, and his face became more serious than her general request to be seated called for. Without question, the current was still there. His appraisal of her was intense, and she knew that they would have to work hard to stay focused. But at least he was a gentleman . . . for the moment, anyway. She slowly released her breath in order to regain control and shift gears.

"Good, then let's get started," she said dryly after a moment of hesitation, eyeing Victor with a glare of silent reproach before taking full command of the room. This was, after all, *her shop,* and she was not about to relinquish her control of it in front of the team, regardless of how shaky she felt.

Victor watched her as the group settled in. He absolutely loved the way Liza moved to the front of the room with authority. No matter how unnerved, she had a natural air of command that could not be challenged. That simple fact had not escaped him in the least.

It was clear from her stance that she had taken a resolute position. If her territory were to be invaded, then *she* would initiate the signing of the treaty, not he. Liza was as determined as always to save face to the end. He smiled in appreciation of her position. This was what he loved about her style the most. She was almost as good as he was on the boards.

He watched her move with enjoyment, unable to abolish the thoughts of the way she had moved beneath him the night before. It was only when he monitored silent alarm on Liza's face that he checked himself. Trying to drop the steel curtain of detachment that was momentarily beyond his ability, he hoped like hell that she hadn't picked up on his thoughts again.

Liza began with directness, her words cutting through the room, with sterile precision. "As we all know, there has been some dispute between the way Chem Tech International originally awarded this bid. Unfortunately, their decision resulted in bad blood between our firms. Although arguably warranted, our mutual response to the client's decision has been less than professional."

He watched as she picked up a pen before continuing. She looked tired, and he wondered if she had gotten any sleep. He sure hadn't.

"And those reactions to date have cost both firms time, money, and manpower. If we don't get back on track, it could ultimately cost us our reputations in the industry as well as the risk of being removed from the account altogether. Neither firm can afford the stain of being ousted on the basis of contractual noncompliance."

Liza's remarks fell on the room with a deadly accurate pall, and there was no visible sign of resistance from anyone. She was, indeed, in command. Beautifully, sexily, in command of her audience. He couldn't take his eyes off her. Somehow the danger of discovery, combined with the openness of his assessment, made his secret knowledge of Liza all the more titillating.

There she stood, so close, yet so unavailable at the moment. The rational side of his brain was definitely losing the battle with his libido, forming a granite wall to reason in his loins. Not now . . .

Although she glared at him with unharnessed fury in her eyes, Liza's voice still held its original matter-of-fact intonation. The dichotomy was electrifying. He could tell that she felt it, too, but would never, ever, drop her guard willingly again. She was challenging him openly, but secretly. He loved it.

"Therefore, I am instructing my staff to fully cooperate with DGE," she continued steadily. "That means all files, pertinent information, hunches, leads, office space, if necessary, will be shared by both firms until we get the client's sign off that the deal is complete. We have a massive amount of catching up to do, and I will not be pleased if the delays are due to side issues."

The severity of her warning was unmistakable, and her immediate staff nodded to affirm the directive that was really intended for him. He wondered what she might do to him if he displeased her. Against his better judgment, he allowed a slight smile to come out of hiding. It wasn't intentional, just a reflex at the thought of arguing with Liza on a personal level. *She must be magnificent,* he mused, now totally incapable of escaping from his own mind.

Clearly perturbed, she put him on the spot, ceremoniously yielding the floor. "I will now ask Victor Duarte to *stand* and say a few words about his firm's commitment to our mutual goals. His team can launch the meeting this morning," she added curtly, moving to the vacant seat next to Ron Savick.

A woman's vengeance could be a powerful weapon. How could he stand now and face an entire group, given his state? Victor cringed inwardly and stalled with just a nod.

However, despite her smug return volley, Liza still didn't look quite right. Her normally vivacious coloring was off. She was a little on the grey side, to be exact, and the quiet nonverbal exchange between Liza and Ron concerned him. She hadn't even looked at him after she'd smiled, but had continued to fidget with her pen, appearing as if she would wretch at any minute.

Perhaps the evening before had been too much for her to deal with. It had certainly thrown him off-kilter in a way that he couldn't define. Feeling a bit ragged around the edges himself, he had decided to take a spectator's seat during the discussions this morning. That had been his plan, anyway. However, as always, Liza had thrown him a curve ball and he would have to actively participate in hosting this session. Without much room for evasion, or personal thoughts, he would have to figure out what was wrong with her later.

There was a meeting to run.

Seven

Liza's eyes scanned each face around the table as her mental radar picked up a jumble of thoughts. Everything in the room besieged her at once. It was like taking a drink of water from a fire hydrant instead of through a straw. The echoes that crashed about in her mind were almost too much to handle as she grabbed the edges of her seat to stave off the confusion. She couldn't focus on any one impression. Each team member's voice clamored for attention, even though no one was speaking. All the deafening noises in her head now turned the mild headache into a stabbing pain behind her eyes.

Her gift had never been this strong. Some new catalyst had wrenched her strange ability to the fore and held it there. This time, it wasn't coming from Victor Duarte . . . yet it was linked to him in an odd way.

When Ron turned his attention to her directly, she winced, ignoring his bewildered expression. She was openly blundering. She had to get out of the room before she threw up. There was no escape as she searched her mind for an exit strategy. Ron kept trying to pass her a note while muttering something under his breath. His actions only made her head pound more.

Whispering through the pain, she begged him to stop. "Please, Ron, not now, okay."

Ignoring Ron, her focus narrowed on Victor as he rose to accept the floor. He appeared flustered, but collected himself in short order, which she had to admit was appreciated.

"I would first like to thank Liza Nichols for allowing our firms to come together with a new atmosphere of collaboration. On behalf of DGE, I would like to say that the technical expertise that Risc Systems possesses is, by far, some of the best in the industry . . . and I'm sure that my partners share my view."

She almost shut her eyes as he went on. What was it?

"We concur with Liza's directive wholeheartedly and offer the same openness from our side. If there are any resources that our firm can provide, you have but to ask. Now, I would like to present Ed Gates, who will outline some of the issues that have been baffling our financial people for weeks. Your input into solving that puzzle will be invaluable."

Still looking down at her portfolio, Liza reconstructed the brief discourse in her mind. Even through the pain, she could not register any deception in his statement. Victor's delivery, however, did seem a bit stilted and little less enthusiastic than his normal dynamic presentation. His address to the group had been crisp, direct, and to the point, forcing her to cringe inside as she took in the sound of his voice. Yet there was still a problem in the room. Her radar had finally located the source of the disturbance . . . in Ron.

The meeting looked as if it might go off without incident. Thank you, she breathed inwardly. In her peripheral vision, she noted Ron's sarcastic fishy stare, squelching it with a warning glance. But when Ed finally gathered his materials and stood up to address the group, her fears quickly dissipated. Within moments, she could feel Ron becoming totally absorbed in the technical data that shone on the screen.

Using the overhead projector to display the complex financial information, Ed methodically began in his normal, low-key manner.

"There appear to be some severe inconsistencies between the computer tapes of Chem Tech's financial information and the actual paper files found at their administrative billing offices. From what we understand, the combination of corporate files, local plant site information, and customer records should match perfectly. The problem is that they don't."

Ed appeared uneasy, and he looked in Victor's direction for a nod of approval to continue. Receiving it, Ed moved closer to the screen to illustrate his point.

"We have been asked by the client to build an international network link connecting their order centers, all warehouses that ship product, their sales offices that post commissions, and their customers that are billed and receive the inventory and then to close the loop back to the accounting office at headquarters. The original Request For Proposal stated that Chem Tech's objective was to have one order come in, have that transaction entered once, and then have that data file hit all the departments that need information from that order."

Ed was in his element, and his initial apprehension abated as he became swept up in the presentation.

"For example," he pressed on more confidently, "a customer places an order. From that order, Manufacturing should get notification that a particular chemical must be made. Plant Scheduling can look to see when a production run can be arranged or they can send a request to any warehouse in the country to find out if the product is already in stock. Shipping should get an MSDS—material safety data sheet—and then load up their trucks, rail cars, or barges to send the product to the customer. The customer should be invoiced and billed, and Sales should know what rep, from what region, should get commission . . . and so on. One transaction hits the system, and everything is triggered like falling dominoes."

Ed cleared his throat and rummaged through his papers before beginning again. "This objective will form the basis of the computer system architecture that our teams will build. Risc Systems will handle all the conversion programming to make the myriad systems talk to each other around the world—all the IBM's, Vaxes, HP's, and Univacs. It's a mess, and I have to say that you guys have the tougher part of the job."

Ed put up a new slide and his tone became more authoritative. "From the financial perspective, Chem Tech has too much cash on hand in the Foreign Sales area, given the shipments to the customers that they claim to have made. But the interesting thing is, from the order reports and the invoicing records, they do, indeed, appear to have had this volume of sales. You see, the warehouse inventory records and the production scheduling records don't match what they claimed was actually shipped. Yet the weigh bills show that these products did go overseas. Perhaps we're not looking at this right."

Connie, who was taking notes, raised her hand to interrupt. "Excuse me, Ed. I'm sorry. I know that I'm the only one in here that doesn't understand, but I want to be sure that I get this down right in the minutes."

"No problem, Connie, let me try to simplify. In essence, what has happened is, the invoices look like they billed for a lot of product and the customer paid for them. But there was no way that the warehouse or plants could have made that much stuff. Another way to look at it is this. . . . Suppose you ordered six kitchen chairs from Sears. Sears billed you for six; they claimed to deliver six; and you paid for them. But when we check the records of the Sears warehouse, they never had six chairs in stock to begin with—they only had two. And they didn't manufacture any additional chairs or buy them from another dealer to fill your order. So, where did the other four chairs come from? That's the problem."

The room was completely silent, save for the hum of the projector. Everyone respected Ed's analytical ability, especially Ron, and they waited patiently for him to resume.

"However," Ed continued, almost talking to himself as he frowned with confusion, "if we are to architect a financial network that can link Chem Tech directly to their customers for ordering purposes, we have to be able to track back the shipping costs of each order and compare that to the best warehouse or plant pick site. How can we tell if it costs more to ship from two different warehouses versus setting up a chemical run near the customer, especially if the warehouse and production numbers are off?"

Ed ran his fingers through his neat blond hair. "We're supposed to be making it possible for Chem Tech to do productivity simulations for their financial analysis that will ultimately lead to significant cost savings. That's why they agreed to pay top dollar to have this done. Shipping costs are an enormous burden to their business, and they'd also like to be able to close their books around the world in a few short days, instead of several agonizing months."

Liza felt as though she were turning green. Some problem was radiating through her skull, and she openly massaged her temples.

Ed seemed totally confused as he stared at the blank faces around the room. "The customer invoices have the same or correct volumes, and we can't seem to find the hole in our analysis. If Chem Tech has really only shipped half of the order and our client's customer's are paying for freight costs of the higher X volume, then those customers have been over-billed. That piece represents a significant issue for Chem Tech and could possibly be a source of massive liability if their customers ever found out about this. To not factor it into our client progress meetings would be irresponsible and misrepresentative. Now, this issue only affects a portion of their overall shipments. The sector that we can't seem to tie back financially represents Chem Tech's largest accounts in South America."

"Ed, I think I may have found your money!" Ron beamed, pleased with himself and unable to contain his excitement.

Ron had blurted out the statement that he had obviously been dying to tell her about all morning. Suddenly it became clear. Liza immediately sensed that this new information was the probable source of her nausea. She immediately clasped her hand around his wrist to forestall his revelation. Somehow she knew that Ron's findings would be too dangerous to disclose in an open meeting. The warning registered in her gut; her probe snapped on in reflex, yet oddly, Ron didn't seem affected by it the way Victor had. That was what had amazed her from the beginning—no one, save Victor Duarte, had ever felt the affects of her silent ability.

Too exuberant to pick up her warning, Ron slipped from her hold easily, rose, and walked to the front of the room with his coffee cup still in his hand.

No one moved, and Ed stood stock-still beside the projector. It was as if someone had set the detonator on a time bomb and everyone sat quietly listening to it tick.

Ron had always been openly appreciative of the respectful deference his new colleague Ed gave him. Thrilled about any information that he could provide to the group, Ron wouldn't let the rare moment pass. Only this morning, Liza was not in the mood to humor him. There was simply too much else going on. Plus, instinct told her it was dangerous.

"Ron, this is not the time. We'll discuss this later," she said in a low voice, trying to take back control of the meeting.

Suddenly, without warning, her focus was drawn to Victor Duarte. But this time it was not from a hormonal perspective. She detected extreme agitation, something so close to the surface that his veneer had completely peeled away entirely. What the hell was going on?

"Ron, what new information can you share with us?"

Without regard to protocol, Victor had questioned Ron directly. The breach of professional conduct infuriated her.

It was the first time that she had seen Victor Duarte so unnerved in a business setting. But her glare didn't stop the chain of events that was unravelling. She keyed in on how unsuccessful Victor had been at steadying the anxiety in his voice when he spoke to Ron.

"No theatrics, Ron. Just the facts."

Duarte had openly challenged her. She had given Ron a direct order of silence, and Victor had cancelled it!

Holding the room hostage with anticipation, Ron took a few moments to enjoy the power that his comment had over the group. Before continuing, he glanced at Liza, unconvinced of the new spirit of détente that had just been espoused.

"Well, gang, I'll tell you . . ." Ron began slowly, ignoring her glare. "I've never trusted these Chem Tech guys from the beginning. I mean, as a client, they've been a royal pain in the ass and I wouldn't put anything past 'em."

Stealing some of his thunder, Liza cut impatiently into what seemed like another of Ron's long dissertations. "I told you, this is neither the time nor place," she said quietly in an attempt not to embarrass him.

"Ronald, just get to the bottom line and—*NET* it out. Save the editorial comments for later," Victor shot across the table, ignoring her order.

Visibly taken aback by the heated powerplay going on between both firm principals, Ron began again in a severely churlish tone.

"Don't worry, Liz. I know what I'm talking about. All right, here's the deal. I didn't want to bank the reputation of our firm on the data *they* provided."

As Ron continued, he offered his explanation through the tight line that had become his mouth. "Hey, their Information Systems Department wouldn't let me access the mainframes unsupervised, or directly, to get the information I needed—*when* I needed. They would only give me day-old tapes. Sort of like a day late and a dollar short. So, I felt like, wait a minute, if we're gonna screw up and miss deadlines, then let it be because *we* didn't do the work properly, but not because *they* gave us bogus information blocking our access. At the time, I didn't know what Ed was working on. I was just doing the Risc Systems part of the job."

Ron's new information held the group in thrall as he peeled back layers of complex details. Despite the momentary glory, his eyes flashed hotly at Liza, still seeming considerably miffed by her attempt to stop him from speaking. "So, let's just say that I got the information *myself,* which proved *very* interesting."

Although Ron had added the last parting blow with a scowl, Liza was unmoved by his personal indignation. The severity of the implied issues around a possible unauthorized break-in to a client system floored her. Immediately comprehending what Ron had done, she sat in horror, assessing the full impact of his unspoken admission.

"Ron, tell me you *didn't* access their systems in an unauthorized break-in?" she whispered.

Undaunted, Ron took another sip of bitter coffee and steadied himself against her controlled response. Although appearing nonchalant, she could tell that her warning chilled him, forcing him to explain further.

"Before you pass judgment, Liza, let me tell you what I found out. See, I knew they were trying to set us up. I'm talking about their technical staff versus ours. The computer tapes that they gave us, which were supposed to contain accurate, updated, customer and warehouse files, were all wrong. The set they *gave* us showed that they did a certain X volume of sales at a certain price, X, to all of their regions. However, the *real* file shows that the volumes they had, and prices they actually charged, were *much* less. It was confusing . . . really way off by a long shot!"

Ron was becoming visibly agitated as he wrestled with the fact that the group was probably not following the information which appeared so painfully obvious to him.

"Don't you get it?" he finally exclaimed with exasperation. "They're padding their records to show large volumes of sales that have never really been shipped! Yes, they actually do have customers in those regions and, yes, those customers are buying their chemicals for mining solvents, fertilizers, you name it. But not as much as they are showing on their books or probably to the IRS!"

Ed appeared to understand the implications immediately and graciously chimed in. "It all makes sense now, Ron. They would have to have a way to explain the excess cash deposits in their accounts. If they made it look like they had very large customer orders, it would justify the revenues. The mistake that they made was forgetting to increase the warehouse and production volumes to match the volume of sales they *reportedly* had. If the warehouse or production volumes and shipping volumes had matched, I would have never detected a discrepancy. I would have just continued to work on loading the financial data without suspicion. Fantastically brilliant work, Ron. Let me shake your hand!"

As Ed and Ron exchanged mutual pats on the back, Liza knew that she had to interrupt their premature celebration with a severe reality check. "Ron, let me ask you a question. Have you given any thought to how we are going to *credibly* explain to our client about how we've *fixed* their data-feed problem?"

Ron looked stunned as Ed stood tenuously by his side weighing the possibilities. She surveyed Victor quickly, but his face was impenetrable now.

"And doesn't it make sense that if they've gone to all the trouble to have two sets of books—invoicing the customers for the correct shipments, then showing another false and higher level of revenues on their balance sheet for legitimacy . . . wouldn't you think that there is something *extremely* wrong?"

Ron stood by silently. Obviously he hadn't thought about what would happen after he exposed the information. His naive focus had been to merely solve the equation to make it balance and to probably please her with his brilliance. She hated to go after him like this, but felt it was too dangerous, and foolish. For his own safety, and the firm's, she couldn't let it ride.

Beyond the edge, Liza was standing now as she leaned toward Ron from her vantage point across the table. "Answer me. We are talking about numerous felonies here—possibly international in scope. We don't know what they're really shipping, or hiding. This is an off-line discussion, and it should have been presented to me prior to this meeting, Ronald."

The silence in the room was deafening as Ron stood frozen by her panic-laden attack. Liza could tell from the shocked expression on his face that none of her comments had ever entered his mind before now. He hadn't even considered the consequences before he acted, much like a child playing with a loaded gun. Now that a potential tragedy existed, Ron's fear for his own personal safety, the firm, and the rest of the staff registered as he realized that he'd been playing Russian roulette. Her directness was meant to be a bread-and-butter slap of reality across his face. She loved Ron too much not to make this real for him, and the tactic apparently worked as she watched terror mirror back to her from his eyes.

Victor stood again slowly, positioning himself to enter the fray. His eyes held a cold, analytical warning which confirmed her fears.

"Edward, Ronald, your work here, although unauthorized, has been exceptional. But let us ask ourselves a few questions. First of all, most companies attempt to hide revenues . . . to avoid unnecessary taxation. Correct?"

Liza watched Victor pace as he spoke, circling the table like a predator and challenging her through his slow approach to the front of the room not to interrupt him.

"If that premise is true, then it would stand to reason that, by Chem Tech's taking the unusual position of overstating their revenues, quite possibly the extra cash flow is being provided by some less-than-legitimate source. And if I were to continue with that line of reasoning, the fact that nothing ships *out* of the regions in question—but it is Chem Tech that is obviously being paid to ship something in to them—then we must endeavor to understand what is *needed* most by those regions that have accepted the shipments."

No one moved, much less breathed, as Victor's blasé logic painted a lethal scenario.

"When most people think of illegitimate enterprises in South America," he continued matter-of-factly, "the immediate perception is that it is drug related."

The reality of Victor's concept was not lost on the group. It was written all over their stunned faces, echoing the panic of Liza's earlier outburst.

"However," he went on calmly, "if South America is a primary producer of illegal drugs to the world, why would they accept *in* an illegal drug shipment? No. That is not logical. What we must evaluate is . . . what does the U.S. have as their primary asset? If my hunch is correct, that would be technology and weaponry . . . and customs is much more lenient coming from the U.S. *to* South America, than the other way around."

Victor surveyed his captive audience and returned his gaze to Liza as he spoke. "When we talk about the scope of this possible intrigue, we are now in the unfortunate position of dealing with some extremely dangerous people. Liza's assumption and cause for alarm are very real. My advice, at this point, would be to continue business as usual . . . even to the point of not making Chem Tech aware of our new spirit of détente. If they perceive that we are still at war, they will feel secure that the left hand doesn't know what the right hand is doing . . . which all makes perfect sense now." Casting an intense look toward Ed and Ron, he added, "And I also wouldn't be too terribly surprised if you gentlemen haven't found all of the extra money."

Liza was incredulous. She had to understand, and the only one who seemed to be tying the facts together coherently was Victor. The events of the evening before became irrelevant, evaporating with her growing distress. Hell, her company was at stake, and the award from Chem Tech was the only thing that was going to keep it running.

Facing him, she remained standing on shaky legs and spoke bluntly, determined to get a clear explanation. There was no room for gamesmanship here. Just the plain, simple truth.

"Victor, do you mean to say that this has all been a set-up? That they assumed we'd fight like yard dogs over the bone they threw us; never coming together?"

There was a long pause as Victor considered her question. She hoped that the honest confusion that had come through in her voice would be compelling enough for him to give her a direct response.

"I'm afraid so," he answered finally.

Although it was an honest response, it was not the one that she was prepared to hear. Victor had now taken a clinical position, calmly watching the look of total alarm that she was sure blazed across her face.

"What we have here is classic, and beautifully executed, I might add. I must be slipping or I would have caught it much earlier."

Victor remained oddly removed as he dissected her with his gaze. He was now in a remote place so distant that he was unreachable, even predatory. She felt his mind hunt hers as her thoughts raced, stumbled, and fell as she tried to sort out the new cryptic information without success. His earlier statement was clearly not enough. She needed to know how dangerous their situation really was. He'd read her so well, too well, and once again, she was vulnerable.

"It is very simple, Liza," he continued, expertly using his calm delivery to stem the growing hysteria in the room. "Their key data-base people could not be associated with tampering with the files, in case it got . . . shall we say, *complicated*. As I told you before, Liza, life is very complicated."

She almost gasped aloud at the brazen reference to the conversation during last night's dinner. It was, indeed, a cold dash of water in her face, if that were the intended effect. Appearing satisfied that there would be no additional interruptions, Victor continued, forcing her to be steady with the thinly veiled threat of exposing their liaison. Fury overtook her ego, but not her reason, and she clenched her fists at her sides, remaining silent. Never losing eye contact with him, she waited for an opportunity to present itself.

"In any event, gentlemen . . . *and ladies* . . . they brought in two relatively small, outside consulting firms to work on the job. This situation was just too sensitive. So naturally they shied away from *The Big Eight* firms, which have larger staffs, virtually unlimited resources, and untarnishable credibility in the industry. They played us against one another brilliantly, knowing that in such an environment, we would never effectively collaborate. The unfair contract split of fifty percent to each firm would ensure our mutual animosity, since DGE is only doing twenty percent of the work. That part was a gamble, but well thought out by Chem Tech."

The questions that swirled in Liza's head were making her dizzy, and she sat down to steady herself. "Victor, please get to the point. I have to understand all aspects of this situation."

"Quite right," he agreed. "Simply stated, Risc Systems has the computer-technology expertise to build a network that can tie in all of Chem Tech's plants, customers, and their headquarters to a central repository of information which will make closing their books—or *adjusting* their financial reporting—a much more streamlined process. DGE has the financial expertise to ensure that the network is built in such a way that it will appropriately feed into their accounting systems and accurately update their chart of accounts, which we are monitoring."

Victor outlined the strategy with a surgeon's skill, oddly responding to her silent requests for more to go on.

"As we know, when you have two warring contractors in one account, it's easy to go round-robin for years before actually discovering who caused a problem—should there be an audit. And since Chem Tech is an upstanding, tax-paying corporation, one that even employs *minority* vendors to do the work, the likelihood that they will come under any undue scrutiny is minimal."

"And what happens to us?" Liza asked quietly, her temper simmering down from the absolute shock.

"Well, after your firm builds the network, we will be asked to do the financials, and it's a done deal. However, we were both probably chosen because we were not only small enough to discredit if necessary, but are also indisputably good at what we do. Therefore, if there *were* any loose ends in their plan, surely one of us would point Chem Tech right to the problem in an attempt to show up the competing firm's lack of thoroughness. Then they would close the hole, fire the firm that found the problem, and that firm would go away in a cloud of shame—having lost the favor of a major account."

Victor's concluding statement was the most appalling, and she felt the blood rush to her face in outrage. "How could they be so stupid as to believe that we would stand for this?" She was incredulous.

Duarte was unmasked now, and he seemed openly distressed that her fury might make her engage Chem Tech in outright warfare. She didn't need to have any special ability to understand the source of his fear. What he didn't understand was that she already knew how dangerous they could be. Her father's death had demonstrated that to her a long time ago.

"Liza, I suggest that you understand that this isn't a game," he menaced. "Let us understand who is really at risk here. First of all, if you do go to the authorities, Chem Tech will simply say that it was sour grapes, due to the cancellation of your contract for work slippages—which, to date, have occurred. Second, you only have one print-out, no back up or corroborating information. Plants . . . where? Product . . . sent to whom? Dates these shipments occurred . . . when? Etcetera."

Liza felt as if she'd actually been punched, but Victor continued to batter her senses.

"Am I beginning to make myself clear, Ms. Nichols?"

Jolted, she watched as Victor unloaded the final blow.

"Then, most importantly, they will spread the rumor that your firm slipped on critical contract deadlines throughout the industry and claim that you came up with wild, unsubstantiated allegations instead of facing your fate like a professional. The bottom line is, Risc Systems will never get another contract. Not after being charged with slander by the firm that gave you your first big chance as a rookie minority firm. They'll award your remains to another small outfit—which will be only too glad to lap up your leftovers, and your credibility will have had it."

"I won't allow it!"

"Well, Liza, if all else fails and you get too pesky, they could just kill you. I've seen it done," he ventured in a dangerously low tone.

That was it; the room broke out in a harmonized gasp. But despite the stir, Victor remained calm with unflinching, iron control.

"Ladies and gentlemen, I *do* hope that everyone here understands just what we are dealing with. This is one of the largest corporations in the world, but we are not dealing with ethical businessmen. It's like finding out that the CIA is laundering money." Looking directly at Connie, he went on. "None of the last twenty minutes of this meeting are for the record." Then turning his gaze back to Liza, he commanded, "Therefore, I am advising the removal of all but key personnel from this project— even if it means twenty-four-hour shifts. I don't want people unnecessarily involved."

He surveyed the room with a riveting gaze and held their attention with the severity of his warning. "I do not overexaggerate when I tell you that your lives could be in danger. All discussions stay on a strictly confidential basis from now on. Everything in this room stays in this room. Ed, not even your pretty, suburban wife needs be put in jeopardy with this new information. Understood? Ron, no more unauthorized accesses. *None!* At least not without Liza and my knowing about it and planning our approach in advance."

Victor had taken over the meeting entirely, comprehending that she was momentarily too overwhelmed to function effectively.

"Anyone wanting out now should say so, and it will not be held against you. If you want to leave the firms, we will give you excellent letters of recommendation and you can cite truthfully that the strained working environment caused you to bail out. For now, we will maintain our facade and appear to remain enemies."

His voice barely above a whisper, he delivered his parting shot. "The only logical plan will be to complete our contractual obligations as if we never detected any discrepancies. *Understood?"* The spellbound team nodded their assent as Victor walked toward the door. "Listen, it's been a long and eventful morning. My suggestion is to adjourn and let everyone go home to consider their personal options and commitments. Liza, I would like to speak with you in your office."

There was no time for protocol, and Victor's request was mandatory. Holding the door of the conference room open for her to follow him, he effectively ended the meeting.

After an almost imperceptible hesitation, she followed Victor out of the room. Her mind reeled as she walked briskly down the long corridor to her office, totally absorbed by the new information that could destroy her firm and everyone in it.

Eight

Once the door to her office had closed, Victor took a seat in the chair that faced her desk. He seemed driven by a dangerous instinct. Her gaze shadowed his as he surveyed the room's appointments. She knew he was grappling to understand what made her tick.

How dare he try to manipulate her!

"This is unexpected. . . . I would've thought that someone so engrossed in high-tech would have preferred a more modern decor," he offered blandly.

Victor's weak attempt to let her calm down before getting back to the main subject insulted her. Her thoughts were erratic, and she couldn't focus enough to read him. This time she would have to rely on her intellect, not her extraordinary gift. She felt cornered. Her firm was entangled in a nightmare, and he chose to discuss furniture.

"Don't play with me, Victor. We're not here to discuss my taste or office decor." Her tone matched his—low and predatory.

Unperturbed, Victor took his time to answer. Or perhaps he

was just stalling for an elaborate lie, wondering where to begin. Once again, she didn't trust him.

"You have misinterpreted my comments, Liza. This office reminds me of the chalet where I spent time in Geneva. . . . It's impeccable," he returned, sounding earnestly appreciative despite his flagrant avoidance of the issue at hand.

"Stop it!" she demanded. Liza's gaze narrowed, and she took in a deep breath through her nose. The tightness of her fists drove her fingernails into her palms. *Just like the damned chardonnay!* she thought icily. "I don't give a damn about Geneva. Get to the point."

Victor's jaw tightened. She wasn't going for it. But he needed time. Time to figure out what to tell her, and how to do it. But Liza's stony glare was enough to remind him of her passionate dislike for indirectness and he opted to dispense with the small talk. He couldn't stall her any longer; however, he hadn't factored in the variable of the team's being overtly drawn into helping him on his personal mission. Their limited knowledge escalated the risk.

He looked directly at Liza. A thin sheen now glossed her face, and she appeared positively ill. Directness, she respected directness. There was no point in trying to fool her since he had already experienced her frightening ability to probe his mind.

"Liza, last night I told you that there were a lot of things you didn't know . . . and . . ." he hesitated, not sure of how deeply to confide in her.

"Yes, and after you *screwed* me last night, you decided to finish the job off this morning."

He was stunned. He had thought he knew the range of Liza's artillery, but he had seriously misjudged her fury. Her anger ripped through the unnatural silence in the room.

"I should have known, Victor," she went on, her voice tight and acidic. "You had darkness all around you—I saw it! But like a fool, I chose to ignore it. Then you eloquently explain to my team that we will be used as pawns, though you never once mentioned this garbage to me last night. Let me ask you, Victor—" she railed "—was it the first kiss, or the last, that was the kiss of death for *my firm?*"

Liza trembled as the words seethed within her, scorching her lips, each one burning her throat as she swallowed the tears that she refused to allow.

She took another deep breath before continuing. "Do you think that I don't know how dangerous these people are? I've had direct and merciless experience with how they can destroy people. I don't know what your hidden objective is, but you are *mad* if you think I'm going to allow you to help them while I sit by helplessly."

He had received more vicious blows from much stronger competitors, but her condemnation left him wounded and exposed. Never in his life had he been gripped by so passionate a rage.

"You have twisted a series of unrelated events together to suit your own purposes, Liza! Don't you *ever* categorize me like that or tell me that I simply *screwed* you! Ever!" he yelled, angrily ignoring the propriety of her controlled threat.

Finding himself in the full heat of battle, Victor searched for a way to ward off another attack. He had been totally unprepared for the reference to his lovemaking, which had inflicted a deep gash in his pride. Why did that matter so much? Liza watched him, then flung her glasses across her desk, not uttering a word but rendering him vulnerable. He could just let the remark pass, since there were more serious immediate issues to deal with . . . but to hell with that!

As he moved toward the door enraged, he saw Liza's body shake with anger before he turned away from her. He would not dignify her affront with more explanations, especially since he didn't have any. She was a grown woman, and he was not about to apologize for what had happened the night before.

Advancing quickly toward him, she seemed angry enough to come to fisticuffs.

"Why not?" she exploded, no longer able to control the volume. "You're not so different from the ones who *killed* my father and mother. It's all one big *damned* circle that I can't seem to break. But I won't let you take down my business!" She glowered at him. "Not when I'm *this close* to getting to them."

Halfway into the hallway, Victor stopped in his tracks. Liza's words—and vehemence—made him turn around and look at her, then move back into the office and shut the door. As the tears brimming in her eyes overflowed and streamed down her stricken face, he inexplicably wanted to reach out and hold her— which was, now, totally out of the question.

Moving back into the center of the room, he met her gaze steadily. The tears made her eyes glisten wildly, like those of an animal trapped in a corner and ready to attack. He had looked and felt much the same when his godfather had found him on the campus of London University twenty-five years before . . . when he learned of his family's massacre.

Liza had become completely still. He moved toward her as he would approach any wounded creature. She was only an arm's length away when he stopped and spoke to her quietly.

"Liza, tell me, what did they do to you?" He faltered, realizing that somehow this was part of the pain that had shone in her eyes the night before.

Now unreachable, she abruptly turned away from him and walked to the window, swallowing hard again to stop the steady stream of tears coursing down her face.

Gaining some measure of control, Liza finally wiped at the tears and faced him, her expression full of bitterness. "Last night, I told you that I was all right. That I'm *always* all right, Mr. Duarte."

She spat out her reply, then angrily swung herself back around to face the window. He didn't answer her attack, but slowly walked over to her post by the large glass panels and stood next to her. Looking out at the magnificent skyline, he waited a long time before he decided to speak.

"And you also said that we were both very much alike, you

and I . . . which I now believe more than I did twenty-four hours ago. What did they do?"

"What didn't they do?"

She did not look at him, her words a distant whisper. He knew that she wasn't with him. It was as if she had transported herself to a place of pain far away, and he was forced to turn to face her to fully hear what she might tell him next.

"My father was an honest man and I loved him dearly. His only real quirk was that he could never go to the beach. Since he'd fought in the Pacific in WW II, it brought back too many memories. When I was a little girl, he would push a dollar bill into my hand and tell me to go with Mom and my brother Gerald to the boardwalk. That was before they had the casinos in Atlantic City. I've kept his sword, the Japanese samurai that he brought back, because it reminds me of how much he gave this country, and how little he got in return."

Victor's line of vision travelled to the far wall where the priceless relic was mounted. Initially, he had thought it odd that her office was so well appointed with masculine furnishings. He had attributed them to Liza's commensurate power and authority, never once imagining that they could also be family treasures. Fascinating. They were so much alike, yet so diametrically opposed. Through her quiet admission, she was letting him in, even though she hadn't really answered his question.

He knew that it was best not to speak, his gaze just held hers as he tried to comprehend.

"Both my mother and father marched with Dr. Martin Luther King, right out there," she pointed listlessly, motioning to the monuments that created the skyline.

"They were so naive and idealistic." She smiled sadly with remembrance. "They thought that going into politics was the answer that could bring about change. They foolishly assumed that just because the rules were written down, that was the game being played. Dad believed in playing fair . . . Robert's Rules of Order and other gentlemanly conduct. For him, integrity was everything. It cost him his life."

Liza's tears stopped flowing, but her tone remained weary. It didn't seem to matter to her anymore. Her resignation was all too familiar, too frighteningly suggestive of someone close enough to the edge of despair to jump. He had been there himself, and had to pull her back. As she looked at him, she gave no flicker of life. He knew that Liza no longer viewed him as her nemesis, but as another selfish individual who would take from her. With a long sigh, she went on, clearly not caring how much she revealed. She had died a quiet, internal death . . . and it had happened so quickly, right before his eyes.

"So, in '68, when the politicians decided to get some black faces in front of the angry mobs, my father got a job as an elected official in our hometown, Philadelphia. If he had stayed there, my parents might have lived. . . . But as we know, success breeds the taste for more success and, like a bad drug, it had him."

Liza's breathing had steadied, but her eyes burned with the memory as she unfolded it vividly before him.

"With his new Congressional seat, by the mid-seventies, Dad was commuting back and forth from Philly to D.C. and my mother had become the perfect politician's wife. All was well until he faced his loan-repayment date with the Devil . . ." she trailed off again, overcome by emotion and struggling under the weight of her burden.

"They set him up, simply because he wasn't willing to play dirty politics. He never told me what he was working on—I was only sixteen when he died. Later I found out that it was a foreign aid bill that barred international weapons-build-up. Dad held the swing vote. Lobbyists and his fellow Congressmen with a lot at stake wanted him to vote for leniency so they could ply their military wares. Dad voted with the bill that would deny foreign aid to countries that were building arms. So simple. Can you imagine?"

Without waiting for his response, Liza spoke, almost to herself. "Ironic. Idealism and anti-war stuff probably killed a decorated veteran. . . . Who knows?" She traced her finger along the edge of the window sill.

Inexplicably connected to Liza's story, he couldn't fight his own impatience. He pushed for an explanation.

"Do you know who attacked him? Who killed him? How many were involved? Who was behind it?"

Liza regarded him coolly, her mouth turning up at one corner in a bitter smile. "Oh, they didn't kill him quickly. They tortured him until he killed himself," she responded dryly, then turned from the window to look him directly in the eyes.

"If they had put a gun to his head in the parking lot, it would have been much more humane. No, instead, they assassinated his character, destroying him slowly—in the press and with un-warranted grand jury investigations. They went after him with deliberate, excruciating, skill . . . until they finally entered his soul and broke it. He tried to weather the storm, but was finan-cially ruined through the travesty of the legal system and a host of defense attorneys."

Unable to watch the pain any longer, Victor reached out to her. She instantly recoiled in self-defense.

"They smeared his name because he wouldn't vote a certain way, so that there would be hope of having the bill overturned at some point—and to send a clear message to anyone else who might have the nerve to buck the system later . . . which led to the loss of his seat, the loss of his income, his home, and finally the loss of my mother's mind," she whispered furiously.

Turning away from him again, Liza looked off into the dis-tance. "My mother was gorgeous . . . a rare and genuine beauty who took refuge in alcohol to numb herself from the press and the eventual loss of her home. Her mother, my grandmother, *scrubbed floors* on the Mainline in Philadelphia and was often paid for her years of dedication with cast-offs—frequently an-tiques—instead of money. Those precious possessions, which were so dear to my mother, were sold as the mounting legal fees to defend my father bankrupted us. Over that period, my mother's hair turned white and her liver failed until she just finally gave up and died. He had nowhere to go for help. His political friends and cronies had abandoned him, and the civil rights organizations wouldn't touch him with a ten-foot-pole because his credibility was in such question—they only want to defend the clearly honorable. Everybody guarded their own public image, and in his time of need, they turned their back on him. He was shunned and left with two children to care for."

The calm that had crept into Liza's tone was unnatural. She had spoken this horror in a soft voice, resignation weighting each word. For the first time in his life, he was at a total loss; he had no strategy to cope with such information.

"It's a short story, really, Victor," she explained without emotion. "In the seven years that followed their deaths, Gerry and I lived with my elderly aunt until I finished high school and college. Then, she died, too. Gerry and I had to win our educations through scholarships and full-time work."

Liza had moved from the window to the beautiful antique desk that he assumed was command central for her office. Lovingly, she ran her fingers across the soft inlaid leather that was surrounded by an elaborate border carved into the timeless oak wood.

"Dad didn't even make it to Christmas without Mom. He just sat down at this desk, wrote a short note, put his service revolver in his mouth, and pulled the trigger. I guess in his confusion and pain he thought that his insurance would provide for us. They could barely read the note for all the blood. It just said, 'My Lizzy . . .' "

Suddenly Liza stopped. It was clear that she was battling to steady her voice which quavered with repressed sobs. She closed her eyes and took a deep breath, then looked down at the desk again.

"It said . . . 'Gerald is not strong enough. You have to be the one to go on for me. I'm sorry, Pumpkin. The baton of the future is yours. I just wasn't able to go on. Dear God, forgive me and care for my children. I'll love you, always, Babydoll. Understand and never forget—Daddy.' The words of that note are burned into my brain." After another swallow, Liza gazed up at him. He stood frozen in the pain of understanding, unable to reach out to her lest she recoil again.

"That's why I came to Washington, to rebuild my family financially. Since it was a suicide and Dad had mortgaged the house and used up his older policies for his defense . . . and the one that he had just bought was less than a year old . . . there was no insurance. They don't pay you to take your own life. I had to take care of Gerald, who was younger than I and an artist, and now *have* to go after the assassins that ruined my father. I suppose I kept the desk and the appointments from his office as a focus, to remind me to keep going when I'm tired. And I have been very tired for a long time. So, you see, Victor, for me, anyway, this has *hardly* been a game. The same men behind Dad's death now run Chem Tech. Those same lobbyists now run a major corporation and have hooks into the same politicians who grant them free rein to ply their wares on The Hill. Incestuous business. That's why I fought so hard for complete control of this project."

It was mind-blowing. They were after the same people!

He studied Liza's youthful face. It belied the years of turmoil mirrored in her eyes. He carefully phrased a delicate question.

"You know, Liza, that you are putting yourself and your family at risk. Where is your brother now?"

She shook her head as two large pools formed in her eyes. "Gerry was so kind and so good . . . always. This has been difficult for him over the years. He was just twelve when they died . . . and he must've felt that our parents had abandoned him. Since then, he's repeatedly tried to take his own life—to join them, I suppose. He's institutionalized . . . and he's dying from a disease that has no mercy."

Drawing a resolute sigh, Liza forced herself to go on. "Fate has a cruel sense of humor though. . . . Because ever since Gerry came down with full-blown AIDS, he hasn't had the strength for suicide. He probably won't be here by the end of the year, and I've prayed that God be merciful and take him before he suffers anymore. They hurt him years ago, Victor, when he was just a baby. Killing him now would be an act of pure compassion."

Words dissolved in his throat. What could he say? Liza's account of her family tragedy constricted his chest as he felt the all-too-familiar well of emotion rising within him. She had a way of making him feel each emotion with raw intensity. Whether it was rage, or passion, fear for her safety . . . now, grief—whatever it was, it always broke through some unguarded portion of his heart with impact.

The connection he made with her story was at gut level. He found the coincidence eerie. Her family had been destroyed through character assassination in the same way that his family had been actually murdered during a military coup by the same powerful people who pulled the strings. If his hunch proved correct, Liza was, indeed, the information source that could lead him to the missing Washington piece of the puzzle.

His mind raced to align key variables. It was probable that the two firms were chosen because he and Liza's hidden objectives had already been discovered, which meant that they had been at considerable risk from the very beginning. Maybe they were being monitored, followed, and tracked, and that was why their two firms out of the entire bid process had been chosen for the job. If so, his connection to Liza was hardly coincidental. However, another aspect of their connection went well beyond anything that he could cope with at the moment.

He approached the delicate subject again. "And the men that set your father up . . . the politicians . . . do you know who they are?" he asked, softer this time.

He hated to question Liza about anything that would keep her enmeshed in this painful subject, but he had to know. He was convinced, now more than ever before, that he was close to his target.

Unexpectedly, Liza's eyes burned through him as they narrowed in an angry glare.

"Of course," she retorted. They even came to the funerals. But I had learned their names from my mother well before then.

When I was just a kid, and when she was in her cups, she would hold conversations with them . . . begging them not to hurt her Bill."

The last memory was more than Liza could take. Her stance became rigid as she stepped back from him, suddenly behaving as if he had cornered her again. Perhaps, unwittingly, he had.

"So now you *know* me . . . better, Victor. Although I'm sure you enjoyed last night more than this glimpse of the real me. Then, you should also know that I'll never give up without a fight—even if it endangers *my* life. But I won't have Ronnie or Maureen or the others hurt. I'll only take risks with my own life, not anyone else's."

He knew her position well and understood that removing Liza from the game board at this point, even if it were to save her life, would be impossible. His only choice would be to gain her trust, make her an ally, and teach her how to play to win.

"Liza, we have much more in common than is even possible for you to fathom at this juncture."

"Then be honest. Why can't you tell me what that similarity is? Why is it cloaked in so much darkness? I've revealed myself because *I don't play games* and it doesn't matter anymore anyway. But you . . ."

Her question was reasonable; however, he wasn't ready to incorporate her that fully into his plan or into his life. The risk was too great. Opting to answer one half of what she demanded, he tried to avoid her glare.

"I will help you, but you must learn how to play the high-stakes game right. What's the point if you only set up some low-level flunky? That person has no more direct power than you or I. You have to set a snare big enough to hold the larger marlin, then be prepared to disappear—or die. Can you say that you are willing to do that?"

He was deadly serious and could tell that in her newfound calm Liza had activated her probe to evaluate his honesty.

"You told me that you never use your *ability* unless it's for a good purpose," he stated gently, just to make her aware that he could now sense when her magnet was on.

No sooner had the words passed his lips, then he was suddenly unable to breathe. Anvil pressure instantly forced the air from his lungs, and he clutched his chest as the pain from a violent spasm made him buckle and hold on to the side of her credenza. His body contorted with agony and terror as he searched Liza's eyes, desperate for help while gasping for breath. His heart . . . Consciousness was slipping away from him, but he had to focus on her, make her hear his mind screaming for help.

Liza was only two inches from his face now. As she looked at him coldly, her eyes reflected instant death not rescue. He felt an acute terror.

"Now all bets are off, and saving my own life *is* a good use of my gift. Don't play with me, Victor," she hissed, then turned away quickly.

The sensation of his heart tearing away from its tissue-anchors to slam against his rib cage eased as quickly as it had come upon him. In the seconds of pain and confusion that consumed him, he was both fascinated and horrified.

"Did you do that? Were you actually able to do that!" he exclaimed, gulping large breaths of air while snatching Liza's arm roughly to make her face him. When his gaze locked with hers again, he saw that her face was totally drained and she reeled as she caught his arm to break her fall.

Out of breath and unquestionably frightened, Liza seemed unable to answer. Her complexion had become pallid and cool, with only the slightest new sheen of perspiration forming on her brow.

"I dunno," she stammered. "I've been angry before, but I've never projected it like that. I mean, it felt like I swung at you, and I'm winded . . . tired. I have to sit down."

New tears brimmed and fell in large splotches on the blotter on her desk. Covering her face with her hands, she sank into the chair. "I don't know what's happening! You're the only one that makes everything feel . . . *so vivid!* It's like you're a catalyst.

When I'm around you, it's as if you give me more power—-more wattage. *I'm scared.* I can't believe I did that."

She stared at him in abject apology. "Victor, I was ready to kill you. I'm so sorry. I don't know what's happening, or how to control it."

He returned her gaze with astonishment and fear. Without another word, Liza reached into the drawer and frantically grabbed a silver filigreed cross, clutching it desperately to her breast. Her lips moved silently and she crossed herself, then looked at him again and swallowed. He found her fear ironic in the wake of so-recent a display of her awesome power.

Squatting beside her, he reached out his hand for the crucifix.

"Your grandmother's?" he asked softly, taking the fine jewelry only after she had calmed enough to nod yes and offer it to him for inspection.

"Liza, I am *not* the Prince of Darkness . . . although we probably do have some similar modes of behavior," he teased nervously. "You'll have to trust me on this. I'll even go to Mass with you and take Communion if it will make you feel better. But you have to stop running from your extraordinary ability. It could be a valuable weapon in the fight we're going to embark upon. I won't let them hurt you anymore, Liza . . . and I won't hurt you. But I will teach you how to strengthen your gift and how to execute strategy like a master."

Victor returned the heirloom to Liza and moved toward the door. "Go home and get some rest," he ordered gently on his way out. "Tomorrow you have a chess lesson in Potomac policy."

Although calmer, Liza still appeared unconvinced that he was not some demonic presence sent to harm her. She watched him warily from the doorway, then called after him.

"I'm not Catholic, but if you can deal with an Episcopal congregation, which is close, Sunday services begin at 11:00 A.M. In Philly. You can meet me in front of the Holy Apostles' Church at 10:45. Even after all these years, D.C. just isn't home."

"You're lucky you can still go home, Liza. Not everybody can."

She didn't respond other than to close the door to her office. He shook his head with a smile. Liza was definitely growing on him. Their diametric opposition . . . their bizarre similarities . . . It had been one hell of a twenty-four hours for both of them, and he understood she would never trust him without an acid test.

Holy Apostles' Church . . . how prophetic!

Nine

Leaving Liza behind in a state of hurt confusion had been one of the hardest things he had had to contend with recently. It was difficult, but necessary. Much like everything else in his life. What else could he do? He needed a solid plan that now had to accommodate a new variable: Liza. It had been a mistake to get involved with her; she was a risk factor.

With no way to comfort her and no way to get her to trust him, he had few options available. Victor's mind wrestled with the issues and the possibilities before him.

There had to be a way to establish a common ground, a way to assure Liza that he didn't intend to double-cross her. Liza probably possessed the key names and information that would close the loop of mysteries that plagued his mission, and her personal safety was paramount. This tempestuous beauty held him hostage; he was unable to move forward without her, unable to forget her. He definitely needed a plan.

A contract had brought them together, mutual attraction—or suspicion—had brought out her extraordinary gift . . . something that he had accidentally, and fortuitously, stumbled upon.

His intellect was challenged beyond belief, and he wanted to know more—much more—about her mysterious ability. When Liza attacked him, he had felt the unparalleled terror of his heart beginning to burst. Could she actually use her mental powers to affect the physical world? How accurately could she foretell events, read thoughts, provoke feelings . . . and could her powers drain and diminish her or boomerang and injure her? It was unexplored territory for him, an area of marginal belief before he'd met Liza. Now, he was hungry for knowledge.

Winding through the local traffic, he decided to satisfy that hunger immediately. He had to learn more about this phenomenon before they met again. And her eyes . . . those wonderfully rich, brown orbs of emotion that simply took his breath away . . . had instantly turned as cold as ice, threatening to take his life. Was he mad? Common sense would dictate that he leave this sensual, but dangerous, creature alone. But after last night, that was no longer an option. Her allure was more than sensual. Liza filled a void that he hadn't even been aware of until now. When near her, he felt a sense of completion, a familiar and complementary blend of equals that he'd never experienced with any other woman. Yet she also needed protection.

As Victor cruised down Georgetown's main thoroughfare, absorbed by the strip of eclectic shops, he decided to try the Crystal Bookstore, which had a distinctly arty exterior.

Finally able to park, he walked back down to the little shop, but hesitated before going in. What the hell was he doing? He felt foolish as he peeked into the window of the bright, oddly decorated establishment.

It reminded him of the artist community in Soho. Admittedly, he had always harbored the hidden prejudice that people who indulged themselves in New Age dogma were a tad on the fuzzy side of reality.

But what he'd experienced with Liza had been real and he could not ignore it. Victor's curiosity propelled him forward and he entered the shop. He knew that he looked totally out of place, and when the proprietor grinned broadly at the sight of him, he felt all the more uncomfortable.

"Well, this is *new*," the tall, post-hippy shopkeep quipped, coming from behind the register to greet him. The man wore an oversized, mustard-yellow shirt that covered his slightly baggy, ripped, faded jeans. Studying the shopkeep, Victor noticed that the man's jeans buckled at the top of a pair of dingy sneakers. His graying hair was tied back in a straggly ponytail, and the long crystal and metal pendants that he wore chimed as he walked.

Victor surveyed the establishment skeptically, taking in the candles, crystals, and thick aroma of frankincense. The proprietor watched him cautiously, alert to his every move. Victor tried to shrug off the uncomfortable sense that he was treading on haunted ground. This was, he told himself, merely unknown territory—not a coven of evil.

Looking directly at the clerk, he noticed that the man's sallow complexion made his face gaunt. He should have been in the mortuary business, Victor thought, ready to give up and go home. But something in the way the man looked at him stayed his leave. Maybe it was the stark contrast of his eyes which seemed to contain a youthful brightness, making his age and temperament difficult to gauge.

"You look lost. May I help you?" Although polite, the man still seemed to be critically assessing him from head to toe as he neared.

Victor had to smile at himself as he looked down at his own traditional navy business suit; starched, monogrammed shirt; and conservative, wing-tipped shoes. Breaking into a full grin, which quickly became an earnest chuckle, he decided to lighten the exchange. "Yes, I do suppose that I am lost. Truly lost."

Victor's now cheerful disposition and the certainty of his tone changed the clerk's earlier reserve. In response, the quiet man beamed directly at Victor, totally absorbed in his interesting new patron.

"Well, I was hoping that you weren't from the IRS or something, bringing bad vibes and negative karma into my shop. Who needs that, man?"

It was such an unexpected comment that Victor laughed, unable to catch himself. "No, I assure you that I'm not from the

IRS. I know that I look like the government and not like your normal patron . . . but, I would appreciate your help."

At 10:30 in the morning, the store was quiet. Lunch-time shoppers hadn't come in yet, and only a few knowledgeable browsers were around.

Satisfied, the proprietor smiled. "Sure, what's your area of interest? Health and diet? Holistic healing? A lot of people in the stress professions start dealing with that when confronted with a serious illness for the first time. Tarot cards . . . reincarnation? Most times, new people come in after they've lost a loved one or a relationship has gone awry. Out of body experiences? . . ."

Victor held up his hand as he looked sheepishly at the rows of books denoting myriad subject matter that he didn't have time to wade through. Not really sure why he was in the shop, he began tentatively. "No, I have a . . . shall we say . . . specific incident or series of incidents that have occurred—that a colleague of mine seems to be able to tap into."

The proprietor understood exactly what he was wrestling with and began a series of diagnostic questions like any skilled physician. "Can your friend tell what's going to happen just before the event takes place? It's in the look, the eyes . . . real intense . . . right? Then you feel like a mild electric current running through you, starting at the base of your chakras. I'll explain later. You feel it when the person is probing you . . ."

"Yes! That's what it's called," he exclaimed with excitement. "Probing."

"Hmmm . . . it's rare. Special. Can the person move an object with her mind? Or make a physical change occur?" He trailed off, intent on Victor's short, direct, one-word responses. "She's a natural."

"She? I didn't denote gender," Victor interrupted cautiously.

"This person . . ." the proprietor began again, ". . . has this person ever used crystals to magnify personal power?"

It was evident by his eager tone that he asked the question for more than casual informational purposes. The man's fascination had escalated to a more personal level, and he seemed impatient when Victor merely shrugged.

Perplexed, Victor ran his fingers over his hair. There were a number of questions that he wanted to ask, but he didn't know where to begin. Before he could pull his thoughts together, the proprietor interrupted, not giving him a chance to voice his unspoken concerns.

"You do know that if a person can focus this energy, it gets stronger. Consider the difference between a flashlight and a laser beam. Both are directed energy, both use light. One is diffused light, which can only illuminate things, bringing clarity to unsure, hidden areas . . . like thoughts. The other, like a laser, can be used as a tool to actually change mass. Adding a crystal to a strong flashlight can actually bring focus to the diffused light, and crystals store energy. So, it is *very* important to clean the old energy out of the crystals regularly or you could project something negative."

Although overwhelmed, Victor remembered his most burning question. "Is this . . . gift hereditary?"

His temporary teacher scoffed. "Of course! It's just like any other trait. Were your mother's eyes brown like yours? Why do people make such a big deal about this stuff?"

Indignant, but unable to refrain from giving a brief history lesson, the proprietor went on.

"Look, man, the ancient Asian and African cultures . . . Yorubas, Aztecs, Mayans, Incas, Egyptians, American Indians . . . I mean, all of these great old civilizations believed in this stuff and had this information as the foundation of their life practices. They didn't question their harmony with the universe and, in fact, it was the conquerors of those lands that brought in superstition and made people scared of their own ability. Hey, they *burned* people at the stake for using a natural extension of their minds. It was a power thing. Now that's deep, man."

Confident that he had made his point, the clerk moved to a section containing information on crystals. Victor followed quietly, more intrigued than ever. As he reached up to the top shelf, the man's slender build seemed fragile against the massive book-case as he hunted for a specific volume.

"Ah, that's the one I was looking for," he said, reaching for a book and handing it down to Victor. "It gives the entire history of crystal use, a lot of helpful information, and exercises for beginners."

Moving swiftly between the rows, he settled on a general-purpose book about psychic phenomenon, then quickly looked over to Victor again. "Did I hear you say your friend can move objects . . . or something?"

Victor was stunned. "No, I said it is always a possibility," he hedged defensively.

"But you *are* sure that she can do more than just pick up thoughts—aren't you?—or you wouldn't be here," the shopkeep pressed on, unwilling to let him evade the direct line of reasoning.

"I'm fairly sure that something is going on," Victor admitted haltingly, becoming uncomfortable as this stranger invaded his personal objectives. "And, as I mentioned earlier, I never said *she*. I said a colleague."

The man just smiled. Curiosity seemed to have a stranglehold on him now, and Victor knew that he wouldn't be eager to let the subject drop.

"And this gift has been in her family for a while, you say?" The frail man's smile broadened after he made the comment, while his eyes seemed to take on a direct, open gaze.

Victor's body froze, made rigid by the awareness that he was being lightly probed. "No, I didn't say!" he retorted, furious at the intrusion.

The shopkeep apologetically lowered his eyes. "It's hard to turn it off when your curiosity has the best of you. She probably can't help it either, and has got to be as scared of it as you are. This is weird science for the layman, you dig? Look . . . if she did that to you, almost stopped your heart, then the book I just pulled down will barely scratch the surface of what you're dealing with." Indicating that Victor should wait, he rushed to the back of the store and disappeared behind a bright tie-dyed drape.

Victor was speechless as the man raced away from him. He had never met this man before; yet this stranger had *read* him—accurately assessing his innermost thoughts. It was eerie, leaving him totally unsure about the black-and-white, cut and dried world that was quickly evaporating before him. Now everything was a shade of grey, not exact, and held unlimited possibilities.

The clerk returned excitedly and lowered his voice to make his comments audible only to Victor. "You know, man, not many people have it that strong. Your lady must be really extraordinary. These books are expensive, so I only keep one or two around. . . . I'm not gouging you or anything. These are my personal copies, but you probably need them more than I do right now. I'd have to special-order the set if you wanted brand new ones. But they should provide you both with significant insight."

The proprietor took back the earlier book selection from Victor's hands, giving him the new ones. "You may want to let her try her power with the crystal exercises, to see how far she can go. Just take it slow, and stay positive, and the results could be mind-blowing!" He smiled with a knowing expression that made Victor uneasy, then took the set of volumes again.

As the owner shoved three hardcover books into a recycled paper bag without Victor's consent, he looked over to the crystals on the counter. His expression seemed hopeful.

"Do you need one to work with or do you have your own?"

Victor let out a small chuckle as he paid for the volumes, quickly grabbed the parcel, and headed toward the door. "No, thank you. I have my own. I've appreciated your assistance with my questions, however."

A swift departure was in order before the balance of his inappropriate thoughts about Liza could be read. Calling behind Victor emphatically, the proprietor added, "Remember to clean them first! Call me if you have any questions. The name's Jack."

His last comment was almost lost. Victor was already out the door.

* * *

The drive home seemed longer than normal, and Victor imagined that the night would be even worse. He felt strangely fatigued and was unable to ignore the dull ache that throbbed in his temple. After all, he reasoned logically, he hadn't slept all night and hadn't eaten all morning. Stress. He'd be lucky if he died from it.

Still wrestling with the puzzle pieces before him, he tried to align them serially as he drove. His mind had become a belligerent adversary, refusing to turn off to allow him to unwind. He daydreamed, his gaze continually wandering over to the bag of books on the passenger's seat. What was he getting into? His arms felt like lead as he popped in a classical music CD to help restore his peace. Soon, an entire orchestra unfolded within the soundproof cab of the sedan and he worked his shoulders and lolled his neck, trying to expel the tension.

The day had turned into a bizarre whir of unexpected events and information, which always seemed to be the norm when Liza was involved. Until this moment, he had been able to justify his side jaunt to the bookstore as a clinical exploration of his curiosity.

Pulling into the spacious garage, Victor sat with his eyes closed, taking in the music, his head titled back. Too tired to move, he gave in to fatigue. It was a rare moment of peace. He could feel the tension drain from his body, down and out through the soles of his feet.

As his shoulders slumped, he worked the kinks out of his spine, then stretched his legs out in front of him as far as the confined space would allow. The process of unwinding felt good, and he let out a deep sigh of release. But as his breath pushed past his lips and his ears registered the sound of his own voice, he immediately thought of Liza. She was like a drug.

Less than twenty-four hours ago, she had made him gasp from deep within his chest near that same place in the garage. Now the torrid memory washed over him in an unexpected wave of desire. Annoyed, he sat up and shook his head. He had to get out of the space that harbored her very presence. That part of their involvement was over, and much too volatile to contemplate. Any thoughts along those lines were destined to rob him of the relaxation he needed so badly.

Hurrying out of the car, he grabbed the satchel of books with irritation. Suddenly, his heel crushed something that felt like glass. When he looked down to see what he'd stepped on, he saw the hundreds of tiny beads that still crisscrossed the cement floor.

Each crystal seemed to magnify the memory of his intimate encounter with her. He chastised himself vehemently. Finally closing his eyes against his will, it was impossible not to recall the intense lovemaking that had released him from his self-imposed exile. Standing next to the open car door, he held onto the cold steel to brace himself against the next wave of desire that swept through him. God, she'd felt so good.

The memory of her scent filled his nose. His eyes still closed, he took a deep, involuntary breath, searching the air. He could almost smell her. It took only an instant for his mind to play back the recently recorded image with all the passion that she'd invoked. He had to stop.

But it was too late. The vividness of his careening imagination returned all the tension that he had previously released. Now those thoughts focused mercilessly into a dull central ache.

"Oh, no, Liza," he groaned out loud. *"Querida,* don't do this to me . . . not again. Not now!"

Holding onto the car door for support, he found himself spellbound and trembling with need. To call her was totally out of the question. What would he say? I miss you? I need to feel your warmth wrap around me again? Absurd. She hated and mistrusted him. Now, *that* was logical.

Yet, if her torment continued, he was sure he'd go crazy. He would have to pull himself together. Immediately. There were too many unanswered questions. Could she project thought over such a distance? Was she even thinking about the same thing now? The possibilities were endless, leaving him in complete and utter confusion.

With great reluctance, Victor tore himself away from the vision and found the strength to close the car door. Once inside his bright, modern kitchen, the intensity of Liza's presence subsided. Thankful that the urgency was abating, he resigned himself to one of the half-eaten cartons of leftover Chinese food in the refrigerator.

He scavenged disinterestedly through the limited alternatives and made a mental note to call Helyar to set up a meeting in New York. Get back to business. That had always warded off his libido in the past. Maybe he could call another one of his ladyfriends . . . but who could compare to Liza? Forget it. Mind over matter.

Grabbing a beer and a cold murky carton, he quickly crossed the room and bounded up the back stairs. He would have to take a long, hot shower, then banish Liza from his mind. The plan was to hopefully relax, before delving into his newly purchased wealth of information. He had work to do.

The events of the day had wreaked havoc with Liza's emotions, and no one had even questioned her when she'd left the office. She had given Connie the instructions to screen everyone and everything.

Her assistant had listened patiently when she'd explained that she was a wreck, needed to go swimming, then was going home. Connie had nodded in agreement when she carefully asked her to only call if there were an emergency. As she left, she had told the team that she wouldn't be back until the following morning. It was odd, but she couldn't remember when she had abandoned the office midday, or even taken a vacation.

Liza recalled the brief exchange as she turned on the ignition. Connie had taken one look at her, then chided motherly, "Hon, you've been under a lot of strain lately . . . and it's telling on you. Why don't you work from home for a couple of days? They'll live without you."

The idea of taking time off now was insane. But she really wouldn't be gone. Just home, and away from the office, she had thought wistfully, while allowing the temptation that Connie had presented to lure her.

Detecting a flash of serious consideration in her expression, Connie had urged her on. "I can forward all important calls to you and screen the unnecessary ones. You have a terminal there, and can dial in if you get lonely for us. Consider it, Liza. You won't do yourself or anybody else any good if you drive yourself into the ground."

Liza had known Connie was right, and she had quietly agreed to take at least one day to recover. What in the world would she do without Connie to look out for her? She hadn't even searched for Ron. She could speak to him later. Too tired to argue anymore, she had left her office unburdened by files for the first time in years.

Ten

She awakened with the morning sun streaming brightly on her face. That was new. She never slept past 5:30 A.M. during the week, and rarely past 7:00 on the weekends. She'd come in from swimming the night before, changed quickly, and deposited her leaden body on the bed. The cloak of sleep had been merciful.

Reaching over with a lazy yawn, she pulled the clock radio toward her. "Ten o'clock!" she gasped, sitting bolt upright in the bed. "I never even set the alarm!"

Disoriented, she reached for the phone, annoyed with herself. "I have to call Connie to see what new drama will unfold today," she muttered as she dialed.

"Good morning, Connie," Liza croaked back to the cheerful voice on the other end of the line. "Would you believe I overslept? I'll be in soon."

Connie quickly rushed in, breaking off Liza's sleepy explanation. "Oh, no, you most certainly *will not* be in here soon, not sounding like that! I thought I instructed you to stay home. At least for one day, didn't I? There's nothing critical going on here, and *everybody* came back today. As of now, there are no resignations. So, please, for once, stay out of my hair and get some rest."

Liza smiled as Connie fussed at her. It had been so long since anyone had taken care of her that she had forgotten how good it felt. Connie's slow, Southern drawl poured over her like warm syrup. Sinking back into the pile of goose-down pillows, Liza pulled her grandmother's quilt up to her neck, luxuriating in the warmth that emanated from the massive four-poster. Heaven.

"Connie, you're making it difficult for me to even move. My legs feel like rubber, and I slept like I was in a coma last night. I didn't even set the alarm," Liza confessed.

"Good, then. That was God's work," Connie flipped back. "Now, Hon, if I see you in here today, I'm gonna spank you myself," Connie chided, much to Liza's delight.

Since the firm's beginning, Liza and Connie had developed a special relationship. Connie had almost become a surrogate mother to her. If it weren't for Connie's occasional maternal words of wisdom, Liza probably would have cracked by now.

"Okay, *Mom*," Liza gave in pleasantly. "But only if you promise to let my guys know that if they want to talk privately, they can come over. Really, there's a lot going on now, so don't hold any important calls. . . . They could be critical. I know how you are."

With an air of mock disgust, Connie sucked her teeth and chastised Liza again. "And now you're going to start telling me how to do my job, after all these years? Humph!" she scoffed, without suppressing a chuckle. "I'll tell you, some folks stay out of their job less than one day and want to start taking over yours. I swear to Pete!"

They both laughed, unable to stay in the character of their

role-play any longer, and Liza apologized profusely before hanging up the phone.

As the call disconnected, Liza stretched hard until her muscles hurt. Snuggling into the comforter, she twinkled her toes, enjoying the way the sun made the room warm and cozy as she slipped back to sleep. She thought of Connie's words, "God's work," which brought back pleasant memories of her grandmother.

The easy thought flowed over her, taking her back to when she was just a little girl. She couldn't have been much more than five or six when she'd sat on the needlepoint stool at the side of that same high four-poster, combing her grandmother's exquisite silver hair. It was a piece of Heaven salvaged from the past.

Liza remembered fondly that her Nana's hair had not been a soft, cottony white, but a long, silky elbow-length of pure silver. Nana had kept her hair in one basic style—two neatly braided ropes pinned up and crisscrossed atop her stately head. It seemed so easy to recall the rush of silver against her Nana's dark, reddish-brown skin. The braids made the elderly woman positively sparkle despite her eighty-four years. And it was just as easy to remember how Nana's proud carriage had remained unbroken till the end.

"Nana," she whispered into the vacant room. "You were so wise. I wish you were here now to tell me what to do."

Liza closed her eyes, thinking of the great lady who had always taken her in her arms and kissed her chubby child-face, warmly smelling of lavender water and lemon drops. As the memories engulfed her, tears brimmed and spilled down from the corners of her eyes, lightly dampening the Battenburg-lace pillows that cushioned her weary head.

Pleasant memories encircled Liza as a light breeze blew the lace curtains away from the sunlit window. She loved the fresh air and often slept with the window cracked open just a tad even in the most extreme winter. This crisp morning was just what the doctor had ordered.

Oddly, the gentle stream of air brought with it the distinctive scent of lavender, which now delicately filtered into the room. The new sensory awareness startled her, but she tried to remain calm to hold onto the fragile moment.

In the past, when she'd felt the unusual presence, she would instantly panic. As if sensing her fear, the presence would always vanish as quickly as it had come, leaving her nervous and confused. But this morning, she was determined to hold it with her in the room. She wouldn't allow her fears to chase it away.

Taking deep breaths, Liza focused on the fragrance, trying to bring it in closer to her, not wanting to let it go. This morning, she needed it to wrap itself around her like her grandmother's arms. Her calm acceptance allowed the scent to grow stronger until she also detected a sweet lemony blend to the aroma.

Smiling with her eyes still closed, she said softly, "Nana, is that you? I've missed you so." The breeze passed through the room, and the glass perfume bottles on her vanity chimed softly. She didn't fight the experience.

And for the first time, there was no headache.

"I need your help. I won't be afraid anymore. The gift, I just don't know how to use it . . ." she whispered, hoping for an answer.

Suddenly the aroma vanished, and the curtains became still at the window. Liza sat up, engulfed in unbearable disappointment. She could no longer fight the host of raging emotions that had assailed her over the past few days.

Now she broke into earnest sobs, drawing her legs up to her chest and burying her face in her knees. "I just wanted to visit with you for a little while . . . ," she cried out between sobs like a forlorn child. "Why didn't you tell me how to use it?"

After a time, the rush of shudders that shook Liza's body ebbed with her sigh. Strangely, the tears that she released made her feel lighter, as though they had washed away some of the pain.

Liza sat quietly for what seemed like a long time, no longer feeling weighted by despair. She closed her eyes and fastened her mind on the sensation of calm, absorbing every facet, knowing that—somehow—she hadn't been abandoned.

When the phone rang, it startled her. The noise broke through the elusive peace with a vengeance, removing the last vestige of her morning meditation. *What now?* she thought irritably, thoroughly annoyed by the interruption and losing every bit of the peace that she had just managed to obtain. When Liza pressed the receiver to her ear, Victor's warm, exotic baritone flowed over her senses.

"Good morning, Liza. I was hoping that you would pick up, instead of one of those infernal machines," he crooned good-naturedly. "I'm surprised to catch you at home. I really had to wrangle with Connie to get her to pass me through. She made me promise that I wouldn't upset you today and warned me that my call had better be extremely important."

"Well, is it?" Liza quizzed, her tone deliberately disinterested, if not acidic.

"Of course, it is," Victor teased back, resisting her testiness. "We have a chess lesson today. Have you forgotten already, Sleeping Beauty?" He laughed warmly, sounding relaxed and as if he were genuinely looking forward to her company.

"Are you crazy?" Liza snapped, her nerves still raw from the last forty-eight hours of chaos and the disrupted meditation. "With everything that's going on? I don't have time for games, Victor. Not even a game of chess. And I definitely don't intend to lose the one moment of the peace I've been able to claim for myself this morning."

Liza wondered if he had any idea how severely injured she felt. Nothing was worse than being made to feel like a wounded, frightened female that someone had to coax out of the corner. He'd have to give her something more substantial to go on than a stupid chess game.

"Liza, I went to the bookstore yesterday . . . and stayed up all night doing some research on a very interesting subject. That's why I stayed home this morning, too," he ventured tentatively.

She could tell that Victor was hoping to snare her with her own curiosity and draw her out. Not today.

"You mean you're not calling from the office?" she queried immediately, unable to suppress the surprise in her voice. This was different—especially for a confirmed workaholic within a hare's breath of a complete win.

"No, I'm in Potomac having an espresso and finishing up on my reading," he returned calmly, as if sensing that he was close to his objective.

"What are you reading? *An Assassin's Guide To A Thousand Ways to Kill Your Business Partner?*" she snapped, annoyed by her own curiosity.

He laughed at her, and the rich infectious sound of his voice made a slight smile come out of hiding on her face. "Liza Nichols, you are the most suspicious woman I have ever met! No. I was doing research on *your* behalf, if you must know." He chuckled, seeming to take total delight in their sparring match.

"Okay, okay, okay! So what does your research have to do with me?" she blurted out, no longer able to resist the carrot that Victor dangled before her.

"Ah . . . that will have to be discussed in Potomac with your first lesson. I'll give you my address and home phone number, and I will be there all day," he said pleasantly while she rummaged for a pen and paper in her night stand.

"Slow down." She could barely keep up as he rattled off the information like a Wall Street ticker tape.

"I'll also ask Isabella to make lunch before she leaves. *Hasta luego!*" he boomed cheerfully, then was gone.

"The absolute nerve of this guy!" she fumed loudly, hanging up the phone as she flung herself out of bed. "I still don't know who he is, Nana? He never told me what his angle in this was!" Rummaging through the large mahogany armoire, Liza sifted ruthlessly through the soft fabrics for a comfortable outfit. "I cannot believe him. Chess?" She yelled out loud to the empty room. "When people might be trying to kill us?"

She turned on the shower, and slammed the bathroom door.

As the thick steam curled around her nose, she stepped forcefully into the claw-footed tub, yanking the curtain behind her.

The hot water was soothing, and it slowly began to de-escalate her. "Why do I let him goad me like this?" she snapped to herself critically.

Only allowing herself a quick five minutes to finish, she roughly towelled down her body and snatched her wet hair into a dripping ponytail. Thoroughly agitated, she applied a light dusting of makeup to her face. That's enough, she grumbled to herself. No frills. Searching for a tube of lipstick in her cosmetic bag as she paced the bathroom floor, she finally settled on a neutral shade and impatiently applied the color.

"Why am I even going through all this?" she fussed, turning to take one last quick look in the mirror before she slapped off the light. Where were her glasses? Damn. He's only a man. Just like all the rest. No biggie. Hadn't she successfully dealt with them in business before? "The trouble is, girlfriend," she muttered, "you made the fatal mistake of mixing business with pleasure."

But as Liza moved back into the bedroom, she froze mid-step. The breeze had come back, bringing with it the unmistakable mixture of lavender and lemon.

Liza stood in front of the large oak doors waiting for Victor to answer. Her sudden rush of anxiety didn't make sense. Shrugging off the feeling, she rang again and cupped her hands around her eyes to see in the window. Through the stained-glass panels, she could see him bounding toward her like an excited puppy. He looked curiously less intimidating now, dressed in khaki slacks and a polo shirt. His wide eager grin gave him a much younger presence.

As he managed the locks, it dawned on her that she had never actually seen Victor out of standard business uniform. No longer so formidable, he looked like a big kid anxious for a companion to come out and play with him.

"Liza!" he exclaimed. "I wasn't sure if I had successfully coaxed you out of bed."

She was sure that if the big puppy before her had had a tail, he would have whipped her legs mercilessly as he ushered her through the door.

"Well, I'm here," she responded with a blasé shrug. Fighting Victor's welcome, she suppressed a tiny smile and stepped into the spacious marble foyer. His merriment was infectious, and she could tell that he would be impervious to her snipes this morning.

"Please, come in, come in," Victor said excitedly, escorting her by the elbow into the living room and helping her out of her coat. His exuberance overpowered her against her will. This was not the Victor Duarte she had grown accustomed to. It was becoming impossible to steel herself against his ebullient hospitality, and she almost giggled as she followed quickly to match his long strides.

"An espresso, *señorita?*" he asked happily. Not waiting for her reply, Victor dashed into the kitchen and returned almost immediately with a small tray of danish and espresso. Still looking at her, he set it down on the coffee table, which stood before a large, pewter-colored raw-silk sofa.

Liza surveyed the room with curiosity. She noticed an eclectic mixture of ultra-modern furniture speckled with breathtaking antiques. The strange profusion of colors and periods was oddly tasteful, and strangely familiar. She was surprised that a bachelor had pulled everything together in such an artistic way. He probably had used decorators, she reminded herself. When would he have had the time?

"Victor, your combination in here is extremely interesting," she remarked with genuine appreciation, wanting to know more about him. "Did you do this yourself?" she asked, looking for a polite distraction. Now she sounded as he had the other day. What was going on? Stalling . . . for what?

Liza's view swept past the large built-in mahogany bookcases and the floor-to-ceiling picture window to an antique drop-leaf table where a massive marble chessboard stood. "It's really different." The board was like a magnet.

"Ah, so it is," Victor returned merrily, watching her as she took in the room. "But I thought you didn't like to discuss decor."

She ignored his smile, and his reference to their fight.

"I like it," she said evenly, moving closer to the board. She was not about to rehash the argument.

"I suppose it represents my ambivalence to things. But I can't take all the credit; I did have a little help."

Liza frowned at the first part of his remark. "I would've never described you as an ambivalent person, Victor. You almost always seem to know what you want, and get it," she returned, determined to stay mildly annoyed.

"Uhm . . . not always," he protested, widening his smile with mischief. "For instance, I know that I detest living in the past . . . which for me, holds some painful memories, too, Liza. So, I chose to arrange my office and dwelling with progressive new pieces," he said, directing her gaze toward the twelve-foot, oblong, abstract print that hung over the fireplace mantel. "But then, on the other hand, the past can represent a vast reservoir of strength and heritage . . . so, I keep a few special things around for balance."

His response had been logical, just as she would have expected.

"Makes sense." She nodded in reluctant agreement, walking over to the large chess set that had captivated her when she'd first entered the room. "I still wouldn't call it ambivalence."

"But don't we all have *some* measure of ambivalence to deal with in our lives?" he contended, taking a leisurely sip of the strong brew as he leveled his gaze at her. "Can't I interest you in an espresso?" he offered again, while bringing a cup toward her.

She smiled. Victor was baiting her, and she decidedly would not be drawn in. Taking the tiny china cup, she thanked him, shifting her line of vision to the enormous onyx-and-terra cotta-colored marble chessboard that now separated them. Looking down, she reached out her free hand and ran her fingers over the exquisitely carved set. Each piece was a ten-inch figurine, detailed in the costume of the era. Every one had inlaid silver, small gemstones, and other metals to give definition to their armor and swords.

The queens had finely cast, silver-filigreed crowns, hosting what appeared to be diamond baguettes. The king pieces were not as ornate as the queens or bishops, but the detailing of their robes in the carved marble was impressive. But the most awe-inspiring pieces were the knights. The detailing on the reared horses that they rode could only be described as spectacular.

"This is absolutely gorgeous, Victor. How old is it?" she questioned with honest appreciation. Although it had been her intent to skillfully change the subject when she walked over to the board, the art antiquity was mesmerizing.

Pleased by her admiration, Victor gazed at her and smiled again. "It is a prize piece that was crafted during the days of the Spanish Conquistadors. It's one of the few things that have remained in my family for a long time," he said with pride.

"You can date your family back to the time of the Spanish Conquistadors?"

Even to her own ears, her voice was filled with awe.

"Yes, I can date Duartes from the fourteen-hundreds, when mainland Spain conquered the Inca empire. I am not necessarily proud of that fact, however."

As Victor fed her the tidbit of information, Liza detected a slight current running through her. In response to the sensation, she quickly lowered her eyes. Damn it! She hadn't even tried to activate her probe, and it had turned on by itself again. What was happening to her?

Victor smiled knowingly and took another sip from his cup, seeming to become more pleased as her face flushed with embarrassment.

"I felt that, Liza. Although I do not have the benefit of your gift, I'm beginning to be able to sense when it's being used on me. In fact, someone else did it to me yesterday. So, you're not alone. I've done a little research. Unfortunately, some of us have to go to the library or to the bookstore to get information . . . and that's what I did yesterday after the meeting."

"Oh, God!" she exclaimed. "I *was* doing it again! I'm so sorry. The piece was so interesting and held so much energy . . . I was just drawn to it. I should go. I've intruded. Sometimes it happens without warning, and . . ."

With a graceful gesture of his hand, Victor cut off her tumble of words, then reached over to hold her gently by the wrist. "Liza, please. Why are you so jumpy? I don't mind. Seriously. Your probe has intrigued me beyond imagination. And the feeling it generates . . . that's what I went to the bookstore to find out about."

As Victor coaxed her into one of the high wing-backed chairs that faced the board, he brought over three books that she had noticed on the small glass-and-wrought-iron table across the room. Had she not been so nearsighted, she might've been able to read the titles when she walked in. She'd just assumed that they were nice coffee-table books, not essays on the paranormal! Nervous about what the material might contain, she gingerly accepted the volumes from him. It was clear that Victor had, indeed, done a considerable amount of research. Each chapter was highlighted and marked with sections for further reading.

She sat quietly, running her fingers over the leather bindings. Victor slid into the chair across from her with an expectant expression on his face, but allowed her to examine the books without speaking.

When she finally looked up, she felt an even stronger current of energy race through her. This time, without reservation, she carefully studied Victor's face.

"I just asked for this information this morning," she whispered. "I can't believe *you* are the one bringing it to me."

"Chivalry is not altogether dead," he quipped gallantly, taking an exaggerated bow from his chair. "After all, would the Prince of Darkness go to the bookstore to read about psychic phenomenon?" he teased warmly.

"No, I suppose not. Well . . . if Nana says you're all right, then I guess you do have *some* redeeming quality." She smiled back, truly delighted by the wealth of information Victor had provided.

"Your grandmother? I thought you didn't have any living relatives, other than your brother Gerald?"

"I don't. She passed away years ago. But somehow I know she answered my prayer this morning . . . to find out more about this stuff."

"Good, then we can get started with some exercises to test where you are now and to strengthen your ability. But I have to tell you that one of the biggest things we have to work on is harnessing your fears, and most definitely that *temper!* Although I must confess that I love the way your fiery mind torches everything in its wake."

Looking at her with a big grin, Victor laughed and shook his head. "See! Look at you! Right there . . . there it is again. You're as angry as a wet hen, and we haven't even begun! Your eyes have practically changed color!" He roared with laughter.

"I'm glad that you find my disposition so amusing," she said, feeling the irritation rising in her voice as she sipped her brew.

Still chuckling, Victor reached over and took one of the books back from her, donning a pair of reading glasses that she hadn't noticed resting on the nearby lamp-stand.

"Hmmm, let me see, . . . Ah, here it is," he said. "You may read for yourself that old Victor is not trying to do any behavior modification or mind control on his partner. Or, trying to get you to join a cult. I'm just stating the facts."

Skimming the text, she returned the book to Victor, her ire subdued. She had to exercise moderation. The facts spoke for themselves.

"So you mean that I'm actually scattering valuable energies when I get angry or frightened? And if I focus these explosive emotions, I could put them to better use?"

"It appears so. Although I'm not sure that I want to be the target of such a direct attack again. I definitely do not want to experience a heart attack while still in the prime of my life," he reprimanded with a smile.

In defense, Liza dropped her gaze. "I told you that I was sorry yesterday," she murmured without looking at him. She still wasn't ready to revisit that portion of their discussion.

Undaunted, Victor continued to chastise her. "Yes, but as you get better at this, you might be apologetically dropping a rose on my casket. So, you will *have* to learn to contain yourself, Liza. From what I can understand, this is sort of like the martial arts. You might be able to rip out your opponent's heart, but restraint and harmony must be the foundation for your actions. And Liza, I'm not your opponent. Otherwise, it would be like giving a loaded gun to a child," he continued more seriously.

That phrase rang a bell. Hadn't she said something similar about Ron, using that very metaphor? Contrite, Liza shifted in her chair. She had been furious at both Victor and Ron yesterday, but she most certainly didn't want to harm anybody. Funny thing was . . . Ron hadn't been affected. Victor most definitely had. Yet she couldn't understand why Victor wanted to help her. Rather than using her probe, she asked him.

"Can we talk, Victor? Just straight up?"

"I was hoping that we could eventually get to that point."

"Question number one: Why are you the only person who can ever feel a result of my probe? No one else seems to be affected or even notice."

Victor sat back and grew serious, studying her face carefully. His intense gaze made her wonder if he also had the same gift.

"From what I've read, certain people have more sensitivity to it than others . . . especially where there's a link. Even a past bond."

"But we just met each other."

"In this lifetime, maybe."

"What?" She stared at him.

"I'm not a fanatic, and this subject matter is as new to me as it is to you. I'm just telling you what I've read, and I still remain skeptical . . . although my brush with a heart attack was enough for me to respect what I don't know. But admit it, Liza; haven't you felt something undefinably familiar between us? An eerie *déjà vu* . . . especially during our more personal encounter."

Liza examined the rim of her china saucer, tracing it with a finger. The nervous gesture was her only defense. She didn't want to talk about that evening.

"I thought you wanted complete honesty. No games."

He was baiting her again, and if he only knew what a fleeting thought about their lovemaking did to her equilibrium . . .

"Past lives," she evaded. "I had never considered the possibility of unfinished business in that regard. It does hold certain possibilities that clarify things."

Victor chuckled, accepting her evasion. "Okay. Possible, but no way to prove, and probably not even relevant to the more pressing matters at hand."

"Then given all the dangers, why are you doing this . . . reading about psychic phenomena? Especially when we have so many real things to deal with at the moment?"

Victor studied her face, his expression tortured. He had lost his previously teasing smile. To date, his actions had been erratic and mysterious. If he wanted to gain her trust, he'd have to include her in and share all his data on the Chem Tech deal. If he didn't come clean now, she wouldn't commit.

Leaning forward, Victor extended his arms across the table and covered her hands beneath his. The unexpected action was so forward and earnest that she could only stare at him.

"A while ago, Liza, you said that you and I were very much alike . . . and I agreed. My interest in the Chem Tech project has absolutely nothing to do with the money . . . hard though that may be to believe. This is a matter of justice."

His eyes burned with a sudden seriousness as he looked at her directly and spoke. "Go ahead; turn it on. Look at me, and do not turn away from what you see . . . because we both need each other now to beat them. I am convinced our pairing was not some freak coincidence. There has to be *complete* trust between us."

As Liza leaned forward, her knees brushed his under the table, and he openly braced himself as if expecting an intense evaluation.

"Liza, I have a hunch that some of the same people who were instrumental in destroying your family were also instrumental in the murder of mine," he said just above a whisper. "Although your tragedy culminated in the late seventies, my horror began a decade or so before yours."

Victor knew that he had to tell her. There was no way around it. He stood up and paced toward the large living room window that overlooked the marina, watching the water lash against the rocks that rose behind the house. It helped him to think. How could he determine how much he really needed to reveal about the details of his life? Although Liza's probe seemed to be on at full tilt, he would only give her a surface explanation. That plan made sense. Under any circumstance, the subject had always been too difficult to really discuss.

With nervous resolve, he began again as Liza sat quietly. She appeared to absorb each thought before it had even formed in his mind. The sensation was eerie, but compelling.

"My father was an extremely wealthy man, Liza," he said quietly, hesitating as he watched her expression.

Her look was not one of judgment, but of understanding, making him feel safe to continue. "He had several very successful ventures, from vineyards to mining. Perhaps that's why I'm so partial to good wines . . . but wealth and power has its price," he added sadly.

"I've found that everything has a price, Victor," she returned with a pained expression.

Feeling a little more comfortable, he decided to tell her more. He knew that he could trust Liza, and she had told him as much about herself the day before. It was the first time that he had dared to approach the topic with anyone, except Helyar. Even they hadn't talked about it in years. Looking at Liza carefully, he began again slowly.

"In 1968, the government in Peru was changing. The only

thing that saved my life was that I was abroad at school. Certain factions wanted my father, as I'm told by his best friend, André Helyar, to allow his vineyard operations to produce a *sure* cash crop: Cocaine. It was a good way to generate off-balance-sheet capital. His vineyards provided a perfect cover; however, when he refused, they were confiscated. The new regime also had to find a way to accept large shipments of arms. Since my father's loading docks were above suspicion, they wanted him to allow the contraband to be hidden among the supplies that he imported for his international mining operations."

"But don't they have free elections there now? That was almost twenty years ago. . . . It's not still a military dictatorship, is it?"

"No. Things have changed."

Reflexively, Victor took a deep breath to fight the nausea rising in his stomach. He never talked about these events because the memory was too painful.

"You see, Liza, the U.S. had come up with a foreign-aid policy that prohibited the transfer of monies to developing nations that were actively engaged in weapons buildup. So, if a country wanted and needed U.S. funds but also wanted to build up their armament, they had to develop creative solutions to the problem. Your father's swing vote in '68 was probably the one that made such legislation possible. Ironic, isn't it?"

Unable to tell his story and take Liza's active probe at the same time, he strode to the extensive bar near the far wall to pour himself a drink. He rarely allowed himself anything stronger than wine, and he was even moderate in his consumption of that libation. But he felt an old depression resurfacing. To stem the emotion, he crossed his legs and leaned against the bar for support. Studying the concerned expression on Liza's face, he took an angry shot of vodka that seemed to make her flinch. The bitter substance burned the back of his throat as he swallowed, but he needed something to steady his nerves as he told her about this travesty of justice.

"In return, they would allow my father to remain on *la haci-*

enda, where he could stay wealthy, and remain alive." He laughed bitterly, staring into the bottom of his empty glass. "Only my father, quite like yours, Liza, was too honest for his own well-being. He believed that honesty would prevail. He knew that, in all likelihood, despite the coup, General Alvarado was not directly aware of how his *caudillos*—military strongmen—were financing the unrest. Not to mention, lining their own pockets. So, against André's advice, my father tried to get this information to the general. However, as you say . . . the way the story goes . . . on his way to meet with the general, he had an *unfortunate* car accident. And as one would expect, according to the coroner's report, it was death by natural causes. But the report neglected to mention the bullets that were lodged in his chest cavity and skull. And more coincidentally, as fate would have it, *la hacienda* had an unfortunate fire in the adjoining carriage house—where my mother, sister, younger brother, and cousin just happened to be visiting that day. My godfather said that from the way the bodies were found, they had obviously been bound by the military police and left without any chance of escaping the inferno."

Liza's eyes brimmed with tears, and she swallowed hard. "Victor, I am so very sorry," she said softly, consumed by his grief. "I understand now. This was the darkness that I saw around you. The pain. No wonder you didn't let me trespass there . . . I am deeply, deeply, sorry . . ." Her voice trailed off as she looked down at her hands.

"Liza, I was a nineteen-year-old student in my senior year, ready to graduate from college with honors. I was supposed to fly home that afternoon when I received the call from Helyar. The only reason I hadn't flown home to Peru a day earlier was because I was indulging my hormones with my current girlfriend in London. I had given my cousin François, my plane ticket, and he arrived the day I was originally destined to be there. Of course, my parents insisted that he stay with them instead of at his villa, since his own father would not be coming for another day or so. Because of my lack of restraint, I lost my entire family without even being able to look on them one last time."

Liza watched him in silence. The pain that he had so expertly disguised was ripping him apart, contorting his insides without mercy as he struggled to sound detached.

"This is why I never allow myself to overindulge. The price is too high for the momentary pleasure. Self-control must be exerted at all times. This is why you present such a risk. I have no control around you."

"Victor, you *cannot* blame yourself for what happened to your family. If you had been there, you would have been killed, too. God must have had a purpose for sparing your life."

He noted how she avoided the last portion of what he had said. Her comment made him smile sadly, and her gaze held a fervent expression that almost begged him to let her in. Her voice sounded so earnest that he wanted to believe she cared. It had been so long since anyone had cared. Too long since he had cared. Yet that emotion only made people weak and dependent, and he was neither. But he recognized a kindred soul . . . someone who had walked through the same hell-fire and had come out alone.

Although there was more to tell, he couldn't respond to Liza now, fearing that his voice might tremble and betray him. Instead, he filled his glass with vodka again, and took another forceful shot. He wanted to stop, but felt compelled to go on. Even without her magnet, there was something so natural about sharing this pain with Liza.

Steadying himself, he continued haltingly. "I knew when you told me about your family that you could appreciate the level of devastation. Perhaps, we have been through the same nightmare. . . . I know we're fighting the same demons. Before you even told me, it was in your eyes, Liza. You had the same look on your face that I'm sure I did when Helyar came to London to collect me."

He held up his hand to stop her from speaking. He couldn't look at her as he continued. It was just too hard. "Helyar tried

to tell me this, too . . . that I shouldn't blame myself. But I hated
that the change in government was heralded in the world press
as a bloodless coup. My family had paid in blood, yet their deaths
were considered legitimate accidents . . . not direct military as-
sassinations. He has kept me out of Peru since that time for my
own safety. Otherwise, the government would have made me
disappear."

His hands were trembling and he considered more vodka, then
changed his mind. Drawing a deep breath, he went on, this time
with more control. "For six years, Liza, I was a wreck. Chess
was the only thing that saved my sanity and helped me learn to
control my rage. I was much like you during that time. Angry.
Self-destructive. And openly volatile. Helyar helped me to understand the benefit of employing patience and strategy to get
what I wanted."

Victor fell silent. Liza had a way of siphoning the truth from
his innermost regions, and he was unnerved by the short time
it had taken her to get past his most formidable barriers. He
wanted to stop—to fight the descent into caring. But as she sat
quietly and gazed at him so openly, he had to go on. It wasn't
her ability to probe, it was her ability to care that moved him.

"Geneva was good therapy. I sank my energies into learning
the martial arts; the game I love so dearly, chess; and rebuilding
my inheritance by playing the Big Board on Wall Street. Same
difference. Games. They nationalized eighty million dollars of
my father's assets, Liza. They took everything—in the form of
land, mineral rights, plant and equipment, bank accounts, an-
tiques—*everything* that had been in our family for generations.
I narrowly escaped only because I wasn't in the right place at
the wrong time. Maybe it was fate. Now, I'm the one who sounds
superstitious."

Swiftly, the familiar icy detachment that had always served
as his barrier closed around him. He could not stay this vulnerable. His voice suddenly took on a menacing tone, and Liza
seemed frightened.

"Victor, what do you want now? I mean, how do you expect

me to help you?" she asked, appearing afraid of his possible answer.

It annoyed him that she still couldn't understand how her ability could be used to solve the equation. Hadn't he said enough?

"We have a mutual enemy . . . or, more accurately, enemies, Liza," he responded coldly. "When I finally pulled myself together, I began playing the market. André had only been able to smuggle out a few things when he fled the country. One such treasure was my mother's priceless diamond-and-topaz earrings. I used them along with my dwindling education account in Switzerland for collateral to rebuild my portfolio. By the time I got to Harvard, I was already fairly well established financially, although older than most grad students. But I needed the student visa in order to enter the United States."

Liza's look was incredulous. "Do you mean to say you've been tracking this situation since the mid-seventies . . . when you finally pulled yourself together?" The shock was clearly recognizable by her expression. "I'm in total awe of your tenacity. I thought I was bad."

"Quite right," he said evenly. "I met Ed and Stan at school. They're good friends—my best friends—and now my business partners. I, too, have to trust those I do close business with. I've had to leave the others behind for safety. They aren't even aware of my real ambitions. You and André are the only ones who know. That's trust, Liza. Uncompromising trust. And, with it comes a cost . . . as you have said. Breach it, and I'll deal with you. Understood?"

Liza nodded her head slowly. She seemed too calm.

"As a graduate-school intern, I stumbled upon some information which led me to believe that Chem Tech was a front for this smuggling operation."

Without warning, in a mercurial explosion that shattered his restraint, he crossed the room and grabbed her to her feet by both arms. The sudden aggression bewildered her, and the confusion shone in her eyes. He didn't care. His patience had reached its limit. It was simple. He had to make her understand how serious the situation had become.

"You don't get this, do you? Don't you see, Liza, DGE was supposed to get the bid alone so I could get the rest of the information I needed to hang these bastards! Your firm ruined everything when you entered the bid late and took the controlling interest. At first, I hated you for the intrusion and would have eliminated you by any means necessary! But you still aren't following, are you? When we were younger, we posed no threat. Then both of us, on our own, unaware of the other, started asking questions and making inquiries. So, they baited us with the contract and brought us closer to their operations, where they could control us."

"What? *They know who we are?* I can't believe—"

"We both thought that we were being so clever, but key people in this firm have been manipulating our families for almost thirty years! Don't you find it odd that we, the descendants of the victims, won the bid? It's painfully obvious to me that it's all been a setup. And after we finish the job, they'll finish us . . . as the last surviving remnants of their dirty deals. They'll wipe us out, and their tracks will be completely covered."

Liza covered her mouth in horror. He could see that he had finally gotten through.

"Don't panic; we're not beaten yet. They don't know that we have this information. All we need is a plan. I'm formulating one with Helyar, when he's available during the next couple of weeks. I told you before that I wouldn't let them hurt you, Liza. I couldn't bear to have anyone else's blood on my hands."

Although his fury and revelation had frightened her, his pain seemed to make her open to absorb the information. Liza's warm, brown eyes softened him, and he dove into the limpid pools for comfort. They emanated a strange calm that drained the tension from his body, making him slump against her shoulder for support. She brought her arms up around the expanse of his back and stroked his shoulders and the nape of his neck.

"How can I help, Victor?" she whispered again as he shook his head woefully.

"Maybe I'm just so desperate for an answer," he intoned raggedly, "that I'm clinging to straws. But I just know that there had to be a reason we were thrown together."

They both stood for a while, not speaking, and he allowed Liza to caress the hurt away from his body. It was as if she instinctively knew that he needed human contact, to be held in order to heal and close the wound that his confession had re-opened.

"Your hands have a healing quality, one that cleanses the soul, Liza. I haven't felt like this in years," he breathed against the softness of her neck.

He lifted his face to kiss her, but she stopped him, lightly touching her fingers to his lips. "Confession cleanses the soul, Victor. Not this."

"I thought you weren't a Catholic."

She let the comment pass; and with a wave of resignation, he relaxed his hold on her.

Reluctantly, he let her move away from him, and she returned to her seat in front of the board. "Do you have any part of the plan figured out yet?" she asked quietly, trying to shift his focus back to Chem Tech.

As he returned to his chair, he couldn't take his eyes off her or stop worrying that it might be too dangerous to involve her. But she was already a target. The question was, could he protect her?

"Liza, first we have to be able to name all the senior-level players. Then, we have to get indisputable evidence: Plant sites, shipment dates, warehouses, land leases, bank deposits . . . anything that legitimizes our claims. We will have to have a way to simultaneously alert the proper authorities and press so that Chem Tech doesn't have time to cover their tracks. Finally and, I suppose, most importantly, we will have to figure out a way to vanish . . . if we want to live."

"Victor," she began hesitantly, "I guess I still don't understand how my ability can help."

Watching Liza's mind career from each of the points he had laid before her, suddenly he wasn't sure how she could help either. His reasons now seemed remote, and his logic felt speculative at best. Now everything appeared to be a blur of conjecture. All he could do at this point was to appeal to his original assessment of her potential skill. Gut instinct.

"Liza, listen to me. Every good lead that I've ever had, even playing the market, came from a well-confirmed hunch. You might be able to save valuable time, as well as the possibility of exposure, by concentrating on names, locations, dates, anything that will close the loop. If your feeling is strong on something, we'll follow it and get the necessary evidence to confirm it. The time we could save will be vital. The part that has stumped me for years is the Washington connection. Who is helping to get the arms out of the country, and how are they hiding their payoff?"

He fell silent, searching her face, wondering if she still wanted in on the plan.

"This will be dangerous, Victor. And what if I'm not as good as you think? I could send you out on a wild-goose chase and accidentally get somebody killed. I don't know if I could handle that."

Liza's face was completely open, not judgmental; she merely stated the facts.

"And the part about vanishing . . . How long would it be until I could return home?" she asked. "Honestly, the thought of having to leave behind all that I cherish . . ."

He understood her dilemma all too well and respected her too much to be evasive about this critical point.

"Liza, do you remember when I asked you about Gerald and other living relatives? I was secretly relieved when you told me that you had none and that Gerald's time was short. It was not out of callousness, but out of concern. Because, quite possibly, you might never be able to return; and for their safety, you would never be able to contact them. If you decide to go after the people who ruined your father, you will have the tiger by the tail. Liza, this thing that brings together your battle and mine, is much larger than either of us originally imagined."

He watched her take a deep sigh of resignation as she openly struggled with the turmoil of leaving.

"And what about my firm . . . and the people who depend on me? I may not have family, but I do have dear friends." She was pleading, as if trying to make him understand.

He refused to soften the truth. No games. "Then you must provide for them before you fully embark. There may be ways . . . but it could prove too dangerous. Write a will, and be sure that you have an executor that you can trust. Leave them what they'll need to rebuild. They'll miss you; that part is unavoidable. But at least, they'll survive. You won't, and they might not, if you try to contact them after you've gone into hiding."

He wrestled with the same dilemma, much more than she probably realized, and he hated to be the catalyst to force her to make this deeply personal decision.

"Liza, this will be the second time for me. I almost went mad the first time. Perhaps, that's why I haven't forged any bonds that would devastate me if they had to be broken. I've managed to keep my relationships on a fairly surface level, to date, all except Helyar; and I've paid the price dearly for the lack of human connection to anyone or anything."

The more he told her, the more she absorbed his loneliness. The vacant expression in her eyes made him want to hold her, to gather her up in his arms. In truth, he needed Liza to comfort him again. Anything to stop this pain. He saw such blatant empathy etched across her face that he was sure that she was the only person in the world who could heal the gaping wounds left by the isolation.

Confessing to her, he offered himself up, opening his soul to her for full view. "You see, the first time was in Geneva. Since

they found my cousin's charred body in the burned-out rubble
of the cottage, they assumed that they had wiped out all of the
immediate Duarte family. I didn't even have to change my name.
I just couldn't return home to risk the possibility of being recognized. At least that's what I thought until you told me of your
vendetta against Chem Tech. That's when I realized they know
exactly who I am. This time, when I go into hiding, I will grieve
the loss of Ed and Stan's companionship—they are dear friends.
But we will all recover in time, and I will position them well
financially. What else can I do?"

"I have to think about this, Victor. There's so much at stake.
I don't bond easily either, having been so terribly disappointed
in the past myself. But those few people who are close to me
are more valuable than anything in the world," she whispered.

The reality of their situation sank in slowly. Renewed terror
flashed in Liza's eyes, and he could tell that she had suddenly
become fearful for her friends' safety. But she had to understand
how dangerous this was. They were probably already in too deep
because of Ron's break-in. Liza had to make a choice. She could
drop her idea of seeking revenge and let him go on unencumbered or she could do it the way it had to be done. She had
options. He didn't.

Liza looked like a deer caught in headlights as she persisted.
"I can't imagine never seeing Ron's mischievous face or hearing the lilt of Connie's voice or, worse—much worse, I'd never
get over leaving Letty. She's been like a sister throughout the
years."

Sighing from the mental fatigue, he considered her position
and tried to gentle his voice. "This is a deeply personal decision
that only you can make, Liza. I respect the struggle. You must
understand that I am not asking you to make this decision. I will
never take the responsibility for your isolation—only to have
you hate me for tearing you away from those that you love."
Telling her the truth plainly was the only way to make her fully
understand.

"Then why are we here? Why am I here—trying to learn how to increase my powers of perception for this project?"

Her questions unveiled the confusion that had to be eliminated before they could proceed. Now all of the cards had to be out on the table. There was no room for evasion, and he had to dump the truth in her lap without reservation.

Proceeding without caution, he restated his position. "Liza, when I saw that we had a mutual enemy, I knew that your passion to avenge your family would make you go after these people with ferocity, but with naivete. Let's face it, you're a rookie. I also knew that you had only solved one small piece of the puzzle. In your anger, you might cause *the machine* some consternation—but you wouldn't stop it. You're no match for them alone. More than likely, they would break you, or kill you . . . and I couldn't bear to see that happen. On a more selfish note, I knew that your angry, erratic moves would destroy my chances of completing the mission I began over twenty years ago. I was not about to let you do that either. So, the only logical solution would be to join forces."

He couldn't read Liza's expression. She stared at him blankly, as if she were somewhere far off in the distance. Oddly, she didn't seem to be fighting him anymore.

"Liza, you have to decide whether or not righting the wrongs of the past is worth it."

Victor had forced his voice to remain even. He wanted Liza to know that his warning was real. The brutal honesty of his words had returned her to the room, but she didn't seem angry. Just very, very sad.

"I understand. . . . Justice of this magnitude has its price. But up until now, I guess, I never really faced that part of it," she admitted quietly. "Frankly, I'm torn. I could live a relatively normal, happy life—the price, backing down from an extreme personal injustice. Or I could die satisfied. I don't know, Victor. I just don't know."

He respected that she openly confided in him about her indecision. He'd let her know how much her truthfulness meant to him later, but she'd have to come to some conclusion very soon.

Eleven

Despite the sunshine that cut through the flawless blue sky, it was still a brisk day. She was glad that they had taken a break. Both of them needed some air—some space away from the grave issues that faced them.

As they made their way down the back staircase, the wind whipped wildly, catching the ankle-length hem of Liza's military-olive raincoat and pulling her along to quicken her pace. Before they'd even approached the dock, the salty mist had begun to sting her nose. Breathing in deeply, she let her gaze scan the horizon.

So much had happened in twenty-four hours. She reeled at the magnitude of the changing landscape of her reality. Although she had prayed for years to be in a position to finally avenge her family, now that the perfect opportunity presented itself, she was afraid. It meant an entire life-change, a personal nova. Maybe this day would be the day of reckoning. One question remained: Was she prepared to die for her principles? Shivering at the thought, she stared at the water. Victor Duarte certainly seemed to have no trouble with that concept.

"Are you cold?" Victor asked in a quiet voice as they neared their destination.

He had asked her that before, and she wondered if he remembered. Liza shook off another shiver that was not caused by the cold air and stuffed her hands into her pockets.

"No, this is breathtaking," she replied, trying to give her mind a rest. "The view of the horizon seems endless."

"And so are the possibilities, Liza," he returned softly, as though off in the distance himself.

"I wish you could see some of the real beauty that the rest

of the world has to offer. There are some spectacular sights that are etched in my mind forever, but that, I'm sorry to say, I may never see again," he added, his tone resonant with sadness.

Victor hadn't looked at her when he spoke. He was obviously travelling to a beautiful place far away.

"Paradise, Victor?" she asked quietly, eager for some unknown reason to mentally travel there with him.

"Yes. Some of the most magnificent waterfalls; lush, dense, tropical forests; breathtaking mountains; turquoise-blue skies; vast untouched wastelands that look like lunar landscapes here on earth . . . a million years or more of evolution that could disappear within our lifetime, and I may never get to show it to you."

Returning from his mental journey, Victor turned to face her. His gaze held hers as he studied her face. It was as though he were trying to recognize something, or someone. Or, perhaps, he was trying to burn her into his memory, just like the other scenes that made him so sad. The sensation that his penetrating look caused was all too familiar. The feeling brought an exquisite new dimension to the hollow in her soul. As he stared at her, stray wisps of hair caught in the breeze and whipped about her cheeks. Without breaking their gaze, he reached out and brushed the hair away from her face.

"Liza, what I'm about to say may sound crazy, but somehow, when I think of those places, they seem to require you. You're a natural part of that landscape, just like the flora that makes it so beautiful. It's as if your soul has been there for a thousand years and somehow, by some bizarre accident, you wound up here." Victor shook his head, perplexed, then asked, "Do you understand what I'm saying?"

There was no real answer that she could give to satisfy his question. But she understood the feeling very well. She had felt the pull when he'd told her of those places. It was as if she could imagine all that he described even though she had never actually witnessed the scene herself.

"I don't know, Victor. There are people who believe that we

have all lived somewhere else before, yet we're only able to remember bits and pieces. Reincarnation. Others believe that each generation carries the total mind experience of all of the preceding generations, which they believe can be tapped into for current knowledge. I just wish that so much hadn't been lost during all the wars and conquests. That destruction resulted in such a waste of intellectual property and humanity . . . which might have possibly provided surer answers today."

"Ah, yes . . . the conquests . . . the ugly side of power."

Victor put his arm around her shoulder, temporarily blocking the wind. She had to admit that his warmth felt wonderful, if not like a blanket of protection.

"I was hoping that the weather would hold out a little longer. I was looking forward to taking the *Phoenix* out of her slip today, but I fear that the waters are too choppy. Perhaps, we'll be blessed with an Indian summer for another few weeks."

Again, he had skillfully changed the subject. Victor's evasive posture could always be counted on when a delicate topic had been broached. Liza smiled. Again, he was right. They were very much alike. He was just as nervous as she was, and she no longer felt trapped or cornered by him. She now understood that there was nothing easy about this for him either.

When she had raised one eyebrow and tilted her head, questioning his comment about the boat, Victor had only smiled shyly. Of course he would have a boat in the marina. Why not? Why else would he live way out here? It hadn't occurred to her, but it made sense. Then in an instant, she saw something way off in the distance that made her blink. It looked like a large wooden vessel with broad sails. But the ship wasn't modern. It was like something out of a pirate movie. Dear God, was it happening again?

"You have a ship?" she offered weakly, trying to stem the vision.

Victor laughed. "No, I wouldn't exactly call it a ship. It's a forty-five footer, but it is my one extravagance," he admitted, "to an otherwise moderate life. *She's* beautiful, though."

Affection weighted Victor's every word, and the way he looked out into the water with longing when he spoke about his boat made her smile. She was sure that the *Phoenix* was probably the only real woman that Victor had cared about in his life.

"Do you get out on it much?" she asked, thankful for a benign topic of conversation.

"No, not as much as I'd like to. With the travel and pace that I keep to run the business, sometimes I almost miss the season without even a day on her."

"Then what made you buy a boat, when you travel so much? Isn't it expensive to keep a boat harbored, especially one that you don't use?"

Victor nodded, and his expression had become wistful again. "It is an extravagance, as I said before. But Liza, when I saw her with her sails up and the blue Caribbean water all around her, she took my breath away. It was the flawless wood cabins that made me have to have her. The master cabin is appointed with early Spanish antiquity. You'd just have to see her . . ."

They both stared at each other for a moment, allowing the reference to the wood cabins to fall between the empty space where there were no words.

The passion in Victor's voice that was directed toward the inanimate female object in the water made Liza's smile broaden. Little boys and their toys. It was an endearing quality, really. Victor's expression held the same look of awe and fascination that children have on Christmas morning. She suddenly felt the pull to tease him, wanting to keep him immersed in childlike splendor for a while longer. He seemed so relaxed and so utterly at peace that the earlier conversations almost vanished.

Peering at him with a sheepish grin, she teased, "See, Victor, not all overindulgences are bad. So, tell me how you two first met. Was it in a past life?"

His return smile made her chuckle. She could tell Victor wanted to tell her, but that he'd probably feared that he'd bore her. His hopeful expression had clued her in, not her probe, and his now-excited look told her she'd been right.

"After I made my first million, as I said before, I indulged myself. I bought her as a personal badge of survival . . . and so named her as a toast to having come back from the ashes myself. You should see her when she's on the open sea! The wind, the salt air, the sky . . . There's just nothing like it. But the water here is just not blue enough to do her justice . . ."

Victor was gone again, and this time she allowed him to travel alone, settling into the warmth of his arm as it lay across her shoulders. She could almost envision the *Phoenix*, but the vision of Victor at the helm was even clearer.

Finally, he returned from his mental voyage with obvious reluctance, drawing her closer as the wind began to whip fiercely again.

"We should probably go back inside to eat," he said grudgingly. "Then, let's try to get something done before it gets too late and we both get too tired to think."

Victor, as always, was a pragmatist. It never failed to amaze her that he could abruptly wrench himself back to reality as if he had only been reading the Sunday paper. With her, the process was much different. When she journeyed through her mind, each sensation heightened the next until she was totally transported. Her return was always just as deliberate, allowing each memory to slowly dissipate, leaving her grounded. If she were jolted back before she was ready, it affected her mood for the rest of the day and left her slightly off-balance and annoyed.

"How in the world do you do that?" she exclaimed. "It would totally jangle my nerves, and you do it *constantly!*"

Victor seemed puzzled. "Did I miss something, Liza? What on earth are you talking about?"

As they began their short hike back to the house, she continued with exasperation. "You can change subjects on a dime. I mean, you can time-travel, then poof! Just like that." She laughed with a snap of her fingers. "You give a weather report."

Victor stopped and looked at her, then chuckled. "Liza, surely you are making too much of my compartmental approach to things."

"No, seriously, Victor. You do it all the time," she protested.

Edging toward what seemed like affection, Victor removed his arm from her shoulders and threaded it under hers around her waist. As they walked, she took in the immaculately landscaped view that bordered the back of the house. She imagined what it might look like in the spring with small purple crocuses splashed amongst fuschia impatiens and vibrant yellow azaleas. But if only for this moment, she enjoyed just being near him.

Still chuckling as they neared the deck stairs, he gave her waist a small pull which brought her in closer. "Then I'll have to remember not to be so formal."

When they entered the spacious, sunlit kitchen, Victor hesitated, as if reluctant to let her go. When her body tensed, he allowed her to slip out of his easy hold. Continuing to tease her as he rummaged around for a couple of sparkling ciders to go with their light meal, he smiled broadly, picked up their food, and led her back toward the living room.

"Come on, let's go sit in here where it's *less formal*," he quipped. "I'll start a fire, and you can tell me all about my bad habits. Rest assured, I'll tell you *all* about yours."

Victor was already on his way out of the room and she trotted behind him. Taking off her coat and plopping down on the floor in front of the large glass coffee table, she continued to belabor her point while he cheerfully built a fire.

"You're not taking me seriously. Really, it's amazing. How did you learn to just sever yourself from your deepest thoughts so easily? Was that part of your martial arts training?"

As the fire began to catch, Victor turned to her with an intrigued expression that she hadn't expected.

"Very perceptive of you, my dear. As a matter of fact, that was partly where I learned self-control. I learned the rest by playing the boards," he said, gesturing to the chess set across the room.

"I only allow myself momentary journeys, or fits of anger, then I regain my perspective—and *self-control*. Then I can move on to develop a strategy, that is, if one is called for. I was hoping to teach you how to do the same."

Victor's smugness would have irritated her before, but now it only made her smile. Something had changed between them. It went beyond a mere truce to something akin to trust. But it did irk her that he was also insinuating that he had checked his passion as well . . . even though she herself was ambivalent on that score . . . for the moment.

Admittedly, he had a point about not allowing one's opponent to read too much, and only that which was absolutely necessary to win. She was a master at this in business negotiations, but had trouble applying the technique to the more personal aspects of her life.

Liza munched the watercress and turkey sandwich in front of her. She watched him closely, arming for the light challenge.

"And you mean to say that there is never an instance when one should be completely open? Or, better stated, is it your position that one should never mind-travel emotionally, then return slowly only after the memory, or the *need,* quietly fades?" she asked, baiting Victor into a game.

Piqued that their passionate encounter seemed to have had little or no after-effect on him, she grew introspective. Just because it blew her away didn't mean that it was such a big deal to him. The bleak thought came out of nowhere, depressing her. *It was probably just stupid, and convenient,* she went on to herself. *What a fool you have become, Liz. What a fool!* It wasn't important now anyway. The stakes had been raised.

Completely unaware of the mental conversation that she was having with herself, Victor answered her more audible question and interrupted her thoughts.

"Correct, even if one is laid vulnerable momentarily, complete control of the recovery is essential," he said with caution, becoming wary of the change in her mood during the discussion.

The hit was too close. Victor's answer could have referred to more than some hypothetical circumstance. They were back to double entendres again. Liza let her shoulders slump. For a brief moment she'd actually thought that they'd gotten past games. She had to pull herself together and let the arousing effect he was having on her dissipate. He was not about to make her lose control again, even if they did partner on the Chem Tech problem.

"I will have to work on that." She'd decided on a noncommittal stance while she contemplated the multiple applications of Victor's answer.

Wary, Victor took a seat across from her on the floor at the opposite side of the table. As he began to eat, Liza offered another benign question.

"Then, when we begin our exercises today, will you show me how to do it?"

She was leaving options open, but she also hoped he wouldn't sense it. It was crazy. . . . She wanted him, yet didn't want him to know that she wanted him . . . at least not without his establishing that he wanted her first—beyond the physical. It was making her head hurt and she chastised herself. There were more important things to deal with. Now, *she* was the one playing games!

But she had to know where the earlier passion had come from. Had it been his way of compromising her? Ensuring that she'd side with him and not make waves for his mission? Or had he actually felt something? Maybe it was just pent-up frustration and she was available at the time? He'd said himself that he didn't get close to anyone. But then, neither did she. Maybe she could, just to show the arrogant male before her that there was more than one way to play. She knew how to play chess, and poker to boot. Very, very *well*.

"Of course, I will," Victor went on after a pause, eyeing her suspiciously. "After all, that is why we are here. I know that you understand how the pieces move on a chessboard, but that's not the art of the game. The real game is the strategy, which includes patience and self-discipline. It's not necessary to take every piece just because it's open, which may be a trap, ultimately laying you vulnerable at a critical stage in the tournament."

She nearly choked on her sandwich. Could he be reading *her?* Steadying her gaze, she let him continue uninterrupted and acted as if she were hanging on his every word.

"Another element of the game is analysis," Victor went on with an air of unshakable confidence. "Being able to collate many variables in your mind at one time in order to see a pattern unfolding is important even before your opponent makes a move. Finally, concentration and perception are key. Without them, you cannot keep track of all the variables. This is why this game is ideal for developing your gift."

An arrogant, charming chauvinist she thought, now fully engaged to do friendly battle. Since it was going to be a light-hearted test of wills, she wanted to see just how good Victor was at maintaining his concentration—especially since he seemed so bent on testing hers. Plus, it would be a welcomed diversion from the very real problems that they faced. If she were going to be his partner, then damnit, he'd respect her!

"I think I might enjoy this . . . and I don't think you'll beat me." She smiled.

"I see." He returned the challenge with obvious delight. "I was hoping that there would be some sport to what could otherwise be a laboriously boring lesson."

"No, boring is the least of your worries," she said, taking a sip of sparkling cider to make her point.

"We'll only play a game or two." He chuckled. "Then I'm sending you packing with some homework tonight. We can continue tomorrow, after you've done some necessary reading and have had enough time to regroup."

Victor had flipped the last comment over his shoulder with confidence as he rose and strode toward the massive, marble board. Liza stifled the urge to chuckle as she placidly walked over to join him. *Mistake, Duarte.* Mustering up her most innocent expression, she made herself appear quite doe-eyed and ready for the slaughter. Basic feminine technique. *The fundamentals, my brother. How quickly we forget.* Studying the board critically, she never looked up as she slowly turned on her probe.

She focused one half of her attention on the board and the other half on Victor. Detach. Compartmentalize. Steady. He was probably right: Patience was the key. Just as the texts said. But the fact that he might be right annoyed her no end. Shaking off the distracting irritation, she fine-tuned her strategy. Employing moderation, she would gradually increase the wattage until it was in full force. She had never tried it before. This would be a test run. Okay, it was an experiment. But he was the one who had said he was curious about her gift. So, that couldn't be so wrong.

Besides, it was exhilarating to engage someone who both understood and appreciated her secret. She truly marveled at Victor's keen mind, despite his sometimes rigid position on things. It was odd, but she felt that she could sit there for hours, challenged and stimulated by the new concepts that he shared with her. She knew he respected her on many levels; but then, on others, she wasn't quite sure.

However, there was *always* the arrogant assumption on his part that he would win. That's what she had to contend with, and it was the point that she wanted to prove now. She decided that his sure win wouldn't necessarily be so sure. Okay, maybe that was a rationalization. She couldn't worry about the ethics of her test now.

"Don't count your chickens before they're hatched," she cautioned as he took his time to set up the board. *This really might turn out to be fun,* she thought as he turned serious. "Today, I don't intend to play by *your* rules, Mr. Duarte. Let's see if you can teach me about maintaining my concentration without losing yours," she added. Well, forewarned was forearmed. She'd told him. Sort of . . .

"Would you care to place a small wager, *señorita?* I should tell you that I *never* lose on the boards."

Victor's eyes were alight with challenge, and it made her giggle.

"You keep your concentration, and you get to keep the extra thirty percent you owe my firm."

"Ha! Back to the money again, Liza? Well then, for such a healthy wager, what do I win if *you* lose?"

Terror coursed through her momentarily. She hadn't really thought of the flip side. She had just been getting in a rhetorical dig.

Victor's eyes burned her and his smile twisted into a wanton grin. "Let's see. . . . What could be worth a few million? Hmm. Well, clearly, I don't need the money. And I could be assassinated at a moment's notice. . . . So, I'll have to make this something *really* special. Perhaps I'll invoke my ducal rights and decide what I want later. Fair enough?"

"No way. I never enter into an agreement blind-sided. State your wager or the deal's off," she hedged, becoming nervous but still enjoying the game.

"All right, Ms. Nichols. You drive a hard bargain. Shall I settle for stabilized peace, since I have the unfair advantage here? I'll teach you how to play first and allow you to learn some technique before placing a firm wager. After all, I am a gentleman. Then, if we play a second game, I'll raise the stakes. Does that meet with your approval?"

"We'll see." She chuckled. "Let's understand how much of an advantage you really have first. Then, I'll decide."

Victor's smile was infectious, and she had to admit that she was thrilled by his willingness to be a guinea pig for her experiment. But there was no way that she was going to let him win. He had thrown down the gauntlet again—in her court, no less! Nope. Out of the question. It would be strictly business.

Their chess match labored on as she passed up several opportunities to take the few pawns that Victor purposely left vulnerable to her. He seemed even more astonished when she passed up one of his bishops.

Unable to contain himself, he questioned her moves. "Liza, you do know that is a fairly significant piece?"

"Uhmmm," she answered coolly. "I have a strategy, *señor.*"

Her probe was on at full tilt, but it was having the reverse affect of ruining *her* concentration instead of his. As the time wore on, she wondered if teaching him a lesson would be worth it.

What was she doing now? Victor wondered.

He couldn't follow Liza's erratic moves as she passed obvious openings and closed less important ones. The more he tried to force her into snapping up his most cherished pieces, the more she fled from his aggression on the board.

Her reticence in the game was not what he had expected. In all of his dealings with Liza, he had found her confident, direct, and most definitely aggressive. He was becoming frustrated as he took more risks to draw her out, only to have her recede behind an insignificant piece.

As he pursued Liza around the board, he also found his pulse quickening as though he were chasing her around the room. It was unreal. And as she touched each chess piece, he simultaneously felt a feathery pressure that began to melt his concentration.

When the game rounded the first hour, his mind had begun to wander. Almost as a reflex, he began taking in the rosy glow that settled in Liza's cheeks and watching the gentle rise and fall of her bosom as she evenly drew each breath—a lapse of concentration that he couldn't afford now.

Though she never looked up at him while her brow furrowed in analysis over each move, he could barely keep his eyes on the board. As he watched her, he became painfully aware of her light, seductive scent and drew a deep breath to take more of her in. Madness.

Tension rose cruelly in his body, and he swallowed hard to regain his focus. But his efforts were in vain. Looking at Liza now and ignoring the board, he remembered vividly the satin texture of her flawless skin. Worse yet, each time she moved a piece across the board he remembered her touch.

Finally, she made another paced, analytical move on the board, and he hastily returned the play. He had lost interest in the game and had become impatient to get back to his mental wandering. Something was wrong. This was not his normal behavior during a match. This rookie was beating him! His concentration was shot.

When she shifted in her seat, it stirred him. Feeling connected to her every sensation, he realized that the board had lost all relevance. It was absurd, but he wanted her again. However, remembering her diplomatic rebuff, he reluctantly returned his thoughts to the game. Yet each time he began an earnest analysis of the setup, his mind betrayed him. She'd never go for it, would she? He knew better than that and never let women throw him off his game. Ever. Only fools did that. Weak men. What was wrong with him? Yet if only he could touch her again . . .

Liza's voice interrupted his thoughts, and it gave him a start.

"Victor, it's your move," she said calmly.

Maybe too calmly.

He was sure that he had noticed the flicker of a repressed smile before it disappeared. Now he was beginning to see things. In his heightened state of arousal, he had unwittingly begun to process her benign statement as a double entendre. She'd better not be playing with him. Not like this. It wasn't fair!

Almost without looking at the board, he made another distracted move to pursue her king.

Liza knew she was winning, but was it worth it?

This ought to put him away, she thought with pleasure. The mischief swept through her indecently as the idea crystallized. Yet it could be dangerous and it really wasn't fair. But there was, after all, a principle to address. Weighing her options, she gave in to the temptation for a sure win. She had to do it. Victor's challenge had been the final straw. Bragging that he'd never lost on the boards had been a clear invitation to friendly fire. *All's fair in love and war,* she thought. *Okay, here it goes. Heat-seeking missile, Mr. Duarte. End of match. Checkmate.*

With a sultry, nonchalant yawn, Liza stretched and allowed her knees to barely brush Victor's. She envisioned her hips undulating in a slow, sensuous rhythm while on the surface she forced the appearance of being pleasantly engrossed in the game. The sudden intense look that Victor cast in her direction made her stop abruptly. She had to stop. She'd made her point, and this was definitely an abuse of power. Guilt swept through her. She'd never acted in such an irresponsible manner in her life! What had come over her?

Shaking off a tremor of excitement, she chastised herself. She'd gone too far. Okay, fair was fair. The poor guy was only human! For that matter, so was she. Besides, it was time to stop—way before she got accidentally caught up in her own mischief. Victor's intensity was beginning to burn her, and her own concentration was faltering. Damn. She'd done it to herself again.

Perhaps it would be best to just call the game. She would go home, let Victor save face, and allow both contenders to cool off. She could say that she was getting tired and suggest they pick up where they'd left off another day. That way, no one would have to lose. Both people could save face. Now, that was fair.

Offering the alternative of a stalemate, Liza proffered a drowsy truce. "Victor, I'm getting tired, aren't you? How about if we knock off and pick up another time, huh?" she asked, yawning for emphasis.

He seemed irritated. She couldn't tell whether it was due to his frustration or the way he'd sloppily handled the board. She was winning. A woman. That had to bug him.

Rigid in his position, Victor declined her truce. "Developing concentration requires developing endurance, Liza. Afterwards, we'll break."

He was a glutton for punishment! His stubbornness amazed her. Giving him another out, she responded with an intentional double entendre.

"Victor, pushing past the edge of one's endurance can also rob one of concentration, wouldn't you agree? So, if we're both tired, why don't we just call it a day?"

She could tell that Victor was suffering mercilessly as a light current coursed through his body—igniting her own. But she also knew that his machismo now had the best of him and his fierce competitive nature would never allow him to stop the game before it was over. His lack of immediate response confirmed her hunch.

Victor levelled an annoyed look at her. "My concentration *and* endurance are in tact," he said in a tight voice. However, since this is new to you, we should perhaps call it a day at your insistence."

The tide of mischief pulled at her again, and she imagined kissing down his massive chest, mentally stopping along the way to nip his nipples. She was astonished to see them harden under the soft cotton of his tee-shirt as if she'd actually touched him. She almost needed to pinch herself to be sure she'd seen his response—but she had no doubt about her own supercharged reaction. She had had no idea that she could create such a direct link—which explained *everything!*

Interesting discoveries aside, she was piqued by Victor's pretentiousness and his unwillingness to admit that perhaps they were *both* tired. With that in mind, she decided to let him suffer.

"Nah, I'm not thoroughly fatigued. I just thought that you were getting restless, given the wide open moves you were making on the board. I can hang for at least another couple of hours—that is, if you can."

He didn't answer, but stared sullenly at the chess pieces.

There was one drawback to her experimental strategy, however. Victor's energy-pull on her was not to be trifled with. He had his ire up, and his frustration had begun to warm her during their intense exchange.

Picking up on a nonverbal cue without warning, her mind took his mouth slowly into hers. Again, she had become the unwitting victim of her own secret weapon. In response, he moistened his lips involuntarily as his eyes closed to half slits. *This has gone too far!* she lamented to herself, now caught in an unnecessary test of wills.

Since she'd activated her probe with his knowledge but had taken it in a direction that she knew he wouldn't appreciate, she gave him one last chance to disengage from the futile game. Even now as she tried to turn off her power, it seemed to be locked into the "on" position in her brain. *Oh, God. What now?*

This time, when she broached the subject, she was annoyed and much less diplomatic. "Victor, c'mon. Give up. You're hopelessly checkmated from a variety of positions on this board, and you know it. You haven't been concentrating through the duration of this game; admit it. You let me in mentally to track your thoughts—to see if I could play well even though I'm a novice at the game. Well, I proved that I can. So, now either we call this thing off or we sit here for a couple of hours staring at this silly board. What's the problem? Why can't you admit that a woman can handle strategy as well as any man?"

She was exasperated by his urgent need to win—so male!—and that he seemed indignant at the mere suggestion that she might win. Men!

God help him, she was right.

Victor was furious at her impudence . . . or was it that rage was the only acceptable emotion he could vent? He really didn't give a damn what Liza was saying to him, as long as it was yes. But she had, after all, attacked his pride. He was teaching *her,* not the other way around. He'd regain his composure and take no mercy with her on the boards.

Resuming the play, he nearly growled. "It's your move."

"Have it your way," she said with an indifference that bugged him.

Although he would not relent, heaven only knew why, his objectives had become murky. Women! The more frustrated he became, the more surly he became; thinking had become a chore. Suddenly during Liza's move—or was it his?—his mind-set shifted radically.

Without question, he was now completely focused on a singular goal: penetrating Liza—instead of her forces on the board. He no longer valued Liza's king—not when he considered the alternative she presented. It was almost impossible to keep up the facade, but he had never lost on the boards! Ever! And definitely not to a woman. And not because he'd lost his concentration! Damn her gift; he was a pro.

Liza was enjoying her inevitable win. He could feel it. And he was also certain that she was aware of just how much he wanted her. What had all that stretching been about—when her knees had touched his? But, nevertheless, there was the not-so-small matter of pride, which made saving face almost as compelling as Liza's arms.

He had become accidentally transported as the last shred of his concentration peeled away from him. Liza's normal, even breathing reminded him of the quickened whispers and groans that she had expelled into his ear just a day and a half before. His cherished game was not only wearing him out, but getting on his nerves. He took another aggressive move to snare her provocatively unattended king, but he really wanted Liza—more now then he could have ever imagined. Just as he wanted this infernal game to be over.

God is good, Liza thought, offering up a quick prayer.

"Checkmate," she said smugly, but got no response. "Victor . . . are you okay?" she asked with a note of concern. "I said *checkmate,*" she repeated, realizing that he had not even heard her the first time.

Victor looked down at the board with blatant disinterest then returned his gaze to hers, an expression of unabashed desire in his eyes.

"Quite right. I admit it. I seem to have lost my concentration. . . . You win. I defer to that probe of yours. You're good," he confessed, dropping his wall of defense in bewilderment.

Although her conscience was plaguing her, she knew that Victor would be furious if he thought for a moment that she had been toying with him—*that way.* Her main objective was to diplomatically collect the reading materials and leave well before he became more intense.

Until the game was over, she had been able to remain playfully detached from her exercise. But as Victor's desire seemed to overwhelm him, she felt a new urgency she hadn't expected. It wasn't possible. Not again! How had she become ensnared by her own test? As her self-control edged away from her, she struggled to make a graceful exit, vowing never again to toy with Victor's appetites.

She was outta there.

Liza looked for the nearest escape route. Standing up fast, she offered Victor her hand, but he did not respond. He sat motionless, fighting for composure. *I went too far!* she shrieked to herself. *He's practically over the edge.*

Without a word, Victor rose to get her coat and stealthed back to her like a panther. Even though she had finally managed to turn off her probe, it was easy to read the basic, open request on Victor's face. She was drained. Her internal battery was low. Now, she was in trouble.

Skittish, she tried to ignore the tension that hung in the air between them. She averted her eyes from Victor's face, employing the age-old feminine strategy of avoidance.

"Victor, this was very interesting and I look forward to our continued lessons," she managed, deliberately preventing any direct physical contact as she put on her coat.

"I look forward to getting together again as well, Liza. I have since Tuesday."

He'd responded with an open sensuality that definitely did not refer to their chess game. She was in trouble; that much was clear.

While she rummaged in her purse for her keys and returned to the coffee table for the books, Victor stood frozen, burning her with his gaze. Unable to avoid his stare any longer, she looked up and offered a mild protest.

"I really do need to go home."

He didn't answer, but continued to stare at her. She was cornered with no easy out.

"And I really do need for you to stay, Liza."

His voice was a low forceful whisper as he reached to pull her to him.

She'd opened Pandora's box! Why in the world had she used

sex to distract him? Could she hope that some small margin of Victor's self-control remained in tact? She had only meant to slant her advantage on the board, not totally blow him away. Or had she?

Victor nuzzled her hair and kissed her temple. It was the most exquisite sensation. . . . She had to stop him.

The ambivalence that she felt about the relationship, the directions, all so close to her firm . . . everything made her want to cut and run. She wasn't prepared to be swept up in a tide of passion. The issues were too intense, and Victor's all-or-nothing approach to winning *everything* was too much for her to deal with. Her past experiences had made her wary of falling too deep, too fast. Victor was a tidal wave that she was unprepared to handle.

Liza realized abruptly that she had been reeling in Victor's arms and hadn't answered him. The thud of his heartbeat felt like it emanated from inside her own body. She had to pull back, but Victor was beyond shame or discipline. He wouldn't let her go without a struggle. His hands slid down her shoulders and enfolded her, and she melted into his chest. He took her mouth slowly—she made no protest—and his grip tightened. An arc of electricity passed between them. Her heart stopped. She was going to die.

A short, panicked gasp escaped her, clearing her mind. She couldn't fall into this again. It was too risky. . . . Besides, he could vanish at any time! She warned herself to stop again and stepped back from his embrace before she could be swept into his passion. Appealing to his logic seemed her only means of escape.

"Victor, our bodies are betraying us. But with what we have to do and the decisions I have to make, we can't let ourselves be the pawns of passion. We have so much to consider, that a lack of control at this time could cloud the issues. I am going to go home, and you are going to keep your promise to teach me chess while remaining a gentleman . . . or I'm not coming back."

Coerced by her logic, he relaxed his grip. He would let her leave now, albeit reluctantly, even though she was wavering, uncertain.

Several minutes passed before Victor spoke. Without looking at him, she stood very still and focused on the stained-glass panel by the door, but she sensed his tortured recalibration, the battle of cool, mental logic against hot, physical need. She hadn't intended to let it get this far out of hand. She could only ease Victor's anguish by giving in. Since that was not an option, she waited for him to unlock the door and show her out.

His eyes burned with fury and frustration, his gaze focused full blast at the nape of her neck as she walked ahead of him. He had a right to be angry. She heard his mental message loud and clear. *Okay, okay, okay . . . I'm sorry,* she said to herself. *It'll never happen again.* He was resentful, but she was adamant—although, in a way, she wished that she could stay. . . .

Leashing his fury, Victor spoke to her through clenched teeth as they entered the large foyer. "I cannot say that it will be *easy* to keep my promise. But I am, after all, a man of my word."

As they approached the door, she sensed that he wanted nothing more than to snatch her by the neck in retaliation. She had skillfully extricated herself from his arms, and he was positively seething.

With common sense her only guide, she elected to leave on a humble note lest the panther change his mind. Instead of a sarcastic quip about life not being easy, she softened her refusal, reminding herself that they ought to at least get along if they were to be partners.

She formulated the words in her mind before speaking. When she touched his arm, he swallowed again and she could hear him mentally begging her to change her mind. She couldn't. Not now.

"Thank you, Victor. I do appreciate your patience with me on this. . . . It's all so very confusing." Her diplomatic response was intended as an apology.

This woman was making him crazy.

Although disarmed by Liza's unexpected feminine charm, he had to let her go. He hated that he was becoming angry that he shouldn't be angry. It was her decision. It was her right. . . . But God, it was difficult for him: Checkmated for the second time today. What else could he do but concede like a gentleman?

"Of course, you are right," he murmured. "We have more important things to worry about."

There. He'd said it. He'd wrested a chivalrous response from his innards and done the right thing. His father would have been proud. Without further ado, he walked Liza to her car and watched her pull out of the driveway in utter dismay.

"Let me know when you have arrived safely," he called after her, disappointedly returning to the house.

Without Liza in his arms, he suffocated in the confines of the massive rooms. His body tormented by desire, his mind couldn't focus on anything except making love to a woman who positively exasperated him.

"Dear God, I've got to work this off!" he shouted, violently grabbing the telephone from its jack and dialing Stan's number. After three rings, Stan's jubilant voice boomed through the receiver. "DGE. Can I help you?" Victor winced at the chipper salutation.

"I do hope so, old buddy. How about an intense game of racquetball to kill the tension that's been driving us all mad? I'm *sick* of this project" . . . and dealing with Liza Nichols, which was pure hell.

Twelve

Stan was waiting for him, sitting on the floor of the glass enclosure with his legs crossed, his usual reckless grin lighting his face.

"So, this is how you treat your business partners: Stand them up, then call at the last minute—two days later, no less, when your surly ass is ready to come out and play." Stan cocked one eyebrow and laughed, then leapt to his feet.

Victor was at a momentary loss for words, which only gave Stan more ammunition to ride him. It was a prerequisite to their daily sparring match, and Victor couldn't help smiling as he looked at the droll expression on his friend's face.

"I had an important client-dinner, then some critical reading to do, and forgot to inform Barbara . . ."

Why did he feel such a need to explain?

"Nope. I don't want to hear it," Stan cut in playfully. "No excuses can save you now. Ole Stan'll just have to spank you out here in public!"

For dramatic emphasis, Stan had whipped the ball into play on the word *spank,* which brought both combatants into the game with a hearty laugh.

Stan did everything based on dramatic content, following the extreme philosophy—work hard, play harder. Maybe that's why he loved Stan so much. Stan could enjoy life the way Victor couldn't. Time had robbed him of that luxury.

As the intensity of their game increased, Stan's thick, red hair matted into dark-brown, dripping spikes that clung to his face. A deep crimson was beginning to spread over his freckled shoulders. "Gimme a second to whip your tail."

After forty minutes, Stan stopped. Winded, he bent over with his head between his knees and gasped for air.

Victor smelled blood. He was going to win this one.

Standing a short distance from Stan, Victor breathed deeply but maintained his position to resume play. He kept his knees slightly bent and legs spread in a fencer's stance, welcoming the physical exhilaration. From an internal reservoir of adrenaline, he felt a predator's intensity surge through him. He was *on* tonight. His muscles twitched involuntarily as his reflexes remained keyed to instantly attack the ball.

"Serve it, man. What's the problem?" Yeah, he'd kick Stan's ass.

Victor's light-grey, cut-off tee-shirt and maroon shorts were totally darkened now from the steady stream of sweat that rolled down his torso, back, and thighs.

"Okay. I'm on you," Stan panted, still stooped over. "You ain't seen nothin' yet!"

Recovering slightly, his opponent straightened to begin again. After taking one look at Stan's face, Victor knew that his buddy would not be the one to issue punishment on the court today. But he also knew that Stan was a true competitor. If his friend lost the game, he'd have to find a way to salvage his pride. Assuming that they both lived through the match, Stan would probably ride him verbally. And if Stan could find something to get on him about, he would. It had been the norm between the two of them for years.

As they neared the hour-and-fifteen-minute mark on the large, fenced-in clock, Stan finally collapsed in defeat, gasping for air as he ruefully conceded by waving his racket.

"Vic, I'm through! I owe you one."

Victor leaned on the wall taking in large gulps of air. He almost chuckled as Stan looked up from the floor, wiping the sweat from his expectant, green eyes. They both knew what would follow. The game of verbal jousts. He braced himself.

"Vic, I do wish you would get laid soon so I can stop playing racquetball with an android!" Stan offered a wide grin, still wiping his brow.

Victor loved the mental and physical exercise that Stan provided. The two had become so good at pushing each other's buttons over the years that it was now an expected ritual when they saw each other.

"Ah, Stanley . . . I am truly disappointed that a gentleman of your caliber would use the ladies as a shield," Victor volleyed, unable to repress a chuckle.

Although he had accepted Stan's new challenge to a match of wits, he was still careful to avoid his friend's attempt to intrude into his personal affairs.

Stan responded with mock indignation and followed Victor into the showers, riding him all the way.

"What, are you kidding? Unlike you, Victor, I treat *my* ladies well. They would be *more* than willing to be used for a bullet-proof jacket, much less a shield, once ole Stan was done with 'em!"

Unable to keep the banter going, both gladiators broke up in a thunder of riotous laughter at Stan's comment. His buddy was outrageous with the women! How did he get away with it? Victor could only shake his head at Stan's overassessment of his own prowess as he left the showers.

Stan followed right behind him. "Vic, I met a real beauty in the courthouse yesterday. It won't be long." He chuckled, vig-orously toweling dry his shock of flame-red hair, which now looked like he'd put his wet finger in a wall socket. "It's an open-and-shut case."

The sight of him made Victor laugh even more.

Distracted, Stan pulled on his shorts, fidgeting about his locker, smelling his socks in a futile attempt to distinguish last week's laundry from this week's.

Using the lapse in conversation to mentally rehearse a sarcas-tic zinger, Stan looked up from his task and returned to their verbal game with confidence.

"No, seriously . . . I mean, out of corporate concern, Ed and I need to know if our partner is under any type of mental strain that might make him snap or become a liability. You know?"

Still smiling as he continued, Stan added with a wink, "Cer-tainly lack of female companionship for more than a year could possibly lead to brain damage . . . or, at the very least, a hel-lacious tennis-and-racquetball partner. Victor, have a little mercy. I'm tired of getting my butt kicked on the court by you, m'boy. The way I figure it is, you need to expend that energy on a new conquest."

A direct hit. Victor was less than pleased. He hated this topic of conversation, which he considered far too personal. What was worse, he knew that Stan knew just how much it annoyed him. Up till now, the ribbing hadn't affected him. But now, he was really pissed and felt the familiar steel gate begin to close down over his expression, which broadened Stan's smile.

"Maybe you should practice your game a little more instead of wasting valuable energy on the women, m'boy. Then you might stand a chance out here with me one day," Victor parried aggressively.

"Touché!" Stan yelled over his shoulder, sounding totally cheerful and unaffected. "Testosterone jolt? Better have that checked before you come down with prostrate problems, Vic."

Victor's annoyance escalated. He knew that Stan considered it an art to find the right button to push; however, this was turning into an archaeological dig. Under more normal circumstances, when one of his secret goblins had been activated, he could exhibit restraint. That was what *he* had always considered to be the real art of the game: Never showing his opponent that he'd been laid vulnerable. But the look of triumph on Stan's face indicated that Stan knew his comment had struck a vital cord. It wouldn't be like Stan to let such a rare opportunity pass.

Defending his honor, Victor returned another surly volley. "Anyway, what makes you assume that I haven't availed myself? Unlike you, Stanley, I have *always* conducted my personal affairs with the utmost discretion."

Victor hadn't looked at his friend when he snapped off his response. Avoiding a frontal assault, he stuffed his perspiration-soaked clothes into his gym bag. Stan spun around and straddled the bench, aware that Victor was in trouble. Victor looked up with a frown and quickly zipped his bag, then put on his watch. He was now on the ropes. He could feel it. A toothy grin had widened on Stan's face, and Victor groaned as Stan drew his imaginary blade, determining how to make the next cut count.

"As the firm's attorney of record, it is my responsibility to keep us out of litigation. Having an unfired cannon around could be dangerous and present undue liability. *Comprende, Señor Duarte?"*

It was a deep gash.

"At a loss for words, ole buddy?" Stan inquired with a grin.

"This must be a real problem. Normally, you would have countered with a hundred brilliant one-liners. Frankly, I'm shocked! Even I can do better than this. I hope you're not losing your edge, ole man. Who is she?"

He wanted to punch Stan, not deliver a witty exchange. He was, indeed, at a loss for words, and that bothered him. Before Stan could land another salvo, Victor was halfway out of the locker room heading toward the garage. He needed air.

"Hey, slow down! What's with you today? I'm really curious about your attempted escape from our age-old battle of wits," Stan called out, quickening his steps behind him.

When Stan caught up to him, Victor realized that, although Stan wanted to continue the good-natured prodding, his face showed real concern. It was odd, but Victor couldn't remember ever witnessing his friend rendered so totally speechless. For that matter, he couldn't remember when he had ever been at such a loss for words himself.

"Is it still the Chem Tech problem?" Stan asked, his tone now serious. "We talked for over an hour yesterday, and I thought from what you said the situation was controllable."

Stan nudged Victor's arm, trying to sound playful again. "Hey, ole buddy. We've gotten out of tighter spots than this before. Right? Your problem is that you need to get into a *real tight* spot to feel better—it works for me. Know what I mean? Great tension-reliever. Plus, with me as your attorney, you've got the luck of the Irish on your side."

"No need to worry about that, Stan. As I said before, I have a plan." Victor cuffed his friend's shoulder and started walking again. He refused to be baited into a discussion about women and kept the conversation focused on their immediate business problem. "We'll finish the project and get out of that account as quickly as possible. We'll let them continue to think that we're still at odds with Risc Systems; that way, they'll never know that we figured anything out. It's simple, and nothing is in jeopardy."

"Sounds good to me."

An uneasiness crept through Victor, and he changed the subject abruptly. He cared about Stan and Ed too much to burden them with the possible dangers. He turned toward his car, not looking at Stan, who was trying to keep up.

"Right now, Stan, the only liability that we have is your insistence on making a move on every woman that comes through the door. Haven't you heard about sexual-harassment lawsuits, my dear attorney?"

"Look, Victor," Stan said, perking up again. "Ed and I know that you've been a picky bugger ever since college. Hell, even the ones that you left standing all alone were incredible!" he added in a wistful tone that forced Victor to smile.

He groaned. How did Stan do it? It worked every time. College days. Despite his resolve to remain stoic, Victor weakened at the memories.

Stan slapped his back and laughed. "Remember . . . women? It hasn't been that long, has it?"

The outright ribbing had changed a little. There was still a tone of concern in Stan's voice, even though he had couched his questions in humorous banter. Victor wanted to tell him more, but it wasn't appropriate. He'd never violate Liza's honor. And the other information was potentially lethal. He let the fleeting thought go and popped open the trunk of his car without responding.

As if sensing that his commitment to self-imposed exile had wavered, Stan pressed on. "Aw, seriously, Vic. Ever since you started tying up your brain with Chem Tech, none of us see you anymore—at least not outside the office. Hell, you've turned down some of the most luscious blind dates that I could've possibly arranged for a sorry S.O.B. like you. . . . I'll bet you haven't even taken your true love, the *Phoenix,* out for a whirl. You've probably still got her cooped up in her slip. Right? Victor, gimme a break. Hunting season's almost over in the nation's capital. Now, *that's* a crime if ever I heard one! As an attorney, I should know."

Victor hadn't offered a word in his own self-defense as Stan went on comically. Preoccupied, he had only kept the silent icy distance that was his trademark. Nonplussed, Stan leaned on the passenger side of the car roof with one elbow, casually nudging him.

"You can let me take her out of her slip in a week or so for you—to take advantage of Indian summer. . . . I have two indescribable models coming down to do a shoot with one of our clients, and they would just *love* the *ride* up to Annapolis. If you're a good boy, I'll even share."

Stan's eyes twinkled, and Victor felt his jaw lock in response. His cool exterior had defied him all day, despite his attempts to master it. He fired a last warning shot to end the irritating and invasive conversation.

"Stanley, you may have the *Phoenix,* and both women. I haven't the time for either. This project is paramount. When my work is done, I may join you in a little debauchery. But until then, stay off my back with this crap."

Slamming the trunk hood to emphasize his point, Victor moved to the driver's side, jumped in, and turned on the motor as an end to the discussion. Pressing his face to the glass with a grin, Stan stood on the passenger side, tapping on the roof impatiently until the electric windows slowly opened and allowed him to poke his head into the idling sedan. Victor smelled blood in the water, but this time it was his own. Total victory was within Stan's grasp, and he wouldn't stop until the crowd cheered.

Victor went for the bait. "What is it, Stanley?"

"I am *pretty* sure that if you weren't so wound up, you'd have detected by now that our new, and very reluctant partner on that Chem Tech deal, is a drop-dead, stop-your-heart beauty. I mean, even old, conservative, married Ed takes a deep breath when she walks into the room. And that boardroom fire! Man, I'd love to see that unleashed in the bedroom!"

Stan whooped and slapped the hood of the sedan when Victor gave him the finger. A decided victory.

That was it—the final straw. Victor's restraint snapped as his temper flew to the surface full throttle. "Go to Hell, Stanley!"

He had no other immediate defense. If they weren't friends and his liaison with Liza weren't a secret, he would have definitely punched Stan for talking about her that way. Without looking back, Victor shifted angrily into gear. Stan stepped away from the car—impervious to the insult and thoroughly enjoying his win.

Victor tried to shut down his brain before Stan called out another comment. If he could just get out of the parking lot!

"You know, if I were you, I'd spend my time trying to *make it* with her, not trying to fight her!"

Stan's words echoed after Victor as his car screeched up the parking levels and out onto the street. Anger raced through him, and he punched the interior roof for release. Damn! That last comment had totally gotten under his skin. He hated Stan's reference to Liza and understood that it was probably her bitter distrust of such macho innuendos that would keep her remote, and away from him, for the foreseeable future.

Liza would never allow her authority to be undermined because of one sexual encounter with him. That he was sure of. But he didn't want her power or her authority. He wanted her. It was so simple, yet so complex. Why couldn't she understand? For that matter, why had it taken him so long to understand? Clearly, Liza could maintain the facade of remoteness to the extreme in order to preserve her dignity. In that regard, they were evenly matched.

Well, maybe not exactly.

He wasn't sure if *he* could stay away from *her*. He hated to admit it, but this wasn't a stalemate. It was a decided checkmate. She'd won on the boards, and in the cold war. The last thing he had wanted to do was scare Liza off or to make her retrench. But his body constantly belied his awareness of her. He cursed his own lack of control around the woman. Even his usual regime of athletic exertion wasn't enough to completely wipe Liza's earlier visit from his beleaguered mind. Hell, he might even have to stop parking his car in his own garage!

As he entered the house, climbed the stairs, and flung his

exhausted body across the bed, he couldn't stop thinking about how wonderful Liza would feel beneath him. He wanted her so badly that it was giving him a headache.

She had been right. It was getting complicated. Very, very, complicated.

Liza closed her eyes again for the tenth time. She had to get some rest! The way her lashes gently dusted her face was another irritating distraction while she desperately struggled for sleep. Everything kept her awake, and it annoyed her that nothing seemed to dispel her inappropriate thoughts.

Her normal swim hadn't even cleared her mind. In fact, it had cruelly added to her misery. Adjusting her head to sink deeper into the pillows, she pulled the comforter around her, determined to shake the feelings uncurling and then tightening at the base of her stomach.

She'd gone for a vigorous swim, read the books Victor had given her until nearly 1:00 A.M., but the peaceful cloak of sleep still eluded her. True, the books were a relief. It was fantastic to discover that she shared this gift with others. Although her gift wasn't common, it wasn't necessarily weird or crazy either. She was grateful to Victor Duarte for giving her some peace of mind. In that way, he'd helped her solve a puzzle that had been plaguing her since childhood. Finally, the headaches made sense. . . . They'd only come when she'd fought against her power and tensed. Plausible.

Adjusting the pillows again, she thought of her earlier session in the pool. She was still confused about what had gripped her so directly when she'd hit the water. It had been as if her skin had become a shock absorber, registering a thousand tiny tingles from sensitive nerve endings when she'd cut through the surface on her first dive. It was still vivid now.

When she thought back on her forceful pulls through the water and how good it had felt to glide silently under the surface, she remembered how every stroke, each scissor of her legs, had sent a tremor through her entire body. By the time she had reached the far side of the Olympic-length pool, she was openly trembling and had to hold onto the side, fighting against her own feelings.

The underwater silence had actually forced her to concentrate harder than she'd ever wanted to. That had never happened to her before . . . not just from swimming. It was eerie. Ever since her earlier bout with Victor, she hadn't quite been able to turn off her mind. The only peace that she'd found had been when she'd become absorbed in the reading. She had clung to that escape and had continued to use it to effectively block Victor from her thoughts all evening. But that had only worked until her eyes became too tired to go on.

Now, as she lay wide awake in the quiet darkness of her bedroom, Liza felt as she had when she'd first entered the water. Her skin was on fire again, tingling and responding strongly to the array of textures that covered it.

Her pale-peach chemise caressed her skin like a feathery touch. The sensation that the contact produced tormented her. As her breasts rose and fell against the silk, she shuddered. She could remember his touch . . .

Crisp cotton sheets offered a cool contrast to the thick spreads protecting her from the chilly night. Yet the multiple layers of bed linens were a poor substitute for the real warmth that she craved. She could definitely remember . . .

Her thoughts wrapped around her as she imagined Victor's presence. For an instant, she was sure that she could actually detect his scent: Rich . . . earthy . . . male . . . Immediately, her middle wrenched with anticipation. God, he smelled so good. . . .

She couldn't help wondering what it would be like to make love with Victor Duarte in her bed instead of standing up against the wall of his garage. She'd never tell Letty that one. It had been the wildest thing she'd ever done. Too wild. Liza almost chuckled as she tried to force herself to stop.

"Oh, God. I'm a junky," she groaned, turning on her side. "Cut it out, Liz." What was it about this guy? She'd seen good-looking men before. There had to be more to it than that. What about the familiarity? *When or where . . . how did she absolutely know him like this?*

A tiny moan escaped her lips as the throb between her legs returned. Although it had been only two days ago, and there was so much more involved, she desperately wanted to experience his touch again. She had to admit it. Her own probe had betrayed her, keeping her hopelessly locked within Victor's thoughts. Served her right. This was her punishment.

Lightly cupping her hands over her breasts, she shuddered hard. Drawing a deep breath, she felt herself swell and moisten in response to the caress. The sensitive tips beneath her palms stung from the pleasure of her own light touch.

She had to stop feeling like this about him. It was insane. She could go back to being celibate if she tried hard enough. Hadn't she gone for years without a man's touch? But Victor was like a drug . . . a hardcore narcotic.

"This is what withdrawal must feel like," she groaned. She'd have to check herself into a detox program if she didn't stop.

Her thighs burned. No, she wouldn't give in to it. Not while thinking about Victor or with her probe still on. What if he could tell that she felt this way? What if he could read her? That would be too embarrassing. She closed her eyes and removed her hands from her breasts. But as she did so, the hunger became more acute. Flopping onto her belly, she admonished herself, but the change in position tortured her. The contact with the mattress felt like another caress, and a short whimper escaped her lips as she moved involuntarily against the soft goose-down beneath her.

Tossing herself onto her back, she took a deep breath, expelling it with annoyance. Häagen Daz. It was like methadone. She just needed to make it downstairs to the refrigerator. Down to the clinic. She would not go out in search of a dangerous drug by calling Victor tonight. No, that was out of the question!

Liza swung her legs over the side of the bed and steadied herself. The ache was becoming unbearable, and she closed her legs tightly against the sensation as she stood up. Her inner thighs were damp. She'd never make it.

Reflex drew her to the telephone, and she reached for it with her eyes closed. What was she doing? But she was unable to stop dialing, nonetheless. Betty Ford. She should've been calling Betty Ford's!

Victor picked up on the first ring, as if sensing her call.

She tried to swallow away the humiliation and say something that made sense. Her mind grappled with the options. The project, the alliance, the enemy . . . *Think of something, you fool!* Then she looked at the clock. She was busted. What could she say? It was 2 A.M.

After a moment of silence, her words rushed out in defiance of propriety. "Victor . . . I can't take it. . . . I should have stayed this afternoon. I'm sorry." Dear God, she had no pride!

He hesitated, then answered with a deep breath between his words. "I'll be there. Give me your address."

Victor's directness, coupled with the latent desire that she heard in his voice, sent another shudder through her. The truth was out, and she no longer cared. He obviously felt the same way, and she was grateful that she wasn't losing her mind alone.

"Please, hurry," she whispered giving him directions quickly, and hung up.

It was an addiction, and she was terrified of O.D.-ing tonight. Running her fingers through her hair, she remembered the conversation with Letty. Hadn't her best friend made her promise to call with the coroner's report after *the dinner?* She could only hope that by tomorrow morning, Letty wouldn't be the one reading a tag on *her* toe. On the phone, Victor had sounded as though he were as overwhelmed as she. She couldn't imagine how he'd react now. Especially after the garage . . . What would he do with an open invitation? Maybe Häagen Daz, double chocolate chip, would've been safer.

She had to get Victor out of her system. What was wrong with her?

The wait for him was interminable. She didn't even bother

with the pretense of pulling on jeans and a sweater. Her face burned with shame as she paced in the foyer waiting for him to arrive. She had lost her mind! But she could literally *feel* him draw nearer as her desire heightened. It seemed like a lifetime ago that anyone had aroused her senses.

This wasn't just a case of being interested. This wasn't a case of being willing. This was nearly wanton. No one ever had this effect on her. Not her first boyfriend in college. Not her three-month boyfriend when she'd started a real job. Not even Barry. *Ever*. What was this thing between them?

Still standing in the foyer, Liza felt her body sway from the avalanche of emotions. Closing her eyes, she leaned her head back against the wall. She couldn't just open the door and face him like this, could she? She should at least run upstairs and get her robe. Show some decency . . .

Riveted, she listened as his car screeched to a stop at the curb. She was now fully alive, without shame, and wanted him to make her forget her previous inhibitions. Her whole body trembled violently, and she only wanted to experience Victor's caress.

Seconds seemed like hours. She was still leaning against the wall for support when his car door slammed. Her senses now keen, she heard him take the short flight of stairs in two cat-like steps. Her brain never consulted her hand as she reached out and opened the door before he could ring the bell. Their connection was immediate as she drew back into the vestibule to let him enter. She knew he felt it now. Definitely.

The dim light of the foyer cast an amber glow on his rich, dark complexion, momentarily holding her for ransom. Victor looked semi-disheveled, as if he had just thrown on the nearest pair of sweat pants and a tee-shirt and raced to her house as quickly as possible. It had only taken him fifteen minutes. He hadn't even shaved, and a dark shadow stubbled his jawline. The change from his normal immaculate dress was startling, and the raw masculine presence of the real Victor Duarte made her pulse race.

As she stepped from the shadows into the dim light, Victor

drew an audible breath. He looked at her with an electric appreciation, assessing her from head to toe.

"Incredible. Absolutely . . . incredible," he said, holding her with his gaze. A familiar current bound them, paralyzing them. This time, she wanted to feel the full voltage of that current unhindered by her own fears or suspicions. No matter what happened after tonight, Victor made her feel. She had dropped her shield to take in every glorious measure of him.

"I thought you'd never allow me to touch you again," he murmured, still rooted in the foyer.

Liza closed her eyes. "I don't know what I'm doing. But I can't . . ." Her words trailed off as she heard him step closer. "I've never . . ."

He didn't answer immediately, nor did he fill the small sliver of space that separated them. She could feel his breath near her face.

"I want you to be sure," he said in a low whisper. "You have to be sure . . . because I cannot hold anything back tonight. I just can't forget . . ."

For the first time in years she had let down her guard willingly, and quickly. She wanted to experience all that had been denied her, all that she had denied herself. But she was afraid that Victor might assume that her reactions were routine. She had never called a man to her home. Yet, to hold anything back, would be next to impossible now. Instead of turning off her probe, she decided to turn off the analytical side of her brain. Peeling away the last layer of doubt, she approached him timidly and offered herself to him fully.

"Tonight . . . I'll hold nothing back. I've never been here before . . . on such an impulse. But with you . . . I can't seem to stop myself. . . . That scares me," she confessed. "I couldn't stop thinking about you . . . us . . . all day."

"Neither could I."

Overwhelmed and frightened by her own intensity, she turned her back to him and led him out of the foyer. Perhaps there was enough time to regroup. Maybe she'd feel better about the whole thing if they talked first. She didn't really know him. They had to clear their heads. Maybe she could make him a cup of coffee and retreat until she was sure. Ambivalence raced through her as Victor's thoughts hunted her. It was all too familiar . . .

His warmth radiated against her back as he followed her, slowing her escape with his voice.

"Don't run from me, Liza. Not this time," he whispered, placing his hands on her shoulders without turning her around. "I thought I would lose my mind when you left me earlier. I almost begged you to stay. . . . What do you want from me? My sanity?" Breathing against her neck, he murmured, "Tonight, it's all yours."

The heat of Victor's touch melted into her bones, stopping her retreat. Still unable to bring herself to turn around, she leaned her head back against his chest. "This is like a dangerous drug, Victor. I have no self-control around you anymore. . . . You were right." Embarrassment swept through her. She had never opened herself up this way, been this vulnerable.

"I've felt like this from the very beginning, Liza, and fought it as long as I could. I can't tell you how many nights I've fantasized about being with you. . . . We can't go on pretending."

Her will had turned into putty beneath his hands, and she sank back against him as his arms enfolded her body. "I know," she murmured breathlessly. "Just tell me what you want from me tonight . . . *anything.*"

It was as if her admission were his undoing. With her back still to him, she could feel his body respond against her spine. She languished under the deep, sensuous kiss that he started behind her earlobe and held onto his hips for support while he gently captured the curve of her neck. She almost cried out when he brought his hands down slowly to fondle her breasts. She had waited for that sensation all evening, and she gasped as his light contact made her swell with agonizing pleasure.

Just his touch, there, made her arch involuntarily backward

and pull his lower body against hers. The last of her inhibitions fell away as he moved against her slowly, filling her center with renewed waves of anticipation. The hard length of him was insistent and could only be answered by friction. She had to move; he demanded it.

Glorying in the contrast of their bodies, she allowed another small whimper to escape as he feverishly pressed against her. Her whole being needed him. In a strange combination of agony and pleasure, her world blurred. She saw an oak-paneled room and heard the rush of waves around her. But she didn't care this time. She was in Victor's arms.

His soft moan was an assault that her senses couldn't ward off. Helplessly trapped between fear of the inevitable and fulfilling her physical hunger, she couldn't turn around while he continued to worship her body.

"Liza, I'll do anything. *Anything* to make you always respond to me like this," he gasped finally, giving way to their pent-up desire.

Victor continued to enfold her possessively as he emitted a groan from the base of his throat. It was frightening to experience the powerful emotions that seemed to emanate from the very core of his soul. They had both slipped over the edge of reality, landing someplace foreign, yet familiar.

"I've never . . ." she murmured as her will collapsed.

Victor's will crumbled with hers. His urgency had suddenly escalated, and she understood that he was beyond caring about tomorrow.

His hands ravished her as he breathed into her hairline. The sensation of being with him was so intense that she shut her eyes tightly against it.

She could hear his mind formulating words through the passion—words that she had to understand. Abruptly turning to face him, she touched his damp cheek as she stared into his eyes. His breathing was ragged, and he was perspiring as though they'd already made love. She'd felt the same . . . just standing in the hallway.

Victor searched her face before he pulled her to him again. She was witnessing an internal battle that he waged, the effects of which were devastating. Taking in large gulps of air, he rested his head on her shoulder.

"When I close my eyes, I can't shake the fantasy: The ship. The room. Then . . . the four-poster bed. Insane jealousy, and this crazy need to protect you. It's like I'm obsessed, and I can't fight it. Oh, God, woman . . . I can even feel you in my sleep."

Liza captured his hand against her breast. Confusion and desire fought for control of her mind. She knew how he felt . . . the exquisite terror.

"Come with me," she whispered, leading him toward the stairs. Each step heightened her arousal as she anticipated fulfillment . . . his body next to hers in bed.

She could feel the heat of his breath on the small of her back as he followed her. Only a few steps more . . .

"Liza . . ."

His murmur stopped her advance a few feet from the landing. He seemed unable to continue.

Turning her around, he whispered, "I can't go another step without touching you," and buried his face against her belly.

She held his head to her in a loving embrace, running her fingers through his hair as he kissed her stomach through the silky fabric of her nightclothes. Her breathing quickened and she felt the warmth of his hands sliding up her thighs to capture her bottom. She melted into that warmth, feeling her legs give way as he trailed kisses down her body until his mouth made contact with her skin. Grasping the railings for support, she moaned with pleasure as his mouth grazed her.

Lowering her gently to sit on the edge of the landing, he knelt before her and kissed her mouth deeply. Even in the moonlight, she could see his eyes burning with desire—and something else that she was afraid to name.

"I need all of you tonight," he breathed into her mouth just before capturing it again. "I don't care what's causing us to feel this way."

He had barely uttered the confession that they both knew was true. His words described all of the emotions she'd been afraid to admit to herself. He had told her this before—but a long time ago, it seemed. His touch, now so familiar, shattered her into a million pieces of broken light. He trailed kisses down her body, and she fell back against the oriental runner, tears of pleasure brimming in her eyes. "Then, I'm yours," she told him hoarsely, giving in to the intense hunger.

Her own words battered her senses. She had become someone else . . . somewhere else. Victor only emitted a deep groan in response. Finding refuge in the soft folds of her, his tongue recklessly tortured, tasted . . . threatened to consume. She beckoned him with her mind not to stop until waves of feverish sensations swept through her. Her body responded of its own will, arching her spine, bringing him to the place that would ignite her. The back of her head dug into the rug as ribbons of exquisite pleasure overwhelmed her being.

"Victor!"

Hearing herself call out to him from a remote place in her mind, she knew she was somewhere else and couldn't get back. Her cry soon became something between a plea and a sob. His only response was to demand another cry from her. Tightening her grip on the spindles of the staircase, she braced herself for the searing tides that cascaded through her body. She nearly wept when the last explosive shudder brought her to the crest and beyond. She could never go back now. Not after this.

As he landed kisses along the inside of her thigh, the stubble on his face grazed her skin again. She shivered from the renewed want that shot through her. Everything that he did . . . every part of her that he touched . . . he now owned.

His voice had become harsh with need as he nuzzled her ear.

"I need more of you, *Querida* . . . until we both beg for mercy. Let me take you to bed . . ."

Gathering her up in his arms, he carried her into the room.

God help her, she was falling in love with this man.

Thirteen

Dawn poured slowly through the window, and he lightly kissed Liza's exposed shoulder, drawing her closer. Suddenly he needed to seal the space that had opened between them while they slept. Never had he witnessed a sight more beautiful than the quiet breaths she took; she lay peacefully unaware of him as he watched her sleep. Her tousled black mane shone with highlights of copper and red filaments in the early light.

His exile had ended.

It had been more than just a physical release, it had been an unexpected emotional journey. Every barrier had crumbled as he dared to dream of tomorrow with her. Hope had emerged, unmarred by the realities that faced them. And each time he had taken her, they had descended into an inferno, creating a new bond that still held him captive.

He'd never before questioned his experiences or his passion. Now, his reality had changed. His perceptions had shifted. It was as if something had forced him beyond the envelope of self-protection. What gripped him last night went beyond description or comprehension. It was a feeling of total union, a familiarity that thawed the glacial regions of his being—absolute vulnerability, a completely indefensible position . . . a new place where it was impossible to think past the echoes of his soul. This was what he had always feared . . . what he had always hungered for . . . what had always secretly fed his dreams. To possibly trust another human being this way had been inconceivable to him before. Now, that possibility was within his grasp, sleeping quietly beside him.

As he watched Liza take restful breaths, looking so fragile

and serene, he was seized with the inexplicable need to protect her. From the depths of nowhere, he needed to hold her to him tightly, fearing that he might lose her even though she had never committed to being his beyond what they'd shared last night.

Panic surged through him. Liza seemed like a precious treasure that had been taken away before. The feeling was irrational, but devastatingly real. His only defense against the fear that engulfed him was to bury his face in her fragrant hair as she slept.

Nuzzling her gently, he opened his soul, allowing Liza's fragmented light to creep past the dark spaces within him.

"Liza, my sweet—*mi tresora dulce,*" he whispered into her hair. "I'm mad about you. . . . Please don't leave me. . . . Come with me. I'll never be able to live without you again."

Just as quickly as the words had escaped, he issued a silent prayer, hoping that she hadn't heard his soul-felt confession in her sleep. It had come too soon to make sense, but it felt so right. He was sure that leaving Liza behind would be the worst part of his mission. He had to take her with him.

Tracing the curve of her face with his finger, he pushed away the fine wisps of hair that framed Liza's cheek. Immediately, he knew that the priceless gemstones from *la hacienda* had been made for her. As he brushed the lobe of her ear with his lips, he envisioned the exquisite topaz-and-diamond jewels.

It was an odd awareness. Without question, he knew. Through a hundred lifetimes, the stones had finally found their rightful owner.

His kiss stirred her, but she only turned toward him drowsily and drifted off again. The comfort of Liza's adjoining warmth eventually drew him into sleep as well.

When he awakened, the sun brought full brilliance to the room and the busy street-sounds of activity also filtered in. Liza was returning to bed when he focused on her. He, on the other hand, was unable to move from the complete and satisfying exhaustion.

"Well, good morning, *señor,*" she murmured.

Still disoriented from a coma-like sleep, he could only venture a lazy smile. Watching her walk gracefully toward him, he finally managed to raise himself on one elbow to pull her back into bed.

"Buenos días, señorita," he yawned, enjoying the sight of her half robed. "I am glad that you called last night," he admitted, kissing her shoulder. "Or I might have found myself in a somewhat . . . alarming adolescent condition this morning."

Liza expelled an easy chuckle as she fell back into his arms. "Victor, you are *really* awful, you know," she said with mock surprise. "What am I going to do with you?"

Dropping back on the pillows to give his weary body a much-needed rest, he pretended to ponder her question in earnest. "Hmmm, you are a difficult woman to please. Last night I wasn't so terrible. But this morning, you, *señorita,* have lodged a very serious complaint. So, I guess I will have to become more creative to answer your question about what to do with me."

They both laughed as she struggled to get away from him. "No, really! *I can't!* Not again! *No mas!* I'm whipped!" she squealed, laughing as she tried to reach the edge of the bed.

"I believe you said those very words last night . . . and do you remember the effect they had on me, Liza?" he teased, grabbing one of her long legs to prevent her from slipping away from him.

As they tussled and played, their laughter rang out like unruly children, unsupervised and uninhibited, enjoying themselves wildly as they broke all the rules.

Finally giving in to a more basic need, he let go of Liza reluctantly. With a sly smile, he stood up, and issued a playful warning as he crossed the floor. "You are very lucky that Mother Nature has granted you a reprieve. I'll have to consider your sentence for the affront when I return."

Still giggling as he entered the bathroom, Liza shot back an answer. "Well, at least you could tell me my sentence in *English.* Last night I wasn't sure *what* I was in for!"

Chuckling to himself as he closed the door, Victor didn't respond to her comment. Remembering the depth of passion that they'd hurtled into the night before, he was certain that he'd called out to her from the throes of desire. But now, functioning on only two hours of sleep, he had no mental record of what he'd said. His thoughts and words had rushed together wildly last night. Each sensation with her had been vivid, defying translation.

Splashing water on his face, he reflected on their night together. Never in his life had he been so thoroughly captivated . . . and certainly not to the point where he couldn't articulate in English. Liza was destined to make him lose his mind, and for the moment, he was perfectly content to let her rob him of any mental faculty that she desired to claim.

He opened the medicine cabinet. Searching innocently for a tube of toothpaste, he suddenly stopped as a disconcerting thought arrested him. What if he found some other man's possessions?

Agitated, he scolded himself. Why shouldn't a young, vital, attractive woman have a liaison? She was certainly passionate enough. That was rational, to be expected. Were it not for this project, he would have had a woman friend. Liza was not committed to him. Yet as he smeared a glob of toothpaste on his forefinger, turning it into a makeshift toothbrush, logic offered no comfort.

He returned the tube to its shelf in the cabinet with a slight tremor of relief at not having found any evidence of another male's territorial markings. Shaking the uncomfortable thought, he returned to Liza, who was waiting to fulfill the second basic need that insistently required attention when he was around her.

She was sprawled across the bed smiling at him when he entered the room.

"Now, you say that you need your sentence translated, *señorita?*" he asked playfully as he hopped into bed and pinned her beneath him.

Letting out a tiny squeal, she struggled unsuccessfully to get away. "In the spirit of détente, I demand that you take me to my embassy." She laughed sensuously, trying to avoid the attention he paid to her neck.

He lifted his head. "And you did not have to study a second language in school? Hmmm . . . How very, very, unfortunate," he teased, expelling a low laugh strategically next to her ear.

"I can only remember parts of tenth-grade Spanish, and they didn't teach anything too racy in public school," she giggled. "So, *Señor,* if you have any more requests, you'll have to be more direct." She laughed again, easily, squirming under his weight and warming under his hold.

Tenderly kissing her body as he moved against her, he paid attention to all the skin that he'd missed during their sleep. When he sensed Liza's readiness, he penetrated her, holding her lightly under her shoulders as she began to tremble.

Still looking at her with a smile, he murmured, "Then I suppose I will have to remedially address your education. They say it's often better to teach using a *graphic* representation of the foreign phrase."

Liza had closed her eyes, and he enjoyed watching the acute pleasure register on her face as he slowly withdrew and began a casual, excruciating return.

"Really," she questioned in a quiet gasp as he re-entered her, "what did you say to me last night?"

Conversation was losing all relevance as Liza twined her legs around his, making it difficult for him to withdraw again. The momentary shift of her weight and the feel of her becoming more ready with each entry stilted his own breathing.

Garnering his control, he responded just above a murmur. "I asked you to slow down. Correction, to *please* slow down . . . *mas despacio por favor* . . . or we would have had a very limited encounter." He kissed the bridge of her nose. "But then, we have had a number of encounters to make up for it, have we not?"

Feeling Liza close around him with a slight shudder almost made him forget what he was about to say to her. His own pace was maddening, but he couldn't resist teasing her.

"But then again, if you'd prefer that I not take so long," he whispered against her neck, delivering a soft nip between phrases, "that can be rectified, I assure you."

"Please," she breathed, looking at him directly. "You win."

Liza's whole body shook as he joined to her more forcefully. Her only answer was a light whimper of pleasure that nearly made it impossible to pace himself. When she took his earlobe into her mouth, his intention to take his time vanished. He loved her open, ready responses.

Yes. He was sure of it. He had gone mad.

Encouraging him to hurry with the rush of her own movements, Liza began the slow destruction of his resolve.

Taking shallow breaths, she whispered roughly, "Victor, whatever you do . . . drives me crazy. Just don't stop again, *please.*"

Liza's eyes were shut and her head was tilted back. Her request and the passion in her voice demanded that he hold her tighter. He could no longer steady himself against the torrent of pleasure that swept through him, and he gave in immediately to the urge that would stop their torment.

No words were necessary as he filled his mouth with hers. Again, there was no such concept as control, much less self-control, as he bound them together in an unrelenting rush toward the end. When their storm receded, they clung to each other, breathless and giddy.

Peering up at him sheepishly, Liza looked sated and mellow. He could sense from the glint in her eyes that she was ready to tease him again.

"I think I've learned my lesson." She chuckled with a sexy smile.

She was incorrigible, and he had to laugh between the deep breaths required to keep him from passing out. As always, Liza had managed to throw his plans out the window and he would be the one who wound up learning the lesson.

Rolling over on his back to give her room to breathe, he looked at Liza as a grin found its way back to his face. "Do you still want me to escort you to the embassy?" he asked, reaching over to indulge his hand in the warmth of her full breast. He loved the way it pouted and responded beneath his palm, even when he was fairly sure that she was satisfied.

She propped herself up on one elbow and looked down with a devilish wink. He loved the way she worked both his mind and body. Her warmth seeped into his pores as she pulled herself closer to him, creating a heat-seal between them. Yes, he definitely loved her skin . . . the feel of this woman. And that wicked, sexy grin of hers. He chuckled as he watched her mind develop a witty comeback.

"No." She brushed her lips across his chest. "But, please, whatever you do . . . continue, *Señor Duarte*. I am looking forward to getting my masters in the language."

Laughing at the provocative pout Liza offered, he kissed her quickly, giving her bottom a pat as he pulled her on top of him and began tickling her.

"Please, please, stop! No more, no more, *Señor!* Honestly, I can't take it!" She shrieked when he continued to poke her.

"Then you must promise to behave yourself, young lady, and let a weary man have some respite." She waved her hand in defense and nodded her agreement.

Finally collapsing in a gale of laughter, he petted her against his chest until her giggles subsided. When she looked up, he had suddenly grown serious.

"Victor, what is it? A second ago you seemed so happy." Her eyes scanned his face, searching.

His tone was gentle as he responded to her. It had come upon him so quickly . . . he couldn't explain it. The feeling was like a well of emotion inside, and he touched her mouth as he tried to form the words that were so hard for him to say.

"Liza, *Querida,* do you know how very long it has been since I've laughed? Really laughed. Or how long it's been since I cared to wake up in someone's arms . . . never wanting to let them go?"

She looked ready to cry. Perhaps she knew exactly what he was feeling. She had told him of her own painful experiences and had probably protected herself the same way he had—by living life on the surface for a very long time. His heart broke as he looked into Liza's beautiful face and wondered how many years they had both been amongst the living dead.

She touched his cheek and he covered her hand with his, kissing it forcefully. It was as though he were fighting the reality of what was still before them. They had immersed themselves in pleasure all night long and through the better part of the early morning to avoid it. But now, it had crashed in on him without warning. Just like everything else, the timing was terrible.

"Liza, being with you is so wonderful and this feels so right . . . but I can't be sure that I can protect you."

Witnessing his struggle with the serious issues that surrounded them, she told him quietly, "Victor, I have had pain that has caused me to cry rivers, until I literally died inside from the torture. I thought that I could never feel again. Then you came into my life, and I've found that I'm really still alive. That makes me afraid because I know that this time I could die from the hurt. I'd never recover."

Liza's eyes had misted over and a shade of despair eclipsed her once-cheerful expression. Looking at her, he knew that there was more than just her family tragedy that held her captive in the pain. He wanted whatever it was lifted from her—gone, to allow her to trust again.

He studied her face intently, and a basic, protective urge swept through him once again. Feeling an unexpected rush of emotion, he sat up and looked directly into her eyes. He refused to allow anything to claim her beyond himself.

"Tell me, Liza," he demanded, "who did this to you? What happened to make you so afraid to trust me . . . so wary that you can't believe me when I say that I love you?"

They fell silent, stunned by his words and the vehemence with which he had spoken them. He hadn't said that he loved her out loud all night, assuming that she knew. Rather, that she could tell from the way he had let her into his soul, making her a part of him forever. But that didn't make sense. Not after a mere few days. It was impossible.

However, it was too late. The words had been said, and the confession made her eyes sadder. Claiming instant distance, Liza broke away from his grip and flung herself out of bed while snatching up her robe. As she tied the soft paisley fabric together, hiding her body from his view, she sat across from him in the overstuffed chair by her armoire. Something new about her demeanor was strangely analytical.

Her sudden remoteness was confusing. Painfully so. He could only sit there fighting the explosion of conflicting emotions that vacillated between hurt, anger, wanting her, needing her. But in order to draw her back to him, he softened his tone. Her terror told him that he had to allow Liza room to emerge on her own from the new corner in which she was trapped.

"Liza, what happened?"

Her focus narrowed on him, and she fought for control, responding with unnecessary bitterness.

"Why is it that when a man wants something from a woman, he feels he must first take her to bed and tell her he loves her? Giving her satisfaction is supposed to guarantee her loyalty— and pay for whatever he intends to take from her anyway."

He couldn't answer. The coolness of her exterior and the clinical precision of her question paralyzed him. He saw his own old emotions mirrored on Liza's face. It was bizarre. Somehow, the tempered blade of remoteness that had become his most lethal weapon was now the one that she unsheathed against him. He did not understand the reason for her attack, which had come without warning and without provocation. He had bared his soul and found himself hopelessly vulnerable.

This was not like Liza. Up until now, she had played hard, but fair. Had his honesty triggered her battle mode? For self-preservation, he retreated into his internal fortress, answering her coldly.

"That is one technique, but one that I do not prefer." He masked his hurt with outrage.

"Because you're a *gentleman,* I suppose?" she fired back, hitting her target.

They seemed locked in a pattern that could destroy them—or perhaps had, long ago. Their relationship was difficult . . . complicated . . . unexplained.

Moving away from the bed, he addressed Liza with intemperance. "No, because it lacks strategy and ingenuity; it creates too many variables; and, overall, it is too easy to detect."

As she stood up, he realized—too late—that the old battle had begun again, only now with greater passions at stake. He moved toward her, but she recoiled from him, her fury blazing in her eyes. She stood near him, inadvertently revealing the abuse she had suffered long before. He wanted to pull her into his arms, seeing in her an injured spirit, a fragile child that he wanted to protect. But dared not reach out for her . . . not now.

"Victor, what if I told you that this whole scenario is very familiar to me? That the last person who told me *darling, I love you* was supposed to be a friend and mentor . . . someone whom I allowed to understand all my fears, hopes, dreams, the family pain, everything. And this person also held me in his arms and said that everything would be okay."

She had pulled out the heavy artillery, and he couldn't move or speak as Liza decimated him with her logic.

"Yet, even knowing how vulnerable I was at the time," she continued, her voice becoming icier, "he didn't have the common decency to just let it be a physical thing. Instead, he betrayed my *trust,* our friendship, by clouding my perspective and manipulating me for his benefit—On My Job!"

Her anger belied her pain, and she folded her arms over her chest as if to find the support within herself to go on. He could do nothing but hear her out.

She turned from him and walked to the window, her voice barely audible.

"With us, Victor, the stakes are much higher. Barry asked me if I were okay, too, after the first time. . . . Your concern sends chills down my spine. You are both successful men with a mission. Unfortunately, I've learned the hard way that your kind of power breeds ruthlessness. I stand between you and three million additional dollars and a controlling interest in a project that you want very much. Which means, I'll be the one to get hurt—as much as you might hate to twist the knife. So, please, *respect* me enough not to tell me that you've fallen in love in the past forty-eight hours."

Defeated and resigned, she turned to him. ". . . And because I am all grown up now, when you tell me the long story about how it was *necessary* to use me to get what you wanted after all, I won't cry. I'll just become the worst nightmare that you've ever faced in business."

He was stunned, yet understood her crystal-clear warning. Her wounds had been deep and had not yet healed. Would they ever?

"Liza, I have never told any other woman that I loved her," he said. "I consider that bond sacred."

Almost talking to herself, Liza continued. "Barry *also* told me that he had never been with a woman who made him feel the way I made him feel. La, la, la. I was extraordinary, made him dream of the future, et cetera. But he had no trouble getting up out of my bed one morning and kissing me goodbye, because it was *necessary*. And he found nothing odd or questionable about wanting to sleep with me again a few months later . . . after he thought things had cooled down. Been there. Seen it. Done it."

It galled him to be compared to such a shallow human being. He prided himself on his shrewdness, his superior negotiating skills, *and* his integrity. To be compared to a pariah who would sleep with a woman to gain an advantage in a business deal was an outrage!

Yet the parallel was obvious, and he understood all too well her vulnerability and her fear. He forced himself to let the accusations go unchallenged, setting his pride aside. She had been wounded; if he could calm her down, they might have a chance to right things between them.

He approached her with caution, wanting to reassure her. But then, what promises could he actually give her? The devastation still registered in her eyes as he turned her around to face him. His own fears blurred his thinking, and Chem Tech strangely took a back seat to this rival who still held sway over *his* woman.

"Do you still love him?" He became angry with himself as the very question passed his lips.

She looked down. "No," she admitted at length, "but that was the last time I cried myself to sleep . . . and the first time that I really accepted that I was truly alone. That was a couple of years ago."

His relief was overwhelming. He needed to hold her and, unable to resist the urge, pulled her to him possessively, murmuring, "*Mi corazon,* there is so much that we have to overcome . . . must overcome."

This time Liza didn't combat his touch as he cradled her, but she did not respond either. She lay limp in his arms, barricading herself behind an invisible wall of self-protection. There was no fire in her soul, and that was worse than when she had fought him. He had an eerie sense of *déjà vu:* She had done this to him before.

"Don't let them kill your spirit, Liza," he implored. "We have to fight them all or there is no point. Mere existence is not the same as life!"

Liza's passive resistance sent a terrifying, familiar shudder of dread through him. It was uncanny the way her reactions—her analytical coolness—now mirrored his own. Two days before, he would have been remote and aloof. Now he was begging this woman to reach out to him.

Liza smiled sadly as he grappled with his distress. "I'm going to wax philosophical on you, Victor," she said, her voice a monotone. "You have no idea how bitter the taste of revenge can be . . . even when you do win . . . or how much is at stake to make winning even possible."

He didn't understand, but she sensed his confusion. "Let me explain," she said. "I had to leave my old firm. I was upset, depressed, and vowed not to let him beat me. I was tired of being taken advantage of, tired of being pushed around and manipulated. So I spun off and started Risc Systems. Since I had been the one who did all of the work for him in the past, I was well positioned to go against him in the bid fight for the Chem Tech contract. Nothing could have stopped me."

"Wait. Let me get this right. You didn't know who the key officials were in Chem Tech prior to the bid? And you only went after it to prove a point to an *ex-lover!"*

He was speechless. It was a betrayal by omission. *He had given her the link!*

Liza measured her response. "Not exactly, Victor. I had the Washington political names, but had no idea that there was a corporate entity involved until you and Ron confirmed it. I needed the Chem Tech deal to finance an attack against the politicians. That was it. You guys came up with the missing puzzle piece. I didn't. I wasn't even looking for it, but I could feel something wasn't right. Crazy, but . . . actually, an ex-lover did put me right in the middle of a hornet's nest. Maybe it was fate after all."

Victor paced, his rage renewed. "Why Chem Tech? There were a hundred other contracts that you could have gone after." He whirled on her mid-stride. "Answer me!"

Liza tightened the belt on her robe and straightened her carriage. "I was better than he was, and he had used me. I wasn't about to let him present *my* account strategy. It was a matter of principle. So, I beat him to the punch and won. I had started Risc Systems on paper four years before, but hadn't had the capital . . . or anger . . . to launch it until I left my old firm. That's why the Chem Tech contract was so vital. End of story. None of this is really any of your business anyway."

"None of my business?"

"It's my *personal* life."

He tensed with irrational jealousy. He hated that another man had touched her. "And last night wasn't personal?"

"Wear the shoe on the other foot, Victor. Tell me that you've never made passionate love to a woman before, then gotten up in the morning and gone to work—as though it meant no more than satisfying a hunger. Just because I'm a woman, does that mean that I have to be in love?"

He was devastated and speechless. She was so right . . . and so wrong.

"I lost two-and-a-half years of my life," she said. "I've lived without feelings, closeness, or the ability to trust. So let's be realistic and stop talking about love." In spite of her bitter words, Liza looked at him pensively. Had they discussed this all before?

Consumed by jealousy, he stalked away from Liza, searching for his clothes. His sense of betrayal was irrational, but primal. Why was he so goddamned furious? Why had she been so cut and dried? He'd had scores of lovers but had never been in love. He had certainly enjoyed Liza's body, and that should've been enough. In the past, it would have been. But foolishly, he had let himself fall in love.

Seething, he pulled on his sweat pants without comment. He hadn't been prepared to hear that someone else had impacted her so significantly before him. It was easier to deal with Liza as a waif caught adrift in the sea of life, someone that he could save and protect. But now he saw her as injured, yet strong, and quite possibly out of his reach.

Unable to stabilize his anger as he grabbed for his shirt, he aimed and fired at her. "So why didn't you just turn on your damned probe to protect yourself from him? Why didn't you test him the way you've tested me? And why don't you use it now to see what's in my heart?"

He wasn't even looking at her as he snatched on his tee-shirt and roughly pulled on his tennis shoes. He didn't expect an answer, and her soft, considered reply brought him up short.

"At the end, I did turn it on and I saw darkness around him. Just the way I saw it around you. Remember? An impenetrable darkness that raised the hair on the back of my neck. It's still around you, Victor. There's something more here, something I can't explain. Until I do, unflinching trust is out of the question.

I've been burned; I won't be again. Not with my life and my business on the line."

What was she doing? Liza thought in despair. She couldn't stop herself.

She studied Victor and, surprised by his torment, changed the subject. She had turned into Barry too late. How could she admit now that she'd been at such a low point in her life, with loneliness strangling her, that she had dismissed the warning signs, opting for human contact? Besides, her gift was not an accurate science . . . and two years ago she'd thought it was a sign that she was losing her sanity.

However, she was intrigued by the fit of temper that Victor so openly displayed . . . and by the strong reaction that his saying that he loved her had triggered. Turning on her probe was impossible now. She was tired and tense, and the process always escalated emotion. It was too dangerous . . .

But curious about the mercurial change that had just taken place right before their eyes, she proffered an earnestly analytical question.

"Victor," she began, "have you noticed that you are beginning to take on many of my personality traits and that I, unfortunately, am falling victim to many of yours?"

In these few short days, her self-control had improved immeasurably, but Victor now became irrational at the slightest provocation. She found the switch perversely amusing. Control. Was it linked to trust?

Victor shot her a threatening glare, appalled at the inference. He tore around the room, hunting for his car keys. Finally finding them on the floor, he scooped them up and snapped defensively, "That is *complete* bull, Liza!"

His outburst shook her. What was happening to them? Her mind raced, and she grabbed one of the books from her night stand.

Victor hadn't moved a muscle, and she knew that her theory was taking root despite his protests. Not wanting him to leave before she'd made her point, she quickly searched for her horn-rimmed glasses, then settled down in the chair.

"Look, I don't know what's stoking the passions between us, but—"

"It doesn't matter," he said, turning towards the door. "I've heard enough."

"Wait," she said more softly. "I believe they call the process something like . . . uhm, oh, here it is. *Transference*. Mr. Duarte, that will be your homework assignment for tonight. Or at least before you can come out and play again."

How dare she assume that he only wanted to use her body! If they weren't going to have a deeper relationship, then Liza Nichols could go straight to hell!

Begrudgingly, he accepted the book from Liza as he headed down the steps toward the front door. His mind reeled as he tried to process her sudden changes and complexities. This conversation—argument—although different from the others, had a familiar ring to it that had slowed his decision to bolt.

Why had the mere mention of another man actually made him taste blood? He had taken Barry's existence as an actual affront. But he had no right to react as if she belonged to him. Never in his life had he ever wanted to possess any woman.

But the scenario was like a play that he'd seen before but had forgotten the key acts of the performance. He couldn't help turning their responses over and over again in his mind. Nothing made sense. Not her angry outburst, not his jealous rage, and especially not her transformation into cool detachment. They should've been arguing about Chem Tech, but they had stumbled into a more personal interaction.

He glimpsed her from the corner of his eye as they entered the foyer. His anger overrode the excruciatingly pleasurable potential of the evening. He would not deal with this insane creature. He would never be responsible for the excess baggage she carried. Liza needed a therapist, not him.

"Drive safely on your trip . . . to New York . . . and . . . tell André I said hello."

Stopped dead in his tracks, he turned around to face Liza, who sat on the steps massaging her temples as though in severe discomfort.

"Liza, that's incredible. How did you know I was planning a meeting this afternoon in New York?" Victor asked in astonishment.

"I did do my homework before I came out to play last night. But as they said in the book, it's a very weak muscle at the moment. I'll have to do a lot of exercise before I can get really accurate."

Suddenly she didn't want Victor to leave on a sour note after the wonderful time they'd just shared. She wanted to give him some scant measure of peace, but her emotions had tangled like a ball of yarn. If she pulled one thread, she'd find knots, then everything would begin to unravel again. God help her, the man had said he loved her and she knew how much his admission had cost him. Hadn't she thought the same thing, too, last night when he'd carried her into the bedroom? And yet, she'd answered him in a way that was totally out of character. It was as though she were blaming him for some past betrayal that he'd never committed! What was blocking her own simple admission now? Why couldn't she give in to what they both felt?

To hold him, she opened a little more. "Victor, this is not an exact science. As you said, it takes practice and concentration and the ability to relax and trust. Right now, I receive information in dribs and drabs . . . like the static-ridden reception on an old television. I don't know if that'll be good enough for what we need to do."

Still standing in the arch of the foyer, Victor praised her with caution. "Liza, this is exactly what I had hoped for, but now I'm not sure that I want to involve you. I'm concerned for your safety. If that becomes an issue, the deal is off. Agreed?"

She rose to her feet, her cheeks burning. "No, Victor, we most certainly are not agreed. Did you forget that I have a direct stake in this? I could be quite satisfied, and possibly safer, just putting a couple of dirty Senators behind bars, along with a crooked corporate vice president or two. That would square my deal personally with Chem Tech and the good ol' boys. If I go *all the way,* as the phrase goes, I might have to leave my home, my friends, my business—and figure out a way to ensure that my loyal team members are properly compensated. That is a lot to put on the line for a *roll in the hay.* That's the message, Victor. That's what I have not decided about yet!"

Victor's eyes narrowed. Her directness stung him for it minimized the importance of their evening together. That had not been her intention. She had merely wanted to make her point about Chem Tech. But had she? As his temper smoldered out of control, she knew it was too late. The damage had been done.

"Liza, don't force me to choose between a twenty-year quest and you. It was not *that* good! You have a week—until next Monday—to make your decision. By then I'll have had a chance to develop a viable plan. We could have it all, but I am used to disappointment and will act accordingly."

"You don't *own* me!" Liza snapped. Victor's patronizing tone annoyed her. "You expect me to trust you after the lies you've told me?"

"Own you?" he retorted, stunned. "Lied to you? When, Liza? Tell me when!"

Images blurred with the man who stood before her. They were standing in a harbor. . . .

"Everything you've told me has been a lie!" she cried out unreasonably. "I'll never trust you again!"

"Fine. Have it your way. This was insane from the very start. We'll be reluctant partners till it's done."

Her self-esteem evaporated with his words, and she felt as if he'd slapped her.

"I don't have to negotiate with you, Liza—or share you with any man!"

"The hell you don't!"

"My carriage is waiting. Just have your belongings packed for the voyage."

As abruptly as he said the words, he turned on his heel and

stormed out the door. Outrage coursed through her, along with an unspeakable hurt. Then she stopped.

Carriage? Voyage? Wait a minute . . .

The door slammed, and within seconds, she heard the distinctive motor of Victor's car revving as it tore away from its space on the quiet, tree-lined street.

Was she—were they—mad?

Fourteen

Liza stood in the foyer trembling, unable to stop the tide of emotions that swept through her. They'd crossed some invisible line. Text layered with subtext. Arguments in present tense collided with past tense. Each new moment was woven into some mysterious past thread of their existence. Sentences which had begun grounded in reality spun out of control into the middle of a chasm. If Chem Tech wasn't the only issue between them then what else was?

Her flight up the stairs was broken by the chime of the doorbell. Victor! Perhaps the tempest had ebbed. Her heartbeat quickened as she flung open the heavy oak door that closed her brownstone off from the street.

"Ron?" She tried to align her vision with her thoughts as she looked into the unexpected face of her friend and colleague.

Ron fidgeted with the change in his pockets. "I should've called you first, but I was worried. . . . I'll see you later."

As Ron retreated down the steps, she called after him. "No . . . wait. . . . I need to talk to you."

Ron hesitated, annoyed and disgusted, then reluctantly returned to the foyer. He followed her into the kitchen where she mechanically prepared coffee. They didn't speak and she had trouble facing him; but she could feel his laser beam cutting through her back, demanding an explanation.

There were no words.

Liza set a cup of the dark brew in front of him. Ron looked into the cup, seeming to meditate on the steam that curled up slowly from its surface. A breach of trust had occurred. Her fault.

Taking a seat across from him, she began awkwardly, fully aware that he had to have seen Victor leave.

"I know . . ." she said. She knew? Knew what?

She had no plausible explanation for Ron, but she felt a guilty, irrepressible need to explain . . . something. Ron's silence tortured her.

Studying the white formica counter, she looked for a crack in the surface that might allow her to slip away and disappear.

Still not looking at her, Ron was clearly measuring the internal rage that seethed beneath his calm. "Connie said that you had instructed her to let us know that if we had something important to discuss, we could stop by to speak to you personally. But I didn't expect to have to take a number."

Liza's shoulders slumped from the harsh accusation, and she couldn't muster the mental energy to ward off Ron's attack. She had spent her ammunition in the battle with Victor. The last thing she wanted was a direct confrontation with her friend.

"Ronald . . . It's not what you think . . . but I can't explain." Her explanation was weak even to her own ears, and Ron's eyes flashed intense fury.

"It's not what I think! I may be many things, Liza, but stupid is not one of them. You're a grown woman and how you conduct your *business* is none of mine!"

Although Ron's words wounded her, she offered no defense. The hurt in his voice stripped her bare, humiliated her. She had terribly disappointed a friend. Swallowing hard, she determined to take the full blast of the charges stoically. Ron was right; she was wrong. She had jeopardized the firm for senseless personal reasons.

Ron trembled as he spat out additional charges. "Tell me *this* is not what has changed the direction of the firm. Tell me you have not lost your damned mind."

The words caught in his throat, and she retreated to the far side of the room, needing to take refuge in herself.

"No!" she yelled back at him, on the verge of hysteria. What was happening? She couldn't stop the tears and hadn't been able to for the last week. "I don't know what the hell is happening here, Ron, and I'm scared!" she said finally, covering her face with her hands. "You have no idea how dangerous this is."

The admission broke her. Suddenly all the fear and pain in her life converged into one pinpoint of light. She had remained in control for so long—gone through so many funerals, disappointments, heartaches; solved so many problems, all with her chin thrust forward and her will made from tempered steel. Now, everything was slipping away from her. She was so damned tired.

Aghast, Ron stared as her body convulsed and she sank against the edge of the sink.

"Lizzy," he murmured. "I'm so sorry. I just didn't know. Please, honey . . . I've never seen you like this. It's gonna be all right."

The tenderness that replaced Ron's normally churlish tone unleashed a new torrent of tears. Even without her probe, she felt his bewilderment. How easily she had shattered! Perhaps this time when she broke, it really would be over, no coming back. She had carried her burdens for so long that maybe she was just too tired to go on. She was also tired of the inexplicable familiarity that crept into the present . . . the way it was unfurling now with Ron.

Clasping her hands, she gave in to sobs that poured forth with a vengeance. Gulping for air, she shot her reply back at Ron and dangerously kicked the pebbles near the edge of her cliff of sanity.

"Why does *everything* in my life have to be for everyone else? Why do I have to always be in control? Why, Ron? Because I'm an ice princess? Do you think I don't have feelings . . . needs? That I'm a robot that can work sixteen hours a day for years without a vacation, without roses on my birthday, Valentine's day . . . except from my girlfriends?"

Her hysteria full blown, Liza could feel the cords standing in her neck as she pleaded for understanding.

"Tell me, Ron, who's there to hold *my* hand and tell *me* it's gonna be okay? Or better yet, not just tell me but *make* it okay?"

Ron was speechless. Liza's pain frightened him. He stood beside her, and rubbed her shoulders. Her eyes were glassy and bloodshot, and the charges she levied against the people who cared for her were true. Liza seemed so strong, always, that it had never dawned on them to take care of her. And when she disappointed them, they had no trouble letting her know. The sad part was, instead of telling them all where to get off, Liza would only redouble her efforts to shore up the riff and would wind up consoling *them*. Maybe that's why he loved her.

He was sickened that his own selfish need for Liza's attention had allowed him to overlook her needs. He had loved her for so long—from a distance—but until Victor Duarte had come along, he had never had a serious rival to contend with. Yes, Barry Walker had broken her heart, but they had worked together to beat him. She had been his—Ron Savick's. He'd do anything in the world for her . . . even break into a client's system to impress her and help her firm win . . . and that had backfired and caused her distress.

As her waves of grief subsided, Liza shielded her tear-streaked face with a napkin. "I am so ashamed, Ron. I've never behaved like this in my life—I swear to you. But . . . this has gotten way out of control and I don't know what to do!"

He had seen Liza angry, upset, slightly injured . . . but *never* vulnerable. She had just been a beautiful "one of the boys" that he had a special, unexplainable attachment to; but now, he realized that she was a woman—just the way he had always fantasized that she could be—but she was Duarte's.

Liza had always been their fearless leader, the one who led them into battle. She had fought every injustice that plagued her loyal troops like an experienced warrior, and now something had changed. He offered her some coffee and led her to the table, holding her chair so she could sit down. Clutching the hot mug for support, Liza took a deep sip with her eyes closed, as though afraid to open them to face him. When she did, he hoped that she would see that he was no longer an adversary. Liza's forlorn look penetrated him, and he struggled to help her find the answers that he, himself, did not have. Although her deep feelings for him held no passion, he loved her just as he knew she loved him.

"I've seen this happen to commanding officers after they've lost a lot of men," he said softly. The analogy made sense to him. "You've been fighting a long time, Lizzy, and this was bound to happen sooner or later. You'll be all right."

He understood, and she loved him dearly because of his quiet acceptance. That's what had always bonded them. They loved each other as friends, no matter what the rest of the world thought. They had been through the worst of times with each other; perhaps this new trial would also bring them closer. They were both P.O.W.'s of sorts, and she clung to his words.

"Battle fatigue? You think so, Ron?"

"Yep, Fearless Leader. It's about time." He held her gaze. "The guy means that much to you, huh?"

She hadn't expected the question. She couldn't fathom an answer.

Taking another sip of coffee to steady herself, she began slowly, needing Ron's understanding more than ever before. "Ron," she whispered, "this has never happened to me. I'm losing control. It's only been a few days, but my life is turned upside down. There was a hollow in my soul that he filled, and I don't know why."

Ron's brow furrowed as he tried to absorb her meaning. "Liza," he said, "you're lucky, I guess, to still have a soul after all you've been through. I know what being lonely can do to a person. Just don't let him break you, sweetie, is all I'm saying. I've seen his kind before."

"I know, Ronnie," she acknowledged. "That's why I'm afraid."

Ron struggled with her admission; and to shake the depression closing in on them, she steered the conversation to the issues facing the firm.

"Victor is not the only thing that worries me," she confided. "That's personal . . . and done with, over. But Ron, we've got some real problems to deal with. Maybe that's why I'm so stressed out and not thinking clearly."

"Liz, we're in trouble, aren't we?" he asked directly.

When she didn't answer immediately, his raw intellect snapped into gear. Yet Ron's question hit home, lifting the haze of personal issues from her mind and allowing her usual mental strength to race to the fore.

"We're in serious trouble, Ron," she affirmed. "We have a lot to do to ensure our safety." Her authority returned instantly with the fear. "We have to tie this up neatly, carefully. No slipups. We've been put in a tenuous position by the customer, and we may very well have a predator lurking over our shoulder in DGE. I'm not sure if I even trust my own *détente directive* myself. So, if I sense that any individual is in danger, I'll disband temporarily. That way, I can make sure that everyone is all right."

She could tell from Ron's expression that her words had fallen on him like a ton of bricks and that it was a struggle for him to follow her line of reasoning.

"You really *are* scared, aren't you? I mean, for everybody's *personal* safety?" Ron asked, shocked.

Although it was a rhetorical question, Ron needed to hear the answer verbalized to make it real. The fear in his eyes reflected the fear in her own.

"That's why I blasted you in the meeting, Ron, and I'm sorry. I have never done that to anyone on our team before, but these people are dangerous. It's no longer about money; our personal safety is on the line. Please, no more heroics, okay? If something ever happened to you, I . . ." she trailed off, unable to complete the painful thought.

"I'm not about to leave you!" Ron broke in. "Even if you fire me! You're the only family I have, the only person in this

whole screwed-up world that I care about. If you're in trouble,
I'm there. Period."

Ron's flushed face blazed with determination. She adored
him and needed him, but could never allow him to be endangered.

"I love you guys too much. No way will I see you in jeopardy.
That's out. I'll make sure that you, Maureen, Connie, and the
others have a smooth transition into other firms . . . with a substantial severance package, if it comes to that. I have a lot of
favors out there, and it will be safer if—"

Before she could finish, Ron had jumped to his feet, slamming his meaty fist into the table, jarring their mugs, and top-
pling over his chair. His sudden action took her aback.

"I'm not leaving," he shouted vehemently, unmoved. "Send
the other's away if it will ease your conscience. Who's gonna
look after you? Victor Duarte? Who's gonna watch your back
when this escalates, make sure that the information you receive
is correct, then help you rebuild? *Duarte?*"

"Ronald," she began, her voice stern to make him listen, "I
will not have you hurt."

Scoffing at the suggestion, he retorted, "At least I've had
combat training. Your suave *señor* has probably only killed the
ladies with his smile. You, certainly, were a casualty."

Even in his fury, Ron was a trip. His testy remark and sarcastic
dig made her smile, although she tried to hide it. "Ron," she
rushed on, "let's hope we can do this without killing anyone.
Okay?"

Her poorly hidden amusement had revived Ron's normal demeanor. She was glad to see it return. That meant he'd be all
right.

"So, I'll stay, and that's final," he replied. "I may even be
able to bring you a few tidbits of information. There's a lot that
Ed and I found out—while you and *The General* were bonding
in *the spirit of détente.*"

Ron was definitely back to his old self, she mused with relief.
Oddly, so was she. The tears and hysteria seemed to dissipate

as quickly as they had come. She looked at the wall clock . . . twenty minutes since Victor had left.

"So you're not angry with me, Ronnie?" she teased.

"Why should I be angry that the s.o.b. stole my favorite girl? I just work here," he snapped.

"Then you won't mind if I go to Philadelphia to visit Gerald today, dear?" she asked sweetly.

"Not if you can spare a minute to get this information. Then you and your *señor* can go back to playing footsies." He scowled, as though annoyed by her transformed disposition.

"Ron, seriously," she pressed. "Getting involved personally was a mistake. I don't intend to let it happen again."

Giving her a skeptical glance, Ron protested, "Yeah, boss. Whatever you say."

Ron held up his hand to stop her from any further explanation. "Look, it's none of my business, but the current that runs between you two in the meetings could be an alternative source of energy for the nation. The printouts are in my car and I'll drop them in your mail slot."

On that note, Liza gave up.

Once Ron was gone, she busied herself with returning phone calls, giving careful instructions to Connie, and preparing for her short trip. It would be good to get out of D.C. for a while. She needed to put a great deal of distance between herself and her emotions.

Driving was always the best time to clear her head. She looked forward to traveling the long, straight highway that separated Washington D.C. and Philadelphia. Shifting into high gear, she tuned into the radio station that played the loudest, most mind-altering music she could find.

This time she didn't want a quiet mediation. Just a way to forget and let her brain turn off. She knew every twist and turn on Interstate 95; and as the bone-jarring music dulled her senses, she switched her thoughts to autopilot for the duration of the drive.

Two hours later, as Liza snaked down the back streets behind the university, she pulled up to her favorite little shop on Forty-seventh Street. It was a much-needed taste of home. As she entered the brightly lit coffee shop, she stopped to take in the wonderful aroma of the gourmet blends that filled the air. And in keeping with the ritual, her heart filled with anticipation of the warm greeting that was always there to welcome her.

Looking around the busy establishment, she smiled to herself. The stout Jewish woman of Russian extraction that had been the proprietor there for years was the last of the *grand dames* in the area, as well as the last one in Liza's life. After Nana Ethel and Aunt V, there was only Stella.

Immediately, the woman recognized Liza standing by the door and gave an excited squeal as she rushed over to greet her.

"Liza, oh, how wonderful to see you as always, my darling! Please come in! Your Stella has some very good rolls this morning for you to take to your brother Gerald."

Liza loved the Old World, personal touch that made Stella's shop a haven. Ever since she was a little girl, she had pressed her face against the window and waved to the kind matron that ran the shop at peak efficiency. Stella always made time for her, regardless of the general hum of activity that was ever present in the store. Culture, colors of skin, languages . . . none of that ever mattered at Stella's. It was the only place that Liza could recall where it didn't. This woman was like her second grandmother, and Liza realized that she was so much more fortunate than most to not have been isolated from the gifts of friendship that all cultures, races, religions—all people—could offer. Nana had said everybody could teach you something—good or bad. Just live and learn . . .

Staring at Stella, Liza fondly recalled the childhood memories. Stella had been so good to her, especially after her mom died. When she was little and she appeared in the shop, her *grand dame* would wipe her hands on her apron, then press a penny or loose gumdrops in her small hand as she skipped away delightedly. That personal, neighborhood-store feeling was what had brought Liza back throughout her college years, as well as each and every time she came back to visit the city.

Clasping each other's hands tightly, they were joined in a warm reunion. "Stella, how are you?" Liza asked, jubilant at the sight of her dear old friend. "These pastries are sinful. . . . Just the smell alone will make me gain weight!" she continued playfully, taking in an exaggerated whiff of the mouth-watering buns.

Stella's eyes twinkled with pleasure as she moved to the large, glass refrigerator that kept her fresh flowers in bloom and carefully picked a delicate selection.

"Oh, I have something special this week for our Gerald," she chimed, busying herself with the task as her eyes misted from emotion.

Pulling long stems from the case, Stella patiently trimmed each bloom while bringing the selection into a wonderful array of color. The raw beauty of the combination of flowers made Liza draw a breath.

"Stella, you make it all look so easy—so simple. I could never do that. Just like the pastry, everything has your special touch," she exclaimed with earnest appreciation. "I never even learned how to cook."

Not looking up from the task, the old woman twisted the bouquet into a perfect arrangement.

Stella spoke to her softly, offering a bit of wisdom in return for the compliment. "Ah, it is just like life: A little patience, a little love, and everything can be made beautiful or to taste good. *That* is what is so simple."

Stella's philosophy was basic and pure. The words easily seeped into Liza's memory bank, making her again think of her own grandmother. Nana had had the same philosophy, and the two old women had been friends. Even in their day, two people from opposite worlds had found something in common to share.

And they had also shared her. Liza's chest felt tight, and she swallowed away the sadness with a smile.

As Stella looked up from the flowers, her gaze met Liza's. "Oh, my little one . . . Why such a long face?" she clucked tenderly, stopping from her task to take Liza's face in her knotted old hand. "It is Gerald? He is not well. . . . Stella knows."

The tenderness and caring that emanated from the stately old matron brought another wave of memories.

"No, Stella, he is not well . . . but I will always come in here to see you. You are my second *Bubbe*—always, my *Babushka*."

They both fell silent, understanding the hidden meaning of Liza's words. It was in this quiet knowing that they acknowledged the day would come very soon when there would be no need to take Stella's special packages of love to the hospital.

Drawing a tired breath, Stella's eyes shined with tears of compassion. She dropped her hand from Liza's cheek and patted her hand gently.

"My child, you have been taking care of so many for so long . . . When will you listen to your *Bubbe* and allow someone to take care of you? This is not good. We must face these trials with someone *special* to love us. It makes it all so much easier."

Liza's face brightened at the grandmotherly intrusion. "Stella, tell me, how do we always get around to this subject?" she demanded with a light laugh.

"Because, you silly goose, you have not listened to what Stella has told you to do—and so many times, no less. With Ethel gone, I must see to a good match." The elderly woman chuckled and began to wrap a few rolls while collecting the magazines that Liza had chosen.

"But it's not that easy and I haven't had the time," Liza protested softly, following the familiar direction of this subject. "Things are different today. Trust me, Stella."

"Time is not what you need," Stella continued undaunted. "And as Ethel would always say, there is nothing new under the sun. You must open your eyes and use your gift to see," she added casually.

Liza stood very, very still. She thought she had detected a signal—an understanding, something that Stella had never alluded to in all of the years she had known her.

Briskly working in the shop, Stella continued her chores. Finally, when she returned to the counter, she smiled at Liza.

"Ah . . . I see that we have not been using that which God gave us. Hmmm. A pity, as it grows so much stronger every day. I noticed it the minute you pressed your round little nose against my clean shop-window, oh so many years ago. I was about to shoo you away when I saw the shine you had in your eyes. And now look at you . . . all grown up, and so beautifully, my *shayna maidel,* with that same shine still in your lovely, brown eyes. It is a gift, my pet, do not fear what God has meant to be." As an apparent afterthought, Stella tweaked Liza's nose in affection as she left the counter again.

"Bubbe, you believe in this stuff?" Liza asked, her mouth still agape in disbelief.

"Of course! It is common. Why the surprise? Your grandmother had this. It passes on, you know. Most people nowadays pooh-pooh the idea. In the old country it was a great source of wisdom and comfort. Ethel and I would talk for hours about these things. But," she added with a sigh, "the young people only believe in the T.V. news. Achh, modern science! Such a piece of *mishegoss!"* she scoffed, buzzing around the shop.

Stella returned to the counter again and waited on two patrons before coming back to Liza, as though not yet ready to let her go. When the door chimed shut, Stella reached up and took off Liza's glasses, gently setting them down on the counter.

"Why do you cover these beautiful jewels, my pet? They would steal away any man's heart, if you just let him look into them long enough."

Liza broke into an earnest belly laugh as her vision blurred.

"Stella . . . *Bubbe,* I can't drive legally without them."

They both laughed joyfully, and their harmony filled the shop, mingling with the sweet aromas in the air.

"If you used them properly, perhaps Mr. Right would drive

you to wherever it was so important to go," Stella teased, enjoying herself. "But as I see it," she continued more insistently, "this gentleman, the one that you claim does not exist, is very, very fond of you and wishes to show you some beautiful new places. After, Gerald . . . you should go. . . . Let the dark stranger make you happy. Hmm? Your *Bubbe* will understand. After all, I will not be here forever myself, tis true enough . . . even though I promised Ethel."

Liza's mood sobered instantly. How in the world did Stella know about him? "You can *read,* can't you?" she exclaimed. "You know how!"

Stella waved her hand dismissively, clicking her tongue.

"Achh! Who knows what it is that we do? Wisdom comes with age. Perhaps it is my old cataract-eyes that see or it could be the years of experience that let me know what is truth. Either way, truth is truth, love is love, life is life. . . . As I said before, it is all very simple."

"But why did you wait so long to tell me that you also had the gift?" she demanded, not willing to let the topic escape.

Stella shrugged serenely. "Because you were not ready. Everything in its own time. But I think you are ready now, pet. Must be. You need it. True?"

The conversation ended abruptly when another stream of friendly customers filled the shop, each clamoring for Stella's personalized attention. But she knew instinctively that Stella had retreated from further questioning because she had seen something painful surrounding Gerald. It had actually been the brief mention of his name that had stopped their discussion.

Collecting her parcels, Liza prepared to leave and hailed Stella as she moved toward the door. The old woman stopped her transaction, came around the register, and walked with Liza to the door. Gently squeezing her arm as they made their way through the narrow aisle, Stella looked up at Liza, her dim eyes still warm and inviting.

"Come give your *Bubbe* one last hug, my sweet. Ahhh, I have looked upon you for so many years with pleasure and you have replaced some of those I lost when I left my country after the war. One can always start over again, but it's much easier if there is someone who loves you to go along with you to a new place. . . . Do not argue. This I know."

Stella's last words alarmed Liza. "Stella," she protested, "I will always be here to come and visit you. To have you fuss at me . . . *always*."

Stella shook her head as she pushed Liza toward the door. "I will not always be here," she reminded Liza. "But I will always be an angel on your shoulder to care for you if you need me. Your shoulder is getting crowded, however, with so many who have wanted you to ask them for their help."

Stella kissed her again, and Liza felt the deep ache of separation sweep through her. Things were changing.

Clicking her tongue, Stella patted Liza's cheek as she shooed her out the door. "He will fill that empty space, my pet. . . . Then you will not need us so much any more."

Once out on the curb, Liza felt like she was five years old again. Older people often had that effect on her. They seemed to know so much, to have experienced so much. None of her formal education had ever helped with any of the deeply personal issues she'd confronted. She could've grabbed Stella's skirts and cried her eyes out. The effort of concealing her tears made her tremble, and she jumped into her car and never looked back. It was if her whole past were falling away from her, leaving her alone and isolated. She hated change, newness, because it always brought pain.

Fifteen

Liza tried not to let her mind focus on Stella's insinuation that she was leaving as she pulled up to the main parking lot of the Pennsylvania Institute. She was thankful that the roar of the elevated trains deafened her to the sound of her own thoughts.

You've cried more in the past four days than you have in a lifetime, she admonished herself. *Gerald cannot see you like this. Get it together, Liz.*

The guard knew Liza well and spoke pleasantly as she entered. The nurses on the ward greeted her with their usual enthusiasm when she stopped to drop off the arm-load of pastries from Stella's shop, per her normal routine.

She had never had the heart to tell Stella that Gerald couldn't keep the delicious sweets down, so this compromise had evolved. The nurses enjoyed the baked goods, which perhaps gave them an extra incentive to keep Gerald comfortable, and Stella was allowed to think that she was helping in some small way.

Liza approached the open doorway to Gerald's room cautiously, knowing that the physical change in him was sure to be devastating. On each visit, she had to make it a point to steel her nerves, paste on her most exuberant smile, and swallow away the tears before she entered.

Quietly stepping into the room, she saw her brother sitting by the window in his wheelchair, looking out over a grassy section of the estate. His once-robust complexion had greyed in his handsome young face. Now, his eyes looked like distant saucers against the gaunt skeleton that housed them.

Sensing her presence, Gerald turned toward her, but without focusing, simply following her sound.

"Lizzy, is that you?" he asked in a frail whisper.

Grief coursed through her. Forcing it away, she quickly crossed the room, wrapped her arms around his thin shoulders, and buried her face in his neck.

"Of course it's me," she managed, giving him a light peck on the cheek.

Her touch seemed to melt him, and he held onto her arms with unsteady hands.

"Oh, Lizzy, I wait all week for your hugs. . . . They feel so good, and it's the only time anyone ever touches me without gloves anymore."

Liza swallowed hard at his admission. They remained clasped, until Gerry finally let her go and bade her to sit down beside him.

Discreetly setting the magazines down on the floor, she realized that Gerald wouldn't be able to read them. She kissed his cheek and stroked his hair, offering the flowers as a consolation prize to treat his senses.

"Uhmmm, Stella is a gem. She knows how to make everything special," Gerald faltered, genuinely appreciative of the gift. "I'll miss her."

Liza ignored the last part of his comment and pressed on, trying to sound lighthearted.

"Yes, she is special. But she's also still teasing me about not being married yet. I have to fight with her weekly about that." Liza smiled through the anguish, reaching for an entertaining topic.

Gerald appraised her face as though searching for answers.

"She reminds me of Nana," he said offhandedly, "although, she doesn't have the same lavender smell."

Liza sat still, extremely unnerved, trying to avoid becoming visibly upset by the reference.

"Gerry, how do you remember what Nana smelled like? You were only about two years old when she passed?"

She'd posed the question as calmly as possible to stem her growing alarm.

Gerald shrugged, his attention returning to the grassy field beyond the windows. "I dunno. She visits every now and then . . . and leaves a lavender scent. That's how I can tell the difference between her and Mom."

Her brother's casual admission chilled her. Liza held her breath for two heartbeats as she absorbed his blasé confession. She tried to summon a reply, fearing that her lack of immediate response would be enough to expose her alarm.

In an unusual display of authority, Gerald took her hand and spoke in a firm voice. "Lizzy, we have to talk," he insisted. "I don't want to upset you, but we can't continue to act like everything will be all right."

Liza couldn't answer. Tears constricted her throat for she knew full well that Gerald was embarking upon the conversation that they'd avoided for over a year.

"Lizzy, we have to face the fact that I am dying," he said plainly. "I won't be around anymore to fill up the open spaces of your life. Stella is right. . . . You have to find your own way now, but I'll always be there for you. I love you more than words can say."

Two big tears rolled down her face, and her voice quavered as she spoke. "I love you too, Gerry. What am I going to do without you?"

His muted eyes gazed at her face lovingly, gently, and he reached over and touched her clasped hands, which she had withdrawn to hold balled in her lap. Very softy, he began again, speaking to her as if he were already gone.

"Lizzy, I'm tired, honey. So very tired. You have to let me go . . . and, I can't go if I don't know that you'll be all right."

Liza nodded in reluctant affirmation. Tears coursed down her face; Gerald was asking her to release him from their lifelong bond.

"I love you, Gerry," she said again, swallowing down the tears. "So much that I want you to be at peace. I'll be all right . . . if you promise to visit me from time to time, like Nana." Her voice gave way to emotion and broke, and she squeezed his hands to keep her own from trembling.

Gerald closed his eyes, allowed his shoulders to drop, and expelled a deep sigh of relief. "Thank you, Liz. I just can't take it anymore. Maybe I finally understand what Dad was going through and how hard it must've been for him to leave us. I was so angry at him for so long."

Adjusting himself to sit up straight, Gerald looked at her thoughtfully, as though measuring her ability to handle his certain departure.

"Liz, will you put my affairs in order? I mean, I want to make sure that Mark is cared for. This has been so hard on him, and he can't even discuss it with me. I want him to have the art, the dance studio. He'll be devastated and will need an income until he can recover. I hope you understand."

Liza took a pen and some paper from her purse. "I will see that everything is handled; you know that. No matter how much it hurts to deal with this," she murmured, swallowing down another wave of tears.

Still looking away from her, Gerald whispered, "One more thing, Liz . . ."

She immediately stopped writing as he spoke.

"Find paradise for me. That's where I want to go when it's over. Just let me fly away. . . ."

As Liza left the hospital, she refused to give in to the emotions that barraged her. Forcing away the sobs, she called her attorney from the car and set up an early appointment for Saturday morning. There was so much to consider, so much to do, and it was all whirring past her in a blur. Her life, no, her existence, was falling apart. In one short week, it was like some cataclysmic chain of events had started, entering her universe and altering everything.

She couldn't stop the fission, but she could restore some order to her life. She called the office.

After checking in with Connie one last time for the day, she turned to Letty, the only person in the world who could cure the low-down blues. Patiently waiting for the junior sales clerk at the jewelry store to call Letty to the phone, Liza hoped with all her heart that her friend would be available for a dose of cheer.

Letty's response was cool and professional, until she recognized Liza's voice. Then, she broke into her usual greeting with a sonic boom.

"Hey, girlfriend! What's happening?" she screamed excitedly. "Where you been? Girl, you know I'm not even speaking to you—no, don't even try it! I don't want to hear no excuses about why you've been underground for days, chicky. You were supposed to call me and tell me all about your foo-foo-la-la dinner.

And all I get is some dry yang on my answering machine about nothing special happened. I swear! I never do you that way, Liz!"

Both women laughed as Letty went into her normal routine. Finally allowed to get a word in edgewise, Liza spoke quickly.

"Girl, I know, I know. . . . But, if you'd just shut up long enough . . . I'm in Philly and would like to take you to dinner. That is, if you have the time."

Liza had forced her tone to be upbeat, disguising the immobilizing pain. It was imperative that she see her dear friend, just for a quick dose of infectious sunshine. Just enough to get her through.

Not allowing her off the hook easily and this time, unfortunately, not picking up right away on the undercurrent in Liza's voice, Letty continued to ride her.

"Chile, I should give up a Friday night with my man to sit with your tired, no-calling-people self. . . . Now tell me, why I would be *that* crazy?"

They both laughed again, and Liza pleaded with her, determined to get her best friend to give in.

"Aw, come on, Letty. You can give the man a rest *one* night this week." The ribald suggestion got her.

Regaining her composure as the giggles abated, Letty fussed on good-naturedly. "All right, all right, heifer. You gonna to make me lose my job *and* my man. Gotta run, but meet me at Zanzibar Blues around 5:30 okay? See ya, doll!"

Liza smiled gratefully as she hung up, glad that her friend was up for a girls' night-out. It was always a treat to be in Letty's effervescent company, and this week's double dose was needed.

This time Liza didn't pull up to the club until 6:00, remembering that Letty was *always* late. Once inside, she found a quiet table in the dimly lit club where the mellow jazz and tasteful decor were a balm to her raw nerves. As the waitress returned with a glass of wine, Liza looked up to see Letty huffing and puffing into the establishment—a late, whirling dervish of un-settling activity.

"You're early," Liza remarked dryly before jumping to her feet to give her girlfriend a big hug.

Hurling into an explanation that was bound to be a very long story, Letty began without taking a breath.

"Chile, you know what happened? Let me tell you. These people on my job get on my nerves, Girl! I *told* them that I had somewhere to go. Anyway—"

Liza held up her hand to stop her friend's roll. "Letty, Letty, please, honey. My nerves can't take it tonight. And why do you always answer your own questions? Slow down, have a drink, take a deep breath, and just talk to me."

Settling into the booth and arranging her raincoat and numer-ous bags, Letty calmed down momentarily.

"Girl, this job is killing me," she went on, oblivious to Liza's amusement over her antics.

"I know what you mean," Liza chimed in by rote, continuing to sip her wine.

She hoped that Letty would get wrapped up in one of her hilarious stories and possibly overlook that Liza had come to town twice this week. Normally she only popped up to Philly to check on Gerald on the weekends, and she didn't want her choice of travel days to be a cause for alarm. But given her hectic schedule and the fact that she rarely made purely social visits anymore, she was sure that Letty would figure it out: Gerald was dying.

"How's he doing?" Letty asked suddenly, not needing to men-tion Gerald's name for Liza to understand. Her sudden quiet demeanor took Liza by surprise.

Liza stared down at her glass before she answered, no longer on the verge of tears, but very weary.

"He'll be gone soon, Letty. It's just a matter of time. When I saw him today, he asked me to get his papers in order. The look on his face told me that was all he was holding on for, you know?"

"Oh, girl, I'm so sorry. Is there anything I can do?" Letty asked just above a whisper, reaching to hold Liza's hand.

Tragedy was the one thing that Letty didn't deal with well, and Liza knew that Gerald's passing would probably be more traumatic for Letty than for herself. She had come to terms with losing people a long time ago. Letty had not.

As the tears filled Letty's eyes, Liza squeezed her hand. "Honey, I know he was like a brother to you; I mean we all grew up together. But when I saw him today, I knew it was time to let him go."

"You said he was fine the other day. Now you're talking like he's already gone, Liz."

"He is, sweetheart."

Silence engulfed them.

"Liz," her friend murmured at last, "you know the Spirits will watch over him, don't you? It's the people who are left that have it the hardest. What are we going to do without him?"

Liza studied Letty. The eclectic outfit of silver Jamaican bangles, combined with an American Indian turquoise-and-crystal medallion, lush African-print over-shirt, and thousands of micro-braids in her hair made Letty look like an ancient soothsayer.

Responding slowly, Liza nodded. "I know, hon. Someone else asked me that same question today."

Unwilling to get swept into the raging tide of despair and determined to get some of Letty's infectious cure, Liza changed the subject, using one of Stella's tactics, before taking a sip of wine.

"We know what we know . . . but tell me, how are you?"

The new direction seemed to brighten her friend. It was as though they both understood that the first topic was too painful. How did one deal with a loved one's death?

Always ready for an uplifting conversation, Letty smiled. "Me?"

"Yeah, you. How come I just get your machine? *I'm* working; that's why you get mine. Where *you* been, girl? That's the question."

Adjusting one of her six pierced earrings, Letty rolled her eyes toward the ceiling. Liza could tell that she was on the verge of one of her comic rolls and hoped that she'd try even harder this time because they both needed a cure.

"Girl, I met a new man!" she beamed triumphantly, accepting her drink from the waiter and raising her glass to Liza.

"So what else is new?"

"No, chile, this one is different! He's fine as wine sparkling in the sunshine, *baby!*" She laughed, glowing at the description of her new love.

"I *said,* so what else is *new?*" Liza taunted.

Letty took on a mock scowl. "Okay, just wait till you meet him. For real, honey, he is *all of that,* and then some!"

"All right, Miss Thang," Liza baited her. "Tell me about Mr. Wonderful."

Accepting her cue, Letty went into an elaborate description of her new love-interest.

"Yeah, Girl, and I just might go live down in the Islands with him. He plays for this reggae band, and we're artistically on the same groove . . . so, I might just give up all of this hustle bustle, and *roll with it, baby!*"

"You're leaving?" Liza asked in consternation. "You mean you would actually leave your job, your apartment, your dream to go into acting . . . to go live somewhere outside the country with some man that you just met? Letty!" She was indignant. "That's crazy."

Letty became peevish in earnest. Liza checked herself, but it was too late. A lifestyle judgment had slipped out, and their code of honor had been breached. What could she say?

"Liz, look . . . everybody can't fit into that stiff, nine-to-five mess. Especially not me. I don't need the car, the fancy clothes, the expensive dinners, you know. That whole corporate scene just ain't me. And, to tell the truth, I don't see that it has been that good to you either, aside from the money—which don't keep you warm at night."

The last part of Letty's defense cut Liza to the quick, but it was her own fault. She had to keep reminding herself that philo-sophical discussions always erupted into outright, heated debate. They had almost fallen out with each other a few days before over this same kind of mess! Liza swore to herself. Why had she even gone there? They had declared taboo such subjects years ago—when she'd hung up her riot gear. Yet, she couldn't let it go. The fight with Victor, compounded by her visit with Gerry, was too much.

"That's not fair, Letty," she whispered in self-defense. "You know I've been busy and had to do what I could to care for Gerald. That comment about my life was really unnecessary. I was just asking out of concern. Let's forget it."

Liza was more hurt than angry, and just wanted to let the subject of her private life drop. She hadn't meant to hurt Letty either. They loved each other, but had different ways of tackling their environment. The last thing that she wanted to do was cause a riff. Not over something like this. Not now.

Letty, too, realized that she had overstepped their boundaries, and she backed up from her position—slightly. Her goal seemed to be to restore harmony, and she offered a testy apology to right things between them again.

"Okay. Okay. Maybe I went too far myself. But you have to loosen up and stop being so judgmental, Liz. I know you're only concerned and have never lived a free-fall existence. But, Girl-friend, who said everything had to come in nice, neat little pack-ages? Some of the prettiest packages I've ever opened have been the most disappointing. You gotta learn to go with the flow."

Without begrudging that truth, Liza accepted Letty's apology and easily admitted that the point had been well taken as they clinked glasses in a toast.

"So, enough about me. What's going on with you?"

Letty perked up with real interest, and Liza felt her stomach knot in defense. There was no way that she could discuss the Victor fiasco with anyone; not even her best friend. Knowing Letty, she'd probably try to talk her into dealing with the man. Letty was a born romantic. Liza was a born realist. Not wanting to get into a lengthy dialogue about the merits of her sanity, Liza broke the cardinal rule of their friendship and opted not to share.

"Oh, nothing much," she said casually. "Just working on that crazy project that has me under the gun . . . Other than that, it's been pretty boring."

Letty's eyes narrowed in disbelief. "Liz, do you know you've been saying that to me for over two years? Now, either you are hiding the finest man this side of the Mississippi from everybody or I'd say that you and Mother Teresa have a lot in common. What happened to the gorgeous dinner-date?"

Liza burst out laughing at Letty's outrageous analogy. "Dinner was a disaster, like I told you on the tape. We're still at each other's throats, and I don't have any good prospects on the horizon. Boring. Just like I told you."

Letty appeared almost irate at the suggestion. "Humph! Chile, you must be crazy! If I had what *you* had, girl, the women would be stopping me with a police barricade on I-95 . . . talkin' about I was armed and extremely dangerous!"

They both burst into peals of laughter, their mirth spilling over to the adjoining tables. As the reverie went on, Liza basked in the healing friendship and laughter. It seemed long ago that she had been upset. The few short hours with Letty were an expected cure-all. The music was relaxing, the friendship was wonderful, the wine was good, and the food was perfect. For the first time in weeks, Liza felt so relaxed that she could almost lay her head down on the table and fall asleep.

After paying the bill, Liza looked at her friend's glowing face and searched for a glimmer of hope.

"This guy is good for you, isn't he, Letty?" she asked.

"Yeah, Liz. I think this is the big one," Letty said with a rare blush, adding sadly, "I'm gonna miss you, Girl."

"I'm gonna miss you, too. . . . But who knows? I might hook up with some fine foreigner and cruise the world myself. Don't be surprised if you get a postcard from the edge of the earth from me," Liza teased, trying not to tear. It amazed her how easily she had allowed the insane thought even fleeting consideration.

Giving Liza the most skeptical look that she could muster, Letty sucked her teeth and scowled. "You, Girl? Pulleeze, spare me!"

They laughed easily at the outrageous thought, and Liza asked more seriously, "So, when are you leaving?"

Shrugging her shoulders, Letty answered, "I don't know. It's a financial thing really. Since my commissions dropped off on the jewelry sales last year . . . and Renton's band thing is sort-of hit-or-miss with the money . . . it all depends."

Letty jumped in to further explain for Liza, who had fallen silent. "He's not living off me, Liz. He has a day job. We're *both* gonna contribute equally to the bills. But my commission bonuses and his gig money were supposed to help us move and have something to live off of until we pulled things together."

Liza's radar relaxed as Letty went on with her explanation.

"See, I had this crazy client . . . A salesgirl's dream! He would call up the store at least once a month and order anywhere between two-to-five-thousand-dollars worth of merchandise. I'm telling you, the guy was loaded! He'd have me send a pair of earrings, a tennis bracelet, whatever, to his latest chippy. He never came in and would just tell me in this sexy, exotic voice, 'Leticia, you decide. I'm sure your choice will be sufficient. . . . Just send me the bill.' And, boy, did I ever!"

Liza's antennae went up immediately as the relaxation drained from her body to be replaced by tension. Letty went on, oblivious to the change in Liza's posture, which had straightened.

"But he never complained, always thanked me, and said that I had impeccable taste. And whoever the latest babe was, I assume, would always be pleased. When he was done with them, Liz, he would always tell me to pick out something *real* expensive . . . usually around ten thousand. I sold a boat-load of lady Rolexes, and I knew it was the big goodbye—because she would never appear on my list to mail stuff to again after that. So, I would just pull her card from my rolodex, and it was bye-bye, baby. He had at least three of 'em going at any one time, usually. Listen, the way I figure it, the guy does a lot of business in D.C. and New York. He probably picked a store in Philly 'cause we're right in the middle and his stable of women—or his wife, whatever—could never track his butt to giving any other woman anything. But about eight months to a year ago, he either ran out of dough, the cops put his foreign ass in jail for dealing, or one of his women killed him. That was all I could figure, because he stopped calling."

Liza was nauseous. Masked outrage pulsed in her jugular vein as she turned on her probe unwittingly, reflexively.

"So that killed your income stream considerably, I'm sure," Liza commented in an awkward, detached tone.

"Yep, that was it. I thought something had happened to him—until he walked into the store this morning. It was the first time that I had ever met him. He's smooth, girl. He politely asked for his records, said it was a matter of personal discretion, and the manager punked out and turned my client file over to him. Just like that! They didn't even ask me if it was okay. My manager, that greedy little buzzard, was probably hoping that my rich client would bring his business back there soon."

Liza felt like she had suddenly grown fangs and hoped they weren't showing as she questioned Letty in the mildest voice she could manage.

"So, what did this guy look like?"

Letty popped up brightly, snapping her fingers twice for effect. Under normal circumstances, Liza would've laughed at Letty's dramatic emphasis, but all humor had momentarily escaped her.

"Lizzy, Lizzy, Lizzy . . . Honey chile, honey chile, *honey child!*" Letty said, shaking her head and a million braids with it. "This man was the finest, sexiest, hunk of yes-I-would-*not*-mind-being-your woman that I *ever* did see! And I don't even like 'em in those blue suits . . . so you know he had to be too good-looking for me to say that! He's about six-four, dark hair, the body of *life,* and this sexy aura that will *not* stop! Girlfriend, when you look up tall, dark, and handsome in the dictionary, his picture will be right there, Honey!"

Liza was almost shaking with rage, but she was not about to give Letty any room to badger her. Still on a roll, her friend continued describing the events of the day.

"See, all of this mess kicked off around 11:30, just before I went to lunch. My client didn't ask *me* about my files. He just came in, said something to my manager—who pulled these seriously expensive earrings out of the vault, said that they needed to have the settings tightened so the stones wouldn't fall out. I ordered the job and said goodbye. Girl, I had to get out of there before I forgot that I was already in love!"

Laughing at her own joke, Letty went on, oblivious to the sound of Liza's teeth grinding.

"When I was gone, they cleaned out my desk, Girl . . . gave him everything! But I didn't find out until it was time to leave, and so you know I showed off—I mean *performed*—when I found out that they had gone in my desk without asking me. That's why I was late and in a big janglement when I walked in here. Chile, I almost quit my job! Then my manager said that he would handle having the earrings couriered to D.C. before some gala because the client insisted on complete secrecy . . . as if I know anybody he knows and could tell his business! The man is crazy—and such a shame, too, given how fine he is and all."

Pulling the data together, Liza asked casually, "Those must've been some earrings, huh?"

Her friend went right on, gladly taking the bait as she vented. Liza could only sit there speechless as the vision came into focus. She allowed Letty to continue without uttering a word.

"I don't know how many carats each earring had. Diamond and topaz set in platinum . . . maybe they were worth twenty-five thousand dollars. Who knows? Or could've been a great paste job. Maybe fakes. But whoever the babe is that gets 'em, you can well rest assured that she definitely blew his mind! If they're real, she blew more than his mind. Maybe that's where he was all year long—gettin' his world rocked. And when it was over, he had to give the chick a fond farewell." Letty let out a little giggle. "I was about to apply for the vacancy, 'cause, Honey, I've never seen one like this. Those eyes . . . but, nah, not my type. He's probably a control-freak. Maybe I could work it out so you could meet him. He is in the District, and—"

"I wouldn't even consider it," Liza cut in emphatically, wanting to scream. "You know how I hate manipulators. This guy probably thinks he can buy any woman with some trinket; and if you claim to know me, then you know that I'm not down with legalized prostitution!"

Letty laughed in agreement. "You're right. Calm down. I must've been outta my mind to suggest something like that to you, Miss Principles. But, if your contract thief looks anything like this guy, you might be tempted to crack under pressure. I'm telling you, this man was *fine,* Girl."

"Well, he's obviously got a lot of personal baggage if he's runnin' women like water. Who needs that mess? That ain't nothing but heartache, Lady. Fine or no fine. Think about it."

"I see what you mean. The men in D.C. *are* crazy!"

It had to be Victor. As wild and coincidental as it was, it had to be him. But she was not about to ask Letty the man's name. There'd be no way to keep a straight face, and then she'd have to deal with a battery of uncomfortable questions. Letty would bust her for sure.

They both got up to leave, and Liza fought hard to swallow down the rage that was rising quickly to her throat. Fury was making her ears ring. She absolutely hated being worked, and would deal with Victor Duarte *directly* when she returned. But then, Letty had never said the earrings were for her. Clearly, she and Victor had never made any commitments not to see other people. *She* had been the one to tell *him* that. Love. He'd lied. Like every other man. He had some other woman in the cut and was trying to convince her that he was an angel. She'd kill him. No, she'd dissect him . . .

Liza immediately checked herself. She had no right to feel

this way. The fact that she was near violence weighed heavily on her mind. Again, like so many other things, her territorial reaction didn't make sense.

Hugging Letty goodbye, Liza turned to her friend and pushed a stray braid away from her face. "Letty, Hon . . . I told you . . . Gerry is not going to make it . . . and he wants me to leave you something. There will be fifty thousand dollars for you in a bank check Monday. Go to the Islands with your love. But don't you dare put it in a joint account or spend it all in one place. You don't have to go back to that dead-end job if you don't want to, okay? But the money is for you when this thing burns out. Remember what Aunt V would say: The left hand don't need to know what the right hand is doing. Just drop me a postcard one day."

Letty seemed stunned and oddly hurt as she took in the words.

"Lizzy, he isn't even gone yet and you're already doling out his money. Has working in the business world this long really made you that cold? He's your brother, for God's sake!"

Liza took the charge stoically and measured her reply. "He said he wants a very small, very quiet, immediate memorial . . . and doesn't want anyone to mourn him. He gave me full power of attorney to take care of those he loved best and said to be sure that his play sister was well provided for. Seeing you happy is about the best way I can think of to spend his money. He doesn't want anyone sobbing over the side of his casket."

Liza was resolute. She had no words for this reggae man. Yet, she could tell from Letty's pained expression that she didn't have to explain how close Gerald was to leaving them. She repeated her instructions carefully and sternly.

"Don't go to work tomorrow, pack your things, make love to your man, and go to the bank Monday. It's that simple."

Letty hugged her as the tears streamed down their faces.

"Lizzy, I'm so sorry. . . . You know I can't handle death," she wailed. "It's just too intense for me."

Liza held her friend tight for what might be the last time, and stroked her hair. Fighting past the lump in her throat, she soothed

Letty. "I know, Sweetie. That's why you won't have to deal with any of this. It's probably Divine intervention. When you leave on your trip, remember that Gerry and I love you, okay? Just promise to be happy."

When the two parted, they were oblivious to the intrusive glances that their sudden emotional outburst on the curb had drawn. As Letty hailed a cab, Liza returned to her car and sat silently for a while, unable to move.

She was thankful that Letty hadn't pieced together the fact that, by now, Gerald didn't even have enough money to pay his rent, let alone provide her with a fifty-thousand-dollar nest egg. But as usual, she would take care of it all—them all. That had been her role for so long that she didn't know any other way. Protectress. Someone destined to take care of every waif in the wind needing a strong wing of support to cover them. But who'd protect her from the storms of life? The question made her tired. Very, very, tired.

Pulling herself together enough to drive to the hotel, Liza focused on the days ahead of her: Saturday A.M., the attorneys; Saturday P.M., individual calls to her staff—to disband them, place them, and Fed-Ex their severance checks. Saturday night and all day Sunday, time in the office to review Ron's information; next week—project priorities, work out at the club, strengthen the gift, and definitely forget about Duarte—at least outside the mutual interest of their mission.

If she could write it in her daytimer, she could regain control.

Sixteen

The drive to New York by way of Philadelphia had been harrowing. He wasn't even sure why he had chosen to travel in that inconvenient fashion instead of taking the train other than that after the series of crazy events that had unfolded during the last few days, he needed to be in control of his destiny. Driving gave him a sense of mastery.

Being greeted by Miguel at his Manhattan brownstone was like returning to a private home away from home.

"Señor Duarte, so wonderful to see you as always," Miguel intoned in his usual, sophisticated manner. "Señor Helyar is waiting for you comfortably in the study. May I get you anything to make your appointment more pleasant?"

Victor smiled. It was refreshing to get back to a normal environment. "It is always good to see you as well, Miguel. How is your family?"

"Muy bien, gracia, Señor. Now, will you allow me to get something for you?" Miguel repeated as he ushered Victor into the large marble hallway.

The tension eased from Victor's body as the warm reception of his butler flowed over him. *"No, gracia,* Miguel. I will let you know if we require anything."

Crossing the foyer with great anticipation, Victor entered the study where André Helyar was waiting. Each time Victor saw him, the elegant old gentleman seemed a tad greyer and a bit shorter. Rising quickly despite his seventy-nine years, Helyar clasped him warmly in a continental embrace.

"Victor, to look upon you, my son, makes me so very proud. You have been well, I take it?"

Victor smiled at the familiar greeting, the mere sound of André's voice was balm to his tattered nerves.

"Yes, and you are very well, I can see. Please, sit down. Let's visit and enjoy this rare opportunity," Victor answered cheerfully, feeling better already.

Helyar's age had not dimmed his intuitiveness or his subtle approach to life. His eyes sparkled and Victor could sense his mentor's eagerness to edge toward the purpose of their meeting.

"Perhaps, then, as we visit, Victor, you can help me to understand the urgency of your call. I am getting old now and have become fond of directness. It saves one time, you know."

Not quite sure how or, more importantly, *where* to begin, Victor became evasive. "What, no mental chess today? I am truly disappointed."

André offered a wise grin with his quiet reply. "Victor, I may be partially blind, but I can still hear. Your voice gave you away, which was why I made myself immediately available."

Rising to cross the room for space, Victor felt trapped by Helyar's keen mind.

"Since I still follow the markets," his aged mentor added, "I take it that your troubles are not financial. Shall we be direct then, Victor?"

He knew that Helyar's question was caused by deep concern. The aged gentleman's voice held a quiet intensity that could not be ignored—but the issues were extremely complex and there was no way to discuss them without causing André undue alarm.

"I could never best you, could I?" Victor chuckled. "So, I would suppose that conceding is my only option." Victor chose his next words with care. It was important for Helyar to be involved, but he also understood that it would take a bit of coaxing to make him see the need for justice after all these years. From his post across the room, Victor engaged his mentor.

"Let me try to explain this as simply as I can. It would appear that I have uncovered almost all the pieces surrounding the massacre of my family and your son . . . all except the Washington connection. I'm still trying to get hard evidence at this point, and I need your assistance in developing a plan."

Now it was Helyar's turn to become indirect, as was always the rhythm of their discussions. Victor was sure that Helyar wouldn't be prepared to deal with the painful topic that they never openly discussed. He would have to be patient if he wanted to successfully draw his mentor into the subject.

"Would Miguel be so kind as to bring an old man a cappucino . . . and would you join me?" Helyar evaded.

"I'm sure he will and, yes, I will join you. But I also thought that you were not in the mood for chess this afternoon." Victor commented drily, drawing Helyar back to the subject at hand.

"Quite so," André agreed, "but I am also not in the mood to go into things that should be left buried."

Victor summoned Miguel, then allowed Helyar to engage him

in idle banter about the markets and current events until Miguel brought the frothy brew. Upon accepting the cup, André's brow creased into a deep analytical expression. The old man was torn, and Victor could appreciate his struggle. He hated to be the catalyst to raise the dead, but the situation had escalated.

When the door closed behind Miguel, Helyar seemed ready to voice his concerns. "Victor, you have been like a son to me," the old man murmured. "Like a blessing that was sent after François died in the carriage house with the others. Upon hearing of my only son's death, revenge was initially all that I could think of. But, then, you were sent to me, my godson, and I had to make my peace with life or risk losing you as well. Watching you grow and mature as François might have had he lived was more than enough for this old man. Now, you want me to assist you in perhaps killing yourself. Victor, that is more than I could possibly endure. If you must, please wait until I am gone."

The pain that etched André's handsome, elderly face brought back the flood of memories that they always found too devastating to discuss.

"I can appreciate your concern, sir, but I have been following this ever since I recovered from the shock. It has been a thread that has guided my existence for twenty years or more, and I *can't* give it up. Please do not ask me to make a commitment that I will break. I have never lied to you, and that's what such a promise would be."

As the elderly man studied the intensity and passion in Victor's face, they both knew that it had already gone too far.

"When I first collected you in London, I knew the wounds had bored deep into your heart. But I hoped—prayed—that time and a family . . . a normal life . . . would save you from this monster that could consume you. Ah, the rantings and prayers of an old man. *No importa,* not important at all," Helyar said sadly.

Taking an unsteady sip of the frothy liquid, Helyar set the china down with tired resolution. "I watched you develop, aware that you had a mental gift that bordered on genius. I hoped that it would be used to your positive advantage. The way you tackled the project of rebuilding your inheritance, your studies, chess, your martial arts . . . I thought perhaps you would let this vendetta go in time. But whenever I inquired about adding balance to your life with a family, I could tell that something was still awry." Absorbed in his cappucino, Helyar waited for Victor's response.

"I am truly sorry to have disappointed you so," Victor murmured, dismayed. "That was never my intention. I owe you my life."

"How long did I think I could fool myself?" Helyar replied without condescension. "You are a Duarte, and your heritage would not allow you to take such an injustice lying down. You will all be fighting the Mendozas in hell, I'm sure . . . The feud has been with our families for centuries. All because Duarte's were *mestizo* and Mendozas were direct descendants from the mainland without any Inca blood in their veins."

Helyar's expression darkened. "They did not deserve the land, the mines, or the inheritance from anything Amaru-Duarte built. The alliance with the Mendozas through marriage was unholy. Your father, my dear brother and friend, did not deserve to die like a dog. Nor did your mother, your sister, or my beloved son. I cannot even bear my ancestor's surname for fear that my identity will be revealed. Helyar . . . that is a European name, Swiss, not our own! That land was Incas' by right, from God's hand. May the Temple of the Sun still watch over its valleys. To hell with governments and sanctions and land reforms. That is why I could never let Mendozas have the stones. . . . It was a small victory to address this not-so-small matter of honor."

"Your rage is my rage. Your vendetta is my own. Then why won't you let me go after them?" Victor whispered. "I must right this wrong, and yet, I have hurt you by even mentioning it."

"To have held you so dear to me, and so close, for twenty-six years was blessing enough. No, my son, I would have probably been disappointed if you had never approached me with this."

Relief swept through Victor. He'd never dreamed that Helyar would relent and was thankful to God that he didn't have to go around the old man that he loved in order to accomplish his crusade.

"Then you will help me?" he almost shouted, crossing the room to squeeze Helyar's arm in affection.

"May I make a confession to you, Victor?" the old man asked with a sly smile.

Puzzled, Victor nodded.

Helyar's eyes sparkled as he spoke. "I, perhaps, have not been quite honest with even myself. Old age can make one get soft and sentimental, but I was not that way throughout my life."

Taking another generous sip of cappucino, Helyar dabbed the foam from his well-manicured, steel-grey mustache while continuing to study Victor intensely.

"Victor, when they killed François, I was almost insane myself. But, then, I had you and my lovely wife, Katrina, God rest her soul, to consider. As I watched you grow strong, it was no accident that I pushed you to excel in self-defense, or arranged for the best masters to teach you self-control, patience, and analysis. It was also no accident that you were protected and encouraged to continue your studies in the U.S., where you got your first exposure to Chem Tech."

Victor's eyes widened in astonishment. Several pieces of the puzzle fell immediately into place. Now it all made sense.

"I was always concerned that you would either break from the grief or that you would make an irrational move that could kill you. So, I wanted to teach you restraint before you went after your prey. But, then, after Katrina died and I began to grow old, my needs became more selfish. All I wanted then was to have you around to share my life. So, I left things as they were."

André finished his confession just above a whisper and stared into the far distance as if watching the memories unfold.

"And if I had never come to you with this request?" Victor asked quietly.

"I would have died a peaceful, selfishly happy, old man. Ah, old age, it is the greatest castrator of the universe!" André scoffed, vexed by his own impotence to directly assist in the plan.

The momentary agitation broke Helyar's trance, and he returned his gaze to Victor with a sad smile.

"I am glad that you told me. It helps me to understand my own complexities better," Victor admitted in earnest, thinking back on a number of scenarios that dotted his life. "So, where do we go from here?" he began again, anxious to get started.

An eager anticipation came over Helyar's face, as if this new game were what he'd waited an entire lifetime to play. Merriment sparkled in his aged, grey eyes, making him look twenty-years younger. Helyar rose slowly and moved toward the long, mahogany meeting table in the center of the room, indicating that Victor should join him.

"I will need a map and something to write on. You will commit my plan to memory, and then burn this paper. Once I leave New York, you will not be able to contact me directly until you are settled. But I will make arrangements to have your assets and any items of sentimental value transferred to your new location. Understood?"

Victor provided the items Helyar requested. Then, it dawned on him. . . . Helyar was *too* prepared. As his mentor pored over the detailed information before them, Victor chuckled.

"Sir, with no slight to your brilliance intended, I find it hard to imagine that you are just pulling this information from thin air as we speak. How long have you had this plan?"

Caught in his own game, Helyar gave a low chuckle of his own.

"Oh, some eighteen-to-twenty-six years. Why?" the old man asked nonchalantly.

"Just curious," Victor replied. "Just curious."

Then they both immersed themselves in the earnest concentration necessary to perfect such a complex plan. After two intense hours, Victor suggested a break for supper, which Helyar seemed glad to accepted.

"Godfather, we have all evening to complete this. Shall we take our meal in the other room for a change of venue?"

Helyar agreed readily, and they crossed into the salon. Once Miguel was out of earshot, Victor continued his earlier line of questioning.

"How can you pull all this together?" Victor asked, referring to the detailed agenda Helyar had outlined.

Another mischievous smile graced Helyar's face. "You're just like a child," he chided evasively. "You always assume that parents know nothing about life, even though your parents (and I) have given you life."

Ultimately, however, he fell beneath Victor's penetrating gaze. "Ah, not to be easily dissuaded I see," Helyar sighed. "If you must know, I spent my entire life working for . . . various government and *private* agencies. Interpol being one of them. This is how I happened to settle in Geneva . . . and where I met my lovely Swedish wife, Katrina, so long ago."

Victor was incredulous, and his astonishment halted Helyar's wistful trip down memory lane.

"Did you think that I was always a moderate, retired, jeweler?" he demanded. "Please, tell me how such a man would be able to provide his godson with the most proficient self-defense instructors in the world? Victor, your mentors were trained in the fine art of assassination. I always insured that your education was kept at the highest standards in accordance with the sacred promise I made to your father."

Helyar pushed his plate of broiled salmon away and leaned closer to his godson.

"Victor," he said, "you surprise me. Your powers of observation are better than this. Have you never given any thought to where I would acquire enough money to allow you to enjoy helicopter *and* flight lessons when you were younger? All assets from your father's holdings were frozen, remember? Or how I understood what events might take place before they actually happened globally—which gave you a tiny investment-edge on the market? I don't want to destroy your illusions, son, but I could not have born your living in poverty."

At a loss for words, Victor regarded his godfather with new eyes.

"Close your mouth, son," the old man teased gently. "Let's just say that the jewelry business is my day job, and otherwise, I am *very* well connected," he added with a hearty laugh.

They finished their meal without further reference to revenge or strategy. Victor spoke lightly of current events, and Helyar meticulously prepared a cigar of the finest blend.

Once they had returned to the study, the old man picked up where they had left off. "Have you explained *all* of the variables to me, Victor?" he asked. "You are aware that every detail of your life is important . . . and any omissions might jeopardize it."

Victor had not even considered discussing Liza, and he introduced the subject cautiously, watching Helyar for his response.

"There may be just one," Victor began slowly, "but I cannot be sure at this point."

Helyar took a long, luxurious drag on his cigar and countered with a dry riddle. "This is my last vice, Victor. The doctors have told me repeatedly to give it up. Each time I see them, I swear that I will, yes, I lie to myself. But I cannot stop smoking for it has completely seduced me."

Expelling another aromatic puff, Helyar raised one eyebrow, watching Victor patiently. Victor could feel the color rise to his own face in embarrassment. He couldn't look into those wise old eyes that left him naked, and his gaze slid away from the exposure.

Pleased by his own perception, Helyar needled him. "Ah, I see . . . That good, eh? Then, perhaps, my earlier concerns have been unwarranted. It is always the way: One variable replaced by another."

Helyar had hit his target, uncovering the real issue: This new variable would have to be included in their plan.

"I have seen some of the shrewdest agents die because they

had to go back to . . . something important . . . one last time."
André's calm voice held an implicit threat. "Or they were broken
because that important something was used as bait to lure them
to their demise. Let us, therefore, be completely honest so that
we do not have to face such unfortunate eventualities, shall we,
Victor?"

Victor escaped to the window again for air. He was ashamed
at having to divulge his irrational weakness for Liza—in full
detail. Perhaps, he was even more alarmed that he would now
have to admit it to himself.

His answer formed slowly in his mind, and he spoke to Helyar
while facing the window. "It is insane, but I am going to give
her the Duarte jewels. No one else is worthy of them."

He could feel Helyar appraising his carriage . . . contemplat-
ing the wisdom of such a decision.

"She must be quite extraordinary, but could pose an extreme
liability. You do understand?"

Still not looking at Helyar, Victor nodded. "Yes . . . but, I can
never leave her. That would be impossible now."

Helyar didn't respond for what felt like an eternity. "You love
her?"

Victor swallowed. "Yes."

"That is all I needed to know."

"Thank you," Victor murmured. "I won't disappoint you."

"Come, let us go back to work."

The subject had been dismissed, his decision blessed . . . by
the wave of a hand that he could trust. Nothing else in his life
had ever felt so reassuring or been so simple.

Rising to leave amid Victor's protests, Helyar remained firm.
"No, my son, I am weary. I will retire to the hotel for a quiet
evening alone. In the morning, I will return to the chalet. Please
be sure that you have told me *everything* about the both of you
before I have left the city. Because, after that, we may not see
each other for a long while. . . . That is, after all, the hardest
part, yes?"

Victor hugged his old friend, mentor, father, guide with a

sensitivity that went beyond the surface cordiality of a continental embrace. He had to swallow away the emotion that tore through him. Helyar was an old man, and each visit with him like a rare gift. Never promised.

Patting Victor's shoulder, Helyar spoke softly. "My son, you have made me proud, your heritage proud, and I hope that you are happy with the balance of your life . . . having been so robbed in the first half of it. I am an old man now, with a few vices, so there should be no worry about what happens to me. Trust that I will pull out whatever stops necessary to see that you succeed."

As they embraced again, Victor felt an inexplicable sadness at their parting. "Thank you, Godfather, for giving me so much and loving me as dearly as I have loved you. Thank you for giving me back an understanding of who I am."

The old man smiled thoughtfully as they approached the door. *"De nada,"* he said. "It is no trouble to love a son such as you." He studied Victor's face. "I have one last thing for you—I believe you are finally ready for it now—something that I had translated out of Old World Spanish so that it could appraise more easily on the antiquities market at Sotheby's. I will have a courier bring it to you since it might provide some insight to the history of the jewels that you seem so determined to give away. For me to give this to you before seemed pointless, especially since treasures from *la hacienda* upset you so. But, now, I think you can handle it. And, remember, there is uranium in the mines that is worth more than a king's ransom to Chem Tech."

As they parted, Victor stood perplexed in the archway, watching the limousine collect the ancient gentleman. A tremor of excitement coursed through him as he walked back to the study to absorb the plan, memorizing every detail, before casting the papers into the fireplace.

The subtle chime of the bell gave Liza a start. She hurried to the door, abandoning the piles of computer printouts that Ron had left earlier. Peering through the window, she was surprised to discover a uniformed courier impatiently waiting on her steps.

Puzzled, she hurriedly opened the door and signed for the small package. A deep frown creased her brow as she returned to the office in her home and opened the parcel. What in the world . . .

The outer wrapping gave way to a soft, black-velvet box, and her memory snapped back instantly. Lightly running her fingertips over the delicate fabric, she delayed opening the oblong enclosure, afraid, yet excited, about what she might find inside. Unable to resist the temptation, she raised the hinged lid and gasped with an eerie mixture of terror and wonder.

"Victor, what have you done?" she cried in shock, held in a trance by the exquisite stones.

She'd never seen anything like them. The strong afternoon sun magnified their brilliance as each of a million facets dazzled in the light.

Liza murmured the words as she read the attached card. "Use them when you do your homework and wear them at the master's chess game next week. Details to follow. Liza, they were made for you. Victor."

All her resolve to be angry, to throw the earrings back in his face and refuse them, melted at the simple words on the card. She couldn't pull herself away from the box, captivated by the timeless magnificence of the stones, captivated by the thought that Victor had selected her to wear them. They were worth a mint. But more important than their worth, the stones had been his mother's. The sentimental value alone was incalculable. Letty had been wrong. This was definitely not a goodbye.

Uneasy, Liza reached out her hand to touch the gems. As the tips of her fingers grazed the surface of each diamond, a light tingling sensation ran through her hands. Lifting the earrings out carefully, she slipped them on and walked down the hall to the mirror in the foyer. She'd seen these in the restaurant when she'd probed Victor, but hadn't understood . . . in myriad visions . . . large, smoky topaz stones glittering with the hundreds of tear-shaped diamonds that hung beneath them. . . .

Curiosity had her in its grip and she held up her hair to survey their full beauty. But as she stared into the glass, a dull ache overtook her temples. Immediately, the ache grew into a stabbing throb that made her wince and cry out.

The intensity of the pain forced her to pull the gems from her ears. Overcome, she slumped against the wall with the earrings still held tightly in her fist. What had caused that sudden jolt of agony? Questions swirled in her brain as she tried to steady her breaths. She felt as though someone had suddenly punched her in the stomach. Trembling, she opened her hand to a stinging sensation that made her palm feel like it had been cut. What was happening?

When she looked down, her palm had blistered and reddened from a surface burn that faded before her eyes. Terrified, she dropped the earrings on the small crescent-shaped table beneath the mirror, looking from her palm to the mirror and back down to the stones on the table.

Unnerved, she gingerly scooped up the jewelry, ran down the hall to her study, and frantically returned the exquisite pieces to the velvet box. Her hands trembled as she worked the hinge, which snapped shut—along with her eyes. Hundreds of images raced before her mind in the few seconds of darkness . . . horrible, horrible images that threatened to shake the foundation of her sanity.

Nothing calmed the wild beating of her heart as she prayed for deliverance, sitting motionless, traumatized, until the light scent of lavender filled the room. That wonderful, comforting presence gave her enough strength and courage to look for answers.

Pushing aside the computer printouts, she reached for the volumes that detailed crystal energy and voraciously searched the pages. Stilling herself, she took the gems into her hand once more, focusing on the images that came before her. This time she didn't fight the warmth that emanated from her hands and the headache subsided into a dull throb that was manageable.

Hours passed as she watched a panorama of scattered information unfold. Finally, fatigued and unable to hold her head up, she slumped down on the table and drifted off to sleep.

She was sure that she heard the phone ring, and the annoying sound brought her to a groggy awareness. Stumbling to her feet, she searched the dark room for the jarring bleat that pierced the evening quiet.

Tripping over the cord, she located the receiver and pulled it to her damp cheek to answer the call.

"Hello," she croaked.

"Liza?" The now-familiar male voice carried a hint of worry. "Are you all right? You don't sound well. Is everything okay?"

Victor's voice seemed far away . . . as if he were calling out across a roaring sea. In a near stupor, she managed a halting reply.

"The stones. The earrings. Something's wrong with them," she said weakly.

Panic registered in Victor's voice, and he shouted to her through the fog that cloaked her mind.

"I'm coming over immediately. Unlock the door. Don't pick them up again until I get there!"

Flames consumed her as she collapsed.

He found her on the landing. Sheer terror had rushed through him when he'd heard her voice on the phone. Appraising her cautiously, he touched her shoulders to make her look up at him. It was as if she had been drugged, and she swayed and leaned against the wall when he reached for her. His heart raced against time. Holding her jaw firmly in his hand, he forced her chin up, took one look at her stricken face, and demanded an explanation.

"What happened?"

As she sketched the details of her experience wearing the

jewels, he paged through the books for a clue to her extra-sensory reaction.

"*Madre de Dio!* How could you have been so foolish, man?" he exclaimed, closing the last book abruptly.

Without answering Liza's perplexed gaze, he picked up the velvet case and ran outside to lock it in the car. He had to get the stones out of the house and as far away from Liza as possible. Returning quickly, he sat next to her on the landing and stroked her hair.

"*Querida,* I could have done you great harm. . . . Forgive me. This is all so very new to me as well. I was cautioned to clean them first . . . to remove the energy with a sea salt and spring water rinse well before you touched them. You just got hit with several hundred years of trauma that was still held in these stones."

Liza seemed totally disoriented, even with the stones no longer in the house. When he tried to get her to her feet, she wretched and vomited, resting her head between her knees when she was done. She was breathing hard and her brow felt clammy. Placing his arm around her shoulders, he tried to get her to lean against him for support.

"Your words, Victor . . . you're not making sense. I have to lie down. It sounds like you're speaking a strange language. . . . Everything is garbled."

Moving quickly, he lifted Liza up in his arms and carried her to bed. He'd take a post in her chair for the night and read. There were too many unanswered questions, and he needed to be with her just in case something else went wrong. He'd be there to protect her while she slept soundly. This, too, felt familiar, as though he'd been caring for her for a very long time.

By the height of the sun coming in through the window, Liza could tell that it was early afternoon. But she distinctly recalled it being dark outside when she'd fallen into bed. The strong smell of coffee was irresistible, giving her the momentum to swing her feet over the side of the mattress to search for her slippers. Had she left the coffeemaker on overnight? What was happening to her senses? Hearing movement in her kitchen, she quickened her pace and found Victor busily searching in her refrigerator for something to eat.

"What in the name of . . . ?" she began, having only a vague memory of his presence before she'd drifted off to sleep.

"I was getting worried about you, Liz," Victor replied gently, "and I'm afraid we've missed Mass this morning," he added, helping her to a chair.

He smiled uneasily at her, and she could tell that he was worried.

"What the hell happened? I feel like I have one giant hangover. But, trust me, I was not out drinking." She rambled on, holding her temples in discomfort.

"Is something wrong with the project? When did you get here?" Nothing made sense to her.

"This should help," he offered in a low voice, pushing a steaming cup of peppermint tea in front of her.

"What's this?" she asked skeptically. "I thought I smelled coffee." The headache and confusion made her irritable.

Victor smiled. "You did, but the coffee is for me. The tea is for you. Did you know that peppermint is a blood-purifier?"

"I don't start my day without java." Why was she so angry all of a sudden?

Not answering her, Victor took a sip of his coffee and surveyed her appreciatively. She followed his gaze and looked down, mortified to find herself in a sheer nightgown.

"Oh, no! I don't even remember!" How could she have made love to someone and not remembered? It was terrifying.

Victor prickled at her response. "Much to my dismay, *that* did not happen last night. You apparently put on the earrings, which still held a lot of negative energy. I guess the best analogy would be that they drained your battery. When I came over, you were in a lump on the floor. So, I carried you to bed, undressed you, and allowed you to sleep unmolested. So you see, chivalry is not dead, after all."

"I feel like I was hit in the head with a sledgehammer." She winced, rubbing her forehead. "Can it really be that strong?"

"For someone with your latent talent, apparently so. I got worried when I couldn't rouse you, and I called a gentleman at the bookstore and told him what had happened. He suggested that I clean the crystals—the diamonds and topazes—well before you wear them again, and he also said that the tea would help you to feel a lot better. Apparently caffeine will only make it worse. So, suit yourself."

Since feeling worse was out of the question, Liza grudgingly agreed to stomach the tea. After a few sips, which did seem to help fight the nausea, she stared at Victor. "This is heavy stuff."

Nodding, Victor looked at her expectantly. Although his tone was matter-of-fact, his gaze said more. "Despite their depth charge . . . did you like them?"

His face held a hopeful intensity that she hadn't seen in him before. He was like a schoolboy asking his first girlfriend to go to the prom, and that rare glimpse of vulnerability made her smile despite how ill she felt. But she wasn't about to wear those stones again! She didn't want to look at them, much less touch them. No thank you. Not for love or money. She'd already toyed with dynamite, his disappointment notwithstanding . . .

"Victor," she began gently, trying not to hurt his feelings, "they don't like me."

"They were meant for you," he whispered, moving closer to her.

She hoped he could understand, and it really made her feel terrible as she watched his shoulders slump. But, then, wait a minute. . . . Snatches of memory started to come back to her. Letty had said something about this jewelry, hadn't she? Thoughts scrambled in her brain for order. Her best friend had said something about Victor giving his women expensive stuff when it was over, didn't she? Anger reclaimed her as she stared at him.

"You don't expect me to keep them, do you? If you want to break up, then you don't have to spend—"

"What?"

Visibly taken aback, Victor creased his brow in confusion. "If you are afraid of them, I will assure you that I'll take great measure to rid them of any negative energy that they may hold."

He was missing her point, so she offered a calm clarification.

"No, if you clean them, there should be no danger. That's not the issue. The issue is that I do not choose to accept them. You do not have to *pay* me as you paid the others for services rendered. If it's over, which seems to be the pattern when you give an elaborate trinket, then we can just shake hands and call it a day."

His face reddened as he walked away from her. "What the hell are you talking about, Liza? Payment for *services* rendered! Are you out of your mind?"

"No. I'm not crazy. I went to Philly yesterday, too, and bumped into an old friend who told me about your style of giving women expensive gifts . . . *many women*. I don't want to be like all the others, Victor." Her voice had been calm, but the depth of the hurt quavered in it.

"What?"

Typical male response, to go deaf when you don't have an answer. His evasion wore on her like betrayal, even though she knew she had no grounds.

"You heard me. I'm not like that. Casual." Her voice escalated.

"Just the other day, you told me—"

"I don't want to talk about it. You don't have to buy me presents. Okay? Let's drop it."

He seemed trapped by an internal conflict, unable to leave, unable to stay. That he was so angry only stoked her fury. How dare he be angry and then try to play it off and deny everything!

"Who told you about this?"

She looked at him hard. "A trusted source. Does it matter?"

"Yes," he said defensively. "Because the past is the past. It has no bearing on us now. I shouldn't even have to explain."

"Oh, and like you didn't ask me about my old lover and then get all bent out of shape. At least I told you the truth—a word that always comes between us."

"Your probe is way off this time, Liza. By a long shot. I don't have to listen to this."

The die was cast. She had sewn the dragon's teeth; this was war. Victor looked as though he might strangle her if he didn't leave now. Squaring his shoulders, he turned away from her.

"Dealing with your logic, Liza, is like arguing with the Mad Hatter!"

She continued, ignoring his fury, still consumed by her own. "Are they ranked from best to least effective by earrings, tennis bracelets, pendants . . . whatever?"

"I'm leaving."

Random flashes of conversations leapt across her mind as she followed quickly behind him. It was as though something had edited her mental video tape, scrunching all the images into a fast-moving reel. Whole sections were missing. Things were there that didn't connect or make sense. Times changed. Words blurred. All she could grasp onto was the irrational anger that held her as she paced quickly behind him down the hall.

"Then, when you break up with them," she nearly shouted, "if they've been really, *really* good, do you give them an especially nice present, like a lady's Rolex . . . or something? I suppose I should be flattered. You lied to me! I'm no more special to you than, than . . . I don't know what you call them. So, if it's over, then at least be up front about it."

She wanted to teach him a lesson, the one about playing with people's emotions. She wanted him to feel the same sense of disappointment and anger that she'd felt when Letty'd revealed the truth. This time, she'd fight back. Truth was her sword.

Victor stopped abruptly and spun on her. With slippers on, she almost skidded to a halt on the hardwood floors to avoid their collision. The quick movement realigned her thoughts.

Now, only inches from his face, she could see it. Oh, God . . . he'd been falsely accused! Then, she saw them. . . . It was an argument, in what looked like an old bedroom. . . .

"I would *never* give *two-hundred-and-fifty-thousand-dollars* worth of documented antiquity to a common whore!" he raged, stopping her vision. "Nor would I give a valuable piece of my family heritage—*my mother's earrings*—to a woman I was about to leave!"

His mother's earrings? Oh, dear God . . . she remembered.

Turning on his heel, he flung open the front door, shattering the beveled lead glass in the panel above it. For a frozen moment, Liza stood still. Nothing made sense as she tried to catch her breath from their violent outburst. She had almost physically cringed for a second, fearing that he might strike her. The fear rose out of nowhere . . . someplace distant. Past. Their words rang in her ears. He had given her his mother's earrings . . . not some paste copies that Letty was talking about. How could she have forgotten when she'd seen the stones at their first dinner? What had taken possession of her memory, her behavior, her soul? She knew what they meant to Victor. What had she done to him?

Paralyzed by guilt, she looked down at the shattered glass that resembled her life and slowly began picking up the pieces.

She had tried to call Victor for days without success. Either she got an answering machine or his efficient secretary screened his calls. She had considered driving over to DGE, but showing up at his office unannounced would have put their relationship on public display and jeopardized the plan for the firms to appear to be at war—a flagrant abuse of their pact to be discreet. Going to his home had seemed like too much of an invasion, and she had no idea what she would do if he refused to open the door. That option was too humiliating. And what could she have said if she'd reached him? Victor, I was experiencing crystal fallout? I was having a bad psychic trip?

Every day she had tried to stop the nagging fears that plagued her. She hadn't wanted to deal with the very real possibility that Victor could already be gone, having left the country without a trace. If it hadn't been for the small flicker of hope that he was still in the vicinity, she would have given over to full-blown despair. She could still *feel* him near her, and that had been the only thing that kept her going.

But the entire week had still proved disappointing. Only she and Ron were left to man the fort, searching in vain through the piles of printouts for answers. With Connie gone, having been tearfully placed in a safe Department of Agriculture job, and the rest of the gang farmed out to other consulting firms, the quiet in the office was deafening. Liza had only spoken to Letty once, to be sure that she had cashed her check and to wish her good luck on her way to the Caribbean.

Ron had been particularly morose, which hadn't helped. The staff changes had gotten to him as well, and he'd not been his normal, sarcastic self. He'd moved about like a ghost, although he'd worked diligently on the project. And since she wasn't out drumming up new clients, the phone rang infrequently—and those calls, mostly vendors were intercepted by a temp.

Ed had called sporadically, just to tell them he was faxing the standard status reports. On those rare occasions, she and Ron would fight for the phone, welcoming his friendly voice. She wondered why she'd made the organizational changes, since it was now obvious that Victor intended to conclude the mission without her and disappear. There was no longer any chance of a partnership with him. He'd told her his position, that he'd go it alone and work around her if necessary. That meant that she had to do the same, and try not to get in his way. She had to be careful not to make a hasty move that could tip off the enemy, so her explanation to her staff had been that it was getting too dangerous for them to stay while she and Ron put more of the pieces of the puzzle together.

To keep herself occupied when the considerable tension of the quiet became unbearable, she would practice her mental exercises and took great delight in how accurate she was becoming. But now, as she entered the fourth day of solitude, she was practically beside herself.

She hated loose ends. Before Victor had dropped off the face of the earth, she had wanted to tell him about the things she'd seen while wearing the stones. . . . Everything was connected— what she'd experienced had not been a flimsy excuse for poor behavior. The vision had been real, part of the overall challenge they faced. She understood that now, but her understanding no longer mattered. Victor was in an unreachable place where her mind couldn't go.

As she stared out the window trying to concentrate, the large glass doors to the suites opened and a hubbub of angry, voices flowed into the corridor.

Apologizing profusely, the young temp glared at the determined delivery man. "Ms. Nichols, he claims he has express orders to have only you sign for this," she explained helplessly. "I *told* him that it was customary for the receptionist to take the packages, but he said he would have to return it if you didn't."

Victor. Anticipation quickened her pulse as she cut the girl off. "It's okay, Denise. I'll take care of it. No problem."

Within seconds Liza had signed for the small package. She waited impatiently for the pair to leave. She needed privacy, and she shut her door to prevent Ron from barging in. He would at least knock, she told herself, as she tore off the sealed cardboard encasement.

The familiar velvet box slid into her hands, and she held it against her chest. *He isn't angry anymore,* she breathed. It had blown over.

Clicking open the lid, she stared down at the magnificent stones. The way they caught the late-afternoon sun was awe-inspiring. But what truly captured her was that they were so precious to Victor and he'd chosen to give them to her. The gems were an extension of an unspoken bond; they had been his mother's.

Lisa searched quickly for a note and tried to still her heart. The card contained another one of Victor's terse directives.

They're clean now. Have them on at the Environmental Fund-raiser this Friday, 6:00 o'clock sharp, Dumbarton Oaks, glass pavilions. Dress is formal. This is the master's chess tournament that I spoke of earlier. Victor, P.S. What's past is past. Fate.

She had to admit it: She'd really missed him. She loved the way he tried to sound so detached, so formal . . . in case anyone intercepted his notes. Until he was gone, she hadn't realized how much he meant to her. This time, she wouldn't mess up. She'd be honest and tell him how she really felt: Positively crazy about him. They were both beyond shame now. There was nothing left to prove.

Snapping the lid shut, Liza held the card. Reading it over and over, she repeated the message slowly, hearing his words in her mind, not just seeing them. Suddenly, she became aware that Victor's voice had been another precious part of the gift.

The bond still held them. Maybe they had a chance.

Seventeen

By 6:00 o'clock, the circular glass pavilions that enclosed the Bliss Collection at Dumbarton Oaks were humming with dignitaries and the press. Every corridor was filled with tuxedo-clad servers balancing chablis and an array of mouth-watering hors d'oeuvres.

Removing a second glass of wine from a tray with an air of showmanship, Stan continued to rib Victor.

"You have become surlier than I have ever seen you, m' boy! Why don't you give up this monk routine and join me in a night out with the ladies? Forget Chem Tech. We'll finish the project and get paid. Case closed."

Inconspicuously gesturing toward two elegant, long-stemmed beauties who were standing out of earshot, Stan worked on Victor's resolve. "Remember, I told you that I had these two models

coming down to work with one of our clients? Well, you're looking at 'em. Now, tell me that they don't give you a rise."

Stan gave Victor a wink. He needed a partner to make his
planned night-on-the-town work. But Victor could not be baited.
He'd given up a life of crime. Liza had incarcerated him.

Appraising Stan's beauties, Victor nodded his appreciation.
"As always," he said, "you have an excellent eye. But I'm afraid
that I'm going to have to pass tonight. Unlike you, I saw this
particular evening as an opportunity to transact business, and
the ladies would be a definite distraction."

Undaunted by the rebuff, Stan reveled in Victor's positive appraisal. Eyeing the models, each man struggled to make his
point.

"Vic, picture it." Stan waved his free hand in the air as though
painting a panoramic vision of temptation before Victor's eyes.
"Two beautiful, willing babes . . . the *Phoenix* out of her slip . . .
them out of their panties . . . the cork out of the champagne . . .
and they said a man could only die once!"

Victor found that a blasé refusal was becoming increasingly
more difficult. Liza was a risk, and maybe a little diversion could
shake her from his brain. He had to do something to make himself less vulnerable to her.

Sensing his indecision, Stan picked mercilessly at his resolve.
"C'mon, Vic. Where's your sense of pride? How can you pass
that up when I've delivered it to you on a silver platter?"

Victor's resolve began to crumble. "Stanley," he conceded, "I
see why you are one of the best litigators on the East Coast.
Your arguments are very convincing."

But as he looked at the women, he couldn't shake Liza's presence from his mind. Had she ruined him for the sport?

"Come on, Victor! You haven't had your baby transported
from the marina yet. . . . We could pull her out of dock for her
last voyage of the season in grand style. Just *look* at 'em, Vic,
and tell me I'm not dreaming!"

Victor laughed. Stan was positively outrageous in his dealings
with women. He had to get the man off his back. Reaching into

the pocket of his tux, Victor pulled out his key ring, slipped off the engine key for the *Phoenix* and tossed it to Stan.

Victor gave the women a contemplative glance. "Stan, you entertain the ladies tonight. Your reputation precedes you, and I know you'll be able to handle both of them quite effectively. But if you do need help, I might be able to make myself available. We'll see; I can't promise." His ambiguous response surprised even him. Was he starting to vacillate? Never . . .

Aware that Victor was teetering on the edge of acceptance, Stan pressed him until Victor became vexed that the simple decision to enjoy himself had become so unnecessarily *complicated.* He and Liza had made no commitment, none that she would admit to, anyway. Just a "roll in the hay," she had informed him icily, offending him deeply. They had gotten off on the wrong foot, and it was probably best that he go back to his old modus operandi before becoming too involved.

Liza's response to his mother's earrings had pissed him off royally. Therefore, she could wear the stones to give her probe more accuracy, to give him more information and that was all. He had been stupid, even admitted to Helyar that he loved her when she obviously didn't love him. Well, the only reason he'd sent the gems back to her was because she had found out about his past relationships. Returning the earrings to her was a compromise, an admission of guilt. But, then again, he had really no reason to feel guilty. . . .

Almost unaware of Stan's continuing argument, Victor emerged from his own thoughts and caught the tail end of Stan's persuasive pitch.

"Besides," Stan concluded, "can you tell me what you have to do tonight that could be better than this?"

"Stanley," Victor capitulated, "I'll go work the room; you keep the ladies busy, and I'll see you in an hour. Now, are you satisfied?"

Without waiting for a response, Victor cut through the waves of dignitaries, selectively stopping to exchange courtesies and seal important commitments to the firm. Lately, it had become too easy to manipulate the throng of pompous guests at these functions and he had lost the thrill of the game. As he made his rounds, Victor forced himself to engage in the routine discussions that now left him bored.

The only saving grace for the affair lay in the splendor of the glass pavilion, which housed a breathtaking collection of pre-Columbian fine art. Where, he wondered, was Liza?

The crystal-like glass structure gave the impression that the objects were actually enveloped by the gardens and woods outside. The illusion of outdoors seemed to free the ancient Incan and Aztec artifacts from their gallery prison, thus making the evening more bearable. She had to be there. . . .

Mingling with one small cluster of guests, then another, Victor moved with a deliberate speed. He had to find her. Something was pulling him, telling his insides that she was in trouble.

It was 6:45 and he still hadn't spotted her. Liza was always punctual.

Distractedly surveying the room while he engaged in light conversation, Victor took a mental inventory of all the game pieces on the board. His survey was halted by a rare mask from the Olmec period which combined human and feline forms.

The mask eerily reminded him of his own personality, merging normal human reactions with an explosive ferocity that could descend into hellish proportions. Captivated by the beauty of the piece, he wondered if his outburst—warranted though it had been—had frightened Liza. Had she decided to retreat?

Continuing his abstract search, Victor's eyes stopped at the Peruvian funerary exhibit. The gold urns and ornaments seemed to catch additional light from another, undetectable, source. Moving closer to the exhibit to investigate, he saw a goddess. She was standing with her back to him, shimmering as if she were a living part of the exhibit.

Her dark hair was swept up tightly, providing a rich contrast to the soft skin of her nape. The way she wore her hair exposed her graceful neck, which carried her head tall and proud. The bare amber of her shoulders wore like a mantle a million facets of light which sparkled from the dazzling gems that clasped her earlobes.

He was mesmerized.

Her lithe curves made his heart stop. She was sheathed in a sheer, dark-bronze silk gown which cascaded down to mid-calf. He took in a breath, monitoring his actions before he approached her. Incredibly, the color of the gown exactly matched the hue of her skin. Crazy thoughts plowed through his mind. . . . She moved amid the ancient artifacts as though she were a naked goddess amongst the ruins. Suddenly, why he was so angry with Lisa became vague.

Determined not to make eye contact or give Liza the satisfaction of casting her spell on him, he chose a vantage point where he could safely appreciate her beauty from afar . . . except there was no safe distance from Liza. The more he tried to dislodge the vision of her, the more he was drawn to it, compelled by her every graceful movement. But where did her distress come from?

He hadn't even noticed Ed, who had discreetly moved to his side, and he started slightly when his friend spoke.

"I knew she was beautiful, Victor, but the conference room really didn't do her justice," Ed said softly, expressing genuine awe.

Unable to deflect this glaring truth, Victor could only nod in agreement. He could trust Ed to be discreet. "No, it doesn't," he admitted quietly, still drawn to her. "The transformation is absolutely breathtaking. Is Marjorie here tonight?" he inquired, changing the subject although he did not cease his adoration of Liza. "I'm sure she would enjoy this gala."

"She wouldn't have allowed me to come without her," Ed replied. "In fact, I've barely spoken to her all evening. You know she's the real politician in the family."

"It helps to have a teammate to work the room," Victor said. He'd always taken vicarious pleasure in Ed's constancy, certain that he'd never find such peace for himself.

"She'll kill me if I neglect to let her know you're here. She's not far off, and I know she'd like to see you." Ed clasped Victor's arm cheerfully, then left his side to collect Marjorie.

The brief encounter with Ed had cleared his head, and Victor was thankful to have his mental precision return. He had to find out what was wrong. Spotting the target that had been his primary objective all evening, Victor obliquely made his way through the throng.

"Bill Hanson, it is a pleasure to see you tonight," he said with confidence as he approached Chem Tech's Senior Vice President of Foreign Markets, moving beside his quarry.

"Victor Duarte, it is always good to see you. I take it that you have some positive news on the progress of our project," his target responded.

He didn't like the wary tone in Hanson's voice. Trouble.

The master's tournament was now on, and the next move was Victor's. A player's calm settled between the two opponents. As if by instinct, two of Bill Hanson's directors flanked him for protection. The momentary shift on the board gave Victor an opportunity to hone his strategy.

"I believe you've met Bob Gallagher, Director of Manufacturing, and John Blaylock, our finance director," Hanson was forced to add as a standard courtesy when the two men joined them.

"Yes, I believe we've met, on more than one occasion during our award meetings. Gentlemen," Victor returned pleasantly, extending his hand, a necessary rule of the game.

Turning to bring the two newcomers up to date with the play, Hanson gave a brief recap before redirecting his earlier move. "I was just telling Victor Duarte that as senior vice president of the division, it will be my neck on the line if we don't start seeing some results . . . and I must tell you that I'm beginning to get concerned about Risc System's ability to handle this job."

Avoiding a direct response, Victor nodded, leaving the pause open to interpretation. Warming up to the game, he carefully watched the two rooks stand close guard next to their king before chancing an aggressive, camouflaged move. "I have been con-

cerned myself . . . and believe that it may be time to assist Risc
Systems a little more than we had originally anticipated. After
all, it is our primary objective to ensure that our client's needs
are met first." He had to throw them off her trail.

As both rooks returned an approving smile, Victor sensed that
a critical portion of their board was now vulnerable. He was in.
The king was left open to assess whether or not he'd play along
as one of the "good ol' boys."

Baited, Hanson responded with another shrewd query. "That
may be difficult, given the original acrimony that has been obvious between the firms."

The opportunity to penetrate was tempting, but years of experience made Victor hold back to set the board more securely.

"Possibly," he said, looking in Liza's direction across the
room. "They are young and do not understand how much is at
stake . . . should there be complications. But I think if we could
help manage them through the process, this could be completed
without any unnecessary issues arising."

Hanson was smiling now. Victor was satisfied that they fully
comprehended the double entendre implicit in what seemed like
a benign statement. Knight advances king.

"Duarte, this is why we wanted your firm to fully share in
the benefits of this contract . . . but from a more supportive,
rather than direct, role. Should issues arise, your firm needn't
suffer the consequences of a young firm's learning curve," Hanson said in a low tone.

Check, Victor breathed to himself, walking the tightrope between betraying Liza and meeting his objectives. During another
meaningful pause, one of the rooks moved forward unexpectedly
to close ranks around their exposed king.

Appearing wary, John Blaylock interceded. "I still feel very
uncomfortable. I can't see how DGE will possibly be able to get
Risc Systems to make the directional change needed to get this
thing done. At least not based upon the animosity I've witnessed
to date."

Bob Gallagher concurred. "If Risc Systems perceives that

their contract has been aborted before they have been given the normal courtesy to produce against it, I am sure their principal would not hesitate to cry foul. She may even try to make it a civil rights issue. We do not need that kind of public focus right now. Not while things are . . . delicate."

Victor enjoyed watching the strategy unravel as he decided how to dispense with the king's protective pieces on the board. Nodding in obliging agreement, he turned to the last piece that had moved in the game.

"Bob, having borne the sting of the wasp myself, I am sure your assessment is correct . . . Which is why I would not advise any sudden, unnecessary approach to the hive." He had to buy Liza time.

As the circle tightened imperceptibly, Victor knew that it was because Bob Gallagher had been rendered impotent. Knight takes rook.

"Then what do you suggest, Duarte?" Hanson asked, opening himself again for another aggressive move.

"Patience . . . and carefully orchestrated détente—which is well underway," Victor said, repressing a triumphant smile as he watched the second bewildered rook fall.

"I hadn't realized that you were on top of the situation, Duarte," John floundered.

They were going down.

In full view of a checkmate, Hanson extended his hand to Victor. "I am pleased to have you join our team. It could be rewarding for everyone. I think we should meet more regularly now for updates. Golf, Monday, at ten?"

Sealing his temporary win with a handshake, Victor closed the tournament. "At ten, it is. Gentlemen," he said crisply, then moved away from the board.

He had to make his way over to Liza before she said anything that could disrupt the board.

"Victor Duarte! I told Edward that he would be on my list if he didn't make sure I had a chance to talk with you. Where have you been hiding?" piped the impeccable socialite that faced him.

Damn!

Taking Marjorie's hand, Victor forced a smile. "I would not hear of such a thing."

"Victor, don't let her badger you," Ed warned. "She has trouble up her sleeve in the form of a *friend* she wants you to meet."

He didn't have time for this now.

Turning to Ed with mock agitation, Marjorie rattled on. "Now, Victor, you will *not* listen to him, will you? You know how *conservative* my Eddie is, and Elizabeth Templeton is one of the nicest people you'd ever want to meet."

Victor's pleasant facial expression didn't change. His mind raced for a plausible escape from a meeting with one of Marjorie's divorced, suburban bridge partners. He was used to the obligatory introductions by now, but couldn't deal with the small talk tonight. He had to get Liza out of there. He could feel a wall of danger closing in around her, and it gnawed at his insides.

But he could also tell from the expectant look on Marjorie's face that a promise had already been made. A diplomatic departure wouldn't be easy. However, he didn't have time to follow the rules. Issuing one of his more rehearsed gazes, he took Marjorie's hand again and opted for the dramatic.

"But, *señora,* why would I need to meet your friend when I have already met the most beautiful woman at this affair tonight?"

Marjorie's long blonde lashes fluttered lightly, and she purred back demurely, "Why, Victor Duarte . . . really!"

A slight giggle of immense satisfaction bubbled instantly to her surface, accompanying a rosy flush that seemed to make Ed nervous. Very nervous. Well, maybe he'd gone a little overboard. But he had to get away from Marjorie without any suspicion regarding his involvement with Liza. Ed's wife was worse than the CIA when it came to uncovering hidden information. The problem was that Marjorie, unlike Ed, could never keep anything quiet. To have Washington, D.C. abuzz with that kind of gossip was out of the question. He'd make it up to Ed later. Victor touched Ed's shoulder as he strode away. "Ed, you are a *very* lucky man. Stay married."

In his haste to remove himself from Marjorie's well-intentioned social pairing, he almost didn't realize that Liza was already engaged in conversation. He stopped in his tracks.

Liza was facing him, but she never averted her eyes in his direction. The gentleman that had her full attention had his back to him, and Victor was gripped by an irrational, yet familiar curiosity. He and Liza had both been talking and mingling with different people all night, so why the sudden red alert?

Remembering their recent rift, he hesitated, not sure of her response. The last thing he wanted was to become the unfortunate victim of a public snipe under the watchful eyes of Chem Tech, so he opted for another glass of wine and a dull nearby group.

Liza was well aware of his presence, but could not focus on Victor. She had to extricate herself from this nightmare first.

She tried to steady her nerves as she continued the stressful conversation that she had wanted to avoid all evening. Returning her attention to the man in front of her, she searched her mind for the best way to break away. She had to get to Victor to give him the information that she'd gleaned. But how could she without arousing suspicion?

"Look, Barry, I'm flattered that you still find me interesting after all this time," she repeated, "but where's your lovely *wife*? Or is it past her bedtime?" she added more stridently than she'd intended.

Pleased that he could still get under her skin, Barry Walker responded with typical arrogance. Only tonight, he was in rare form, adding a lascivious tinge to his voice that made her nauseous.

"She's right over there enjoying herself. But, in terms of bedtimes, I'm sure it's *way* past yours."

Liza flushed, revolted by Barry's knowing, intimate comment. She hated his smug, self-assured assumption that he could still have her, even though they had barely spoken in years.

The test of wills was on. There was no such thing as fair.

"Barry," she returned, "I've forgotten. I suggest you do the same."

Barry's ego made him an unmovable obstacle.

"How could I forget the unforgettable?" Barry crooned, taking a step in her direction. "Maybe we can get together soon, Liz. Why don't we let bygones be bygones? I have missed those very special evenings with you."

Wiping the last vestige of guilt from her conscience, Liza turned up the volume of her probe, significantly. She'd siphon him this time. She knew he had some details.

Then, she saw it. They were planning to give her firm's remains to Walker! He was in on it, from the back end.

Forcing herself to concentrate, she scavenged his mind. No. He didn't know about the other stuff. As a slight sheen formed on his forehead, she smiled. It served him right.

"Let's get out of here," he said quietly, apparently unable to control the irrational impulse.

"I don't think so."

Her satisfaction from Barry's torture was immediate. She watched him twist and become unmercifully tangled in his conflicting emotions, and she enjoyed every minute of it. Consumed by her newfound power, she pushed the exercise to its limits. She'd never done this to anyone before, hadn't even known that she could until Victor had shown her how.

Only she hadn't factored in the extra boost that the stones might give her and had no idea of the range of their effect. When Barry seemed to be struggling for air, she stopped. She just wanted information. Well, maybe just a little revenge, too . . . but what was wrong with Victor? He was crossing the room without regard to decorum. His eyes blazed with the fury of a jealous husband. He wouldn't . . .

Victor felt ready to kill him. How dare Barry Walker even speak to her, let alone stand so close? It was an outrage, and he'd never allow it . . . not while there was still breath in his body.

He didn't know why he was crossing toward her, moving through the crowd more quickly than social grace allowed. All he could focus on was an immediate blinding rage that was triggered by something primal. He halted at Liza's side, almost out of breath.

"Liza," he said, more sternly than warranted. "I have been looking for you for the better part of the evening."

That she didn't answer promptly torqued his rage even more. In reflex, he took an aggressive stance across from Walker, no longer able to undertake the controlled strategy of a chess game.

The two squared off without uttering a word. Furious at the encroachment, Barry drew first.

"Duarte, I'm sure that the gentlemen from Chem Tech would be more pleased to see you than Liza at the moment." Barry's terse comment seethed through clenched teeth as he threw down the gauntlet.

How dare the bastard challenge him? Unsheathing his blade, Victor cut back effectively. "And I'm sure your *wife* would be more anxious to see you as well."

Panic etched across Liza's face. He wanted to tell her that a scene was not out of the question. Her game had backfired; he could feel her probe clearly, and he wanted to be sure that she understood that he was prepared to do public battle if necessary. The consequences would be her problem, an eventuality that she had obviously never considered.

A sudden rush of realization swept through him. Liza's thoughts, her words, her tension echoed in his brain as her probe ignited his emotions like a torch. Barry Walker. Another firm in the same industry. A powerful male. It had to be Walker. Walker had hurt Liza.

"Don't you have more contracts to maraud?" Barry asked through his teeth.

Liza looked at him quickly, tension measuring her words. "Like giving a child a loaded gun, Victor."

Her soft voice brought him back before he could respond unwisely. She had obviously used her probe, but he couldn't understand why she'd focused it on Walker. Or why it had affected him this way. A jealous public display? Totally out of character. Issuing Liza an intense look of disapproval, he shifted his glare back to Barry.

Liza stepped into the space between them, and when he glanced over to her briefly, her eyes gleamed with distress.

"I didn't know you two knew each other," she stammered, as if hoping to defuse the tension.

Barry spat back an immediate response. He was fully engaged and totally lost to his emotions. "Of course. We've met in competition over some of the most precious accounts on the East Coast."

Victor took a defensive, territorial stance. His rational self was bound and gagged by fury. He found himself taking her elbow, making it clear that he and Barry would literally fight if the invisible line of possession were crossed. Appalled by the sudden move, Liza drew a sharp breath. He checked her resistance with a lethal warning glare and immediately returned his focus to Barry. The line of demarcation was clear.

"We have met on more than one occasion, but the Chem Tech bid was the most recent," Victor parried, suddenly recognizing the present connection.

Barry Walker had irreparably damaged Liza. Adrenaline rushed through his body like a torch to a powder keg making his ears ring. If this were the good old days, he would have insisted on a duel. *What?*

Picking up on the flash of recognition in his tone and desperately trying to avoid a scene, Liza interceded again. Her voice became balmy and sensuous. She cast him an intimate look. Why was she doing this, especially now? He was in the midst of battle, and Liza was sending him confusing signals! Giving Victor another long, serious look, she spoke to his adversary without ever turning around to face him. Victor approved.

"Yes, that does seem to be where some of the most unlikely meetings have occurred," she said, not losing eye contact with

Victor. Barry was becoming less of an issue with each passing moment.

Victor stepped closer to Liza. Her simple statement and the way she'd looked at him when she'd said it had ended the war. He'd won. Liza's comment had been like a dash of cold water on the impassioned mongrel called Walker. Barry's eyes narrowed in contempt, openly vented his frustration.

"I might have known that you would have bled the account for *all* it was worth, Duarte," he seethed before turning to Liza. "And I hope that *you* won't be the one left bleeding when that project is finished."

A low menacing tension still resonated in Victor's voice, and he advanced on his opponent one last time as Barry moved away.

". . . and my regards to your lovely *wife,* Walker."

Liza's mind screamed. What had she done? And what was wrong with Victor? She was incredulous. A wild animal-like ferocity still gripped him. As the danger of an incident passed, her curiosity returned, compelling her to question him about his uncharacteristic behavior.

"Victor, what's gotten into you?" she asked in an urgent whisper. "Do you realize that you two were on the verge of a scene—in one of the most inopportune places imaginable? Do you realize how crazy that would have been, not to mention how dangerous?"

Victor looked away from her. She could feel his senses bombarding him at once. The avalanche of emotions was overwhelming. He appeared totally dismayed that he couldn't disarm or fight the logic of her charge. She knew that Victor's next move would probably be to distance himself. Under normal circumstances, she would've given him that option.

"Victor," she continued in a more severe tone, her voice still lowered. "I don't give a damn about what happened between us last week, but to carry on this way in public—especially in front of Chem Tech—is totally unacceptable."

Victor's rage had a stranglehold on him. The more he looked

at her, the more charged his emotions became; but it was still no excuse for a public display like the one she just averted.

Immune to her argument, Victor answered her icily. "Liza, don't start this out here. And most definitely, do not talk to me as if I were a child being chastised. They were my mother's earrings." Straightening his already rigid spine, he stalked away.

She stood alone, still floored, and the last part of Victor's sentence registered, reminding her of the emotions that had engulfed her only a few days before. Touching the gems as she moved behind him, she wondered how Victor had become caught up in her struggle with Barry. *Could the magnification of the crystals be that strong,* she wondered, almost aloud, *to have hit him clear across the room?*

She quickened her pace to catch Victor before he merged into a new section of the crowd, touching his elbow when she met up behind him. It didn't hurt her feelings when he shrugged her off and kept walking. He had a right to be angry, and she'd just have to weather the storm.

As she followed Victor's long strides, she thought about the issues that stood between them. She owed him an earlier apology, after all, and she might have inadvertently contributed to this last scene. To get his attention as he continued his brisk pace, she whispered, "It was just business."

"Just business?" he whispered back, spinning around. "Why didn't you tell me he was the one?"

"You're jealous. I can't believe it! Is that why you came over?"

"No. It was just business. Or have you forgotten about that tonight?"

"I'm flattered."

"You're flattered?"

Victor's look was incredulous as he tried to moderate his voice. "I never suspected that you were given to such feminine trifles, Liza. And I suppose if I had hit him, you would have thrown a rose down from the coliseum!"

The inane analogy made her chuckle because they had, indeed, appeared to be two gladiators engaging in battle for the timeless reason.

She watched Victor intently as his ire dissipated.

"I'm glad that at least there's something I can do to make you smile, even if it does seem to be at my expense," he said testily.

She shook her head at him, feigning dismay as she teased him. "Victor, I still have yet to decide what to do with you. We've gotta talk. There's so much that I have to tell you. I picked up a lot of tidbits tonight. Really. And I *am* sorry."

How could he be angry? Liza had captured him from the moment he'd seen her this evening. The glow of her smile warmed him under her rich, genuine laugh. He couldn't look away from her as he watched a million tiny lights catch in her brown eyes. Involuntarily compelled to allow his emotions to hurdle the stone wall within him, he told her the truth. "You look beautiful tonight."

The simple admission quelled her mirth, and she looked away, flattered in earnest this time.

"Thank you, Victor. I hope I did them justice." She smiled wistfully. "They're beautiful, and I'm sorry. I was jealous, too. I wanted to be different from all the others. I said some really ugly things to you that you didn't deserve. Your women and their jewelry was none of my business. It wasn't the probe," she added. "I found out by chance. Letty Jones is a close friend of mine."

At the mention of Letty's name, he pictured the energetic, professional, black woman who had always conducted his business with the utmost of discretion.

"Is she a friend of yours?" he questioned cautiously, hoping that Liza really hadn't probed to find out any more. He shuddered at the thought of her knowing about his past overindulgence—the other one he'd neglected to tell her about. If she'd found out, she had every right to be angry.

"Yes, that crazy, wild woman is my best and dearest friend from the old neighborhood." She laughed confidentially. "Really, I didn't probe you for this. This one is just an incredible coincidence, maybe even Divine intervention."

"Crazy?" he questioned. "And wild? Are you sure we're talking about the same person?" Perhaps there had been a mistake.

Liza giggled. "Yeah, she's studying to be an actress, and all of that sedate, professional demeanor gets dropped right at the door when she leaves the store at 5:00."

"I went there to remove the names of anyone they might think was involved with me and to remove the stones from the vault. I would hate for anyone to get hurt. Really, that was all. And the stones hadn't been worn since my mother died. I wanted to make sure that they were perfect, and set right, before I gave them to you."

"I'm honored, and please accept my apology."

For a moment he forgot that he was standing in a crowded room of dignitaries. He wanted to take Liza in his arms and show her how deeply her apology had affected him and that she really was different from all the others in his past.

But as reason fought its way back to the fore, he offered a quiet verbal response instead. "Liza, I said *you* were beautiful tonight, not the stones. I only wish that I could properly accept your apology right now to show you that you are truly beyond compare."

The intensity of her gaze sent a familiar rush of anticipation through him. The electricity that passed between them made Liza look away again. She appeared to be as bewildered as he by the tense quiet that engulfed them. Only moments ago, he had wanted to kidnap her and she had only been talking to another man—though this man had felt like a rival, someone who'd made him want to draw swords. What had gotten into him? Into them? He'd never been jealous or possessive. Up to this point, he'd never understood that emotion. No woman was worth that much energy. But as he stared into Liza's eyes, he was certain that he'd move mountains for her—and that she felt the same about him.

Their unspoken exchange might have gone on forever, if

Stan's brisk interruption hadn't broken through their protective shields.

"Hi, Liza!" Stan boomed, extending his hand for a hearty shake. "You look incredible. Enjoying yourself?"

"Oh, I suppose so, as much as one can at these affairs," she remarked dryly, forcing herself to appear calm.

She was definitely a pro. He had been mistaken when he had called her a rookie.

Oblivious to any abnormality in the exchange, Stan pressed on good-naturedly. "Well, will you mind if I borrow Victor for a moment then?" he asked mischievously.

Stan's request came with a big friendly smile, and he shifted impatiently, waiting for them to respond. Stan's mood was as contagious as always, spilling over to make them both grin in assent.

"Sure, no problem. There's a bunch of folks that I have to talk to before I leave," Liza returned, then blithely slipped away.

Victor's eyes followed her as she glided through the throng and submerged into the wave almost out of sight. His reaction was involuntary. Turning to Stan with annoyance, his voice became tense again. "What is it, Stanley?"

Taken aback, Stan's jubilant expression drooped. "You said an hour, didn't you, old buddy? Or am I getting hard-of-hearing? It's been almost two, and the ladies are getting restless."

Producing the key for evidence, Stan reminded Victor of his prior nebulous commitment. How could he have forgotten? Agitated and concerned that Liza was now out of sight, his attempt to camouflage himself was painfully transparent.

Stan stared at him, finally picking up on the obvious source of Victor's distraction.

"Get out of here!" Stan exclaimed in awe as he looked at Victor, then into the crowd where Liza had disappeared. "No *wonder* you were so blasé about the babes!"

Although annoyed and embarrassed, Victor was at least glad that Stan's last comment had been said in a confidential whisper for once in his life. But he couldn't bear the thought of Liza as

the irreverent topic of one of Stan's Monday morning weekend
updates, and so he protected her honor, dodging the subject.
"It's not what you think, Stanley. I'm just enjoying the view
from afar. But about the women tonight," he added more firmly,
"I can't deal with them." At Stan's skepticism, he returned the
conversation to business. "I'm meeting Hanson for golf Monday, which means I have a lot of reports to prepare."

Stan's disappointment was laced with concern. "I wouldn't
have minded if you'd told me you were going big game hunting
tonight," he said. "But this obsession is not healthy."

Victor offered a complimentary protest to divert Stan from
further speculation about Liza. "I know the ladies will be in
good hands," he said. "I just hope the *Phoenix* can withstand
it. You know *she* was only built to take the punishment of the
high seas."

"But look at 'em, Vic. Two gorgeous, willing—"

"Please, oblige me tonight, Stanley. I won't be a monk forever,
I promise you. Nor will opportunities like this continue to knock.
So make the best use of your time. You can handle both of them,
I'm sure," he cut in with a genuine laugh. "Or so you've been
telling Ed and me for years."

"All right," Stan shot back, giving in. "I absolutely hadn't
thought of it that way. Well, old buddy, don't say I didn't try."

Victor slapped Stan on the back, and the two shook hands,
but a fleeting worry flashed through his mind. He shook it off
immediately.

"Be well and have fun," he called after Stan, but his friend
was already out of earshot.

For the last week or so, everything had felt off-kilter, so he
let the uncomfortable feelings dissipate as he searched the
throng for Liza. An irrational panic seized him. Could she have
gone? Moving quickly through the crowd to avoid lengthy conversations, he tried to steady his pulse and drown out the low
buzz in his ears. After several unsuccessful rotations through
the room, he gave up, his nerves unstrung.

Noticing Marjorie trying to pick her way toward him with a
Potomac matron in tow, he bolted toward the fresh air. He could
call Liza when he got home.

Eighteen

Moving through the lush gardens of the outer terraces, Victor
plotted an inconspicuous escape route. His progress was
abruptly halted when he caught a transient, familiar fragrance
as he passed a garden column.

"Victor?" whispered the low female voice from behind the
column. "I couldn't take the crowd anymore and was hoping
that you would come out here."

The relief of finding Liza almost took his equilibrium. The
sight of her, coupled with the beauty of the moonlight against
her skin, was almost too much to bear. The entire garden seemed
to perfectly frame her in a backdrop of profuse flora. She was,
indeed, a goddess amongst the ruins.

Emotion caught in his throat, and he couldn't answer her immediately. The indescribable need to touch her had transformed
itself into an involuntary reflex, something akin to breathing.
The feeling had taken priority over everything else. Time, space,
appropriateness no longer mattered.

Still unable to speak, he crossed to Liza without reservation
and drew her near for a deep, memory-filled kiss. Liza's yielding
response burned him. Stirred by her warmth, even after they'd
parted, he leaned down again to take her mouth. As his tongue
eagerly found hers, he was unable to stop himself, now totally
unconcerned about who might see them.

She withdrew shyly, as if sensing his passion about to take
full tilt. Disengaging from their embrace, she moved away from
him so that she could better study his face.

"Victor . . . the stars shimmering . . . these columns . . . do
you find all this familiar? I do."

Although he didn't answer her, he did not dismiss her words.

But his passion had momentarily consumed the operational side of his brain and he was not prepared for a lengthy, philosophical discussion. Taking a moment to clear his head, he leaned against a small figurine before answering.

"Liza, there have been many times that I've felt . . . an inexplicable knowledge of you. I must confess that it's alarming, yet intoxicating. I've never felt such a loss of control in my life or such a sense of having known someone before."

Although true, the admission made him feel too vulnerable. Countering the sudden exposure, he moved away from the figurine for psychological distance. As he felt her approach him from behind, his mind reeled. He closed his eyes and took a deep breath against the wonderful sensation of vertigo that she produced. "It was that way the first time we made love," he whispered.

When he turned to face her, he touched her soft, warm cheek. "The fights with you are even familiar, Liza. Your perfume, the texture of your skin, and now the stones you're wearing . . . I know it must be so." He moved his hand gently to her throat as he took her mouth again, breaking away only at her insistence.

"Victor," she began breathlessly. "Please, I can't think when you're like this. But I believe I can explain some of it."

How could she?

"I've felt it, too, but could never understand it until now," she told him.

"I'm glad you understand it, because the whole thing is unfathomable to me," he interrupted, still grappling to regain his composure.

"While you were gone for a couple of days, I practiced," she began again, keeping her distance as she spoke. "Then, when you gave me the earrings, I tried the exercises with them on."

Curiosity overcame his passion, and he walked toward her. "What did you find out?"

"I expected to see all of this Chem Tech stuff, but I only got spotty information. What I found out about was me and you . . . or them . . . whomever. It all runs together."

Confused, he pressed her to go on. "Who are you talking about, Liz? Who's *them?*"

"Us . . . Now, this may sound crazy, but bear with me."

Chuckling, he shrugged. "Haven't we already lost our minds? Nothing sounds crazy anymore."

"Pictures . . . impressions started coming to me," she explained. "First it all came in a jumble. Then it sorted itself out, like in a daydream or at night. I kept seeing a couple. . . . They had horrendous fights. . . . She was crying at one point, and he was pleading for her to understand. Everything was out of time—past. Old clothes . . . carriages . . . nothing modern. There was also a younger man. I could tell that he loved her. It was just an impression, but she didn't feel that way about him. At one point, he looked ill—the younger man, that is. The couple had more fights. There was also a man on a boat, a captain, and I sensed danger. . . . He also wanted this woman, and I could tell that she was at risk. At the docks—"

"Docks?" He was amazed. "In one of our arguments, I blurted out something about a voyage, didn't I? But I was so angry, it never registered. It was as if something overtook me. I wasn't myself, and I picked up in the middle of a sentence about something unrelated to what we were even talking about."

"Yes," she replied—as if from a distance. "It's been happening like that between us from the beginning, hasn't it? Like we're operating on two planes of existence at once, and neither of us can pull out of it when it happens. . . . I saw a harbor . . . an awful argument between the couple . . . then gem stones broke loose from a small pouch and fell at her feet when he slapped her and grabbed her arm. And, Victor, I was in the room—the wood-panelled room that we both saw. It was so vivid. . . . I could actually feel them together . . . feel their passion . . . and all that was at stake. But I can't fit it into Chem Tech at all. I'm sorry."

Victor closed his eyes, and the impression washed over him. "You've dreamt about us being together, too. . . ." He trailed off, remembering his own recurring fantasies.

"Okay. Okay. Stop it. We've got to be serious here."

"I am very serious, Liza."

"Will you stop and just listen for a second? It all makes sense now."

Rebuffed, he let her go on. "All right. It's just so difficult being around you. It has been awhile."

"Only four days." She chuckled.

"Five. But it feels like much longer than that."

"Let me finish!" she demanded, pacing as she spoke.

He forced himself to behave. "Go ahead," he pouted. "I apologize."

"They had a fight."

"Who?"

"Let me finish. The two lovers," she said, glowering.

"Sorry. No more interruptions."

"It was horrible," she went on, her voice subdued. "The first clash I saw, they were near the docks. She'd hurled the stones at him, and he'd slapped her."

"What? The earrings? And he hit her?"

"No. They were loose . . . in a pouch around her neck. But when the bag hit the ground, the gems spilled out. I got the sense that he didn't want to slap her, but had to. There were others standing around. I could feel that he had somehow deceived her and she didn't want to board the ship. The next snatch of information I got was in a bedroom. He was trying to make love to her, and I could feel that she was very angry but didn't resist. . . . Then he stopped and walked out. The next thing that I could make out was the ship's cabin . . . the one we both saw. This time, she gave in to him of her own will."

Victor walked away from Liza, awed by her story. From anyone else, it would have been unbelievable.

Looking up from her shoes, Liza pushed back the tears that filled her eyes. "I don't know who these people were by name, Victor. I can only feel impressions of the emotions they felt. She couldn't trust him until it was too late, and he died."

Victor swallowed away his fear as he prodded her for more information. "He died? How?"

"There was a storm. She was in the cabin after they made love, and he was up on deck. A mast broke; the captain pushed him in front of it, and it swept him into the sea. He drowned."

He stared. It couldn't be possible. He'd felt like he was drowning in emotion each time he'd looked into her eyes. "What were they fighting about?" he whispered.

"I don't know. He'd made her a promise. . . . There was some sort of breach of trust . . . and he'd broken it."

Liza covered her face with her hands. "Don't you see? It's been the same way with us? I don't know if we were these people or if I'm seeing their ghosts or channeling their spirits. But I can definitely feel their emotions at times . . . and I know you can, too. Sometimes, it's so strong that I can't even concentrate on important things."

"Guilty as charged, Liza. . . . Perhaps, I am well past the point of concentration myself."

The admission stunned her. Never would she have expected such an admission from Victor, not when he had fought about that very point tooth and nail only a week before during their chess match.

His eyes never left hers as he approached her, and the low resonance of his voice held her. Closing the distance, Victor rested his hands on her bare shoulders. She could feel him tremble as his fingers moved down her arms.

When he leaned into her this time, he didn't take her mouth, but slowly, deliberately, followed the trail of her scent. He inhaled deeply as though burning her scent in his mind.

"Tell me. Help me understand. What is it about being with you that makes me this way?" he murmured. "No one has ever had this affect on me."

His caress began torturously behind her ear. He nuzzled her, descending into a delicious place that he found near the curve of her neck. The faint tantalizing aroma of their scents had been borne on the evening breeze and were now wonderfully concentrated before them.

"I love the way you smell," he whispered, his voice husky. "It's almost like a memory and not just a perfume."

She could feel the warmth radiate from Victor's face as his mouth and nose continued to nuzzle the most sensitive regions of her neck. Panic seized her as she felt him becoming unglued. Here of all places? It was just not like him! It was happening again.

Speaking urgently into her hairline, he caressed her arms. The tenderness of his touch proved a sharp contrast to the low, forceful whisper that escaped from his chest.

"*Querida,* I need you and I don't care why. Come with me after Chem Tech. Don't ever leave me again."

When he spoke, he expelled a warm current of air that burned her ear. He lingered over the scent that assailed him. There was no question now; Victor had been affected by her probe.

Nuzzling her more aggressively as his passion overwhelmed him, Victor spoke harshly into the curve of her neck. "I would have killed the bastard if he'd touched you tonight."

The comment snapped her back. She saw it. The captain's face merged with Barry Walker's then was gone.

"The captain and the other man . . . The captain wanted her, but her lover *owned* her, Victor."

"What?" He allowed her to draw away from him with reluctance.

"She was a possession—her lover's possession. Chattel. That wasn't their agreement. He was supposed to marry her."

"No. *She* possessed *him,*" he whispered, pulling her back into his arms.

She couldn't respond, not while Victor's attention to her throat and shoulders bombarded her senses. Unable to answer him, she closed the small space that remained between them. The heat from his body formed a blanket around her, and he held his breath when she wrapped her arms around his waist until an involuntary gasp escaped to burn her again.

She held onto him to steady herself. Her breathing was no longer even and paced as she fought for reason. The din of the crowd seemed so far away, so remote, and he felt so good against her. Hidden in an alcove behind the columns, they had created a small haven. Rational choices were becoming blurred; but when she felt him unzip the back of her gown, her good judgment returned.

Moving her hands to his chest, she stopped him gently. In response, he brought his head up from her neck, his hair disheveled from his earlier attentions. Tenderly, she ran her hands through the thick, dark mass, pushing the loose strands back into place. Running her thumb over his mouth to block another kiss, she murmured, "I want you again, too, but not here."

He seemed to tremble as much from her touch as from her admission. Holding her face in his hands, he breathed to her urgently.

"Where then, *Querida?* It's already been too long."

Forming words was becoming difficult as she struggled in vain for clarity. "I'm in Georgetown; that's closer than Potomac, don't you think?"

He began to reason clearly once more. Liza was right. What the hell had he been thinking? The results could have been disastrous. Reluctantly, he let her go and spoke to her in a more controlled tone. "It would be best if we left separately, then. I can follow behind shortly."

Although the plan seemed logical, he dreaded the return to the crowd with Liza waiting painfully out of his reach. He watched her leave, morosely retracing his steps. He had no choice.

Entering the pavilion, he made the rounds one last time. He even endured Marjorie, who had become unavoidable, mouthing the hollow promise to call her friend.

It had been his only means of escape.

Idling his car in front of Liza's door, he steadied himself. They needed to talk. She had disclosed so many mysterious things;

and yet, they hadn't gotten down to business. They needed control; he needed information. There were too many other things to deal with right now. He couldn't allow either one of them to be jeopardized by passion. He could never forgive himself for something so foolish.

Alarm coursed through him as he imagined the tragedies that could have befallen Liza on her way home. When she answered the door, this time his responses were tender. If anything had happened to her . . .

Their kiss blended them as familiar lovers, uniting them in a bond that went beyond time. He felt as if he were travelling somewhere with her, somewhere safe, somewhere that felt like paradise.

"I hope you can now see how truly sorry I was. . . . I do care, Victor. So much, that it frightens me," she whispered, leading him from the foyer. "Come and sit with me by the fire and just hold me tonight. I have so much that I want to share with you."

It had felt so natural to fall asleep in Victor's arms. Snuggling into his warmth, she watched the dying fire from her cozy spot on the sofa. He hadn't even stirred, exhausted from the sheer emotional impact of the last few days. Neither of them had really slept well. . . .

By now, the fire had burned down to deep-red embers, smoldering eerily to an erratic pulse. The dim light that the embers cast had a hypnotically tranquil hold on her as she slipped from Victor's grasp and sat quietly before the ashes. Letting her mind clear of the thousand thoughts that usually besieged her, she focused on the light, feeling vaguely at home with its presence.

The initial images that the angry embers revealed were disjointed and abstract. But as she endured their presence without fear, they became clearer and connected. The combined images were both wondrous and horrible, and she fought to take in the vision without interpretation.

Floating further away from the present, she felt her soul being lifted and carried on a breeze—as though travelling effortlessly beyond the horizon.

Roused when Liza left his arms, Victor quietly lifted himself to one elbow and watched her. Somehow, although her back was to him as she sat by the fireplace, he could tell that she was nowhere in the room. The image before him was both alarming and fascinating, and he had no explanation for the certainty that she was gone.

After a while, the curtains stirred against the window sill. As though she had re-entered the room with the breeze, her body seemed to regain life. The scant straightening of her spine, a minute movement of her head, a light sigh of breath . . . made him wonder where she had been.

Liza started when she saw him watching her closely.

"How long have you been awake?" she asked tenuously, as though afraid to admit to her journey.

"I felt as if you'd left me, and I woke up suddenly to see you by the fire," he said with concern.

Her gaze slid from him to the embers.

"I did it, Victor," she whispered. "I've been afraid to do it all my life. When I was a little girl, I would fight the sensation of leaving my body, then wake up screaming. But I felt safe with you here."

He got up from the sofa and moved wordlessly beside her, slipping a supportive arm around her waist. Then his curiosity got the better of him.

"You were gone," he mused. "I could tell. Strange, but I can sense so many things about you."

"That's because we're connected. And every one of us has this ability. We mostly tap into it for the people we care about."

He fell silent, pondering her statement.

"Do you ever have a strange feeling . . . like a worry about someone . . . then it comes true. . . . You find out that there was something wrong or you know that you must call them, and when you do, they were expecting your call?" he asked uncertainly.

"Happens to me all the time," she murmured with a smile.

"Well, for me, it's very unusual. But ever since I've been with you . . . it sort of happens regularly. Even with other people. I used to call it gut instinct. But now, I'm not sure what it is."

"Does it have to have a name?" she asked quietly, brushing his lips.

"No."

He wanted her, but knew she needed just to be held. The feeling that she gave him was so strong, though. . . .

"Where did you go? What did you see?" he asked, trying to stem the tide of his own emotions.

Drawing a deep breath, Liza spoke softly, continuing to look into the glow of the fire. "It felt like I was flying, and I saw them all. . . . Nana touched my face and told me not to be afraid. She was the first one I saw, and she held my hand to help me see better."

Unshed tears made her lashes sparkle, but Liza's expression remained calm. "I saw the men who hurt Dad . . . all of them," she whispered in the voice of a pained child. "I saw the city again . . . a vast metropolis that looked like New York, but wasn't. The people spoke another language . . . not Spanish, but close."

"Portuguese?"

"I don't know, Victor. I don't speak the language. But I saw a sign . . . Paulo?"

"São Paulo. It makes sense. That's in Brazil!"

"That's where some of the payoff money is . . . in banks," she said in a voice that was too calm.

He wanted to yell with excitement, but didn't want to break her vision. He'd known she could do it! His gut instinct had been right! It was absolutely bizarre.

"I flew over a place that was breathtaking . . . a waterfall of unbelievable dimensions—crashing and thundering over the cliffs and the lush beauty that surrounded it . . ." She trailed off, her face in her hands. "It was paradise . . . and it made me so sad."

Gulping back sobs, she sought his shoulder. He could only hold her, not knowing what it was that caused the pain.

"Liza," he urged her gently, "what was it, *mi dolce,* that made you so sad?"

Liza wiped at the torrent now coursing down her face, but she looked directly into his eyes.

"As I crossed the falls, I turned into a powerful bird—an eagle? a condor? A strong bird of prey with an enormous wing-span that almost blocked out the sun. But my call was a long, lonely cry. I knew, somehow, that I was searching for my other half, a soul that would make me whole again. As I crossed the fertile valleys and flew past the wastelands, I kept circling near this one mountain. Then I lost my ability to fly."

Although confused, Victor didn't blink. Her tale was too sketchy to absorb, but all-too-familiar to ignore as she went on.

"I felt very strong, almost masculine . . . but something was chasing me and I was terrified. I ran into the side of a mountain and I was trapped and couldn't breathe. A little light came in through a crack, but I was too big to get through . . . and I couldn't breathe."

She stopped momentarily, her breathing labored at the sheer memory. Finally able to resume, she fought a rising hysteria.

"But I wasn't afraid for just myself. You were dying, Victor. I could feel it! I knew that I had to get to you. . . . They had separated us. It was as if I could tell that we would never be together for a thousand lifetimes if I didn't reach my destination in time. This time. You were dying again!" She sputtered through the tears.

The wild look in Liza's eyes held him in a calm terror. He struggled against the impulse to make her stop, lest the process take her over the edge, but he couldn't tear himself away from the story that seemed so familiar but had nothing to do with his life.

Liza clasped her trembling hands to her stomach as she spoke with deliberate resignation. "There were flames . . . fire everywhere. A boat went up. They'd tied her to a stake and burned her . . ." Her voice had become a hoarse whisper.

Trying to understand, he reached for her hands. "Focus. You said the boat was in a storm. But there was a fire?"

"Yes," she said, breathing heavily. "I can't pick up any more, I'm just too tired."

He kissed her wet lashes tenderly, consumed now more than ever before with the need to protect her. "I don't claim to understand," he began softly, "but I know that your vision is a part of some answer that has haunted both of us for a long time. We have to go to Brazil."

Her gaze looked haunted as she touched his face. "Victor, I've known you since forever . . . and I'm afraid when I look into your eyes. The first night you gave me the earrings, I actually felt myself burning," she said quietly, too detached to feel the horror of her words. "Then an old man scooped me up—my ashes. None of this makes sense. But something terrible happened then . . . I'm afraid it could happen again now."

Her vision was beyond him. She had a gift beyond his ability to comprehend. His only means of reaching out to her was to bridge the void of understanding by his touch.

Gathering Liza into his arms, he lowered them both to the rug before the fire. "Don't ever be afraid of me," he whispered. "Whatever I was, whatever I did to you . . . God help me. But in this lifetime, I'll never hurt you."

Daylight edged through the window, bringing a light-grey haze to the dim surfaces of the room. The gentle rustle of the curtains stirred him, but it took a few minutes before he regained his bearings.

Disoriented, he eased away from Liza's side. He needed to stretch and to make the critical phone call that would end their bliss. The events of the prior evening flooded his mind with a wave of confusion.

He sat down on the settee in the hallway, scratched his head, and ruffled his hair, trying to shake the fog that still settled over his brain. Rubbing his shadowed face briskly with both hands, he tried in vain to bring back the normal clarity that always guided his judgment. After a moment, he reached for the phone and struggled to remember the number that was supposed to be etched in his mind. He dialed with great difficulty.

"It's done," he mumbled into the reciever. "You may begin the process."

Liza was lying on her side facing him when he returned. It pained him to watch her warm expression grow worried as he neared her.

"Is everything all right?" she asked hesitantly.

There was no way to delay the inevitable.

He sat down beside her, but couldn't look at her as she ran her fingers over the emerging stubble on his cheek. Dear God, she trusted him. Her probe wasn't on; she seemed relaxed and open. . . . Again, the timing was terrible.

Clasping his wrists to form a lock around his bent knees, he hung his head, staring hopelessly at the floor. With a resigned sigh, he broached the subject that he felt sure would end their newfound happiness.

"Liza, since everything has become so good between us, I almost hate to bring up what we must face. But I have to, *Querida*. I just hope that you won't hate me before it's all over."

Shifting away from him, she sat up straight, as if the slight distance between them would protect her. She looked at him . . . and waited. He didn't even have to glance up to understand what she silently asked of him. He hated what he had to do to her.

"You have to let Risc Systems go, Angel. . . . It's the only way," he said, still unable to face her. His statement had been flat, direct. . . . She'd probably accept it as well as a slap in her face.

He watched Liza rise and move to the sofa, pulling the throw that rested on the far arm around herself. It was as though she were trying to block the chill of his invasion. The distance that she put between them said it all, and he began to dress, conscious that what they had was now in serious jeopardy.

"I met with Helyar last week, as you know. We went around the subject a million times, but it's the only safe way," he said with resignation.

"I see," she said, but the tone of her repressed hurt stung him.

"You have to let Chem Tech think that the job was too big for you and that you are eager to have DGE assist you in order to maintain the contract. It's the only way to not have your name ruined in the industry. I have already started staging the board in that direction. Last night, I spoke with Hanson. I'll see him on Monday for golf."

She was too tired. She couldn't read him. The effects from the journey last night still drained her. What was he talking about? Hadn't he said he wouldn't hurt her? Why did her firm have to be the one that was positioned as weak and ineffective? Plus, it was all too soon. She hadn't committed to going, yet. He'd said there was time. A lot more time. He hadn't told her about any of this last night. Now, what was going on? More secrets . . . Lies?

She stood by silently and allowed Victor to disclose his plan. Had this all been a well-orchestrated strategy? Suddenly, all her perceptions focused on darkness. The deception, she gasped inwardly, what if this were it?

"Liza," he went on, his voice unsteady, "this is the only way we can both stay on the account long enough to get the information that we need. Otherwise, they are going to replace you— by whatever manner necessary."

She blanched at the thinly veiled threat. The man who had filled with emotion had turned to stone right before her eyes.

Unable to control herself any longer, she turned to ice. "And when did you come to these convenient conclusions, Victor?" she demanded coldly. "When was I going to be notified, or even consulted, that my company was going to be extinguished? And who is this Helyar to destroy my business without my consent? I thought we were partners. No secrets. No games."

She watched Victor closely as he gathered his car keys. He'd made no attempt to interrupt, and his calmness frightened her.

"After this week, we will collect the remaining data. I will go back to South America to finish what is necessary. You will go to the chalet in Geneva, temporarily, to await transport to a safe place. Once it is possible, I will join you and we can decide what happens from there. But the interim step is unavoidable."

Liza's body tensed with fear. "What if I wanted to drop the revenge? To call the whole thing off? I've done a lot of thinking, and healing. There're too many other people at stake, and I'm—"

"You have no choice now. You can't have it both ways. It's gone too far. It's done."

"You can't force me to go . . . to accept your way out."

Victor took a step toward her. Standing inches before her, he remained firm, although his expression seemed pained. "It is unavoidable, Liza, and I will not have you hurt. This is even riskier than we had imagined. This is not a debatable subject. A courier will bring your airline tickets, a new passport, and new identification by Monday afternoon. I want you gone by Wednesday, no further discussion."

"Who do you think you are?" she whispered in shock. "You come into my life for a couple of days and think you can order me away from everything I've built, everyone I know. My entire life must change, just because you say so? And just like that," she added, snapping her fingers, "I'm supposed to go on some wild escapade with you around the world—using a plan you developed without ever consulting me. Yes, we talked in Potomac and I said I would consider it. But by what right do you reorder my life? It was supposed to be my decision, not yours. Isn't that what you told me?"

Stepping closer into her sphere of hurt, Victor's focus on her intensified. "I told you from the beginning not to make me choose between you and the need for vengeance that has possessed me for twenty years. This is not a choice. It's what has to be."

"You lied to me. You said you'd never hurt me. . . ."

"I never lied to you, and I'm trying desperately to keep you from harm. But you must stop fighting me."

"I'm not leaving. Not like this."

Grabbing her suddenly by both arms, Victor gripped her so hard his nails bore into her skin. "Am I hurting you, frightening you? Well, I hope so, because that's not even near what they'll do to you if they need to extract any information regarding my whereabouts!"

His eyes continued to burn with desperation as she struggled against his hold. "What do you think you can do? Take some little report to the police or to the mayor? This is high stakes, back-alley poker, and you don't have a damned thing in your hand to play with. I told you at the outset—don't start this if you can't finish it! It's just too late for both of us."

Victor's chest heaved with fury. His eyes burned through to her soul, flashing black with a knowledge of the ugly things that she had never witnessed. She could see it, or part of it, but her fear still blocked her second sight. Jamming his hands into his pockets to find his keys, he turned from her and left the house.

Who was this new person? She didn't know him!

Suddenly, she became aware that, for the first time in her life, there was no one that could help her sort out the intense emotions that bombarded her. Letty was gone; Gerald was seriously ill, and Ron would *never* understand—much less forgive her.

Ironically, she had thought that she was alone when her parents died, and more so, as she'd slowly watched the old guard in her family pass away quietly, one by one. But there had still always been loving friends around her, until now, and the new isolation was devastating.

Although her firm had been temporarily dismantled by her own hand, Victor's directive struck a chord of defiant horror in her. Originally, she had sent her team away for the expressed purpose of ensuring their personal and professional safety. But she had been safeguarding them from the aftermath of the plan that *she* had intended to pursue. Not Victor's all-or-nothing way, but her own.

She had fully adopted the idea that the two plans would have to merge eventually—but with the full disclosure and acceptance of both parties. Yet, Victor had transacted meetings in secret, and his clandestine approach frightened her. Who was he . . . really?

Her plan was one of damage control with minimal risks. She had positioned her staff to be able to return to Risc Systems once the smoke had cleared and her firm was on solid footing again. Her plan had been a temporary measure and was totally removed from Victor's talk of finality, intrigue, and escape to faraway lands. It had never dawned on her that she could be swept up in a tide of complete madness.

Clasping the afghan to her body, she headed for the stairs. Then she stopped, detecting the light fragrance of lavender as the phone rang.

Nineteen

She had been numb as she'd watched the other mourners from a remote place in her mind. Gerald was gone, his existence reduced to an urn of ash that his lover was too distraught to accept. Was that it? For a brief spark in the continuum of time, one breathed, loved, lived . . . then it was over?

Letty and Stella had stood by her side like two guardian pillars of strength as the service commenced. They had held her hand as people filed past her . . . but she hadn't heard what anyone had said. She was somewhere else now. It was as though the last vestige of who she was, and what she was, had been stripped away. Everyone, and everything, was gone. . . . Where did that leave her?

Alone.

Her entire reality had sped up, whirring past her in a frightening blur. Gerald had passed away early Saturday morning, and by Monday, she was holding his remains in an urn. Her best friend was leaving. Her company was about to fold. Victor had walked out of her life, virtually threatening to kidnap her to a foreign country. Her life was in jeopardy. . . . She had been hurled into a dark maelstrom of change, each new perception altering her way of life and battering her into acquiescence. It was simply too much to absorb, and there was no way to stop it.

As she held the urn, she ran her fingers lovingly around the gilded edges and whispered, "Oh, Gerry . . . I will find a Paradise Lost and let you gently fly away." Then she turned to leave.

It was over.

Stella was the last person waiting for her at the edge of the small chapel gathering. Seeing Stella again was the one thing that finally made the tears brim over the edges of her eyes, and she held the old woman tightly in a deep embrace for comfort.

"Bubbe," she whispered, never wanting to let the old woman go. "I am so tired."

When Stella raised Liza's face with two arthritic hands, she looked deeply into her eyes.

"We both know that we can *see* things, child . . . some so very sad, some so very good. True?"

Liza nodded tearfully, and the comforting hands never left her face.

"Then this time, you listen to what Stella can see. This is the time for one last look back, for you to visit all that you need to see here, to remember all that you need to remember. Then it will be time to leave, with no more looking back. You have served your purpose well, child. But, now, is the time for you to have happiness in your life . . . and this gentleman friend, please go with him . . . Hmmmm?"

"How did you know about Victor?" she questioned. "How long have you known?"

"Ever since your grandmother showed him to me," Stella replied, her eyes filling with tears. "Let your heart guide you now."

"Nana showed him to you?" Liza was spellbound. "But Nana's been gone for years . . . long before I knew him."

Stella kissed her face. "Ethel has always been with us, the same way you have always been with him. It is time."

Liza placed her hands over Stella's, and the tears streamed down Liza's cheeks again, as she whispered, "But it's not that simple. You don't understand. . . . There's so much to this that I can't even explain, and I'm really scared."

The old matron clucked her tongue, smiling gently and kissing both of Liza's damp cheeks. "Ah, it is simple enough. . . . But if you are afraid, remember to ask for an angel to journey with you. Go visit your mother and father before you leave the city. Let your tears fall on their graves. Then be done with it, my darling. All will be well."

Liza inhaled the changing season and gazed at the once-brilliant azaleas that dotted the browning landscape. Nearing the section that marked her family plot, she walked past each grave, saying a silent prayer, bidding goodbye to each one as she touched the names.

"So young and so full of promise . . . why?" she whispered, approaching her parents' joint headstone.

Hot tears rolled down her face and dripped from the tip of her chin onto the lush carpet of earth. Memories claimed her, seizing her with grief, mixing with the salty taste that filled her mouth.

"Things were bad . . . but they were so much worse without you. Why did you leave us—leave everything on me? I was just a child!" she lamented in a bitter whisper.

Sinking to her knees, she knelt on the dried grass that covered the site and talked in a low voice to the dear ones now far beyond.

"Gerry is gone, and there's nobody left to be with me," she sobbed. "What am I going to do? I don't even care about revenge anymore. I'm just tired, so tired that I could just lie down here with you."

As she leaned against the stone, she hid her face in the bend of her elbow. Her shoulders shook quietly, letting go of the river that had been running deep for what felt like an eternity. In her despair, she hadn't heard the footsteps that came near her. Bleary-eyed, she looked up and started at the dirty old work-boots that stood before her.

"Are you all right, Miss?" drawled the elderly man who looked down at her.

His boots and overalls were caked with deep-orange clay, from a recent grave that he had dug. His dark ebony face was streaked with dirt and sweat as if he had labored hard all morning. The heavy lines in his aged face marked the years of the difficult life that he had seen. Liza looked into his dark-brown eyes which had the bluish, non-focused haze of severe cataracts.

Wiping his hands against the back of his pants first, the old man extended them to her and helped her to her feet. As she rose shakily, his voice soothed her.

"There, there. Yous too purty to be layin' on the ground out here like that. Don' cha know people is crazy t'day, an it ain't safe? Cryin' shame, too, that folks cain't even say goodbye to a loved one wit out trouble comin' they way."

Studying her face, then looking down at the markers, he went on. "Theys been gone an awful long time . . . and yous a young thang, too. Musta been a terrible shame for a small chile like yo'self."

Nodding, Liza tried to collect herself before the dignified old man. She didn't want to alarm him. She'd be all right. She was always all right.

Adjusting his dental plate with his tongue, he took her by the elbow and walked her back to the edge of the grass near his truck. Weak from grief, she allowed him to guide her away from the stones. He stopped and looked into the distance, not focusing on anything in particular.

"Can I give y'all some advice, darlin'?" he asked with great care. Nodding, Liza signalled for him to continue. "See, I's seen a lot of thangs in my day. I ain't no spring chicken, if'n you know what I mean. But my old grandma—she come up from the South, and you know people had some terrible times in them

days. Two thangs she told me, which I know by the grace of d'
good Lord t' be true. First is, He don' take wit one hand lessen
He give ya somethin' back wit de other. Second is, He don' put
no more on ya than you kin bear. And some thangs that happens
is a sign of eidder one or de odder."

Liza smiled weakly, soaking in the aged wisdom that she so
dearly missed. The drawl of his voice and the prophetic parables
that he spoke in reminded her of Nana and a time now lost to
her forever.

Fully engaged by her smile, the old sage went on. "See, young
folk done forgot all about de Good Book . . . and things being
greater out there den da eye kin see. So you jus keep yo purty
eyes on the sparrow, honey . . ."

Affection overwhelmed her, and she embraced the grungy old
man with respectful appreciation of his knowledge of life. Stepping away from him, she smiled, which made him beam with
pride.

"Sir . . . you have been a blessing today, and I thank heaven
that you found me, and helped me. Thank you."

He was visibly moved as she turned to leave him, but he
seemed unable to let her go just yet. He touched her arm lightly,
as though to forestall her departure, and the small gesture made
her stop and face him.

"Naw, I ain't so special. Ain't no blessin' neither. But, ya
know, ain't nobody called me Suh in many a year. Young folk
don' respect yo age much no mo. And dey mos definitely don'
lissen to what an old man wit dirty hands an' work-boots gots
to tell 'em. But, ya see, I could tell by how you was jis soakin'
it all in that yous special like."

Liza stood very, very still. What was sending these people . . .
these old people to her?

Walking over to his truck, he opened the cab and returned
with a bunch of flowers, slowly moving toward her. "Chile,
plenty powerful angels is on yo side. Matter fact . . . theys what
cha needs to watch over ya. So, no matter which way life take
ya, know that they'll be up there for ya—iffen you pray direc'ly.

So, now you take these, an put 'em in some water. Then, you sure up yo purty face an put the straight in yo back an you be okay—jus like the res' of us was."

Giving her arm a pat, he moved away with a labored gait, hoisted himself up into his truck, then drove slowly down the cemetery road.

Liza watched as his vehicle got smaller, knowing that his wisdom was what had gotten generations of people through some of the worst inhumanity ever witnessed in this country. Here it was the nineties, and this old man still looked like he worked on a plantation. Her heart wrenched at the thought that nobody ever called this man of great dignity and knowledge *sir*. Yet, his spirit still shined brightly through his dingy clothes and he had the unshakable peace of a sharecropper's faith. Looking down at the bouquet that rested gently on her arm, Liza's soul melted as she realized that it was a sweet, out of season, fragrant bunch of wild lavender.

When Liza entered the office at 9:30 in the morning, Ron greeted her immediately, his voice full of concern.

"Lizzy, I'm so sorry about your brother. . . . I know it's hard. If you want to knock off, I'll pick up the slack. You don't need to be in here."

Liza shook her head. "Ron, thank you. It was hard, but then, not as hard as it would've been had he not suffered so. I'm really okay with this now. He couldn't go on in such agony. Seeing Gerry that way was what really broke my heart. Not his death."

Ron nodded in assent. "I think I understand, having witnessed the agonized pleading of men in battle, left half destroyed and begging to die. It was those voices that hurled me into this hell I can't escape from," he said softly, closing his eyes for a second as if to jettison the creeping memory away from him. Returning to her, Ron asked quietly, "Are you sure? I mean, there's so much to do . . . and you may be better off avoiding the strain for a few days."

Shaking her head avidly no, Liza tried to make him understand. "Ronnie, I'd just as soon lose myself in some work that requires every bit of my brain and energy. The thought of sitting at home, alone and depressed, is unbearable."

On that note, Ron let the subject drop. She could tell by his expression that he fully understood her method of coping. Probably more than she could ever imagine.

As he crossed to the doorway, her eyes settled on a small exotic arrangement on the side table. She wondered how she had missed the delicate spray of birds of paradise and anthuriums. The arrangement brought a sudden shock of color to her dulled, grey senses, and she knew how hard it must have been for him to select them. Ron always stayed away from hospitals and funerals. To pick out something like this had to be a true trial for his soul.

Looking at Ron with deep appreciation, she said softly, "Thank you, they're absolutely beautiful."

Ron didn't look up, but cast a sideways glance at the table, then down to the floor. He hesitated, then admitted quietly, "Lizzy, the DGE team sent them. Our gang made a donation in your brother's name to research. We took up a collection. I left the cards from Connie and everybody on your credenza."

Liza surveyed him quietly, her voice just above a whisper. "How did they know? I didn't speak to anybody over there. I didn't think it was really necessary at this point."

Shifting nervously, Ron avoided her gaze. "Liz, I called Ed . . . because I knew they would want to know. I'm sorry for the intrusion . . . but . . . I thought that it was the right thing to do at the time."

The empathy in his voice soothed her as she considered what he was really trying to say. He did understand, and she knew that he'd wanted to inform Victor as well. Watching Ron struggle with his conflicting emotions, she recognized even more how valuable a friend she had in him.

Sensing her need to be alone, Ron left, pulling the door closed behind him. She stared at the flowers, thinking of the remaining friendships—and the new directions unfolding in her life.

When she rose from her desk, she crossed to the arrangement and moved it to a sunny station by the window. She opened the card slowly, and the simple words made her chest cavity feel heavy.

We are deeply sorry for your loss and hope that you will find peace in new beginnings.

—DGE.

She had to go on . . . had to deal with the condolences and go forward. Forcing herself to cope with the sad task, Liza opened the remaining cards. As she read each kind condolence from the team, she wept at the fifteen-hundred-dollar certificate that they had collected and sent in Gerald's name.

The last card in the group was actually a business-sized letter on plain stationary. The words were brief, and a certificate fell out of the jacket into her lap as she opened and unfolded it. Reaching for the certificate with one hand, Liza held the letter closer to inspect it with the other. The message was short; and although the letter was unsigned, the author was unmistakable.

Querida, I would have been there for you, had I known—no matter what. Please let me in. This is a time for new beginnings.

Refolding the correspondence, Liza turned over the certificate as she placed it with the other. Her gaze scanned the front, and she almost dropped it in shock as her mind registered the five zero's that followed the one on the donor-information line.

A hundred thousand dollars . . .

She closed her eyes in confusion, trying to assess whether this was something done in earnest or just another one of Victor's carefully orchestrated ploys to wreck her life.

Emotionally drained, she returned to her work and put away the gnawing questions for later rumination. The only distraction that she allowed herself after that was to notice Ron's quiet entry and exit to slip lunch onto her desk. His silent unrequested offer sat uneaten, and she hadn't even realized that an hour had passed since it had been put there.

The discordant sound of the phone broke the barrier of her isolation in the office. Picking up on the first ring, per her normal reflex, she was greeted warmly by a resonant male voice.

"Liza, I wanted to call to express my condolences directly. And I would like to talk to you, just talk, about a number of serious issues."

The tone of the statement was even and unaltered, possessing neither hesitancy nor aggression. It was familiar, yet absent of the usual business-like detachment that would be customary coming from an adversary.

"Okay," she said, then hung up quickly, returning to her task. A new hollow opened up in her soul, and she closed it. She would not allow her mind to dissect the request. She was too drained, and far too busy, to give in to that luxury. She had to rebuild her firm.

When Victor entered the semi-abandoned office suites, he was shocked. Before the temp could buzz Liza, Ron appeared and stopped her, then stepped in front of him with a skeptical scowl.

"It's all right, Denise. I'll take Duarte back. I'll buzz Liz from my office," Ron said, seeming perturbed.

Without further discussion, Victor followed Ron into a small corner office down the hallway from Liza's suite. Generously offering him a seat, despite the considerable tension between them, Ron gestured for him to sit down as he closed the door.

Immediately challenging him, Ron spoke with a low warning. "Look, Duarte, she's been through a lot . . . a lot more than you could ever imagine. That tough exterior that she gives everybody is just a facade. So, do not—I repeat, do not—screw her over, Duarte. She just can't take it this time."

Victor assessed Ron's vehement loyalty with approval. He would've felt the same way had he been in Ron's shoes. How could Ron suspect that his intentions toward Liza were honorable? Oddly, he could identify with Ron's need to protect her, and, thus, purposely didn't arm himself when he responded.

"Ronald, Liza means a great deal to both of us," he began in earnest. "I assure you that hurting Liza is the last thing I intend to do. She's in possible danger if she doesn't make the correct strategic move. And, frankly, I am at a loss as to how to convince her of the seriousness of her position.

Ron sat back, suspiciously mulling over the information. Victor hoped that he wouldn't be able to ignore the quiet urgency of his statement. For the first time in years, he had been direct and told a near-stranger something that sounded vaguely like the truth. Yet, Ron's general skepticism still seemed to keep him unconvinced and Victor was not surprised when Ron pressed him further.

"It's a fundamental question of trust at this point, Duarte. If she follows your lead, she could lose everything—even herself. And her sense of self-preservation tells her that trusting you is a serious and unnecessary risk."

Victor nodded in agreement, much to Ron's surprise. "Quite so," he returned openly. "But this is one of those instances where the lack of time and the lack of evidence of my trustworthiness present a dilemma. Simply stated, Ron, your unauthorized entry into the Chem Tech mainframes has been detected and the top brass is nervous. These people are extremely dangerous, especially when they presume that a risk is present. Now, Liza is a likely target. Under my plan, the worse thing that could happen is that they pull the contract from Risc Systems. I have been trying to get her to allow that to happen under controlled circumstances, but she's fighting me on it. It would offer her a graceful departure from the account instead of an untimely one."

Ron sat with his mouth agape, taking in the full meaning of the threat. Victor watched Ron carefully as a wave of anguish came over him and his plump face blanched with the recognition that he had, indeed, been the one to endanger Liza.

Leaning forward, Ron stammered in distress. "Victor . . .

How can I fix this? How can I make it right? If anything happens to her because of me . . ."

Victor leaned forward to meet Ron's intense gaze, responding in more of a command than an answer. "I love her, too, Ronald, although she doesn't believe that. I'm trying to get her out of the country to a safe place until things cool down. But I need to know the actual shipment locations and transaction sites in South America. And that may take more time than we have. We only have two days; then, it would be advisable for you to take a vacation as well. She cares for you deeply, Ron, and it would kill her if anything happened to you."

Reaching into his breast pocket, Victor pulled out an airline portfolio and handed it to Ron. He felt sorry for the man and wondered what it might have been like to have gotten to know him. Ron was, indeed, a decent person. As he watched Ron open the folder and peruse the documents that contained a round-trip, open-ended, ticket to Geneva and an envelope containing several thousand dollars, he couldn't help but wonder if it were all worth it.

Still in a state of shock, Ron questioned him closely. "This really is serious, isn't it? And you really *do* love her, don't you?"

"Ronald," he suggested, "go to Europe. See the wondrous sights. Take your camera, and fill yourself with delectable entrees. Follow the instructions carefully. If you leave before Liza, I can make it appear that her entire team abandoned her, and possibly save your lives. Then a total disappearing act on your part may only need to be temporary."

Ron immediately grasped his implication and his expression froze as he considered how much more had been left unsaid.

"But, Victor, what about *her* life?" he asked at length. "Will we ever see her again?"

He had expected the question, and it was the hardest one to answer. Without a doubt, the most difficult part of the equation lay in the separation from loved ones and friends, in the severing of the ties that bind. "Ronald, I will guard her life with my very own," Victor promised. "That you can be assured of. But as for the future . . . only if everyone survives can there *be* a future."

Although reluctant, Ron showed no signs of resistance, and Victor did his best to help him cope with the devastation that losing Liza would bring to his life. "Ron, I understand that you served in the military," he commented.

Ron was neither shocked nor offended that Victor had researched him. He was not so overwhelmed that he couldn't recognize the high stakes and the gamesmanship involved in playing with the "big boys."

Victor kept his voice calm. "From your own experience, Ron, you should be able to read between the lines when involved in a dangerous mission. I'm sure you've heard commanding officers try to dispense hope. But within the context of the obvious realities, they could issue neither a promise nor an absolute disappointment, only a slim possibility that one could cling to. This is all that I can offer now, Ron. It is my goal to save your life, her life, and my own. If I'm successful, somehow I'll arrange for you to see her again. That's the best I can do."

Victor rose to leave, and Ron stood behind his desk in a rare gesture of respect. "I'm only sorry that we met under such bad circumstances," he said as Victor reached the door. "I misjudged you; you're okay. Just please take care of my . . . my favorite girl. She's all that I have that matters anymore, and I'd give my life for her, too."

Victor nodded, appreciating the depth of Ron's feelings for Liza and the unbreakable bond between them. He himself had lost all reason when he'd first met her, and the love they shared diminished any fear of retaliation from Chem Tech, as long as he could be with her.

He did not look back at Ron as he slipped through the doorway and sped down the long corridor to Liza's office, anticipating a hostile greeting. He had dealt with so many unpleasant situations, so many negotiations, but he had never felt as nervous as he did now, preparing to see Liza. He knocked on the door and waited for permission to enter—and a miracle.

Liza's grief-stricken face was lined with defeat and resignation. Anguished, he stood before her, expectant, yet respectful of her need not to be led or pushed to choose.

"Liz, I had to come. . . . I am so very sorry." He willed her to come to him, but gave her free rein.

Instead of filling his arms, she walked away from him and took a seat behind her desk. The distance wrenched his gut, and he was forced to accept her retreat and refusal of his support.

"It was a matter of time. . . . Everybody knew that. Thank you for the flowers . . . and the generous donation. But that doesn't change the way I feel about your plan to drive me out of business and kidnap me," she said wearily.

Unnerved by her total retreat, he recalled his morning meeting on the golf course with Hanson. The situation had drastically worsened, and he had no time to mince words or spend weeks convincing Liza of his intentions. For him to save her now, she had no other option than to follow his lead—without question.

He appealed to her intellect. "Liz, they found Ron's entry into their databases," he informed her without preamble. "They are covering up the hole, even as we speak. They plan to remove you contractually from the account—physically, if you put up a fight. I know you're concerned about Ron's welfare, and therefore, I have provided him with a safe exit and re-entry strategy. The only one in jeopardy at this point is you . . . simply because you refuse to trust me."

Liza's calm demeanor made him wonder if she had heard what he'd said.

Finally she responded in a cold, matter-of-fact tone. "Trust, Victor, is a commitment that I have a lot of difficulty with . . . especially when the stakes are so high. How do I know that you aren't painting an elaborately fabricated scenario based upon my fears and weaknesses? You could've planned to have me run off to the ends of the earth in hysteria while you recouped the balance of the contract."

"Yes," he acknowledged. "That's a logical assumption, but we are not up against a logical situation."

Ignoring his dismay, she continued. "Perhaps the information that you shared about your family tragedy was true. But the part about staying on the case for twenty-some years and coincidentally finding a link within Chem Tech, in hindsight, is inconceivable to me. For all I know, you might even be working for them."

"Then probe me. If you can't trust me, turn on your magnet."

She studied him intently before allowing her gaze to wander to the window. "I can't," she confessed. "My radar's down, and I'm flying blind . . . ever since I took off the stones."

Bewildered, he pressed for an answer. "Then wear them. Put them on, and tell me what you see."

Liza smiled sadly and returned her gaze to his face. "I tried once more after you left, but I got only darkness. Nothing came to me. Maybe it was too much of a jolt at the affair or maybe it was the visions I had while wearing them, or the soul-journey I took by the fire that burned out my sensor." Issuing a hollow laugh, she ran her hands through her hair. "It's funny. All my life, I wanted to be just like everyone else. I even prayed for that. And, now, I'm blind. Just like they are. Nana used to say, be careful what you pray for, 'cause you just might get it."

Guilt swept through him. Had he, so bent on his quest, crippled her?

"Maybe it will come back," he suggested.

"I don't think so, and I don't care, Victor. I'm of no use to you now, so I'm expendable."

"You were never expendable," he contradicted, reaching for her.

Liza's body closed against him. Her slight movement was almost imperceptible, yet undeniable. She had frozen him out. He could sense her attempts to analyze his character without the aid of her second sight. Her struggle was heartrending . . . like a paraplegic trying to lift her weight from a wheelchair.

"Give this rookie some credit, Victor. Even *I* know that any good negotiator worth his salt must balance a fabrication with a shred of truth to make the entire picture more credible. So, you see, I looked for balance in the equation before I made my decision. Now, you have everything to gain and nothing to lose if I go along with your plan. And the one thing that *seemed* to interest you is not a rare commodity these days—or so I've been told. Your words. Not mine. There'll be other women. So, overall, your proposal is an unacceptable gamble, that could result in your total possession of me. And that, Victor Duarte, is my *worst* fear."

He had never thought he'd find himself in this position, praying to Almighty God for her probe to return. If she could just look past the darkness . . .

Without armor or blade, he laid his vulnerability before her, hoping that she would do likewise. It was the only way.

"Liza, do you think that it is so very different for a man—this fear of being totally possessed? Do you think that the terror of being completely, helplessly . . . insanely beyond your own control is a fear only you can indulge in? What is so different about your need to protect yourself from betrayal and hurt, fearing that people want something from you instead of something special within you, from mine? If you can make me see the difference, then I will go away."

His admission made her look down. He could feel the terror of the unknown seize her as she began slipping into trust. Dear God, *he* could sense *her!*

Unable to withstand her emotional retreat any longer, he abruptly came around the desk and forced her to look into his eyes. As he held her firmly by the shoulders, she peered up at him nervously, then closed her eyes and turned her head away.

"Liza, if I could disengage Chem Tech, I would; but I can't. It's too late. There is no alternative, and I will not argue with you on this point anymore. Although I may never have the satisfaction of hearing you say that you love me . . . at least if you're alive, I can continue to hope."

He laid an envelope on her desk. "Follow these instructions to the letter, and destroy them . . . or I will have you abducted. Case closed." He met her shocked expression. "Check with your bank. You have a three-million-dollar line of credit backed one-hundred-percent by capital from my personal account—not DGE's. I have said a lot of things that I regret. We both have. But remember that I told you once, a long time ago, that this was not about the money, Liza."

The door closed firmly behind him, and he left Liza to her careening thoughts.

Twenty

There was so little time to tie up the details. Victor reached for the mobile phone unit in his car and dialed the DGE offices. Everything was unraveling.

He could barely pay attention to his administrative assistant. The list of client meetings, dinners, conference calls, and nuisance messages that she efficiently rattled off now seemed insignificant.

Absorbed by the unsettling golf game with Hanson, Victor focused on the hidden messages in their deadly conversation. Something wasn't right. Perhaps the break-in had been detected earlier than originally anticipated. He was seized by panic at the thought. His mind leapt forward, re-arranging the variables. Risk factor. High-risk factor.

Could he and Liza have been followed? Fearing for her safety, he sat paralyzed, his mind closed to all other thoughts.

"How could I have been so stupid?" he spat out in anger.

"Excuse me, Mr. Duarte. I don't understand," his assistant stammered, clearing her throat to gain his attention.

Recovering quickly, Victor apologized. "Barbara . . . no, I wasn't talking to you. Please repeat what you just said. I'm on the Beltway, and you're breaking up."

With a short sigh of impatience, Barbara repeated her last remark. "Mr. Duarte, I said that Stan called. He said that you should've been there and he would be pulling into dock around four-thirty this afternoon. He said to make sure I told you that a man can die twice and that he was living proof—whatever that means. But you know Stan," she giggled. "Who knows what he was talking about?"

Victor dismissed Stan's cryptic message, too distracted to deal with it. Checking with Barbara for any other messages of importance, he signed off and idled the engine in the driveway.

Reviewing his conversation with Hanson once again, he reassured himself that he had ample leeway. In an attempt to reduce the panic that coursed through him, he rationalized that the information he'd fed Hanson should have insured a few days of safety before the opposition got nervous.

But Hanson had questioned the state of his détente with Risc Systems, chilling him. Victor had fabricated a meeting with Liza on the *Phoenix* this afternoon as a hedge. Distance. They needed distance.

Hanson's line of questioning had made him nervous. His strategy would be to direct Hanson away from Liza's whereabouts at all times. Besides the *Phoenix* seemed like a safe diversion. *She* was out of the harbor, already on the water. If anyone approached the dock to check, *she* would be gone. He reasoned that the diversion should've allowed him a safe cover to visit Risc Systems' offices without a tail, even if things had, indeed, gone that far.

But he absolutely hated being rushed into play after twenty years of careful planning. As he had originally feared, Liza's involvement was clearly the problem. Her staunch refusal to go into hiding was like a nightmare. Ron had unwittingly tipped off his opponent, and now he would have to maneuver quickly to cover that exposed portion of the board. Not to mention, protect his unwilling partner.

His brain hurt. In short, Liza Nichols had compromised his judgment and patience. A twofold problem.

Pulling the keys out of the ignition, he ran up the driveway and entered the house through the garage. Once in the living room, he anxiously routed through important paperwork, collecting the false passports, tickets, and carry-on luggage that had been packed days ago. He had to be ready to move at a moment's notice and would only give Liza one last chance to relent before making the other necessary calls.

His nerves were frayed. He didn't have time to negotiate with her, but the thought of having Liza abducted for her own safety seemed extreme. Picking up the cordless phone in the living room, he attempted to call her for the last time. Suddenly, he heard the sound of his printer engaging. He stopped and craned his neck toward the den, disconnecting the call to Liza. Senses keen, he approached the room cautiously, alert to the slightest movement.

Kicking the door open, he surveyed the room for hidden alcoves that could harbor an intruder. He was relieved to find that the only thing which had come to life was his workstation and printer.

Victor moved closer to the equipment and inspected it with quiet horror. The screen scrolled wildly, moving too fast for his eyes to comprehend the data, forcing him to grab at the cascading sheets.

The message made his blood run cold. His heart slammed against his chest as the unexpected variable fell into his hands. "This is a kamikaze mission," he read. "I have accepted it on my own behalf. (stop) I love her, too. (stop) Will attempt to make it to Geneva—then will travel south to toast you on the Riviera. (stop) Told her I was tired/needed a break. (stop) Use this info wisely. (stop) Working from home if questions. (stop) Take care of my favorite girl. (stop)."

Terror swept through him as he riffled wildly through the printout. "You bloody fool!" he yelled to the empty room, while the information relentlessly poured into his hands.

Page after page of locations, ship dates, and warehouses filled his hands while the impending danger attacked his mind. Looking at the system that thrashed wildly on his desk, he realized that Ron had again found a way to break into Chem Tech's mainframes. Dear God, he had even sent it to the disk, providing two copies of the dangerous information.

Immobilized by fear, Victor reached for the second phone line to call Risc Systems. Abruptly, the printer stopped, the data on the last page half finished. The transmission had been interrupted. He almost couldn't breathe.

It was 4:30, and no one, not even the temp picked up in the Risc Systems office. Snatching the loose computer sheets and popping out the diskette, Victor tore through the living room. He had to get out. He had to get to Liza. Brutally shoving the contents into his bag, he dashed into the living room to collect the remaining vital papers. *Time. Please, God. Just a little time.*

From the large picture window in the living room, he could see the *Phoenix* pulling into dock. In the seconds that passed, it seemed to take Stan an eternity to bring *her* into the marina. *Negotiate the vessel! Damn it!*

Hailing Stan impatiently through the window, Victor tried to develop a strategy. It was imperative that Stan quickly remove the ladies from the ship, and the premises, and that he agree to stay away from the office for a short time.

Victor turned towards the door but took only two steps before the earth gave way under him, hurling him forward in a shower of glass.

The tiny slivers of debris were everywhere, clinging to his hair, his face, his clothes. The impact of the blast shook the house to its foundation. His ears rang, and as he wiped his face, his hand came away with blood. Springing to his feet, he rushed out the front door, around the side of the house, then down the back-deck stairway toward the dock. Halfway down the steps, he was forced to stop, squinting against his forearm. Billowing black smoke blew in his direction from the inferno and scorched the air from his lungs. *Madre de Dio* . . . Liza had seen it . . . the boat burning . . .

Victor looked on in horror, choking and heaving while orange flames caught the remains of the dock. The *Phoenix* was completely engulfed in a dark, angry cloud as she went down on her side. Against the sting in his eyes, and the pain in his heart, he tore back up the stairs, taking three at a time, instantly locked into battle mode.

Raking through the debris of the glass-strewn living room floor, he searched in panic for the bag that contained the vital information. Swiftly retrieving it, he dashed toward the garage, jumped into his sedan, and careened wildly out of the driveway. His destination: Liza.

Still unable to get Liza on the phone, Victor called back to the DGE offices for Ed. When Barbara pleasantly picked up on the second ring, he cut her off.

"Find Edward Gates immediately!" he barked. "It's an emergency. It's urgent!"

Ed picked up in seconds, frantic with questions. "Vic, what's the matter? You scared Barbara half to death!"

Beside himself with grief, Victor answered tersely. "Listen," he ordered. "Collect Marjorie and the children immediately. Go to your father-in-law's house in Virginia. ASAP—do not pack! He is extremely high up in the State Department, and you may need his help. Something has gone very wrong with the Chem Tech situation. I will contact you tonight. Stan is dead."

Unable to believe or assimilate the erratic information, Ed pressed fervently. "Stan is dead? Dear God, man, was it an accident? What happened? What the hell is going on?"

Impatient, Victor repeated the directive. Ed had to understand the need for swift action. There could be no more loose ends.

"It was not an accident. It was intended for me. They mined my dock in Potomac, and Stan pulled in. He's gone, Ed. There was nothing I could do. You, Liza, and Ron are in significant jeopardy. Ron went back in, and it tipped them off. He did it because he was trying to help. Go to your father-in-law's now, and I will have more information for you by tonight."

Ed hesitated, then asked nervously, "They won't hurt Marjorie or the kids will they?"

Victor's voice became harsh. He had to cut through Ed's serene world. His friend's life depended on it. "Edward, you must tell the staff to leave, collect your family, and go. Two young women and our best friend are lying at the bottom of the harbor burned beyond even dental-plate recognition. This is no game. Age and gender do not make your loved ones exempt."

Ed was silent, numbed by fear and grief. Victor knew the reaction well.

"Where's Liza? Does she know what's happened?" Ed finally whispered through his shock.

A new wave of terror wrenched Victor, and he tried to steady himself to answer. "No, Ed. I can't locate Liza, or Ron. Do you have Ron's address and telephone number? If so, give it to me now, then get out of there."

Punching in Ron's number, Victor dodged out of control through the rush-hour traffic. His heartbeat matched the acceleration of his vehicle. *C'mon, Ron damnit!* The line was busy, sending a new wave of terror through him as he screeched up to Liza's house.

When Victor mounted the steps and banged on the door, it creaked open eerily. He stood frozen by the wake of destruction that lay before him. Without regard for his own personal safety, he ripped through the house, calling to Liza desperately, searching room by dismantled room for any sign of her to no avail.

The destruction before him left no clue to her whereabouts. *Please, God . . .* Maybe she had gone to Ron's. He had to get there. She was not in the house. His car engine was still on, and he swerved out into oncoming traffic. As he drove frantically, he clung to the shred of hope that he'd find them both working together, unharmed.

Double parking in the street, he jumped out of the car and rang the apartment buzzer. *Jesus, Ron, c'mon!* He shifted from foot to foot impatiently; no one answered. How the hell was he going to get in there? The apartment looked like Fort Knox, with barred windows and no fire escape. *C'mon, Ronald!* That goddamned apartment was on the fourth floor!

Finally, an elderly tenant came to the door to enter. She looked up from her heavy burden of plastic bags with a scowl. Victor steadied himself and took on an official posture. Thinking fast, he removed his passport and travel documents from his breast pocket.

The old woman edged by him warily, but he stopped her with an institutionally authoritative look.

"Excuse me, madame. I am with the Internal Revenue Service. I must gain access to this building to serve a Mr. Ronald W. Savick with a subpoena for tax evasion. Would you show me the direction of his apartment?" Flashing the passport quickly and pulling out his travel portfolio, then returning it immediately, Victor waited with his heart pounding in his ears for the ploy to work.

Eyeing him skeptically, the old woman snarled, "I damn sure will show you where he lives! The ornery you-know-what deserves to have the Feds on him. I shoulda known he wasn't a tax-paying citizen!"

Briskly following behind her, Victor drew a brief sigh of relief as the elderly tenant opened the door and pointed to the fourth floor. He bolted up the stairs, unable to wait for the elevator.

"I wish I could see the look on his face when you show up at his door, mister!"

Casing the hallway, Victor stalked toward Ron's apartment with caution. The door was slightly ajar, and he could see an iridescent light on in one of the back rooms. With no sign of foul play immediately apparent, he moved toward the light silently, appraising every detail of the sparse, meticulous surroundings.

No show of force was evident; everything appeared to be in its place.

Moving quietly toward the second bedroom, which seemed to double as an office, Victor saw Ron sitting with his back to him, facing the terminal. Relief washed through his body. Without waiting for Ron to acknowledge him, he boomed out, "Ron, I was so worried about you! Where's Liza?"

But Ron didn't respond. Typical. Victor's nerves were in no

condition to withstand the man's peevish game. Victor was on him in two strides, grabbing his shoulder violently and spinning him around in his chair.

The sight took a moment to register. Horror trapped Victor's breath. *"Madre de Dio!"* he whispered as he peered into Ron's glassy, bulging eyes. The thick black goo that dribbled down Ron's chin made Victor draw away from the body as if he'd been burned.

Frantic, Victor's eyes canvassed the room, now concerned for his own safety. As he backed out of the small office, his foot mashed something slick and soft. He jerked back in reflex, almost afraid to look down. Revolted, he covered his mouth with his hand, trying to purge himself of the sight that lay at his feet.

Dear God, they had cut out the man's tongue!

A lump of purple-veined flesh held him in a trance. What would they do to Liza? He nearly wretched at the thought and swallowed hard to fight the nausea.

Breaking into a full run, he fled the building. They had tortured the poor bastard without mercy. It was a nightmare, and he couldn't wake up. His mind darted from morbid spectacle to morbid spectacle as the gruesome sight replayed in his brain: The thin telephone cord wrapped around Ron's neck . . . the mutilated stub that had once been a hand . . . the way it dangled by his side, containing only two fingers. . . .

Blind with fear for Liza's safety, he dared one last, futile search for her at the house. . . . He couldn't leave her. To hell with the plan. She had to come with him. Dear God.

This time when he mounted the stairs to her home, the door was locked and he banged on it, out of control.

When she answered, tense, he barreled inside like a madman. Dragging Liza forcefully by the arm, he tore through the room. "Get your purse! We need to trash the I.D. Move now! I have your passport and documents. We're gone!"

Fighting fiercely against him, Liza wrenched away and fled across the room. He knew that his irrational behavior terrorized her, but they had no time. No time.

"What are you talking about?" she screamed. "I've just been robbed. Calm down. This is Washington, D.C. It's a fact of city life, and my number was up. I'm not about to leave my house because of that. I have a locksmith on the way, and the police were already here. That's where I—"

Victor crossed to her in seconds, grabbing her upper arms and shaking her like a rag doll. "Liza, four people are dead, goddamnit! Wake up. This was no burglary!"

His sudden burst of words stopped her indignant torrent. She stood before him dumbfounded, trying to make sense of what he'd said.

In a whisper that was almost inaudible, she asked, "Dead? Who? Why?"

Overcome with the grief of his own loss and the pain that he would now have to inflict upon her, he turned his back to Liza, unable to withstand a probe.

"Stanley . . . he took the *Phoenix* out for the weekend . . . with two lady friends. They mined the dock at my house after I came back from golf with Hanson. I'd told him that I was going to take you out on the boat for a meeting later this afternoon. We were both supposed to go up with the explosion. There was nothing I could do to save them."

It was back. Instinctively, he felt her probe go on, this time much stronger than he had ever felt it before.

"Don't. Please, Liza," he implored. "You don't want to see this. That's why you had the blackout. God was sparing you."

She touched his shoulder and whispered, "Victor, I'm so very sorry. . . . It was not your fault."

He could feel her stop, her magnet de-activate. Anguish bolted him to the floor and numbed him to her touch. He felt his voice quaver with emotion as he whispered through his teeth, "He died like an animal, Liza. He never stood a chance. This is the second time someone burned in my stead. . . . Tell me, how can I live with that?"

He spun around to face her, searching her face hopelessly for the absolution of his sins. Closing his eyes momentarily against the power of her penetrating gaze, he felt her gasp pass through his skeleton as she drew closer to him.

"Victor!" she screamed. "Where is Ronald?"

He pulled Liza to him and crushed her head against his shoulder. "Don't look at it, Liz. Don't look past the darkness." Holding her tighter, he tried to protect her against the words. "Liza, when I got to his apartment . . . it was too late."

"Please . . . Dear God, no! Oh, Victor, tell me he didn't suffer. Please . . . tell me they didn't torture him. He was a P.O.W. That was the only thing he ever had nightmares about!"

Liza's sobs washed over him like a burning sea of agony as he struggled for a way to stop her pain. Holding her tightly, he lied . . . forcefully and directly. It was the only solution to her misery.

"Turn it off, *Querida,*" he said quietly, squeezing her to him as he spoke. "Let yourself go blind. Hear me. You must only listen to me, not the probe. It was quick, and painless . . . at the very least."

He took her face and wiped away the tears, heeding the urgency to press on. "We have to go, *Querida.* It's all gone. . . . There's nothing left, except us. Ed is safe; the rest of your staff is gone. . . . We have to finish this, or die. You can't even go to the chalet since they know from Ron's transmission that he was headed toward Geneva. You will have to come with me."

She picked up her handbag and begin digging in the fireplace as he dialed the telephone. "Geneva is out of the question. The location has been compromised. There's been a variable. Plan B," he said into the receiver and hung up, studying Liza.

She took a funeral urn down from the mantel . . . her brother's remains.

"The stones," she said, unfolding her dirty hand. "I didn't have time to put them in safe deposit. And I have to take this. I promised my brother. Find us paradise, Victor, or watch me die a very slow death in my mind."

She moved behind his frantic pace like a zombie, stricken with pain. Her large, leather satchel swung haphazardly over her shoulder as they jumped into the car, and she clutched Gerald's ashes to her chest the way a frightened child would hold a doll. As they lurched toward the northbound extension of the Beltway, her voice was distant, her attention unfocused.

"I knew something terrible was going to happen. I couldn't see it, but I could feel it . . . so, I sent them all home early today. When I got home, my house had been ransacked . . . and I was relieved to have only been burglarized! I should have fought through the fear and looked directly into the darkness. . . . Maybe Ron would still be here, if I had. I've been blind."

Too consumed by his own grief and guilt, he could offer Liza no consolation. His mind whirred with the logistics of a plan to save their lives. The plan was the only thing that blocked the pain.

He looked at her, answering unspoken questions as they pulled into BWI Airport. "We take a private charter to Miami, then transfer to a commercial flight to Rio. Once in Rio, we'll have to take the airbridge shuttle to São Paulo. That's where the first bogus customer site and bank account are listed. Just as you saw it. Ron confirmed it. You'll need to remember to answer only to your married name, Mrs. Hernandez, and remember your new profession—collecting antiquities and precious gemstones."

He studied Liza carefully, watching his warnings fall on her like the weight of the universe. She offered no response, just closed her eyes and let him continue without questions. When he found the designated landing strip, he took her purse from her. In the remote, unpopulated area, he riffled through her bag, removing all old identification, credit cards, correspondence, photos—anything that would link her to her previous existence.

Approaching the steps of the small charter, he halted her advance, going in first to ensure that the interior of the jet was empty. Then motioning Liza to join him, he situated her quickly and began to taxi out, examining the flight log and landing documents one last time.

* * *

Liza sat motionless. Her life was spinning out of control before her in a web of tangled horror. The short flight to Miami seemed as if it were a dream, while she peered listlessly into the rose-orange haze of the fading evening sun.

Muted by shock, she didn't ask any more about Victor's plan. She didn't want to know.

As the light engines powered down, he directed her again flatly. "Put on the stones. You will have to wear them into the country in order to get through the metal detectors without incident. I have duplicate insurance papers and documents for twenty-five thousand to help us get through customs on the other end. Put them in there."

He motioned to a small bag in the seat next to her, adding in a too-calm voice, "You'll have to change . . . and appear to be the wealthy wife of a well-to-do businessman. The silk pants suit and duster go better with the earrings. Touch up your makeup or they might think that I've been beating you and not let us out of the States together."

Liza followed his instructions, mechanically changing into the new garments as Victor took away her old suit. She watched with detachment as he wrapped the clothes and old identification into a tight knot for disposal.

Commenting dryly, she retouched her streaked face and murmured, "If we're stopped, you can always combine a shred of truth with the lie, Victor."

She intended for her words to wound him. Had they followed her plan, people might not have gotten hurt. If only they had followed her plan! She would never forgive him for Ron's murder. Her words were pure venom. How could she love this man whom she didn't even know? She needed to detach from any emotions that could blind her to his real objectives—or the darkness that could be within him. Fear stunted her reason, and her probe registered only sketches of the information that she des-

perately needed. She'd have to use her intellect. *He's not normal.*
This stuff does not happen to normal people.

As she put on the stones, bitterness tinged her voice. "After
all, I *am* in mourning," she reminded him, gesturing towards the
urn. "And you *have* beaten me, or at least my spirit."

Not addressing the comment, Victor motioned again for her
to leave. His expression seemed pained; and although that had
been her intent, it hurt her, too.

His voice was now soft, his tone concerned. "I know this is
a lot for you to take in at one time, but you'll have to trust me.
It will be a long flight. I suggest that you get some rest. We
don't know what lies ahead, and you'll need to be fresh."

Skillfully negotiating through an inconspicuous entrance,
Victor discarded the last vestige of her old identity. Taking on
the guise of normal passengers, they meandered at a tourist's
pace, found their terminal, and negotiated airport security without incident.

Who was this man? Who did he know that could have arranged all this?

Standing by the enormous plate-glass window, Liza looked
out at the approaching and departing planes. She couldn't look
at Victor as confusing emotions thrashed her. She kept her face
to the window and her back turned against him. Maybe, just
maybe, she would wake up soon.

From the corner of her eye, she saw Victor finish the last
transaction at the boarding desk. Her stomach tensed as he
neared her, and she felt him move behind her. She sensed him
reach to touch her hair, then change his mind.

Standing only inches from her, Victor leaned in closely, as if
to allow his confidential words to fill her ear and mind. "Liza,
this is what I wanted to avoid from the moment that I understood
you were so deeply involved. My heart breaks for your losses . . .
and for having turned you against me. I now understand what a
bittersweet triumph revenge can be—as you once tried to tell
me. But I was so caught up in it that I couldn't listen. After this
is all over, I will leave you . . . and see to it that your life is

rebuilt substantially—without any interference from me. *Querida,* what I say contains no fabrication when I tell you how truly sorry I am."

She could feel his heart wrench at her stoic acceptance of his words. Yet, she didn't flinch or face him or utter a sound. This was the way it had to be. The price was too high, and a basic apology would never be enough to cover the debt of such a loss. He had violated her trust, her trust that no one would get hurt, and she let him torture himself in the silence.

When their flight was called, they moved in tandem, joining the rest of the passengers and taking their assigned seats. Liza settled in, robot-like, then she turned away from Victor towards the window. Closing her eyes, she followed his instruction to rest, stroking the urn for comfort. Filled with resentment, she drifted off from the mental fatigue.

She was caught up in a nightmare.

The drop of the jet's landing gear jolted her back from the comatose cloak of forgetfulness that had shielded her. Startled, she sat up quickly in momentary disorientation. Looking down at herself, then to her dozing partner, she slowly became aware that the horrible events which tormented her had not just been a painfully realistic dream.

The cheerful boom of the captain's announcement of their arrival roused Victor. He looked worse from the deadening sleep than he had from the trauma of the dock explosion.

They joined the long, slow file of passengers disembarking from the plane, and a blast of heat from the tropical climate immediately enveloped them. The brightness of the morning sun made Liza squint, and she had difficulty adjusting to the equatorial glare.

Once inside the airport, she situated herself for a lengthy customs process, nervously repeating her new name over and over in her mind. To her relief, Victor—in fluent Portuguese—negotiated their passage efficiently, producing documents that moved them quickly through the throng towards the airbridge.

Then she saw it. The sign. The portion of the sign that she

had seen in her vision. It had a string of words she didn't understand, but what had caught her attention was São Paulo. Christ. Her mind had locked on both the past and the future . . . old visions of past events colliding with the present and the future. The blasts . . . the fires . . . the deaths.

"The shuttle runs every half hour or so, but during festivals of the season. . . . One never knows," he noted, prodding her forward. He watched her with concern until he could contain himself no longer. "Liz, are you going to be all right?" he asked. "You don't look well. Maybe it's the sudden change of climate. It *is* quite warm."

He put his hand to her forehead, but she immediately slapped him. She prayed not to be sick and held onto her belongings more tightly for support, but she reeled and her vision blurred.

"No. This time I'm not so all right, Victor. I have to sit down." Finding a vacant seat, she slumped with her head on her knees, trying to stave off the waves of nausea.

Victor felt her brow again and stooped beside her. This time she didn't protest. Her whole body felt too cool for the thick, humid weather that encased them, and a shiver ran down her spine.

"Should we wait until tomorrow?" he asked, alarmed. "Can you tell me what's wrong?"

Swallowing again, she looked up and answered him sharply. "No—get me out of here a.s.a.p! It's not illness; it's another link in your chain," she hissed. "It doesn't start in São Paulo. Howell, Senator Howell . . . and someone named Sanders. That's your Washington connection. Those were the names my mother gave me . . . but . . . I feel that they have property all around here, and it makes me sick to my stomach."

Victor stared at her in awe. His lack of insight annoyed her. Hadn't he been around her enough to understand how, or when, this new piece of information had come to her? It was too horrible to be true.

"Liza," he ventured, not masking his absolute fascination. "Two questions. Why are you so willing to give this to me . . .

if you don't trust me? And can you tell me *where* this property is?"

Sitting up straight, she leveled her cannon at him. "Look, I want this whole insane mission to be over as quickly as possible, so I don't intend to draw the process out any longer than necessary. I'm already *sick to death* about the way it's been handled . . . and you said that once it was over, you'd leave me alone! So, if I only have to contend with a migraine for the duration, that'll be the least of my worries."

Victor refused to react outwardly to the mortal wound and turned his attention to the schedule board. Rising shakily next to him, Liza massaged her temples.

"Tell your people to start somewhere around a lime," she suggested, then shook her head, perplexed. "No, that doesn't make sense. It's all blurred. I dunno. It's the language barrier. I get fragments of words I don't understand. Maybe it would help if I could write them down. Anyway, this is where they're getting a large chunk of their payoff. It's property: Lush, palatial villas . . . probably worth a mint."

Snatching the stones from her ears, Liza shoved them into her bag, visibly relieved as the pain in her temples receded. Despite the sting from her earlier attack, he posed another question.

"It's coming back. You've gotten a lot stronger, haven't you?" he said casually, conversationally. "And it seems strange, but here, your probe seems more penetrating." He put a short distance between them, but not enough that she couldn't hear or that others could. "This time when you cut, Liza, it's to the quick," he reminded her. "So, please be aware that there may be innocent bystanders before you draw your blade."

"I don't care if I hurt your feelings," she replied curtly. "I'm being assaulted by emotions, so drop it." Distractedly taking a pen out of her bag, she added with annoyance, "Shouldn't you call your *contact?* Give him the new names, and tell him it's near something called sugar . . . and limes? Who the hell knows?"

The acid in Liza's voice wore on him, but he couldn't deny

his reluctant admiration for the accuracy of her visions. "Liza, there's a large estate called Sugarloaf where a lot of significant governmental entertaining takes place. It's in the province of Leme. I'll make the call before our flight."

Upon his return they boarded. He felt as if his nerve endings were a frayed cord, too sensitive, and much too on edge. Unable to deal with the constant invasion of his mind, he turned to Liza to request a moment's peace.

"Liza, I know that you're furious, hurt, and frightened. But you're going to burn yourself out. Save it for the real bad guys, not me. Please . . . if you want to know something, just ask me."

Oh, yeah, right! she thought. Ask him? Who the hell was he? Flies his own plane, comes up with false identities on the spur of the moment, is involved in some sort of international weapons thing! He was probably CIA. Yeah, ask him, and get a straight answer. Right.

Victor's tone was weary, and the dark shadows that appeared under his eyes lent a grey cast to his normal vibrant complexion. The thick, dark stubble on his face and the cut in his eyebrow, combined with the tension in his carriage, made him look all the more strained.

Appraising him unceasingly, she finally conceded. He did, indeed, look exhausted, if not ragged. And she was tired. Bone weary. She didn't know how she remained upright, and she was too numb to fight him.

"So, where're we off to now, and what's the itinerary?" she snapped, totally on guard with all shields raised against him.

"I have been advised to only give you one location at a time . . . in case anything were to happen . . . and you were abducted. For you to know . . . would not be good."

"Who's advising you? The ghost of J. Edgar Hoover? That's as much sense as all this is making. What the hell am I doing down here in South America?"

Victor listened patiently to her outburst, but didn't answer. She eyed him with renewed skepticism, but her resolve was beginning to waver. Damn the fatigue!

Victor rubbed his eyes with both fists and ran his fingers through his hair in obvious irritation. "Could you just accept a logical answer for once? Because, in truth, I just don't have the energy to battle with you anymore. My main objective is safety and rest. Then we can start again tomorrow."

Her expression remained impassive, and she trained her gaze on him like a gattling-gun.

"Please don't think I'm being evasive," he said quietly. "I know you have the right to know . . . but it *is* dangerous, Liza. Okay?"

Victor's eyes pleaded for understanding as he rested his head back against the seat. Eyeing him warily, Liza consented, and she felt the slight current let up as she released his mind.

"We're going to São Paulo. It's the central business city for Brazil, much like New York is for the States, only larger. We'll stay in the Caesar Park Hotel, which is just a few blocks from the U.S. Trade Center and the Avenida Paulista business center. In keeping with our new identities, Mrs. Hernandez, I'll be taking you to one of the finest jewelry chains in the world, Stern's, at the Hotel Brasilton. *Not for an elaborate goodbye trinket,* but for your wedding band, and to make a contact. Satisfied?"

Battling with Victor was an enormous energy drain, and she was glad that he just wanted to keep the peace. Satisfied, she reclined and fell silent again for the rest of the short ride.

When the shuttle touched down, Victor moved them quickly through the massive Congonhas City Airport. Yielding to his familiarity of the environment, she allowed him to negotiate them safely to the curb to hail a cab.

"Rua Augusta 1508, Caesar Park, muito obrigado."

Liza steeled her nerves during the congested, hair-raising *auto flight* to their hotel. She almost kissed the ground when they stepped out of the cab.

"That's why I learned to fly. It's safer in the air than on the ground around here. But then I thought you liked driving fast."

The droll comment did not impress her.

She ignored Victor's attempt at civil conversation as they

stepped into the sumptuous environs of the deluxe accommodations. Air-conditioning. Blessed air-conditioning.

However, the spectacular hotel did not ward off her strange feelings. It was the first time that she had ever travelled so dependently with anyone. The experience was paralyzing.

Not to know the language, where they were going, what the currency was or how to exchange it, who was after them, who was safe . . . The situation required her total dependence on Victor's lead.

Maybe she'd have to trust him. . . .

Twenty-one

It felt good to get a hot shower and a decent night's sleep. Having effectively banished Victor from the bedroom, she could at least dress in peace and avoid any additional emotional strain. She couldn't deal with that now, which was why she had forced him to take the sofa in the outer portion of the suite. What was going on between them paled in comparison to the loss of her brother and Ron. And even though she didn't know Stan well, his loss weighed heavily on her mind.

Liza dressed quickly and slipped on her flats, taking a large gulp of the strong coffee before she ventured out into the living room. She needed to know the plan.

When she peeked into the small, lavishly furnished anteroom, Victor seemed nonplussed about his ousting and her presence. He was reading a newspaper and sipping his *cafezinho* and didn't look up as she stood in the archway of the door. Despite a twinge of irrational resentment that he could be so serenely composed, she was thankful that at least they didn't have to begin feuding first thing in the morning.

He seemed totally engrossed in his reading, and she studied him, amused. Mouthing the words, *Folha de São Paulo,* she tried to enunciate the name of the paper that he held.

Without looking up, Victor braved a civil conversation. "I

would love to be able to show you the culture here. In my home of Peru, the language is different. You were reading Portuguese; in Peru, it would have been in Spanish."

He was cagy. How had he seen her? He hadn't even looked up.

Victor's dry comment coaxed a smile to her face. It was hard to stay furious at him, especially when the whole situation was so bizarre. Neither of them seemed to be in control of their destinies anymore, and she wondered if Victor felt as hopelessly trapped as she did.

Feeling better after a good night's rest, she considered that possibility for the first time. "I was just thinking how ironic this is," she told him. "I mean, here we are on a dangerous mission, but travelling as a married couple. If you look at the way we're behaving this morning, I'd say we're pretty authentic."

Victor put down his paper and surveyed the scene before him. Looking at his coffee, the paper, then back to her, he chuckled. His response was a sorely needed tension-breaker, and his laughter was a better option than the hysteria she felt bubbling inside her.

"Absolutely true," he quipped as she edged her way into the room. "But perhaps my wife and I won't always be so *estranged*," he added.

Liza ignored his comment. It was preposterous. Too much had happened, and this was no vacation, much less a honeymoon! How could he think that they'd be just hunky-dory? There was no way, and she was sure that her shocked expression would be enough of an answer. He got the message and picked up the paper, putting an icy distance between them again. But before he shielded his face with the alien print, their eyes met.

"Look in the bedroom drawer. There're a few changes of clothes and toiletries there. You'll need a sweater. It gets colder here than in Rio, especially at night. We'll collect ourselves and go over to Stern's . . . but after we scatter your ashes," he said, his voice now gentle.

It was almost as if he intuitively understood that she had to part with Gerald's ashes before she could function. As long as his burial went unresolved, she didn't have the energy to press on. Victor's unexpected kindness amidst the danger of their situation, not to mention the tension between them, melted her outward display of hostility toward him. Even if his behavior toward her were a sham, it was a nice one. He was a decent warden.

Without a word, Liza retrieved her purse and the urn. As they moved toward the door, Victor gave her arm a supportive squeeze, and then asked her for the earrings.

"These are our ticket into Stern's," he said quietly, looking into his palm as she handed the gems over to him. "The person meeting us has been advised to only speak to whomever brings these in. I also need to take the original authentication journal and altered insurance documents as well. But we have time to go somewhere special for Gerald first."

Victor's voice was warm and filled with emotion as she absorbed the much-needed comfort of his understanding. She appreciated that, despite the tight and treacherous schedule they were on, Victor had taken the time to deal with her unspoken special request.

They breezed down the few long blocks to the U.S. Trade Center and took the elevator up to the roof. This time, she wasn't on red alert, but her curiosity was clearly piqued. Touching Victor's arm, she questioned him with her eyes.

"We're taking a chopper to the falls. . . . I called ahead at the airport," he responded succinctly.

Amazed when Victor got into the pilot's seat, she stared at him, wondering about all the new dimensions that she was discovering about him. Even if he might be CIA.

Victor, how did you learn to do all these things? I mean, when did you have time to learn how to fly a plane *and* a chopper?"

Her excited questions had a decided effect on him that was almost endearing. She noticed that after her remark he sat up a tad higher in his seat. All anger aside, she was truly impressed.

Handing her a headset, he showed her how to adjust it for her hearing and how to speak into the thin, wire microphone that was attached.

"I had six years of grief to work through myself, Liza, and I spent it doing all the no-holds-barred things that I wanted to do." Powering up the craft and creating a whine of turbine as the blades engaged, he added, "Life is too short not to experience it."

"That's a long time to work on yourself—by yourself," she said into the mouthpiece while he worked the intricate panels.

Not addressing her comment, Victor gave the necessary information for airspace clearance. Even though he spoke in Portuguese, she could tell that he was saying the flight was for a sightseeing tour.

"We're going to the Iguacu Falls. The area is bordered by Brazil, Paraguay, and Argentina. Along the way you can decide. This is totally your choice, *Querida*. I just wanted to show you some of the most breathtaking natural wonders of the world. Tomorrow is not promised."

She was awestruck as they hovered over the terrain.

"Just look at this sky, the mountains, and the lush green valleys as we go along. I knew this was where you had to be that night you flew away from me."

Peering out the glass-paneling, Liza listened to Victor's tour with her heart beating fast. It felt like freedom—complete, utter freedom. Her eyes filled with reverent wonder as she took in the phenomenal spectacles of nature below them.

When her voice finally returned, she was compelled to turn to him. Perhaps she'd been wrong. He had taken the time to show her paradise.

"Victor, I have never in my life seen anything so beautiful. I feel like this must be the route to heaven," she said into the microphone, watching one half of his face smile at her approval. "I was here. So was Gerry."

They journeyed in silence, meditating on the indescribable panoramic beauty below them. Approaching the falls area, Victor hailed her again.

"Liz, look out here. This represents the merging together of some thirty rivers and streams coming from somewhere in the interior of Parana. The precipice is approximately two-hundred-feet high. By April, it will be in the flood months, making this even more spectacular."

She gasped at the awe-inspiring view and yelled excitedly to him, "This is it! Victor, you found it! This is just the way I imagined it! The way I saw it!"

He looked at her as he circled the area and patted her knee with his hand. It was a gentle touch of friendship, one of comfort and support, and she felt her eyes fill as they hovered just over the five-hundred-foot spray. Victor bowed his head in a respectful gesture of silence. When she opened her eyes again at the conclusion of her prayer, they crossed themselves together.

"I'd like to leave him here, Victor," she said, so quietly that she was sure he could only see her mouth move with the words.

Nodding, he let her know that it was safe to open the window, and she was grateful that he allowed her to perform the difficult task unaided.

She dropped the entire urn out of the craft unopened. The pain of such a final parting forced her eyes closed before she could see the ashes fly away. "Goodbye, Gerry," she whispered ardently. "Remember to visit me. Remember your promise."

Victor's heart turned as he watched silent tears stream down Liza's face, and he brought the chopper around to make the quiet journey back. When the craft had fully powered down, he came around to Liza's side and helped her to the ground. Guiding her into the building, he kept his arm around her. He was thankful that this time she didn't fight his platonic demonstration of support.

Time was his nemesis. It hurt him deeply to have to rush Liza through the painful process of grieving. But their safety was paramount. He could only pray that by some miracle his Liza would someday forgive him for all her losses and find peace. Hailing a cab as they exited the building, they made their way to the Brasilton for the next strategical stage.

The interior of the plush establishment was a hubbub of activity; and at that time of the day, there was a substantial business crowd milling about.

Time . . . He forced Liza to match his hurried pace. Walking past the large mall of expensive shops, Victor directed them into the jewelry store and looked around casually for their contact. When a stocky older gentleman approached, he guided Liza to the wedding bands and engagement rings.

The jeweler welcomed them into the store with a raspy German accent.

"Please, come in. May I help you?" he asked in a pleasant tone, but with an intensity that suggested he might be waiting for a coded greeting.

"Of course. Thank you." Victor responded politely, returning the man's riveting stare. "I am looking for a replacement band for my wife."

The jeweler's gaze narrowed as he moved in closer. "Did you have anything particular in mind?"

Reaching into his pocket, Victor produced the velvet case. "Yes, something to match these."

The stout gentleman greedily reached for the case and snapped open the lid with a smug, pleased expression. "And I take it that you have the authentication documents as well?" he lisped through his thick dialect.

Producing a small leather journal from his breast pocket, Victor handed over the requested information. He could tell that Liza was freaked out, but he steadied her with a reassuring squeeze to her elbow.

When the jeweler looked up from the journal with a leer, Victor pulled Liza closer, aware that the man had raised her hackles. They'd talk about it later.

"Good, then I believe that I have what you've been looking for," the man said, never taking his eyes off Liza.

"She doesn't go with the earrings," Victor menaced, still watching the jeweler warily as he retreated into a back room of the store.

The man's intense assessment of Liza unnerved him, but his barrier was up and Liza was safely behind it. There was no way he'd let her enter this part of the negotiations.

With a few moments of privacy between them, he spoke to Liza under his breath. "See anything you like?" he asked, trying to steady her. "I suggest that you find something that interests you. Something elegant that suits your taste. Because, no doubt, you'll be wearing it for a while."

Moving away from the bands and over to another counter, Liza looked through the cases with nervous distraction. "How in the hell does he do it?" she murmured as though talking to herself.

He was forced to smile as he watched her browse, awkwardly trying to blend in as a casual shopper. Spotting a ring in a case by itself, she studied it. *Topaz. She likes topaz.* It was a large eight-carat, square-cut, smoky topaz stone with diamond baguettes complimenting the high setting. It was perfect for her.

He neared Liza, his smile broadening as he leaned into her closely. "You like it?"

His palms felt suddenly sweaty, and a knot of anticipation twisted in his stomach. The transaction with the jeweler had felt much less intimidating.

"It almost matches the earrings . . . except for the gold setting. How much would something like this run? Is it real or one of those made-to-look-expensive CZ's? Get the cheapest thing you can buy, Victor, since it's only temporary. Then let's get out of here."

Too unnerved to detect the eager current that ran through him, Liza had again broken the spell. What else had he expected?

Before he could answer her, the jeweler returned with a small gym bag, interrupting their conversation. "Everything appears to be in order. Mrs. Hernandez, have you made a selection?" the old man asked dryly.

Victor motioned toward the setting that had caught Liza's eye. "I believe so, but I would like it changed to a platinum setting."

Smiling broadly, the jeweler removed the ring from its solitary case and examined it carefully. "She does, indeed, have an excellent eye, and perhaps I can embellish it a little more for you. Return tomorrow and it will be ready—although it is a bit more than our original agreement."

Victor nodded with irritation, and the jeweler immediately picked up on the unspoken cue to leave the financial transaction to another time. Without further discussion, Victor moved them toward the door and exchanged a tense look with the jeweler, indicating their departure. "Aus Viedersehen," he murmured.

It was madness. Victor had her looking for rings, CZ's at that, and they were supposed to be on a mission. She was, indeed, trapped by a lunatic.

Out in the open mall, Liza curiously studied Victor's face as she stepped double-time to keep up with him until they had reached the curb. "What in the world was that about? And where are we headed now?" she asked, slightly winded by his pace. "I have to sit down to take this all in. And aren't you even going to check the earrings? That guy had them out of your sight and could have switched the stones."

"We'll go back to the hotel for lunch and a break. We'll talk there, and then we'll hit the art gallery on *Rua Verbo Divino*," Victor said, not allowing her to stop.

He hailed a cab and fell silent. There was not much for her to do but to follow suit.

Once in the suite, Victor busily opened the satchel. Removing a collection of photographic equipment, he rummaged through the bag without looking at her.

"Between now and the Friday after next, we have roughly ten days to collect the information that *our jeweler* needs. Each day we will take a jaunt to customer sites and warehouse locations—by helicopter, preferably. You will be able to assist by taking pictures while I pilot whatever mode of transportation is necessary," he said, sounding irritated.

Liza listened quietly, absorbed by the intrigue, as Victor assembled an impressive array of cameras.

"I'll show you how to use these, and you must keep this one in your purse at all times. Hide it in the lining."

His tone was strictly business, and she marvelled at his mercurial temperament as he handed her a small, silver camera.

She studied the instrument carefully. "Microfilm? How did I ever end up on a 007 mission in South America?" she whispered in genuine astonishment.

"This will be the one that gets back your earrings. I'm sorry that I had to use them as a security deposit," Victor added, still sounding annoyed. "At the time, it was unavoidable."

She couldn't close her mouth, but gaining enough contról to speak, she blurted out, "You gave that creep two-hundred-and-fifty-thousand dollars worth of jewelry in trade for a bunch of lousy cameras that we could have bought on the street?" She was incredulous. Truly, he was insane.

"We got more than cameras. We got safe passage, covers, a few interesting things worth the money—like our lives."

Liza fell quiet, and Victor filled in the blanks as he unpacked the gym bag.

"It appears that Sanders, gunrunner for your Senator Howell, has a few additional enemies. Our jeweler is one of them. The stones were a deposit for some information that he requires for his own personal vendetta—which I could give a damn about. But he felt that since we would be in the air, we should take care of his needs while we were up there. It was part of the deal. This is turning into a damned photography safari!"

Victor seemed agitated by this caveat to his mysterious agreements, but she could tell something else was pulling at him, and, for the first time, she felt safer with Victor than with anyone else.

Moving to Victor's shoulder to more closely watch him unpack the balance of the equipment, she touched his arm.

"I'm sorry that it couldn't have been avoided. The earrings, and all. I know how much they mean to you. Is he trustworthy? I mean, will he return them?" Her question brought a trace of alarm to Victor's face, and she quickly reassured him. "No, I didn't see a double cross . . . not exactly. But he was extremely pleased to have them. It was just a casual thought."

Visibly relaxing, Victor returned to the task of putting the long telephoto lens on the cameras and loading film into each one without addressing her question about the jeweler.

"Throw me yours." He motioned, referring to the small silver camera that she had just tucked away. "Yes, it takes microfilm."

Becoming wary as Victor discontinued unpacking the rest of the bag, she stooped down beside him. "What else is in there?" she asked, not accepting any evasion.

Unable to avoid her, he tersely pulled open the satchel and the silvery gleam from a revolver sent her racing away from him.

"A necessary precaution that couldn't be taken through the airport metal detectors, Liz. Don't be alarmed. I hope we won't have to use it, but I do feel safer with it in my possession."

"We?" she asked, astonished. She was going to wind up starving to death in a dank cell in a South American jail!

Snapping the bag shut, he returned the camera to her and deliberately changed the subject.

"Each day after we have gone *sightseeing,* we'll stop at a different gallery to drop off the film. Key people at the galleries will courier it to the correct deposit site. It's in keeping with our cover to collect art, and it may even prove enjoyable. I understand that you have quite an appreciation for art and antiquity."

Liza didn't turn around to address Victor's trite attempt to calm her. She was still mentally focused on the revolver.

"Where do the pictures go? I mean, the information that we collect," she murmured, trying to put the pieces of the large jigsaw puzzle together without much success.

Victor put his hands on her shoulders. The terror running rampant through her body made her lightheaded, and for an instant she was sorry that he had resisted the urge to totally enfold her and protect her from her fears. This time she didn't draw away when he rested his chin against her head, and he soaked in the comfort of as much closeness as she dared allow.

"Querida, this is a cancer and it spans several countries and governments. We have to move throughout a vast network to assure safe passage. Many of the people we will meet along the way are less than honorable. I want you to stay close to me at all times . . . please."

She didn't flinch at his words now and he marvelled at how much she had mellowed. Touching his hands with her fingertips, she longed for a security that he could not promise her.

"Victor, will this ever tie up and end?" she asked. "Where do the pictures go?"

Acting on impulse, Victor enfolded her in his arms and looked out with her over the congestion of the city.

"It all has to be done by June, which is several months away," he explained. "Everything. All the data must be compiled into a dossier which Helyar will assist in pulling together from the information we send. We'll be in hiding during that time. Then, the report will be copied and distributed throughout key countries prior to the next World Earth Summit and the Global Environmental Forum. Over one hundred heads of state will be there—along with the world press, ten thousand delegates, and more than twenty thousand environmental activists. We'll leak the story from the initial standpoint of Chem Tech's horrible abuse of the environment. No politician will be able to withstand the public scrutiny once the hounds are set upon them. Then, the more critical information about the weapons will be leaked at strategic intervals, keeping our predators extremely busy mopping up the mess."

"Abuse of the environment? Chem Tech has an excellence record of compliance—worldwide."

Victor expelled a sigh. "Liz, I told you that it was bigger than expected; trust me, it is. There's uranium in the mountains near the old Duarte lands that they want. That's why my family had to be removed . . ."

"Uranium? Like for atomic weaponry? God in heaven . . ."

"Yes. A most valuable commodity on the open black market when found in dense, pitchblende deposits. There was more in my father's mines than just silver. Although uranium is not a rare element, it's not found in dense concentrations except in a few places in the world. Mining of that rare uranium ore is highly regulated and tracked by all governments—and all U.S. corporations must sell to, or have their sale be approved by, the Atomic Energy Commission. The U.N. wouldn't stand for it, and it could even be the basis for war. Chem Tech has their mining operations, and the nationalized silver plants on my father's land are managed by individuals . . . either way, both sites could be used as a cover for uranium-concentration plants to produce plutonium."

Liza broke his hold and paced. "What the hell does this stuff look like? How will we know what we're trying to find?"

"Liz." He smiled. "Again, Chem Tech has a wonderful cover. Pure uranium looks just like silver, but it's highly reactive and can spontaneously combust with air. I think it's ironic that you, of all people, with your combustible nature and penchant for visions of fire, should be searching for uranium." He chuckled. "God help us all."

She let the dig pass and went on with her questions. She could not believe what she was hearing. This was definitely espionage. "But surely the Peruvian government isn't involved. They wouldn't stand for it, would they?"

"We don't think so, but that's a variable, Liza. You see, the Southern Hemisphere has locked horns with Northern Hemisphere countries over the issue of environmental and technology expansion for years. The problem is that the North industrialized first and as a result is relatively wealthy and strong compared to South America, Africa, India, and the like—whereas Europe, Canada, Japan, and the U.S. et cetera have their industrial infrastructure already in place."

"But, Victor, that means the South also has the advantage of virgin territory that is still unspoiled by waste, doesn't it? Pretty soon, these countries could be the food baskets and medicine cabinets for the world. That's their strategic advantage. Why would they want to blow it by following the destructive path of the Northern countries?"

Victor was patient. "Tell that to the starving masses," he said simply. "Without a solid economy, you have constant turmoil and political upheaval. For a variety of reasons, mostly colonization, the South got a late start building its economies. You should know this since the United States got its jump by having a free labor pool for four hundred years."

"Slavery . . ."

"Then, financially strong, they transitioned from an agricultural base to an industrial economy after the Civil War. Now, the so-called Third World, and I hate that term, has to choose between feeding their starving masses, hyper-inflation, and the ecology. Lumber, mining, and industrial plants provide quicker solutions than long-term building through agriculture. Thus, many times, a blind eye is turned to extreme environmental abuses or the financing of projects through high-margin cash crops like cocaine. In this case, however, it's about more than the rain forests or drugs. The powers that be at Chem Tech are positioning themselves to strip-mine uranium ore and sell it to the highest bidder—regardless of the consequences. That issue will grab any government's attention. The technology that they were shipping was for this project. The cash they received was for deposits on future uranium sales to several non-governmental terrorist organizations. The weapons they shipped were basically to protect the mining site, to set up defense outposts."

Turning to face him in amazement, she looked at him with a dawning respect. "Victor, I really have to give credit where credit is due and say that you're brilliant. I never understood the magnitude of this at all, and I owe you another apology. I find it astonishing that our personal quests touch upon global events. Until this moment, I never really believed that 'no man is an island.' But these people have been abusing more than just our tiny space in the universe. They've raped the *world* at their leisure."

She was incredulous, and her opinion of her captor shifted

dramatically. That there was some honorable intent behind the man she couldn't trust made her believe that perhaps there was some sanity behind the madness.

Victor hesitated, then enfolded her again. She felt his arms tense around her and sensed that he was about to broach a more difficult subject. She braced herself.

"Querida, until I met with Helyar, I didn't even know how involved this situation really was. I have to be honest with you. He has been very instrumental in this whole plan. This was not an ill-conceived, spur-of-the-moment scheme. His hopes that this World Summit might be a way to leak the information led to his political environmental lobbying efforts in Geneva, Nairobi, New York, and at the Environmental Conference in Rio in '92. He needed to get on the inside in order to understand how all the pieces were set on the board." Victor chuckled. "The sly old man didn't even tell me, Liz. That's why he was in New York and it was so easy for me to catch up with him there. I couldn't trust you with the little bit that I did know. . . . That has been the hardest thing between you and me, hasn't it?"

Avoiding the reference to their relationship, Liza answered, her tone thoughtful. "I suppose God has a plan for everyone, and it makes me feel better to know that Stan and Ron didn't die for a selfish reason. They gave their lives for a universal cause. If we can stop one large polluting conglomerate from prostituting the beauty of the earth, then at least they won't have died in vain. Not that that's much of a consolation," she added, feeling her throat tighten with fresh despair. "I never looked past my own small issues to see a larger picture. And in a crazy sort of way, I have to thank you for forcing me to broaden my perspective."

Moving away from him to sit down, she left Victor's arms vacant but both of their hearts hopeful as she continued to ruminate. Now nothing seemed as it once had, and everything had new possibilities.

"It's odd, don't you think?" she went on, less cautious. "We came together in battle with selfish objectives. But in order to reach our own goals and possibly even to save our own lives, we'll also have to give something back to a larger community. This information that we'll provide will not only bring down a few very greedy individuals, but could put a dent in the machine that fosters war—financed by pollution and drugs. Absolutely incredible . . ." She trailed off; her thoughts had taken her far beyond the confines of the hotel room.

Victor took a seat across from her on the bed. His tentative whisper brought her back to a more personal dilemma.

"Mrs. Hernandez, I only hope that one day you will be able to open your heart to me as easily as you have just been able to open it to the world," he said.

Not yet ready to cope with the dual dimension of what faced them, she countered with a question. "How much is enough, Victor? Isn't there enough water, food, clean air, clothing, housing . . . you name it . . . for us all? It's just the fair distribution of these things that's in short supply. I could never understand the insanity of wars over resources. It seems like it would be so easy . . . so natural . . . to share when there's enough."

He looked at her for a long time. Liza's statement was so naive, yet so profound, that the purity of it reawakened a deep sadness within him. "If the peoples of the world could have come to terms with this, perhaps we would all still be in Eden . . . Paradise."

Again, he watched her study his face and wondered if the tears he saw brimming in her eyes were real or imagined. Quite possibly it was his own vision that had become impaired from unshed tears, reacting to the compelling question lingering on her face. A childlike intensity flickered in her expression. Once more, he'd captured a glimpse of the sad goddess who could not comprehend the madness that eclipsed humanity. Then she was gone.

As though speaking to herself, Liza whispered, "I guess hatred and greed aren't biodegradable. That's what we really need to recycle—and turn into something useful."

His arms ached with the need to hold her tight against his

chest. "If I could shield you from all this, I would, *Querida* . . . but my arms aren't big enough . . . and you are so far away now."

Her expression softened, and she let out a weary sigh. "No, that's not fair to you or any man. *God's* arms don't seem big enough at times. . . . How can you expect more than that from yourself?"

This time he had no answer, but a small level of comfort came with her words. Perhaps she would forgive him for this nightmare. In their unspoken language, an understanding passed between them. She had at least forgiven him for not protecting her from the world. But was that enough? . . .

"And you and I." He hesitated. "Do we waste the only human resource that is doled out evenly and measured fairly? Time."

Avoiding his intense gaze, she looked down and spoke softly. "I don't know, Victor. My heart is all that I have left . . . and when people are in life-threatening situations, they tend to come together out of desperation. But that's not a permanent state of being."

Her thoughts careened ahead of her, trying to assemble a rational explanation for her resistance to him. He had opened himself so totally, and had even reinforced his position with a healthy deposit at her bank—just to show good faith, to show her his word was his bond. He had told her the most incredible truths. . . . So, why was it so difficult to just give into the free-fall experience of caring for him? It didn't make sense.

Without warning, his expression darkened and his voice became tight and angry. "I am sorry that I had to come after someone who has wasted that precious natural resource—which now appears to be on the verge of extinction. Liza, I'm human, too, and cannot be in your company without wanting what we had to continue."

Bewildered by his own words, Victor physically distanced himself from her. She felt dizzy and held her arms around herself to stop the sensation of falling, unable to speak. She watched their discussion escalate in a small bedroom.

It was back. Overtaking her brain with a stabbing pain.

A well-dressed man in a red, paisley smoking jacket was standing by an armoire in tears; a young woman was standing by a window. They were arguing, and he was imploring her. The woman walked out.

Liza blinked twice and shook her head to clear her mind. It was happening again.

Watching the raw emotions tear through Victor, she tried to offer salve to his injured pride. "Victor, I was just trying to be honest. I know what we had was intense," she murmured. But now, after the vision, she was even more resolved to remove her heart from the equation. "If you want to, we can enjoy each other for the time being, but I cannot guarantee any commitment. We can't commit to even living beyond the moment."

It was a compromise, she thought, needing to ease into the idea of accepting such a frantic relationship. She hated being pushed—no, *thrown*—into any situation, least of all, matters of the heart. It was time that she required, and patience until her frayed nerves could deal with Victor's all-or-nothing position and this all-or-nothing situation. She had to understand her vision first. . . . what it meant to them and their lives.

Victor was stunned by the terms Liza proposed. Her words were frighteningly similar to those he'd offered too many women in the past. It was as if a role-reversal were taking place. His mind grappled for an answer—had they changed bodies sometime during the night?

Unable to contain himself, he spat back bitterly, "I don't want to just have *sex,* Liza. I want to make love, and to be loved. So we can forestall *that* part of this slanted relationship until it's right. If you can't tell me that you love me, I honestly don't want that from you. Why should I indulge my heart so unnecessarily and have my feelings debased? Why, so I can be hopelessly possessed, only to have you ultimately leave me?"

His voice had risen against his will, and Liza sat, detached, watching him from a clinical perspective.

"Never in my life could I have imagined saying anything like this to a person—much less being able to calmly watch the hysteria from the sidelines," she said, still sounding calm.

"I don't understand any of this. What is so wrong with my caring for you? And what in God's name do I have to do to prove that I care?"

"You know, these sudden intense feelings that you've allowed yourself to reveal to me are extraordinarily out of character for you, Victor. Although I feel the need to say something to comfort you, I'm too fascinated by this process to shift gears. . . . I had a vision."

Victor stared at her blankly, too exposed and bewildered to respond. She only watched and shook her head as if trying to solve a mystery while he struggled to return to his internal fortress to nurse his wounds. He had never been laid so vulnerable and had *never* expected to have his deepest emotions handled in such a sterile fashion. His only option was to retreat, and to never broach the subject again. It was quite clear that she was crazy.

Changing the subject, Liza remained calm. She was obviously trying to break the tension. "We've both been under a lot of strain. Let's go get some lunch, and plan the rest of the day. I think I'm going to enjoy our so-called *sightseeing* in this wonderfully stimulating environment—and I can't wait to visit the galleries."

He could easily have strangled her.

"Tell me about the vision."

"I have to process it first."

He could tell she was hedging; something had definitely spooked her. It was in the room with them. He could sense it.

"It's stronger here, isn't it? Here in South America. You can't run from whatever this is, Liz. It'll haunt you, thereby haunt me . . . until the next time we meet. That much I'm sure of."

He was right. She groaned. What had come over her? Ever since she'd seen the vision of a couple fighting in the room, she hadn't been able to connect with Victor. It was too strange, and he was right about the strength of the visions here. Everything felt magnified. She was afraid to even talk about it lest she give it more power over her mind.

"I just need a change of venue. I almost can't breathe in here. . . . Can we work a little while and discuss it later?"

He conceded reluctantly, stalking from the room and ushering her into the elevator. She could hear the mental conversations of the other passengers. It had never been like this before.

The blast of sunlight and street congestion hammered at her skull. The only benefit that the deafening noise offered was to block Ron's death from her mind.

Maybe there was a God.

Twenty-two

He was tired of fighting. Why did everything with Liza have to be a struggle? Navigating the small plane toward their destination, he gave his thoughts free rein. For almost a full week they had managed to avoid each other, politely passing casual commentary over meals and keeping strictly to the business at hand. He saw to it that there were no more open battles and had let the subject of her visions about their personal involvement drop. There wasn't enough time for that crap.

He allowed no deviations in their discussion per their mutual, unspoken treaty. Each evening they parted, mouthing civil good-nights—only to lie awake for hours gripped by cruel tension. *Something had to give.*

The only exceptions to their polite co-existence came in the form of the comforting hugs that staved off the painful sad memories of their loss of Stan, Ron, and Gerald.

Every now and then, during an occasional break in the schedule, he had allowed Liza to get her toe in the hotel pool. But outside of that, their days were filled with a hectic itinerary of flights and long trips to official-record centers. He was grateful that he wouldn't have to endure her much longer.

However, despite the strained brevity of words that passed

between them, one positive change had not escaped him: Liza actually was blooming under the rich rays of the tropical sun. In the structured, hostile environment of Washington, D.C., she'd reminded him of a carefully pruned hothouse orchid—beautiful, fragile in her emotions, and tense beyond reason. He had always witnessed Liza with every hair in place, her makeup immaculately applied, her wardrobe carefully coordinated, and her glasses firmly perched with authority on the bridge of her stubborn nose.

But she was slowly opening under the sun's rays as would a wildflower, full of life and exuberant toward each new change that presented itself. Now, she abandoned her glasses more often than not, which gave him full access to the deep-brown eyes that she had almost always hid. The humidity had transformed her once-silky bob into a wavy lush profusion of texture that she now wore twisted up. The mere thought sent a shudder through him. He missed her delicate nape. Perhaps, too much.

Every day he'd watched Liza turn into a richer golden brown with a glowing undertone of rose that made him know that she had, indeed, been created by the goddess of the sun. Now, she only adorned herself with a faint hint of color on her lips and cheeks, which gave her face a less formidable appearance. The color of her hair had even changed under the sun's ardent attention, bringing out shimmering highlights of gold, copper, and cinnamon, warming its original onyx color to a deep, vibrant brown.

The change had been gradual, and she almost seemed to travel back in time before his eyes. That vision made him start with anticipation each time he saw her. Ironically, Liza seemed oblivious to the change in herself as she took in her new surroundings with nervous excitement. Perhaps that was what he loved about her most, her childlike adoration for everything new.

He was changing. Liza couldn't put her finger on the difference that she'd noticed in Victor. Peering at him from the corner of her eye, she found him . . . changed.

His urban formality had dissipated. Although his mastery of

the environment remained unaltered, he displayed a more even authority than in his previously abrupt style. Perhaps it was the ease with which Victor converted his stiff, military-blue business suits into lighter fabrics with less-tailored lines. Or maybe it was the way he folded his tie up and kept it in his pocket—only to be used when they went out to dinner. Whatever the case, it gave him a more comfortable control, an aura that almost bordered on relaxed.

But since the conversation remained strained and a treaty of separation was in force, she had been left alone with her thoughts as they made their routine treks.

She always took the passenger's seat out of necessity—given that most of the time they were forced to choose a mode of transportation that she wasn't skilled in operating. At least she had become proficient in the use of the variety of cameras, and that helped her to feel like more of a contributor to their mission.

Watching Victor closely as they made the last pass over Leme, her mind, left to its own devices in the silence, began to draw mischievous comparisons. He had the uncanny ability to make whatever craft or vessel under his command vibrate and respond. She hid a smile at the thought as she watched him power-drive another engine.

What else had she expected? Liza closed the bedroom door and walked over to the window. They were going to Peru in the morning, their task in Brazil complete. All the photos had been carefully deposited at different art galleries, and Victor had retrieved his earrings without incident. Perfect. Then why did she feel so bad?

They had escaped danger in the States. No one seemed to know who they were, and Victor seemed to have every aspect of their plan under control. So, what was the problem? It wasn't like there was anyone to go back home to. Victor had promised to try to get her in touch with Letty and Stella as soon as it was safe. She loved Maureen, too, but there was no way she'd be a party to jeopardizing a child. And, Lord knew, Connie had so much family, there would be no way to protect her. So, what else was left, but this?

Maybe it was the strain or the fact that lavender didn't come to her anymore. Her gift had been a waste, except in the beginning of this whole crazy scheme. Sure, she could now begin to pick up things. Strongly. But not much about the project. . . . and wasn't that the paramount issue? All this other stuff rumbling in her head was a side-bar.

Liza scanned the room for something to read, something to absorb her mind before it absorbed itself. Noticing the velvet case on the nightstand, she shoved it into her handbag.

"No more dreams," she murmured. "No more crazy visions. Ouch!" She felt a prick against her palm, and when she withdrew her hand from the leather satchel, it was bleeding.

"Damn. A paper-cut. I'll probably get malaria or something down here. Knock wood." She grimaced and sat down on the bed.

Annoyed, she dumped the contents from her bag and sifted through them. "Okay. Who's the culprit?" She sighed. "Oh, shit! Wouldn't you know it?" she added with disgust as the translation report for the stones fell out traced with blood.

She took the report into the bathroom to try to clean it up. As she turned on the water and wet a tissue, she stopped suddenly.

Holding the report to her chest, she began to process a stream of quick images. She had to sit down on the edge of the tub, lest she fell. . . .

With the water running, she heard waves. The stones in the adjacent room almost created a beacon as flames caught the hem of her nightgown. She felt a slap, and tasted blood. . . .

"Victor!" she cried out. "It's in the book! We've had it all the time!"

"Liza, snap out of it," he shouted, rushing to her. "You're screaming. What's wrong?"

She handed the translation report to him, and he sank onto the toilet, facing her, holding her arm.

"Open it," she commanded. "I know it's in there."

Victor's hands trembled as he followed her instructions.

"Read it as I tell you, honey. I understand now."

He appeared afraid to take his eyes from her face, but did as she requested without protest.

"It started with a curse," she stammered. "The flames . . . the Duartes and Mendozas."

"Please," he said fervently, looking at her and discarding the journal in his lap. "Just tell me. I can't read it while you're like this."

She felt herself travelling and her voice becoming distant as she spoke. "The Mendozas and the Duartes had been feuding for years . . . for control of precious lands under the crown of Spain. They intermarried to stop the bloodshed. They had slaves . . . miners to unearth silver deposits, the same ones that your father made his fortune on. A black Moor brought from Brazil . . . and a native Indian woman—both owned by the Mendozas. They had a child. They hid the baby with an old man in the hills. The mine collapsed. The Moor was trapped with many others."

Liza's breathing was too labored, and her body literally shook. He had to make her stop. She was going to break or pass out.

"Stop it, *Querida!* You can't do this to yourself. It doesn't matter any longer. We have everything we need for our safety now."

"No," she went on. "It will only haunt us, like you said, Victor. Mendozas called an inquisition and burned the Indian woman because they found her chanting in her native language near the entrance of the mine. They thought she'd created the collapse, but she was just praying for the safe journey of her husband's soul."

Incredulous, he opened the report. "This is Julio Duarte's journal . . . he kept it from the time he was twelve. I never read this. When Helyar gave it to me, I thought it was just to authenticate the stones. *I never read it.* There just wasn't time."

"Read it now. . . . He had an older brother named Victor."

They looked at each other as he closed the document.

"He was fifteen at the time of the burning," she said in a far-off voice. "Julio was twelve. In the ashes were the stones."

"The stones?" Victor paced the room, dropping the report on the floor.

"They were the woman's tears. That's all that was left after they burned her. The old man cleaned up the pyre and hid the stones. He put them in a pouch around the girl-child's neck. Fifteen years later, she still wore them when Victor first saw her."

"I don't understand," he said, raking his hands through his hair. "I have to read this to understand."

"Listen to me," she said quietly. "The feuding began again . . . as soon as the Indian woman died—the child's mother. The Duartes were losing, and Julio and Victor had to escape the country. The entire region was at war."

"The last Inca uprising . . ." he whispered, picking up the journal and flipping through the pages. "Tupac Amaru II, 1780 . . . It was the worst rebellion, and put down brutally by the sword and the cross of Spain. The original bond from years before that was between the Amaru-Duarte line, creating *mestizos*. Still Duartes. This is what Helyar was talking about. . . . The Duartes had married with Mendozas only to hold onto the lands, to further legitimize their claim with a mainland family name. Otherwise it would have reverted back to the viceroyalty."

"Your Inca bloodline . . . That's why you can read me, sense me, feel me. Victor, that's why you're a catalyst."

"The girl. Who was the girl? Dear God, help me understand."

Liza's eyes never met his as she spoke in a distant voice. "The eldest Duarte brother had seen the young girl. . . . He wanted to marry her and take her with him to North America, even though she was so young. She didn't know who he was, nor did he know who she was. They fell in love long before they knew. Julio also loved her deeply, but she only loved him like a brother . . . the way I loved Ron. When Julio became ill—smallpox—he couldn't go on the ship with them to the new world."

"Ron . . . They're all connected, aren't they? All of us. We've all done this dance before . . ."

"Yes," she murmured, covering her face. "Julio never made it out of the country with them. They left the stones with Julio to help him finance a small mercenary army to protect himself and Duarte land. He hid the stones in the house . . . and they weren't found for generations. He died shortly after he hid them, but he'd just fathered a son . . . Victor Duarte—the one who actually kept your line going, in honor of his dead brother. The eldest brother died on the ship, in the storm. The Duartes eventually won and maintained the house. Apparently, the magic worked. Julio's diary led the occupants to the jewels."

"The ship, Liza. What happened to them on the ship?" An inexplicable grief swept through him.

"Each time they were together, she would question him about his parentage, but he wouldn't tell her. He had secrets—a dark secret: The burning done by the Mendoza side. They argued in a small rooming house the night before they were to leave."

"The argument in the bedroom . . ." His voice trailed off into a whisper.

"At the docks, she found out about his lineage, and what they had done to her mother and father. She refused to go with him or take the bag from around her neck. They fought bitterly. He slapped her. It was his brother's life versus her superstition. . . . The old man had said to never separate her from the stones or the curse would wipe out the Mendoza-Duarte line. She had to keep them for the peace . . . but he gave them to his brother and invoked his rights to take her on board as his chattel. He changed her name. Julio told him it was a bad plan; but if she had stayed, she would have been found out and made Mendoza property. Her parents had been owned by Mendozas. But he couldn't marry her there, even though he had taken her virginity. Victor couldn't bear to see her used and enslaved by another man—any man."

His voice was barely audible. "He couldn't bear to leave her . . ."

"He kidnapped her and made her his slave. She hated him for it. She didn't understand . . ." Liza gasped, and again hid her face. "He'd promised the old man that he'd marry her. But when she fought him, he loved her so much that he had to find a way to force her to come with him. His plan was to marry her in the Americas, and then wipe out her slave record. They were headed toward Florida."

"Which was still a protectorate of old Spain." Victor's eyes filled as the pieces began to make sense. "Then, there was the storm . . ."

"Yes. After months of her silent resistance in the cabin, he broke. . . . He had only been with her once and needed her again; he loved her so much. She finally let him explain . . . and he gave her a ring. They made love, harsh and furious . . ."

"Against the cabin wall," Victor finished.

"All available men were called up on deck. The storm got worse, a mast broke. . . . The captain who'd suspected she was Mendoza property and who wanted her physically pushed Victor in front of it. . . . In the garden, I saw Barry Walker."

"I've hated him since the moment we met, Liza. It was inexplicable, but I despised him."

"She, and only a few others, survived. The ship sank off the coast of the Florida Keys, and because she had slave papers, they sold her into bondage in the states."

"Earlier, during the week, as we took in the surroundings, you told me in light conversation that your family history started in the Florida Keys." He gazed at her in amazement.

"Neither soul has rested since. This wasn't supposed to happen, Victor. She was supposed to be his legal wife. They were supposed to right the injustice by a marriage of their two worlds."

Victor pulled her into his arms. "The distrust . . . the feelings of betrayal . . . the love . . . the vendettas . . . knowing that you'd leave me . . . even this journey back under abduction and aliases, all happened before?"

"That's as far back as Nana could remember. This was our bedtime story when I was a little girl. I just never made the connection because I could never see past the darkness to the end."

Gripping her more tightly, he felt an inner wall crumble under the weight of his emotions as she melted against his bare chest. His voice faltered with repressed sobs. He had trapped her before. Had taken her freedom. God save his soul from damnation. . . .

"Mi tresora, how can I make this right? This time, forever, so you'll never leave me. Won't want to leave me."

Her hands left a warm impression on his shoulders as she stroked the pain away from his body. "We can go back to where they were—before the darkness—and start again."

He didn't understand. Sensing his confusion, she laced her fingers through his and guided him into the bedroom. His nervous system was overloaded, and he felt a small depth charge go off within him as she untied his sweat pants and dropped her gown to the floor. Yet, he dared not move. This time, he would follow her lead.

"I've always wanted to travel with you . . . to understand your journeys inward," he whispered as her touch obliterated him.

"That's where I want to take you," she murmured and slid onto the bed, still holding his hand. "Let me show you where I go when I'm with you. . . so that we'll always be connected, no matter what happens."

His body formed a blanket around her and he sank against her warmth as though it were a refuge. He was home. His incarceration had ended. Their shudder became one as he fused with her. "I will always be connected to you, Liza. You have possessed me since the beginning."

She opened her eyes and looked at him without blinking. Her pupils eclipsed her wide irises, creating a gravitational pull that felt stronger than any lunar cycle. "Travel with me. . . . feel every sensation that you release in me. . . . I'm yours. Always. Of my own free will this time."

Liza's admission took his breath, and the feel of her bonded him to the marrow. Every movement against her softness reverberated through his soul. His gaze never left hers as the tide overcame him. Suddenly, she closed her eyes as she began to wash against a shore of pleasure.

"Don't. Don't pull away now," he pleaded in anguish, and a moan escaped his throat as she opened her eyes again. "Please," he whispered. "We're almost there. . . ."

"It's too intense. . . . I can't," she murmured. "Never in my life . . ."

Raising himself on his elbows, he stroked the hair from her face and kissed her eyelids. "Stay with me." Each movement against her burned him with renewed urgency. "He loved her. . . . The first time, he tried not to hurt her. . . . It felt like this."

"Yes," she whispered, and wrapped her legs around his waist. "This is how he made her feel."

His kiss deepened with his return to her body. Nothing mattered. Not the past. Not the present. Not the future. Only the way Liza made him feel at this moment. His body followed hers as she hurtled into a void of repeated climax. The first sensation rocked him, sending a multiple ripple of long-awaited release through him. Burying his head against her neck, he moaned sending another torrent sweeping through her and then through him. Her voice vibrated rhythmically within his soul, which set off another chain reaction of tremors. He was crying. Sated. Semi-conscious. They were one.

It was a long while before he could move, before he could lift his head to brush her mouth with a kiss. He scanned her face, burning every detail into his brain.

"That's what you do to me every time," she murmured. "That's what a journey in your arms feels like."

His response was plain, with no room for eloquence. Winded,

he could barely speak, but he uttered what he felt in his heart. "Marry me, *Querida*. No more games. No more lies. Only truth."

Twenty-three

Liza stretched her legs over to the still-warm spot that Victor had vacated. Forcing herself awake with a drowsy groan, she reached across his side of the bed and pulled his pillow against her. Still warm . . . God, did he smell good!

She couldn't decide whether or not to wait for Victor to return with his customary morning paper before she called room service for coffee. Maybe she'd wait . . . until after he'd left her arms again.

"Hold it, Liz," she murmured, sitting up suddenly. "The man asked you to marry him last night." She laughed at herself. "Oh, you never even said yes, you fool!"

She had to shake her head at her own stupidity while she swung her legs over the side of the bed. As she ruffled her hair with her hands, a glimmer of light caught her attention. What in the world? . . .

It sat in a clear crystal case atop a piece of hotel stationery. Almost afraid to approach it, she reached out her hand slowly and picked up the box first. A mixture of pleasure and awe washed over her as she turned it in the light. Snapping open the lid with care, she drew a breath as the facets of the ring caught and refracted the sun.

Liza slipped the large, platinum-set topaz on her left finger and opened the note, murmuring the words aloud as she read it.

"Querida, *the terms of my proposal are firm and will not change with the cold light of day. Marry me. I love you. Victor. P.S. This expensive good morning is authentic, not a CZ.*"

She immediately clasped the note to her chest and laughed as she fell back on the bed. He was, indeed, a madman! Absolutely out of his mind. Then, it all came into focus. No wonder he had been so cagey about the negotiations when they'd gone back to the jeweler. She'd assumed that he was too distracted to deal with buying a ring for appearances' sake. Once again, she owed him an apology. How was she ever going to make up for all their misunderstandings?

They had found each other again.

With a new burst of excited energy, she rushed into the bathroom to take a shower before he returned. She'd be fresh, vibrant, and ready for him when he came back.

Cutting her shower short when she heard him open the door, she wrapped herself in a towel and, still dripping wet, entered the bedroom. Her eyes could not immediately connect with her brain. Traumatized, she didn't try to cover her semi-nakedness. The nightmare was back.

"He's a lucky bastard, don't you think? I wonder if Cortes will mind if we handle his merchandise before we deliver it?"

"Don't be foolish. We do not have time. We deliver the bitch and pick up our money. No deviations to the plan."

Liza stood frozen as two vultures dissected her with their eyes. A new dampness covered her body, and a stream of perspiration ran down her back.

"Get dressed. Where are the stones?"

She couldn't respond as one of the predators approached her. Her mind sent an instant reflex to her arm to cover her face, avoiding the direct slap.

"Don't even think about screaming," one said, drawing his hand away and shoving her to the bed. "Get the stones and get dressed. We go through the lobby like friends. Without incident. Or you die."

"Don't forget the journal," the other man said. "He wants everything they've got."

Liza stared at the man who'd assaulted her. Black aviator-sunglasses made him look like an angel of death; he smirked at her and rifled through Victor's canvas bag.

"Throw me the cameras. Pull out the film. And look what

else we have here . . ." he said, brandishing Victor's revolver. "Well, well, well."

Her mind only registered black now. Nothing would come into focus as she produced the earrings and slipped on her pants and a sweater. When he took the jewels, turning them over and over in one hand before plunging them into his pocket, she felt physical pain. Terror gripped her. One thought resonated through her soul: Victor.

A new rush of adrenaline cleared her brain. She had to find a way to survive.

"Where's the microfilm unit?" the second man bellowed. "Don't play games with us, lady. You're in no position."

Swallowing hard, she forced her gaze to remain on their faces. Sweat now dampened the front of her sweater as she fought not to look in the direction of her handbag. If they found the camera in the lining where Victor had stashed it, she was dead.

"He handled everything," she stammered, appealing to their male logic. "I was just his woman."

They studied her.

"She doesn't have it," the mirrored one said. "The stupid son-of-a-bitch was in love with her. He must've stashed it along the way. Women . . . always a damned risk." Producing Victor's note, he read it aloud to his partner, laughing. "Here." He tossed her purse to her. "Put the journal and computer printouts in there. We walk out real slow." He nudged his partner to hurry. "Leave the cameras for the maids," he ordered brusquely. "Just take the gun. Kill her with it if she makes a false move."

She sat by the window, watching the world disappear below her, her breathing labored. The hours passed, and the flight droned on. The first vulture piloted the craft, the other sat next to her, rubbing the revolver against her inner thigh. Nausea brought acid to her throat, and a thin line of perspiration coursed down her cheek.

She was nearly suffocating . . .

Closing her eyes against the skull-splitting pain, she recognized *the feeling of masculine, oppressive strength while flying somewhere far away . . . mountains . . . a large bird of prey that blocked the sun . . . her lover dying . . . .*

A flurry of angry foreign words tightened the piano wire within her.

"I said *no!*" the pilot shouted in English.

"What Señor Cortes doesn't know won't hurt him. We are already in the air, so no time will be lost."

The man began to fondle her, and she squeezed her eyes more tightly shut. Her mind screamed for him to leave her alone as he parted her knees with the gun. Unable to stand the violation, she glared at him. Daring him with her mind was her only defense against his touch.

"Por Dios!" her assistant yelled, standing up and bolting from her side. "Put the plane down," he continued hysterically to the pilot, who had turned around in his seat.

"What's wrong with you? Put the plane down? Have you lost your mind?"

Her assailant crossed himself and pulled a small bag out from beneath his shirt, clasping it so tightly that the leather thong popped. "She's evil! A witch! It's in her eyes . . . death."

The pilot's voice dropped to a snarl. "Sit down. Stop this superstitious shit. We land in less than ten minutes. You can give me your half of the money if she scares you."

"I'm not staying in here with a witch! Put it down!"

Levelling a revolver at his partner, the pilot spoke through clenched teeth. "Either sit down or lie down."

The sun from the window reflected off the pilot's glasses, and a scream fought its way to the surface against her will. Covering her face with her hands, she balled herself up tightly in the seat.

"Ron!"

More angry words swirled about her as screams emanated from her soul. . . . A gunshot brought back the darkness. Uncovering her face slowly, she looked down the barrel of a revolver.

"Scream again, and you die . . . like that stupid bastard on the floor."

She tore her gaze from the gun toward a body clutching a parachute. The back of the man's head lay next to him on the floor. A new terror took hold of her as she watched Stan burn in the dark reflection of the pilot's sunglasses . . . then she saw Ron's torture in detail. From the depths of her being, she felt another wave of screams overtake her, along with a red sea of rage. She couldn't stop. They had killed him like an animal! She covered her face to block the terror.

Then blackness came again, obliterating the river of blood that coursed through her mind. Slowly lowering her hands, she looked into the pilot's face, perplexed by the sudden calm that came over her.

His expression hadn't changed. . . . He hadn't uttered a word. His arm dropped to his side, and the gun rolled to the floor as he slid from his seat. The stones fell out of his pocket, and she knew he was dead.

Instinct propelled Liza to the window. Mountains loomed beneath her, coming closer . . . and faster.

It was a flash . . . more like a quick ray of sun.

"Gerald?" she questioned hysterically. He'd waved for her to join him. She'd seen him in the glass.

Survive. The word seared itself into her brain as she rushed toward the parachute on the floor. Struggling with the complex fastenings, she finally got it on and heaved her full weight against the door. It wouldn't budge!

Sealed in a tomb, she fought against the vacuum pressure until her hands bled and she begged for deliverance. As the craft's altitude shifted, the gun and stones rolled across the floor. Her line of vision connected with the earrings . . . and her panic subsided.

Almost too calm, she picked up the gems and dropped them into her bag. An eerie tranquillity engulfed her when she looped the satchel over her head and arm. Lunging against the door one last time, she felt it give way.

She saw nothing but darkness as she jumped.

* * *

"Señor Cortes, we've lost radio communications with the plane."

Victor stood by the large picture window that framed what used to be his father's study. His ears rang with panic as he watched the craft fall.

"Try again. I can see them in the air from here. It must be equipment-malfunction."

All three men were frozen as they witnessed the unnatural descent of the aircraft. He could tell by the way it leveled that something was wrong.

"They're going down," Victor whispered, horror catching the words in his throat.

Cortes leaned forward with a grim smile. "Then, if we don't have the woman any longer, we'll have to extract the information from you more creatively."

Victor refused to face his captor. His gaze was riveted on the quickly falling altitude of the craft. He closed his eyes as an explosion shook the foundation of the house and a billow of angry smoke rose from the far side of the mountain.

Tears stung his throat. His judgment snapped. "I'll kill you!"

"Restrain him!" Cortes ordered, and four armed men wrestled Victor to the floor. "Search the crash site for the diamonds. They should have survived the fire."

A string of explicatives deafened him as he fought against the guards, immune to their blows. Grief had numbed his nervous system.

"May you die like a dog in the street, Cortes! May they rip you to shreds and eat your remains! A curse upon you," he bellowed as they dragged him from the room. "In hell, we meet!"

"Make him understand my displeasure," Cortes said evenly. "But do not damage his head. We need information before he dies."

Victor spat on the floor. "May your own mother rebuke you from her grave."

"Let's discuss it in hell when we meet again, Duarte."

* * *

Twigs, branches, leaves cut her face as the bottom of the world dropped from under her. Then contact and a searing pain shot through her leg. But she was moving too fast and no foundation held as she slid. She dug her raw fingers into the dirt despite her increased momentum and stopped with a thud that nearly cracked her skull.

Darkness eclipsed her vision. Dust choked the air from her lungs. Ammonia stung her eyes. A blast sealed her fate.

She could barely move as gravel filled in the opening of the small cavern, blocking her exit. Coughing against the plumes of dirt, she covered her eyes against the falling debris with her forearm. Pain riddled her left side, wrenching a groan from deep within her until she wept. *Dear God, help me!* she prayed more urgently than she ever had before.

She could hear angry voices in the distance, but she was just as afraid of the squeals of unseen things that scurried overhead . . . bats!

She knew she was going to die. Injured. Hunted. Trapped. There was no way out. *Just like in the vision.* Death and darkness.

"Follow the light."

Liza looked up and rubbed her eyes, craning her neck toward the sound of the whisper.

"Follow the light."

Adrenaline pumped through her veins at this new terror.

"Follow the light."

Squinting, she tried to adjust her eyes to the darkness. A crack in the wall produced a yellow filter of brilliance.

Immediately moving toward it, she plastered her nose to the small hole, trying to breathe. Fresh air filled her lungs. One prayer had been answered. Lowering her head to peek through the crack, she saw row after row of military crates and chemical drums . . . equipment everywhere. Angry guards yelled out commands. . . . She'd hit the motherload!

No longer able to feel her leg, Liza reached into her bag and ripped the lining. Cold steel hit her palm, and she put the camera to the hole and held down the button. Machine-gun-speed clicks vibrated against her fingers, then stopped. This might be all she had left to bargain with.

"Follow the light."

The whisper renewed her terror. "Who are you?" she whispered back, almost afraid of the answer.

"Bondage never conquers the soul of the Moor."

"What?"

"Praise Allah, The Beneficent. My daughter is home."

The words didn't make sense. She saw a glimpse of a tall black man, and as suddenly, his presence was gone.

Then, she felt a strong push forward. *Something* had touched her! Clawing at the sealed entrance, she panicked as the dirt and rocks replaced themselves. She could feel something behind her. . . . Growing more frenzied, she panted as she worked at the front of the tomb. It touched her again gently. . . .

Her scream began low in her throat as a small point of light opened in the dirt. Heaving large mounds away from her face, she fought to escape. It was behind her. It was not a vision. It was not human! Tears blurred her sight. The opening grew bigger. Her efforts increased with her terror.

"Follow the light. Wear the jewels. Your mother did not burn in vain."

Too stricken to turn around, she clawed recklessly. The bright sun blinded her. Two figures appeared on the other side of the hole. They wore robes. She couldn't see their faces. Just silhouettes: A man and a child. The man reached for her hand.

"Jesus, deliver my soul," she whispered, as consciousness left her in the dark.

Thick smoke swirled above her head, and she could hear a low rhythm of voices. Male voices chanting in a harmony that she had heard before in her mind.

"You will live," a young voice said in English. "Let the elders heal you."

Liza peered at the old faces that smiled at her. Elderly, aged, compassionate faces had formed a circle around her.

"Do not be afraid. They have waited for you to come home," the boy whispered, bringing a hot cup of bitter liquid to her lips. "For the soroche. The height of the mountains brings sickness."

Her mind couldn't process the scene. How had they found her? Who were they? Why didn't her leg hurt anymore?

"I work in the mansion," the boy said with a smile, processing her question before it had formed. "I must take orders from all the guards. From many places in the world, they come. Give the elders your tears, and they will make magic for you."

Her frown made the old men chuckle. The most aged of the group came to her side and lifted her satchel from her neck. Working with gnarled hands, he removed the Duarte gemstones. Tears filled his eyes and he laughed, exposing blackened gums in his toothless grin. His excitement spilled over to the group, intensifying their eerily familiar chants.

"He will make a *panchama* bag for you. Do not remove it until you are safe. You have to go down the mountain to the hillside. Watch him carefully, for he will show you how it's done. Learn fast. Learn well. It is the only way."

She looked on with awe as the aged men sang. Dropping feathers beside her, they made a circle with their fists and released a fine white powder around the perimeter of her body. A heavy-scented fragrance covered her as the smoke burned her eyes. Tears ran down the side of her face, increasing their frenzied chant. They touched her injured leg, and their palms gave off an unnatural heat. She could feel her body lifting, as though borne on air. . . . They held a silver cup against her cheek, catching her tears. She was gone. . . .

Liza awakened to silence. The room was empty. A multi-colored layered skirt and white blouse lay at her feet. As she sat up, she fingered a leather pouch that had been slipped over her neck. Confusion tore at her mind. But her leg no longer hurt. Reaching down to inspect the once-broken limb, she drew her hand away slowly in awe.

"Wash. Dress like the others. Then, we will take you to your *señor*. He is dying. He is part of our own."

The timid voice of a young girl startled her. Liza could not comprehend what had just happened, but the reference to Victor propelled her past her fears and she quickly followed the girl's instructions.

A gathering of old men stood outside as she left the hovel. They met her with wide, toothless grins, nodding fervently when the eldest approached her. He spoke in a foreign tongue, a flurry of words, then he opened her palms, which were no longer cut, and dropped a handful of tiny diamonds inside them.

"Your tears . . ." the boy stammered. "They said these must go in the bag with your mother's. Pass them to your first child one day."

Stricken, Liza did as they requested, not allowing her mind to doubt.

"Hide your other large sack under your skirts," the boy murmured, leading her by the elbow. "Come with me to the kitchen entrance. You'll take him water. Do not speak. Just nod. The elders will pray for your safe passage. Your ancestors guide you now."

Her mouth went dry with fear as the boy left her side. Blending in with the other women, who also carried burdens, she hesitated as an old woman's gaze bore through her.

It would never work. And if she found Victor, how would they escape?

She stiffened with panic as the woman approached and inspected her. When she chuckled and took off her dirty kerchief, offering it to Liza, she relaxed. The woman was going to help her get in.

Pulling her to the door, the old woman smiled shyly and

pushed her through. To Liza's horror, she'd been thrust into the middle of a kitchen-guard outpost.

Six heavily armed men sat around the table eating. What the hell was she going to do now?

"Take the sonofabitch some water, girl. I'm not babysitting him."

Another guard glanced in her direction. "Move. Are you deaf? He can't die before we need him to." Rising quickly, he pointed to an urn and grabbed her arm, brutally shoving her toward the basement door. "I hate these stupid Indians!"

Ducking into the entrance, she slipped into the dank stairwell. She almost dropped the water as the lock turned behind her. Holding onto the slick wall for support, she edged toward the bottom of the steps. The sight of a blood-stained body stopped her in her tracks.

He was bound and lying face down. His shoulder wasn't properly aligned. Turning Victor onto his back, she cringed as the joint moved loosely under his weight. When she saw his face, she drew in a sharp breath that cut through the silence. It was nearly swollen beyond recognition. Both his eyes were a black-purple, and a deep gash accentuated his already-cut eyebrow. His jaw bone moved unnaturally as she touched his cheek. They had beaten him nearly to death!

Time conspired against her while she tried desperately to rouse him. Wetting the hem of her skirt, she wiped his bloodied lips. "Please," she whispered urgently. "You can't die!"

Responding for only a brief moment, he coughed, sending a dark trail of liquid down his cheek.

"Oh, God, he's hemorrhaging!" she gasped inwardly, trying not to make a sound.

Frantic, she applied more water, but got no response. His breaths were no longer detectable, and she gave in to resigned despair. He was gone . . .

"I never told you *yes*," she whispered against his cheek, her tears wetting his face. "Promise to meet me again . . ."

Touching Victor's eyes with the tips of her fingers, she drew

away. Reality. She had to leave him. Yet, somehow, fear for her
own life had diminished. She already felt dead.

Leaning over his body, she kissed him one last time, holding
the small, magic bag back with her hand to keep it from hurting
his wounds. No more pain. No more plans. No more running.
Go to the light, my darling. "Follow the light."

Her gaze lingered on him in the dim room; and as she studied
his face, the bruises seemed to lift where she had touched him.
His shut eyelids now had a fiery-red color instead of dark purple.
The cut over his eyebrow was no longer a running gash. It had
closed and was deep crimson!

They had shown her how to heal with her hands. Nana had
shown her. . . . It all came back. Arthritis . . . the old Indian
men . . . Victor's words . . . "Your hands have a healing quality,
Liza" . . . Gerald's need for her touch . . . Just remember . . .

Liza wiped her damp face with her fingertips and ran them
gently over his mouth. The gash in Victor's bottom lip sealed as
she removed her hand. Holding the bag against her heart, she
leaned over his body, touching each damaged part until agony
swept through her.

He was surprised to have ever awakened. The last thing he
remembered was being hurled down the steps with his hands
tied behind him. When his shoulder snapped under his own
weight, he'd passed out. Disoriented, he looked down at his
wrists. Who had untied him? Maybe they'd thought they had
gone too far and had decided to revive him. The bastards still
needed answers. He'd die first. Especially after what they'd done
to Liza.

The memory pierced his heart. Returned consciousness was
only a curse. What did his life matter, anyway? She'd burned.
Like his family, like Stan. . . . He'd already died while helplessly
witnessing her death through the window. Now, he was just the
living dead.

Looking about the wine cellar to see who was still guarding

him, Victor's gaze stopped at a heap on the floor. Christ Almighty . . . They had even abused a worker-woman.

Moving to her side, he turned her over and felt for a pulse. It was strong, but her face . . .

Nauseated by the sight, he almost turned away. They were animals! What could this poor woman have done to warrant such abuse? Tearing off a piece of his ragged shirt, he tried to staunch the blood. But as he inspected the wounds, they seemed to fade . . . What in God's name?

As the woman's face returned to normal, he practically dropped her. He saw Liza and wept and turned from the body. He was hallucinating!

Her cough brought him around slowly. Her eyes opened, and he drew away from her again and crossed himself.

"Victor," she whispered to his horror.

She even sounded like Liza.

"Don't be afraid. It's me," she said quietly, trying to lift herself.

Rushing to her, he swept her into his arms. "Please tell me it's you," he begged into her hair. "Make me know that it's you! What's happening here?"

"They took me from the hotel. We were flying, and the pilot threatened to shoot me when I screamed. I saw Ron and Stan . . . and the screams just came anyway."

A sob racked her body and he crushed her more tightly to his chest. He could only lean his head back and thank the Almighty she was alive.

"Then, the pilot had a heart attack."

Victor held her away so that he could look at her face as she spoke.

"I think I killed a man, Victor." Her terror-stricken expression was consumed with guilt as she plunged on. "I parachuted to safety. Old men in the hills found me, just like in the journal. There's too much to explain . . . but we have to follow the light. That's what the voice said."

Heavy bootsteps overhead stopped their hushed exchange.

"We have to get out of here. If they come down, act like you don't know me," he whispered. "At least, you will get out alive."

"No!" she hissed. "Never. Not without you! The voice said *remember your past and follow the light!*"

"Don't argue! There's no time. If they find out who you are . . ."

"No!"

He heard the locks turn. He had to get her out! Shoving Liza away from him, he tried one last time. "There is no light down here, Liza!"

Untangling her arms from his as the guard's footsteps hit the landing, he threw her across the room with all his strength. Her body fell against a wine rack, jolting it and exposing a cool current of air.

Working in tandem, they heaved their weight against the wood until enough of a passageway opened to permit them to slip through. Cobwebs clung to their faces as they ran down the long tunnel, and they repeatedly lost their balance on slimy rock surfaces as they fled. A grey filter of light shone at the end of the dark corridor. Freedom.

"Remember the past. . . . I had forgotten," he huffed, out of breath. "All feudal families built escape routes into the mansions. My father must have blocked it so the children wouldn't play there."

"I saw a chopper in the courtyard," she blurted out through pants.

"We might be able to make it if they all converge on the cellar. If they think I've escaped, they'll search the house room by room. That'll buy time." A new fear accosted him. He didn't know if Liza could keep up. If she got shot, he'd never be able to leave her.

"I'll go first. If there's gunfire and I fall, leave me. Stay in the alcove until dark."

"No. We run together," she said, gripping his arm tightly. "We run toward the light together."

Against his better judgment, he conceded. He knew that if he fell, she'd run out behind him and die anyway.

Waiting until Liza had caught her breath and the mass of guards had gone into the house, he gripped her elbow. "On three."

"On three," she repeated.

The chopper was at least fifty yards away. Her heart slammed against her chest. She let fear propel her as the layered skirt whipped between her legs. Victor pulled her along savagely as the angry voices neared. Rapid gunfire almost paralyzed her, yet she pushed on.

"Keep your head down!" he screamed, hurling her into the chopper.

Holes riddled the windows. He couldn't get it off the ground! The craft bounced and dragged against the dirt as Victor tried to lift off too soon, almost tipping the chopper on its side. Then, finally, they became airborne, leaving *la hacienda* in a lopsided escape.

Screaming over the engine whir, Victor warned her, "We only have enough fuel to get us to Ecuador! Then we have to charter a boat to the Galapagos Islands! That wasn't in the plan! The charter is a risk! We were supposed to make a flight contact in Lima, then go directly to the islands! If our timing is off, they'll leave us for dead!"

"Risk is not an issue at this point, Victor! We've already experienced that!" she yelled back over the roar. "The real risk is in paying for the boat. We look like shit! We have no money! The earrings will tip them off!"

As she wiped the perspiration from her face with both hands, she suddenly knew what they had to do.

"Well, it's not my job to ask questions, so I'll just be happy with this."

She could tell by Victor's expression that giving the charter captain her ring had pained him deeply. When the man jumped down to the deck, Victor squeezed her side.

"I'll replace it, *Querida*. Just as soon as we're home."

She didn't answer, but touched Victor's face gently and hoisted herself down to the charter.

Rounding the one-hour mark, their captain was beginning to wear on her nerves. The man babbled incessantly, as though they were tourists on a whale-watching cruise. She hated the way he assessed her, his green eyes never leaving her body, and the way he constantly ran his hands through his shock of dirty red hair . . . disgusting. But his lewd references to women got under her skin the most.

She closed her eyes against his voice and leaned her head on Victor's shoulder, too tired to respond.

"Hope you folks won't be at this remote location overnight."

She could feel Victor shrug, but he didn't answer.

"Heard they got Komodo dragons on the island, ol' man. This Aussie's seen 'em back home, but researchers might have flown 'em in. Don't know where the ugly bastards came from. Where your headed used to be an outpost for researchers. Those sonsabitches get up to fifteen feet long, I'm told, and weigh up to three hundred pounds. Stand waist-high and hunt in packs like wolves. Can run down deer and boar alike. Man doesn't stand a chance."

Liza opened her eyes, and Victor's body tensed against hers.

"No shit," he went on in a thick Australian brogue. "So keep an eye on the little lady. When they're ready, they'll run you down."

Yet, as he spoke, she was drawn to Victor's expression. He smiled sadly back at the man. Gentle . . . Full of compassion . . . Stan.

"Who knows, Victor?" she murmured as he pulled her nearer for support. "No spirit or energy disappears. . . . Maybe it's all just a continuum."

Victor brushed her cheek with a kiss and turned to address their captain.

"Well," Victor said softly, "a man can only die once, you know."

"Depends on the woman he's with," their captain laughed, issuing Liza a lewd wink.

"We're two hours late," Victor said nervously, pacing near the remote landing strip. "The late charter and the walk five miles inland had taken too long. It'll be dark in another hour, and based upon what the captain said, we should find shelter."

Fatigue had turned her limbs to putty. "Maybe they'll make one last pass," she pleaded, forcing herself to remain hopeful. "Just a few minutes to rest, okay?"

Too keyed to sit beside her, Victor continued to pace. "Well," he said with resignation, "I guess this is paradise. At least, I kept my promise. We can fish and eat native plants for the rest of our lives."

She stared at him. The strain had rendered him senseless. Their gazes met. Immediately, they both burst out laughing.

"Dragons, Liza! Can you believe it?" he roared. Was he hysterical?

She couldn't answer, for an irrational wave of laughter overcame her.

"Stop! I demand to go to my embassy!" she screamed, leaning against a rock. "Bat pee, Victor! I parachuted into bat pee!"

Wiping tears of laughter from his face, Victor dropped to the ground. "Liz, you wanted revenge . . . action . . . adventure. . . . This tour was not in the brochures, but it's a *must-see.*"

She could only wave her hand for him to stop. "You once said you loved the way I smelled. . . . Care to take a whiff of my latest fragrance?"

He covered his face with his hands, roaring at her outrageous comment. It was a release.

Jet engines immediately stilled their hysteria. Jumping up, they ran toward the small plane and waved frantically. Her prayers had been answered! She was so weary. . . .

As the craft circled and landed, they rushed towards the doors, squinting against the setting sun's orange glare.

Immediate horror iced the blood in her veins. She couldn't even gasp as three gunmen descended the steps.

"Mr. Duarte, you are becoming tiresome. Where is the film—and my stones?"

"Cortes," Victor spat back. "Go to hell!"

"I believe we have had that conversation already." Turning to the gunmen that flanked him, Cortes' voice became even. "Kill the woman and make him understand."

Liza clutched the small medicine bag around her neck and closed her eyes. At least they'd die together. It would be fast. They wouldn't be tortured.

"What are you waiting for?" Cortes demanded, leveling his revolver at his guards.

"That's right; she's a witch," Victor said in a low tone, responding to the men's flurry of Spanish. "That's how your pilot died. Very slow."

Liza gasped. "Mendoza. You are the Mendoza!"

"My mother was a Mendoza, and the stones belonged in our family, not Duarte's. It's not just the money; there is a principle involved."

"Then, since you know where they came from," she whispered, ignoring Victor's warning glare, "come to me, over in the glen, and let me show you how they're used with a woman . . . how they were used before. Duarte could never appreciate the power."

She fought against the fear, focusing on the darkness. Walking away from the group, she turned her back. "Are you afraid of me, too?"

"Liza! Don't!"

Machine-gun fire ripped a dividing line between Liza and Victor. She turned back only once and forced a smile at Cortes.

"They're in my magic bag. I am only interested in a man who is the best. I'll give them to you. He endangered my life, and can go to hell."

"Stay with Duarte. I want to see his face again before I kill him," Cortes grated, following her trail into the thicket. "Maybe I'll enjoy this as much as I enjoyed your mother and sister in the carriage house before it burned. The boy was a disappointment, however."

Victor blanched at the confession, and venom surged anew through his body. Liza didn't know whom she was dealing with . . . the extent of the brutality. Using herself as live bait to buy time . . . to save his life . . . It was an impossible plan. She was too tired. . . . There were three of them. . . .

Sudden gunshot sent an adrenaline spike through him. Liza's scream broke his reason. In one move, he was on the man who stood at his left, snapping his neck and hurling his body against the second guard. As he grappled for the weapon, Liza's screams blurred his vision. He heard Cortes yell. A round went off in Victor's hands. The body above him went limp. He had to get to Liza!

Bramble tore at his clothing as he raced toward her screams, weapon held above the dense thicket. Snarls and deep hissing sounds brought him to a skidding halt.

Less than ten feet away, Cortes' corpse lay in the center of feeding beasts. They had drawn and quartered him. Liza was treed. Forked tongues flickered over their bloody meal.

Speaking to her quietly, he implored her to come down. "Liz, *Querida,* come to me now while they're eating. Don't look down or make a sudden move. Trust me, and follow my voice."

Shaking, she crept down from her safe post and edged by the carnage to take his hand. When one of the dragons snapped in her direction, he squeezed her hand tighter.

"On three," he whispered, pulling her into a full dash behind him.

As they neared the plane, he held her hand even tighter, forcing her not to look down at the bodies.

"It's all over now," he whispered, powering up the engine. "We don't have to ever look back."

Liza stared at him for a long time until her trembling abated. The dying sun lit his profile. "When will this end?" she asked.

Victor's response was not immediate, and he didn't turn is head to look at her.

"Never."

"We have to look back," she murmured after a long pause. "Don't you understand? That's what saved us—looking back to a time and culture that we had forgotten. We have to look past the darkness, draw on the wisdom that the old ones gave us . . . use that strength to follow the light. We can never forget."

"What light is there after this, Liza?" His voice had become gravelly with emotion. "This is my second exile. Stan was correct; a man really can die twice. The isolation can be crippling."

Her gaze took in the natural beauty below her as their small plane ascended. "We've both been stripped of so much in such a short period of time, but have been left with the rare gift of a second chance."

"You healed my body and saved my life, but, Liza, you also healed my soul. . . ."

A sense of peace enveloped her. "And you returned the favor, Victor. No more games. No more lies. Only truth. Remember?"

Reaching for her hand, he clasped it tightly.

"You're my light. You're goodness. That's paradise, Victor. Our paradise lost and found. I do love you."

"Yes, and I remember how much . . ."

Epilogue

Four Years Later . . .
The Cayman Islands

Victor smiled and put down his *Wall Street Journal* next to his coffee as he saw the elderly man approach the veranda.

"How was your flight from New York?"

"Pleasant," Helyar said, allowing Victor to help him into a seat. "And lucrative."

Victor chuckled.

"And how is Mrs. Hernandez feeling these days? Did she enjoy the last bundle of letters I couriered to her?"

"It was the best medicine you could have given her."

The old man looked at him with a wise smile. "It won't be long, son. Patience. Remember the fundamentals."

He had to laugh. "Yes. Patience. I recall that, I believe," he added, pouring Helyar a cold glass of fresh juice.

"Well, Victor, once it was done, it didn't take long for the explosions to seal the mountain . . . with Sanders inside during one of his illegal deliveries. Or for a senator to commit suicide while awaiting grand jury. Or for corporate raiders to descend upon Chem Tech to divvy up the remains, did it? Hyenas keep the delicate balance of nature after the kill. They, too, have learned patience."

Helyar took a sip and wiped his mustache. "Age teaches one patience. We were also very patient with the disposal of Hanson, Blaylock, and Gallagher. . . . We'll be just as patient with Walker. Regrettably, Cortes was not as patient with our jeweler. We couldn't save him."

A shiver passed through Victor. He hated even the slightest reference to the morbid topic, revenge now completely foreign to his existence.

Shaking his head, Victor conceded with a nervous chuckle and redirected the conversation. "But eight weeks . . ."

Helyar winked. "I have something else to take your mind off the wait . . . a proposition that should get you out of the antique gallery for a few weeks."

Victor raised one eyebrow. "Should I be concerned?"

"Ach," Helyar scoffed. "Always a skeptic. No. This is simple. What would you say to investing in a dessert-and-coffee house? One that opened late in the afternoon and played calypso all night? I'd need a permanent band. . . ."

"A dessert house?"

"Yes. I met this wonderful widow during the flight layover in Florida. She makes the most fabulous pastries . . . with Eastern European authenticity. But her eyes . . . enchanting."

"I see you have not given up all your vices, despite the doctor's orders." Victor laughed. "Nor your flair for chess. And who will run this establishment?"

"Well, let us just say that a Leticia Jones has a special flair for—"

"Papa! Papa!"

Before Victor could stop him, the small boy had nearly tackled Helyar. Waving off Victor's admonishments to the child, Helyar grabbed him up into his lap.

"François," the old man beamed, "give your Papa a kiss. Now, we must keep our voices down and not wake up your mother."

"Aw, she's always asleep these days," the child protested, getting comfortable in the old man's lap.

"She needs her rest until the baby comes," Victor chimed in automatically. "So, keep it down."

"Yeah, Dad, I know. But who wants a dumb old baby sister anyway? Why couldn't I have a brother?"

Helyar and Victor exchanged a nervous glance.

"François," Helyar said quietly. "How do you know? Maybe it will be a boy?"

Taking a slice of melon from the table, the child shrugged. "Nah. It's a girl. The old lady told me."

Again, Victor and Helyar looked at each other.

"What old lady?" Victor asked cautiously.

Filling his mouth with the fruit, the child wiped the juice that dribbled his chin on his sleeve. "You know," he mumbled. "The one who smells like flowers . . ."

Afterword

Think of the possibilities . . .

If matter can neither be created nor destroyed, then how can the light that shines within a soul be extinguished merely by the passing from one dimension to the next?

How many kisses, sighs, or tears has this earth borne witness to . . . leaving countless souls adrift, looking for their other half or that which can make them whole?

The secret is believing in the possibilities and knowing that the beacon of a familiar embrace is always in the eyes . . .

So, trust that there will one day herald a signal, for those whose flame burns bright . . . navigating them through the stars to recognition, beyond all their fears, guiding them to a paradise lost.

May we all rise from our own ashes like the mythical Phoenix and fly home, dancing in full rapture amidst the brilliance of the sun.

. . . If not in this lifetime, my love, then in the next . . .

About the Author

Leslie A. P. Esdaile holds a B.S. in Economics as a Dean's List graduate of The University of Pennsylvania's Wharton Undergraduate Business Program, with a dual major concentration in Marketing and Management. She worked as a top ranking Sales Executive for a number of Fortune 100 firms before she became a freelance consultant servicing clients in the microeconomic development arena. Currently, she is pursuing her Masters of Fine Arts through Temple University's Department of Radio, Television and Film, with an emphasis on documentary film-making. She lives in Philadelphia.

Look for these upcoming Arabesque titles:

October 1996
THE GRASS AIN'T GREENER by Monique Gilmore
IF ONLY YOU KNEW by Carla Fredd
SUNDANCE by Leslie Esdaile

November 1996
AFTER ALL by Lynn Emery
ABANDON by Neffetiti Austin
NOW OR NEVER by Carmen Green

December 1996
EMERALD's FIRE by Eboni Snoe
NIGHTFALL by Loure Jackson
SILVER BELLS, an Arabesque Holiday Collection